"I stayed up late into the night reading *The Hero Stone* on my vacation.

"I was riveted.

"You got right inside the heads of the three protagonists, including Melanie.

"The insects and snakes scene was quite compelling!"

— *Colleen Isherwood, Editor, CLN*

The Hero Stone

What if you
could become your
favourite superhero?

Bruce Gravel

Wigglesworth & Quinn
Peterborough

The Hero Stone

Copyright © 2015 by Bruce M. Gravel

This is a work of fiction. Names, characters, places, and incidents are products of the author's overactive imagination or are used fictitiously and are not to be construed as real. Any resemblance to actual events, locales, organizations, or persons, living or dead or undead or alien, is entirely coincidental.

All Marvel Comics characters referenced herein are copyright and trademarks of MARVEL. All DC Comics characters referenced herein are copyright and trademarks of DC Comics.

All rights reserved. No part of this book may be used or reproduced, scanned, or distributed in any manner whatsoever without written permission from the author, except by a reviewer who may quote brief passages in a review.

For information, contact: bruce@brucegravel.ca.

Published by: Wigglesworth & Quinn, Peterborough, Ontario, Canada
Ordering Information: bruce@brucegravel.ca
Printed in the United States of America

First Edition: July 2015
Second Edition: May 2016

Library and Archives Canada Cataloguing in Publication

Gravel, Bruce M. (Bruce Magnus), 1952 -, author
   The hero stone: what if you could become your favourite superhero? / Bruce Gravel

ISBN 978-1-5075-7996-1(pbk.)

I. Title.

PS8613.R369H47 2015   C813'.6   C2015-900583-3

Dedication

To Frances and Scott and Elizabeth,
the bestest support group
any scribbler could wish for.

Books by Bruce Gravel

Novels

Inn-Sanity: Diary of an Innkeeper Virgin
The Hero Stone

The "Condiment Series" of short story collections

Humour on Wry, with Mustard
Humour on Wry, with Mayo
Humour on Wry, with Ketchup

Non-Fiction

The Innkeeper's Reference Book

Author's Note

The character of Michael is based on a next-door neighbour friend of my youth, a great pal who taught me the finer points of chess and checkers, and that living with an intellectual disability does not make you less of a person. I have the utmost respect for anyone living with a disability, intellectual or physical.

Besides being an homage to the real-life Michael, this story is also an homage to superhero comics and the pleasure of growing up with their colourful world of capes, tights, angst, villains, and earth-shattering explosions.

The innkeepers portrayed in Chapter 17 are based on a real-life innkeeper couple, who operated an inn in Ontario.

Acknowledgements

This story has been lurking in my head for decades. It is thanks to the gentle persistent urging of my wife, Frances, that it has finally seen the light of day.

The front cover art was done by artist and writer **Ash**. Contact him at: facebook@GCPBooks.

Huge thanks to Frances Gravel for her great job in the formatting and lay-out of the entire book, getting it all print-ready.

Many thanks to Scott Gravel for designing the covers, and electronically enabling the printing of this book by means of arcane voodoo, which I cannot begin to understand.

Bruce Gravel
Peterborough, Ontario
July 2015

Table of Contents

Prologue 9

01—The Wind and the Flame 12

02 — This Man, this Monster 26

03 — The Green Goliath 31

04 — Deadly Rage 42

05 — Plastic Revelations 49

06 — Shadow of Death 59

07 — Miracle Blood 67

08 — Detour to Hell 79

09 — The Angel and the Maiden 90

10 — Visitors Strange and Wicked 99

11 — Death Comes to Clearwater 105

12 — When Titans Clash 124

13 — The Price of Power 135

14 — Three No More 145

15 — Looking for Love 151

16 — The Black Widows 165

17 — Inn-cidents 183

18 — Deadly Shadow, Desperate Quest 194

19 — The Eagle Flies Again 207

20 — Oh My Goddess! 224

21 — Comes a Killer 234

22 — Communion 241

23 — Confrontation 255

24 — Confession 265

25 — Gauntlet of Terror 282

26 — Show and Tell 302

27 — The Titanic Battle of Fetterley's Cliff 310

28 — Armageddon 323

29 — Explanations - of Sorts 340

30 — Memorial Flight 357

High Flight by John Gillespie Magee 362

Epilogue 363

PROLOGUE

The old man stopped, gasping for air. Who'd have thought it would be so bloody hard to crack a thin stone in half? Damn, he'd been pounding on it forever, with hammer and chisel, and it hadn't even been scratched. His ears were ringing from the sound of his blows on the stone, lying flat on the anvil beneath it.

He sat down and waited for his heart to stop pounding. He passed a hand along the top of his head, through hair that was no longer there. He *tsked;* he'd never get used to being bald. He looked around the workshop. Under bushy white eyebrows, his eyes lit up. There! If chisel couldn't do it, that surely would.

Wincing at the pain in his arthritic joints, he stood and shuffled to the big vice bolted to the workbench. He clamped the flat stone straight up between the jaws of the vice, with half of the stone protruding above. The old man fetched the hammer he'd been using, and stood before the vice. He took a deep breath, then started hitting the exposed half of the stone, as hard as he could, trying to break it in two.

The stone wasn't that big. It was oval, about four inches long and three inches wide, and about half an inch thick. It was very smooth, like a stone from the bottom of a rushing brook, polished by eons of water. Except it had been found in the Australian Outback, miles from the nearest riverbed, which was dry most of the year anyway. At least, that was the story told by the guy he'd stolen it from.

And then there was its colour. That's what had attracted him to it in the first place. Such a beautiful unusual colour: shades of pink and yellow, with streaks of deep purple and white running through it, and tiny flecks of gold here and there.

Yeah, beautiful to look at, horrible to keep. He knew that now.

He whacked away with the hammer until his arms ached and his breathing grew laboured again. "C'mon ... ya bloody bugger ... break!" he gasped, between blows. "You're much ... too dangerous ... too powerful ... to leave intact."

He stopped and sat down heavily. He glared at the rock. Not a scratch.

Leaving it clamped in the vice, he tried drilling it. Broke every drill he used. Then he tried cutting it, first with a reciprocating saw using metal-cutting blades, then with a grinder. Broke every saw blade and grinder wheel.

"Damn!" he muttered, as he rested again. "Yer gonner need a laser ta cut that bloody thing, mate!"

He realized that he really had no choice. With a great sigh, he rose and released the stone from the vice. He gripped it with both hands, thumbs on top and fingers curled beneath, holding it flat before him. He closed his eyes and cried out in agony as he accessed the power. His arms changed from spindly thin with loose skin to thick with corded muscle. His wrists doubled in size and his fingers became huge.

Grunting with effort, he pressed down on the stone with all the massive strength of his impossible new arms funnelled through his thumbs. Long seconds passed, stretching into eternity. Then, with a loud *KRAK*, the oval stone broke into two halves. Oddly, the break was neatly in the middle of the stone, with no jagged edges. A nimbus of white energy, like an electrical discharge, sprang up as the rock broke, and surrounded the two halves. The air was filled with the stench of ozone.

The glowing nimbus slowly faded. When it was gone, so were both halves of the stone.

But the old man never noticed. He was kneeling on the floor, clutching his chest and fighting to breathe. Then, with a wretched groan, he slumped forward.

When Rob Owens, owner of the workshop on the outskirts of

Melbourne, Australia, opened for business the next morning, he followed his usual ritual: deactivate the alarm, hang the keys on the hook inside the office cupboard, switch on the coffee-maker and, in tribute to his habitual big breakfast, crack off the foulest fart this side of a toxic waste dump. He'd be the only one there for another hour, and he was the boss, so who was going to chide him?

Office christening done for another day, Owens walked into the workshop proper, and his morning routine shattered. He found an emaciated senior citizen lying dead on the floor, arms as thin as sticks grasping his chest. Owens was so shocked, he farted again. The body reminded him of pictures taken during World War Two of Holocaust concentration camp victims: half-starved, rail-thin, gaunt-faced. Walking skeletons.

He couldn't understand how the old guy had gotten in past the burglar alarm. Nothing had been stolen; the only things damaged were a bunch of broken drills, saw blades, and grinder wheels.

Owens called the police. After the cops arrived and proceeded with their investigation, they made a startling discovery. The wizened intruder's wallet contained a driver's license featuring a photo of a young man with a birthdate that put him at 28 years old.

Chapter 1

The Wind and the Flame

On that sunny morning in early May, Doris Tweedle knew it was going to be a helluva day when she looked across the street and saw the teenaged Johnson boy walk out of his front door, stark naked. She coughed and almost swallowed her cancer stick.

Doris Tweedle was the neighbourhood busybody. Every neighbourhood had one, and Doris had elected herself to the post for this street. First thing each morning, rain or shine, summer or winter, weekday or weekend, Doris was up and watching through her living room window, while she sipped her too-sweet coffee and chain-smoked her foul-smelling cigarettes. (There was no Mr. Tweedle; hadn't been for years. One night, he'd driven off to the corner store for milk and drove right off Shamper's Bluff. Or so it had appeared. But he'd been well insured.)

Everybody knew that Michael Johnson "lived with an intellectual disability". "Developmentally-delayed" was another current terminology. "Mentally challenged" said those folks who were not up on the latest politically-correct euphemisms. ("Mildly retarded" said others who didn't care about people's feelings.) Had been since birth. Now 17, Michael was a tall, well-built boy with the mind of an eight-year-old. Harmless as a kitten, though, and just as friendly.

But he knew enough not to parade around in his birthday suit. So what the hell was he doing standing outside starkers? And was that steam coming off his body? Did he just come out of a hot shower or something?

He looked very distressed, like he was about to cry. Doris soon heard the reason why; he was being ragged on by his mother inside the house, yelling at him through the screen door:

"WHAT DO YOU MEAN, YOU DON'T KNOW WHAT HAPPENED TO YOUR CLOTHES? AND GET BACK IN HERE BEFORE THE NEIGHBOURS SEE! I SWEAR, MICHAEL, YOU'RE GETTING MORE STUPID EVERY DAY! I DON'T KNOW HOW I PUT UP WITH YOU!"

Doris winced. Ruth Johnson had a mouth on her. If angry words weren't spewing out, then vodka was going in. Poor kid.

Michael hung his head, mumbled something Doris couldn't hear, and went back inside the house. *Sweet Baby Jesus,* she thought, *that boy has a nice butt. Nice equipment in front, too.* A movement to her left, at the Fisher place, distracted her. She turned the full attention of her unblinking owlish stare on Hank Fisher and watched him load a suitcase into his car, ready for another business trip. Man took a lot of trips, and never suspected what his wife got up to while he was gone. Each time, about an hour after he left, a white service truck from a major department store showed up and parked in their driveway. Lisa Fisher needed a lot of servicing.

Inside his house, Michael stood mute, head hanging low, as his mother screeched at him some more. It hurt his ears. He couldn't tell her what really happened. She'd never believe him, and she'd whack him with the long ruler for lying. But it would be the truth: his clothes had burned off as he did his morning run today. Once he got home and stopped running, he realized what had happened, and then became scared at the steam rising from his body. He had stepped outside until the cool morning air dissipated it, so he wouldn't alarm his mom.

Michael Johnson stood six feet, one inch tall, with a shock of unruly dark brown hair adding another inch. He loved to weight-lift and it showed. Broad-shouldered, he had a barrel chest, flat stomach, and muscular arms and legs. He had a pleasant face, with a ready smile and intense blue eyes. Though he often spoke slowly, his words came out clearly and his eyes bore into you as he talked, as if he was making sure you understood him.

To his great relief, his mother finally ran out of words and ordered him upstairs to get ready for school. As he showered, Michael could barely contain his excitement. Just wait until Billy and Melanie heard what had happened to him!

    ❧ ❧ ❧ ☙ ☙ ☙

"No way!" said Billy, when Michael finished his story.

"Way," said Michael, nodding vigorously. "Oh yes!"

Billy McDonnell looked up at his friend as they walked to school. Two years younger than Michael, Billy was also a head shorter. He had close-cropped red hair, a heavily-freckled face, and serious grey-blue eyes. He tended to worry too much, and was self-conscious about his looks. At 280 pounds, he was very overweight for his height, almost obese, and no diet or exercise regimen ever seemed to work. He had watched helplessly as he grew older and his body ballooned out. But how he looked never bothered Michael and that was one reason Billy liked him so much. Plus, Michael shared his love of board games, especially Monopoly, and he was the most challenging checkers and chess player Billy had ever faced. In fact, Mike had taught Billy how to play chess; since then, Billy had never defeated him, despite years of trying. He said:

"C'mon, Mike, it's not April Fool's, okay? Tell me what really happened."

"But I already did, Billy. I runned so fast, all my clothes burneded off! Honest! You know I don't lie. Buds don't lie to each other. And it was SO neat! *Whooosh!*"

"That's impossible, buddy. You'd have to run faster than a race car to do that. You'd have to run as fast as the Flash. Y'know, the superhero with the red costume and the yellow lightning bolt on his chest."

"Duh, Billy. I *know* who the Flash is. And yep, that's who I was," said Michael, nodding some more. "The Flash."

Billy snorted. "But that's just comics, Mike. I know ya really like readin' 'em - me too when I get a chance - but remember, that's not real life."

"Yes, Billy, I knowed that comics are just make-believe. But

I runned that fast anyway. *Whooosh!* It was COOL; and as I got super-fast, everything got real slow. An apple falled from a tree and I had time to catch it, even though I was a block away when it started to fall! And I runned past Officer Tim as he walked and ate a bagel. I zoomed right by him while his foot was in mid-air, and he never even saw me, I was just a blur to him, a wind, but to me, he was not even moving."

Michael paused and his brows wrinkled. "But I was so excited, that I forgot one thing. I knowed my skin wouldn't burn because the Flash's skin don't burn when he runs, but my clothes burneded right off. I forgot his costume never burns off because it's made of special material. And of course I couldn't create that."

"Oh, of course. Ah, listen Mike, I think you've been over-imagining things. Look, it sounds like you're getting those costumed superheroes mixed up with the real world. I mean, c'mon, no one can REALLY run THAT fast!"

"I did."

Billy opened his mouth to protest some more, but a chirpy female voice cut him off.

"Hi guys!" Both boys stopped walking and turned. Melanie Van Heusen crossed the street and came up to them. She was the same age as Billy: 15. In fact, their birthdays were only two weeks apart, and they'd both turned 15 just three months ago. However, she didn't look anywhere near as gawky as he did. She was what Billy's dad called "real easy on the eyes" (when Billy's mom wasn't in earshot): sparkling blue eyes, cheery face, great figure. Yeah, about that figure: seemed to Billy that it was just yesterday she'd been that skinny flat-chested tomboy with scraped knees and dirty fingernails who always beat him at sports.

There were two unusual things about Melanie. One was her glasses: they had extremely thick lenses. She was very myopic; so short-sighted that without her glasses, she could only see things right in front of her nose. The other unusual thing was her hair. Six months ago, she'd decided to dye it. Blue. To the shock of her parents, friends and teachers, her auburn locks were now shades of light and dark blue. After the initial surprise, Billy had come to regard her hair as quite attractive; some of the blue streaks matched her eyes, which was cool. Not that he'd ever tell her, of course.

"Hello Melanie," said Michael, grinning broadly, impatient to tell her his big news. Billy mumbled, "Hi Mel."

"So, guys, what's new?"

"I runned REAL fast today on my morning jog. *Whooosh!* So fast that all my clothes burneded off," announced Michael proudly.

"Really? Wow, that's, ah, something." Melanie patted his arm, then looked at Billy with a half-smile.

"Um, well, he sure believes he did," said Billy, trying hard not to stare at Melanie's chest pressing against her crisp white blouse.

"Aw, Billy, you don't believe me? You know I always tell the truth, yes I do, 'cause it's the right thing to do, yes it is. C'mon, I thought we were buds," Michael said, sounding hurt.

"We are, we are. But c'mon, Mike. You're asking me to believe something that's completely fantastic. Look, I don't know of any other kid that reads as many comics as you, and you know all about the superheroes' powers and stuff. But you can't really be the Flash, okay? He doesn't really exist; he's only a comic book character, f'God's sake! You're ... you're over-imagining things again."

"I knowed what I did," said Michael stubbornly. "I was the Flash. Yes I was."

"Yeah? Then do it now. Right now, in front of Mel and me. C'mon."

"Oh, I can't, I'm all dressed for school. Besides, Mom'll kill me if I wreck another set of clothes."

"Cop-out!"

"Listen, guys, stop arguing. We're at school," Melanie said, and punched Billy lightly in the shoulder before running off to join some girlfriends at the side door. She called over her shoulder: "See ya in Second Period, Billy! 'Bye Mike!"

"So I'll see you after school and we'll walk home together,

okay?" asked Michael anxiously, as he did every day before the boys parted, he to go to his Special Needs class in the north wing, and Billy to go to his classes in the regular high school. Routine was very important to Michael.

"Yeah, yeah, you bet, don't worry," said Billy, watching Melanie run toward her friends, the short pleated tartan skirt of her school uniform rising and falling around her thighs. He sighed. Girls. When had Mel changed from the tomboy he'd known since kindergarten, into someone with a body he couldn't keep his eyes off of? Yet she could still beat him at arm-wrestling. And running. And everything else. He sighed again. Being 15 sucked. You didn't know whether to play video games with her, or try and kiss her. Girls.

Billy and Melanie had grown up together in the same middle-class neighbourhood in the north end of the small Canadian city of Clearwater. Actually a town that thought it was a city, Clearwater was surrounded by rolling farms, sparkling lakes and rivers; most kids learned to hunt and fish before they learned to ride a bike. Clearwater was nestled in Eastern Ontario; a speck on a map, almost an after-thought. It had lots of tree-lined streets and a slower pace of life. Too slow, according to many teens, who couldn't wait to graduate high school and move away to someplace - anyplace! - more exciting.

A common teenage complaint about Clearwater was: "Nothing exciting ever happens here."

Soon, no one would ever say that about Clearwater again.

Billy and Melanie's neighbourhood was an older development, built between 30 and 40 years ago. The houses were good-sized and well-kept; most had been renovated with upgrades to keep up with the times. Yards were cloaked in the shade of big mature trees, some of which, due to their age, had the distressing habit of crashing earthward in high winds.

Paul McDonnell, Billy's dad, was vice-principal at Clearwater High, a mid-sized high school built in the 1960s that was showing its age. The school was notable for its indoor swimming pool; quite a novelty when it was built and quite a headache today because of its tendency to crack and leak.

Things were very awkward for Billy at school. Besides his weight earning him lots of cruel unwanted attention from his high school peers, having his father as the vice-principal added to his stress-level.

Billy's mom, Janet, was curator of the Clearwater Museum and Archives. Originally from Nova Scotia, she often pined for the salt air smell and restless waves of the Maritimes coast.

Melanie's father, Gord, owned the Big 'n' Tall clothing store in town, an establishment that counted Billy as a regular customer, much to the lad's embarrassment. Her mother, Brianna, a former Olympic silver medallist rower, was manager of one of Clearwater's banks.

Melanie lived two streets over from Billy. They had been best friends since they were five, even though Mel was more athletic and daring, while Billy was cautious and more sedentary. As they aged, Mel stayed thin while Billy started getting chubby. Though other kids taunted him about his weight, Mel seemed not to notice at all.

When they were ten, Michael Johnson and his family had moved into the old Carstairs house beside Billy. Though Michael's parents creeped Billy out, the two boys had become fast friends, and it never mattered to Billy that Mike was classified as "living with an intellectual disability". Billy's parents were concerned at first, because the new boy was older and stronger in body, yet much younger in mind, and they worried that he might accidentally hurt their son. They were well aware of the positive Community Living approach: to focus on the strengths, abilities, and independence of people with intellectual disabilities, not their weaknesses. However parents were parents, and they couldn't help worrying. But when they saw how much the boys enjoyed playing together, and how pleasant Michael was, they shelved their concerns.

Besides sharing Billy's love of board games, Michael also enjoyed many computer games. He liked the same foods as Billy, though Mike could wolf down three hot dogs with all the fixings in one sitting without gaining a pound, while Billy put on five pounds just by looking at them.

The duo of Melanie and Billy soon expanded to accommodate Michael, and the threesome were usually seen together around Clearwater. "The Misfit Trio" some older folks called them, behind their backs. "The Three Freakos" some classmates sneered, often within earshot. "A retard, a whale, and a four-eyed bluehead." Whenever she heard those comments, Melanie scowled and delivered a withering retort. Billy tried to ignore the taunts, though the words hurt him deeply. Michael just frowned and ground his teeth.

Ontario government legislation, the *Accessibility for Ontarians with Disabilities Act (AODA)*, was the most far-reaching legislation of its type in North America. It's regulations were meant to ensure equal accessibility for everyone living with a disability. The AODA defined "disability" as "encompassing everything except left-handedness and the common cold", according to senior provincial government bureaucrats. That broad definition meant all three teens were living with disabilities: Melanie because of her acute myopia, Billy because of his weight, and Michael because of his intellect.

The three friends couldn't have cared less.

By noon, the entire school had heard about Michael's running story. During the mid-morning period change, a group of regular students passed by his Special Education class and heard him regaling his classmates about it, with full sound effects, while his teacher looked on, bemused. It spread from there.

During lunch period in the caf', Monster Mack and his Gang of Four sought out Billy, who tried, unsuccessfully, to stay invisible. Monster Mack (given names Charles A. MacKenzie, with the middle initial standing either for Anthony or Asshole, depending who you talked to) was the worst bully at Clearwater High. He particularly enjoyed tormenting kids who "looked funny", and Billy certainly qualified. He was also one of the school's celebrated sports jocks: a feared defenceman on the senior boys' hockey team, known not for his skating and puck-handling, but for his vicious body-checks and brawling. Three years older than Billy, he was even taller than Mike, with a face that had seen its share of fights. His mouth had a permanent sneer.

"Hey there, fats," drawled Monster Mack, helping himself to Billy's chips. "Hear your retard buddy thinks he ran as fast as some comic book sooper-hero this morning. S'matta, the retard forget to take his meds?"

"Mike doesn't take medicine," mumbled Billy, wishing he could hit a *Star Trek* com-badge and get teleported out of there. "Besides, it's just a harmless story he made up."

Monster Mack finished off the last of the chips and leaned forward until his face was inches from Billy's face. "Look, retard-lover, don't you dare contradict me. Everyone knows retards need drugs to keep 'em from flippin' out. Now, it may not be pool-itically-correct to pound retards any more, but fat boys are still fair game. Ain't no bleedin'-hearts give a damn about fat boys. You don't want me to find you after school, do ya?"

Billy wished he had the courage to say "screw you", but his courage had eloped along with his appetite when Monster Mack arrived. He hung his head and mumbled: "No."

The bully snorted. "Damn right, porky. Haw!"

Taking the rest of Billy's sandwich, Monster Mack moved on, targeting another hapless victim. Billy fled the lunchroom, hoping that none of Melanie's girlfriends had witnessed that encounter. If they had, they'd blab it to her when she finished her lunch-time tutoring. He envied Michael; the Special Needs kids got to eat in a separate lunch room, safe from bullies.

After his last class, Billy was late in meeting Mike. He had to stay and talk with Mr. Wendell, about his History essay mark that was way lower than it should have been. Wendell finally admitted that he hadn't read the centre section of the essay, and promised to review it and adjust his mark.

When Billy finally emerged from the back door into the afternoon sunshine, he saw a crowd of kids gathered around two people. With a shock, he recognized one as Michael; his friend towered over most kids. But he wasn't taller than the kid facing him: Monster Mack. The bully had an inch on Mike, at least. His heart in his throat, Billy raced forward, elbowing his way through the press of yelling teens.

"So, c'mon, retard! Let's see you run fast, huh? Or are ya just a big liar, huh, retard?" snarled Monster Mack.

Michael stared, unblinking, into Monster Mack's eyes. "Don't call me that. That's the R-word. That's as bad as calling a black person the N-word. The R-word is a very rude word, yes it is. I'm not that at all. I'm special."

"Yeah, 'specially stupid." The bully spat on Michael's shoes. "Well, c'mon, ya big nutbar. I'm gettin' bored; show us somethin' special or I'll show ya some of your own blood."

"You just leave me alone. I've done nothing to you."

"Oh yeah, you have, retard. You're at my school, pretending to fit in, to be normal, when ya really ought to be locked up somewhere away from us regular folks. Burns my ass, it does, seein' all the special treatment your type gets."

"You just leave me alone."

Monster Mack's gang kept the crowd back. But Billy squirmed around one of them, and stepped inside the open space next to Mike.

"Billy!" said Michael joyfully. "Can we go home now?"

"Yeah," replied Billy and turned to Monster Mack. "C'mon, leave him alone, okay? This isn't fair and you know it. It's not right to pick on Mike."

Monster Mack suddenly lashed out with his huge fist and connected with Billy's chest, sending him flying backward to crash to the ground. "Haw! Told ya never to cross me, fat boy! But ya convinced me. I'll leave the retard alone. I don' give a rat's ass that your dad's the vice-principal; now that you're here, I'll pound the living crap outta you instead." He took a step toward Billy.

"No, Mister MacKenzie, you most certainly will not!" Like the Red Sea before Moses, the crowd parted and Principal Eugene Dore strode forward, followed by two male teachers. Monster Mack's gang suddenly remembered other places they had to be, and disappeared. The hulking jock was led away by the principal, yelling over his shoulder: "This ain't over, dweebs! Remember that!" One of the other teachers came up to Billy and Michael, and made sure they were alright.

"Principal Dore will punish MacKenzie for this incident," said the teacher. "At the very least, he'll be banned from the Spring Dance. This school has a zero-tolerance policy toward bullying. Your father shall also be informed."

And all that won't do any good at all, thought Billy as he nodded at the teacher.

The students dispersed. Billy and Mike gathered their things, again reassured the teacher that they were fine, and started for home. Melanie joined them just as they were leaving the school grounds.

"Wait up, guys!" she called. "I just got out of Biology lab; I hadda stay late to redo my friggin' frog dissection. What was all the excitement?"

After they told her, anger and concern clouded her face. "That Monster Mack is such an ass! You sure you guys are alright?"

"Yes, Melanie," said Michael. "The bully just pushed me around, though he did hit poor Billy in the chest awful hard. Awful hard. Knocked him down."

"Aw, I'm okay," Billy said, not wanting to show any weakness before Mel. "I hope Dore throws the book at that Mack bastard!"

"Don't count on it," replied Melanie. "That goon has a powerful family. And he's one of the school's sports heroes, as if that excuses his behaviour! He's gotten off lightly so many times before."

"Yeah, dammit, you're right," said Billy, rubbing his chest. "And you can bet he'll be gunning for Mike an' me again, after this."

"He's a really bad person," said Michael, frowning. "I don't like him at all. No sir."

But the altercation was forgotten when the three friends turned the corner onto the street where Billy and Mike lived. There was a crowd of neighbours in front of Doris Tweedle's house, watching huge gouts of flame and smoke spew out.

"Holy God!" Billy yelled. "Nosey Tweedle's place is on fire!"

The three teens raced to the scene. "What happened?" asked Billy of the first bystander they reached, Mrs. Dumfries, who lived two doors down from Nosey Tweedle.

"Oh hello, kids," she rasped with her usual dry cough. "It's awful! You know that Doris - Mrs. Tweedle - smokes like a chimney. Well, she's had close calls before, but today her luck ran out. She screamed out to us that she fell asleep on her couch with a lit cigarette and woke up to find her livingroom ablaze and now she's trapped in there! Can't come out the front, can't get to her kitchen to use the back door, can't get anywhere! Listen, kids - you can hear her screaming!"

And they could - a high wail of panic and hopelessness.

"Oh God, that's ... that's awful!" gasped Melanie, hand to her mouth.

"Yeah. Makes ya sick. Bunch of us tried to control the flames with our garden hoses, but it didn't do much good and now it's too hot to get near enough. And no one can get through them flames! Mr. Harris tried, but had to give up; the heat was too much for 'im."

"What about fire trucks?" asked Michael, eyes fixed on the hungry flames. "Firemen save you from fires, yes they do."

Dumfries coughed. "Can't get here for at least another fifteen minutes. Hunter Bridge is closed for repairs and they have to take the long way around. Poor Doris will be dead by then. Burned alive."

Melanie gave a choked cry. "That's horrible!" Billy nodded numbly. Mike started noisily sucking on a knuckle, a habit he had when he was thinking hard about something.

The teens fell silent, along with the rest of the crowd, watching the flames devour the house. The wails within had stopped.

Suddenly, a blazing fireball streaked high across the sky, wobbled, stopped and hovered, then arced down and crashed into the Tweedle house, punching through the roof and disappearing inside. The crowd yelled in shocked amazement.

Several minutes later, the flames escaping from the windows and doors started subsiding. The fire grew smaller and smaller, as if a valve was being slowly turned off. Then, with a throaty roar, a massive geyser of flame erupted through the hole in the roof of the house, soaring hundreds of feet skyward.

"What the hell is going on with that damn fire?" someone in the crowd said.

"Who cares?" said someone else. "The front door's clear! Let's get in there and get Doris out now, while we've got the chance! There's no flames in the living room!"

Several men charged in and emerged minutes later coughing and swearing from the smoke and heat. Between them, they carried a limp smoke-streaked body.

"I think she's alive!" called one of the rescuers. "C'mon, we need some help here!"

"Oh, that's wonderful!" said Melanie, tears in her eyes.

"Mel! Look up there! What's up with that?" said Billy, grabbing her arm and pointing skyward.

At the very top of the flame geyser, the fireball reappeared. It moved to one side of the column of flame, and hovered there unsteadily for a moment. Then it flew off, with a touch of wobble, streaking a beautiful red-yellow tail of flame behind it. When the fireball had disappeared from sight, the geyser collapsed. Seconds later, big tongues of flame reappeared at the windows and doors, licking more hungrily than ever, as if angry at being interrupted from what it had been doing earlier. Within minutes, the entire house was wreathed in fire.

"Mel," said Billy slowly, "Did that fire comet thingy look human-shaped to you?"

"Yeah, kinda, I guess. I dunno, I'm totally freaked out by all this."

"Don't think I'm crazy, Mel, but that fire thing looked an awful lot like the Human Torch."

Melanie fixed Billy with a look. "The Human Torch. C'mon."

"Yeah! Y'know, from the Fantastic Four?"

"I know the Fantastic Four. I saw the movies. But c'mon."

"Well, besides flying, the Torch can control flame. An' that's what that fire-thing just did! Aw hell, I forgot to take pictures with my smartphone! An' so did you!"

Melanie shrugged. "Whatever. I'm just glad Nosey Tweedle is alive. What do you think, Michael?"

But Mike had disappeared. Frantic, Billy and Mel started searching for their friend in the milling crowd. From afar, came the wail of sirens.

Across the street, in his backyard, Michael came out from behind the tool shed, naked. He walked to where he'd left his clothes on the back porch. He was proud of himself for thinking to remove his clothes beforehand. Wouldn't do to upset Mom again; she was probably still mad at him for this morning.

His left hand was balled into a fist, clutching its precious treasure. He held up his right hand. A tiny flicker of red-yellow flame danced across the top of his index finger. It didn't hurt at all. Michael grinned, blew it out, and started to get dressed.

Chapter 2

This Man, this Monster

The roadside diner was the only thing breaking the monotony of the Interstate that bisected the arid landscape in an unending straight black line. The diner squatted there, its faded paint and worn-out roof baking in the Arizona noon heat, waiting doggedly for the coolness of the desert night to return.

The bright orange BMW Z4 convertible pulled in and parked. A black-haired Caucasian man of average height and average build, with average looks, got out from behind the wheel of the decidedly-not-average sports car and stretched. Dressed in jeans and a featureless dark grey t-shirt, he looked to be in his mid-twenties. He sauntered into the diner and sat down at a booth.

Kate Stefaniak had been waiting tables for almost 22 years. Now 39, she could size customers up quickly, and usually tell who would be a good 'un and who would be a bad 'un. This new arrival, despite how ordinary he looked, would be a bad 'un. It was the tilt of his head, the half-sneer on his lips, and especially his cold, cold eyes.

Still, she had to make the effort. "Here's a menu, hon. Want some coffee to start?"

The cold eyes looked her over and she flinched slightly.

"No menu; just bring me whatever's got the least grease on it. Coffee'll be fine," said the man, in a voice like oil.

Kate swallowed and retreated. Before she left, she noticed his bare left arm. The forearm had a long tattoo of a nightmare creature, inked in black: dragon's head and wings, snake's body, and a scorpion's tail tipped with a wicked long barb. The dragon's mouth was open, revealing black needle-teeth, and the snake's undulating body had red words inscribed on it: *Life Ain't Fair.*

The tat, a grotesque chimera born from his dark imagination, was the only unusual characteristic of the ordinary-looking man. He had had it inked when he was 16, the day after he walked out the front door of his parents' Albuquerque home for the final time. The day he had bludgeoned his drunken abusive daddy to death with his baseball bat, right after daddy had beat his momma to death with his massive fists.

Nobody mourned his daddy's death. Folks knew what he was, and knew that his wife and son cherished the days he was away on one of his long-distance trucking runs. It was only after his death that folks had found out what they knew of him barely scratched the surface. The police had linked his DNA to a string of unsolved kidnappings and rapes across the United States and Canada.

The cops had wanted to question his teenage son about the man's violent grisly death, but the boy had disappeared. That was almost 10 years and a string of odd jobs ago.

One-Eared Jake, one of the regulars at the diner, said from his perch on the stool at the counter: "Helluva good-looking car ya got there, pard."

"Yeah, 'pard', thanks," replied the man in a bored monotone, giving One-Eared Jake a quick glance.

"Had 'er long?"

"No, just got it yesterday," and he thought: *They'll never find the bodies of the couple I took it from, so there's no danger of anyone reporting it stolen. I washed the leather seats afterwards and the blood came right out. Latte-lovin' yuppies musta had the leather treated.* It pleased him that his fearsome forearm tattoo was the last thing his victims had seen before life quit their bodies. The tat also reminded him every day of the lesson that life had ground into him, which was why when he saw something he wanted, he took it.

"What kinda acceleration she give ya?" continued One-Ear, determined to strike up a conversation.

"Fast enough to get the hell away from ugly hicks like you asking stupid questions that keep a man from sitting in peace."

One-Ear sat back as if physically hit, face reddening. A few of the other regulars spoke out against the stranger's harsh rebuke, and one started to rise, fists clenched, before his wife restrained him. The man ignored them all, staring out the window at the bleak desert shimmering in the heat.

After several minutes, he got up and walked to the bathroom. The other diners glared at him stonily as he passed. The stranger smiled at them. A smile as cold as the Arctic.

Two of the people glowering at him were the Winslow twins, good-looking girls in their late teens. His eyes lingered on them as he walked by, especially on their breasts, barely covered by tight tube tops. It was obvious there were no strapless bras underneath. His cold smile broadened.

He went inside the men's room and relieved himself at the urinal. Then he zipped up and his hand went into his left pocket, wrapping around The Gift.

The bathroom door opened, but no one came out. Nobody noticed. The tube top of one of the Winslow twins suddenly came down around her stomach. A pair of pale breasts tumbled free, and the girl squealed in shock. Sitting across the table, her sister gaped, then hooted with laughter. People turned to see what the commotion was about, and the men roared their approval.

Then the other twin stopped laughing as her own tube top abruptly fell to her waist and her own breasts went on display. The men redoubled their roars of approval. One called out: "Gotta git yerselves better-fitting clothes, gals! Yore bustin' right out! Haw!"

Both sisters hauled their tops back up. Faces crimson with embarrassment, they fled the diner. They piled into their battered pickup truck and took off.

The man who had arrived in the orange BMW emerged from the washroom and resumed his seat at the booth by the window. He was grinning from ear to ear.

Kate really hoped Cook wouldn't screw up the order, and really hoped the Beemer guy wouldn't complain about it if he did.

The man with the cold eyes took one bite of the steak, then the potato, and pushed his plate away. He snarled: "Hey, waitress! Steak's burnt. I'm eating charcoal here, f'God's sake. And the potatoes are cold. Take it back and tell what passes for a cook to do it right!"

Kate relayed the message to Cook, word for word. A washed-up football jock with a fondness for the kitchen wine, he didn't take kindly to such comments, and came out to have a word with the complainant. The diner grew deathly quiet; the regulars knew what had happened the last time Cook had emerged from his sanctum to confront a customer. Hospital did manage to reattach the customer's finger, though.

"Ya don' like mah cookin', Mister?" growled Cook, in a voice that scared small children. He was a mountain of a man, with grizzled beard, huge stomach, and arms like tree trunks. He towered over the customer.

"Not true, Sir. In fact, I *loathe* your cooking. That meal you sent out wasn't fit for a dog."

Cook reddened and his hand - the one holding the razor-sharp cleaver - twitched. "That a fact? Well then, why don't you jest get yore lily-white tourist ass outta here, before I hurts ya, ya wise-mouth bastard?"

The man in the booth sighed. "Because I was hoping to get something edible to eat in here. But you're right. Must be another diner with better cooking down the highway somewhere. So I'll just kill you all and go."

After a moment of stunned silence, the other patrons erupted in gales of laughter. Any one of them, including the women, could whup this rude asshole single-handed.

As the laughter swelled around him, the stranger slid his hand into his left pants pocket and closed his eyes. A violet aura seemed to shimmer around the man, then the air suddenly crackled with ozone; static electricity made everyone's hair stand up. The laughter died away. Cook stared down at the stranger. The rude man's eyes snapped open. They were now entirely white; the pupils had disappeared. With a sound like a thousand cellophane bags being crunched at once, bolts of jagged blue-white lightning burst forth from the stranger's eyes and shot through each person in the diner. It was over in seconds. What had been living, breathing people were now charred, steaming husks. The stranger smiled and removed his hand from his pocket. His eyes returned to normal as the ozone dissipated.

He rose and went into the kitchen to fix himself some sandwiches before hitting the road again. Later, as he left the kitchen, he took a heavy ladle and hit the thin pipe supplying propane to the stove, breaking it. Propane gas hissed into the room.

The man got into his Beemer, flinging his bag of sandwiches onto the passenger seat. He placed the two beers he'd grabbed into the drink holders. He started the powerful 300 horsepower V6 Turbo engine, drove to the edge of the parking lot where it met the highway, and stopped. Seconds later, a streak of blue-white lightning arced from the car into the open kitchen window. There was a tremendous explosion as the gas ignited, engulfing the diner in a massive fireball.

The man smiled. There. The fire will hide the evidence of what he had done to those people. Authorities will figure they died in the gas explosion. So he'd stay invisible to the law as he continued his journey. He was being drawn somewhere, and he knew he would get no peace until he found what The Gift urged him to find.

He was heading north. Which, by happy coincidence, was also the direction those twin teenaged fillies had taken. On the subject of staying invisible, he grinned as he relived the fun he'd had yanking down their tops. Very nice view. Matched pairs.

The BMW's engine roared as he sped off up the highway. Car handled like a dream. Yeah, he had time for a little diversion. Those girls couldn't be too far ahead. In this orange rocket, he'd catch up to their old pickup in no time. He grinned an icy cold grin, like that of a wolf trying to be sociable. He popped open a beer and took a long swallow.

He had no problem mixing pleasure with business.

Chapter 3

The Green Goliath

It was two days after the fire at Nosey Tweedle's before either Billy or Melanie would talk to Michael again. They were extremely cross with him for ducking out during the fire, causing them to search for him with mounting concern through the crowd of onlookers. Finally, they thought to check his house across the street, where they had found him in his basement working out with his weights.

"Holy crap, Mike!" Billy had exclaimed, "why didn't you tell us where you were going? We've been looking all over for you!"

"Yeah," said Mel. "We were afraid you'd wandered somewhere and got hurt. That was an awful fire."

Michael had looked at them and wiped the sweat from his brow with a towel. "Sorry ... sorry, but I had to slip away. That's how it's done, you know. The hero always slips away, to protect his secret identity."

"Slip away? For what?" barked Billy.

"'With great power comes great responsibility.' That's what Peter Parker says in the Spider-Man comics, yes indeed," intoned Michael.

"What are you talking about?" asked Mel.

"A rescue, of course. And it worked real good too, didn't it? Okay, I did have trouble with the flying part, but it was only my first time as the Human Torch. But I did control the fire, didn't I? *Fwaash!* And that let the grown-ups save Mrs. Tweedle. Is she gonna be all right?"

"Yes, they say she'll recover. Inhaled a lot of smoke, though," said Melanie. She had looked at Billy with raised eyebrows. "So now you're going on about the Human Torch?"

"I *was* the Human Torch," said Michael eagerly. "He was the perfect hero for that 'mergency, yes he was."

"Oh hell," Billy had said with a heavy sigh. "Here we were worried sick about him and he's off in his fantasy world again. Just like that running thing this morning."

Michael had protested, but his two friends refused to believe him. They had stormed out, leaving him alone in his basement, hurt that they thought he was lying and, worse, that they were mad at him.

ぬ ぬ ぬ ぬ ぬ ぬ

The following Friday was the night of the big Spring Dance. Melanie had harangued Billy into going with her. He was not looking forward to this; even though he was going with one of his best friends, dances made him feel more self-conscious than usual. Not just because he was a chubby kid, but because he couldn't dance to save his life. And he worried about being a Grade Niner in a mob of senior kids.

Michael would not be joining them tonight. He had little interest in dances and zero interest in girls and, besides, his Friday nights were sacrosanct: this was his time to flip through the week's new batch of comics that he picked up every Friday afternoon after school. The new comics actually came out every Wednesday, but his parents only permitted him to go to the store on Friday, at the end of the school week. Short of a nuclear bomb, nothing could pry Michael out of his bedroom on Friday nights.

Stuffed into a "smart casual" suit (where the pants actually matched the jacket) and trying desperately not to sweat (a foregone conclusion since he exuded heat because of his size), Billy walked over to meet Melanie at her house. He found her waiting on the front porch. Through the open livingroom window, he heard CNN reporting about some gas explosion that had destroyed a roadside diner near Tucson, Arizona. Melanie smiled as he came up her walk.

"Well, well, if it isn't William Butler McDonnell in the flesh. I'm so glad you really did come, Billy. I kinda thought you'd maybe, I dunno, chicken out. Hey, ya look nice tonight; you even wore cool new running shoes, I see. Goes well with your suave suit."

Ignoring her friendly needling, Billy mumbled "thanks" and stared at her. She looked fabulous, her hair had been permed and she wore a sleek blue dress that really hugged her curves. The dress complemented her blue hair perfectly. She took his breath away.

"Billy? You OK? Say something, ya look goofy," said Mel, coming down the front steps. She wobbled a little; Billy looked and was further stunned that she was wearing high heels.

Billy finally found his voice. "You ... you look ... ah ... great tonight, Mel. Wow. Awesome dress. High heels. And nylons, too. They make your legs look really nice. I don't think I've ever seen you in nylons."

"Yeah, well you probably won't ever see me in 'em again, either. I've decided that I can't stand pantyhose! It's so *tight!* I don't know how my mom puts up with wearing it all day at the bank. Ugh!"

Billy laughed, a little embarrassed at this talk of pantyhose. As they started off, Gord Van Heusen, Melanie's father, called out from the livingroom window, drowning out the news announcer talking about a search for two missing teenage girls whose abandoned pickup had been found several miles from the burnt-out diner:

"Have fun, kids! And Billy, you be sure and bring Mel straight home after the dance, okay?"

"Absolutely, Mr. Van Heusen," replied Billy. He felt funny: *What Mel's dad just said, did that mean we're officially on a date? A date? But we're just pals! Augh!*

"Bye, Pops! Love ya!" sang out Melanie. The two teens walked to Clearwater High, Mel chattering away, oblivious to the turmoil in her friend's head, turmoil made worse by the strange new sounds Mel made as she walked: the *clack-clack* of her heels and the soft *swiff-swiff* of her nyloned legs.

"Y'know ... um ... I've rarely seen you in a dress before either," said Billy.

"Yeah, well, my girlfriends - an' my mom - talked me into it. But it goes down to my knees an' my legs really feel trapped in this tight thing! I dunno if I can even dance in it, an' I sure as hell can't kickbox."

Billy laughed. "I very much doubt that dress was made for kickboxing!" Mel laughed too; a sweet musical sound to Billy's ears.

The dance wasn't as fearsome as Billy had thought. The school gym had been transformed into an undersea wonderland, and the Video DJ really knew his stuff. There were a lot of Grade Nines there, and they congregated together, apart from the older kids. Mel actually got him to dance with her a few times and it wasn't so bad. At least no one laughed at him.

Billy looked nervously at the throngs of seniors, searching for Monster Mack and his goons, but he didn't see them. Mack must have been banned from attending and his goons had stayed away in solidarity. He heaved a sigh of relief. One less worry.

At 11:00 p.m., the dance ended. Melanie and Billy said goodnight to their circle of friends (well, mostly Mel's friends; Billy envied her ability to make friends). Then the twosome started for home. As they left the school grounds, Melanie said:

"Well, that was fun, now wasn't it, Billy?"

"Yeah, Mel. Sure was. Much more fun than I figured. Thanks for talking me into coming. And I really liked dancing with you. You really ...um ... look very nice tonight."

Melanie cleared her throat and said, somewhat shyly: "Thanks. Ah, ya wanna ... like ... hold hands?"

He almost swallowed his tongue in surprise, but finally managed: "O ... OK."

So, awkwardly, self-consciously, they did. After a while, it didn't seem so weird at all.

They were about a block away from Mel's street when a black and red van roared up and screeched to a stop in front of them. Billy and Melanie recognized it instantly: Monster Mack's infamous van or, as he proudly called it, his "sex machine".

But there were no girls in it tonight. The van's doors snapped opened and Mack and his four cronies piled out. In seconds, the two fifteen-year-olds were surrounded.

"Well now, what have we here?" drawled Monster Mack. "Two little lovebirds. Though I dunno what a babe like you sees in a tubbo like him."

"Leave us alone," said Billy, in what he hoped was an authoritative voice. "I'm walking her home and her house is just down that street there."

Monster Mack smiled and there was no warmth in it whatsoever. Billy could smell the beer on his breath. "Walking? On this cool, dark night? Why, let's be neighbourly, boys, and give the lovebirds a lift home."

"We don't want a lift; we're fine walking, thank you," said Mel. Holding Billy's hand firmly, she pushed forward, but stopped as the boys in front of her refused to give way.

"C'mon, guys! Let's take 'em fer a little ride!" yelled The Monster. Before they could react, Melanie and Billy found themselves being grabbed and shoved into the back of the van.

"Hey! Leave us alone," yelled Billy.

"Watch those hands, you creep!" shouted Melanie.

Their protests were cut off as the doors slammed shut.

Strong hands held them in place as Monster Mack drove. He cranked the CD player very loud, with lots of base. The gang paid no attention to Billy and Melanie's demands to be set free, and their yells were drowned out by the music.

After a long drive, the van stopped and the eighteen-year-olds got out, dragging their younger captives with them. Two goons held each youngster firmly between them, gripping their arms hard.

Billy saw they were at the end of a long dirt road on the shore of Serenity Lake. An icy dread started building in his stomach. They were miles outside of town and this part of the lake was deserted. He looked at Melanie and saw in her eyes that she was scared too.

"Look, you guys, enough is enough, OK? We don't wanna be here, so just take us back, OK? We won't say anything, if you take us back right now," said Billy and was disgusted with himself at hearing his voice break.

"Our parents will be looking for us, so you jerks better smarten up and let us go," said Mel, and tried to dig in her purse for her smartphone, despite the hands grasping her arms. One of the boys holding her wrenched the purse away, tossing it into the bushes.

Monster Mack had fetched another beer from a cooler in the van and took a long swig. He walked up to Melanie and leaned in close.

"You're lookin' real sweet tonight, babe," he leered. "That's quite some rack ya got there under that tight little dress. Too bad you're underage."

One gang member guffawed. "That ain't never stopped ya before, Mack!"

The gang all laughed at that, while Mel's face went white. "You, you better not dare try anything. You'll get in so much trouble. My dad - "

"Can't do dick-all, compared to *my* dad," sneered Monster Mack. "When ya own the biggest factory in this jerkwater town, that employs half the people here, ya get to call the shots. My old man can get me out of anything."

"Yeah, even Ashley's accidental pregnancy," chortled a goon.

"Hey, stupid!" snarled The Monster. "I told ya never to mention her no more! She's history an' we don't talk about history!"

Melanie gasped. "So the rumours at school are true. You got your old girlfriend, Ashley Thomas, pregnant! We all wondered why she suddenly left."

Monster Mack leaned close again. Melanie winced at the stench of beer on his breath. He said: "Don't waste time on rumours concerning Ashley, sweet thing. Tonight, I'm gonna start a whole new rumour about you."

He took another pull from the beer bottle, then reached out

with his other hand towards the girl's chest. She recoiled with a little cry, but the boys holding her pushed her back toward The Monster. Her left breast went right into Mack's big paw, and he squeezed hard.

"Ow! Stop that! Hands off!" shouted Melanie, and tried to knee him in the groin, but her confining dress hampered her leg. Monster Mack evaded her knee with ease, released her breast, and slapped her face. She yelped in pain.

"Hey, you leave her ALONE, you damn asshole!" yelled Billy, squirming with all his might in the grip of the two thugs holding him. Monster Mack turned and, quick as a striking cobra, hit Billy square on the jaw with his fist. Billy's head snapped back and pain exploded in his head. He sagged at the knees. Through the roaring in his ears, he heard Melanie scream: "BILLY!"

The Monster laughed and finished off the beer, tossing the bottle away. Tasting the copper tang of blood in his mouth, Billy choked out:

"Look ... it's me ... you have a mad-on for. So ... so just let ... let her go, OK?'

The bully barked a short laugh. "Yeah, it was you who we was waitin' for after the dance, fat boy. But your delicious little friend here is a bonus, and when I'm done with you, we're gonna have her for dessert."

He turned to his gang, smiling broadly. "And y'know what, boys? From what I just felt, there's no paddin' in that bra; them boobs are all hers." There was a chorus of hoots and guffaws. Melanie blushed crimson and looked away.

"Why ... why are you doing this to us?" said Billy.

Monster Mack brought his face right up to the younger boy and whispered: "Because I can."

Then he started hitting Billy, hard, in his stomach, head and chest. Helpless in the grip of the two thugs holding him, Billy gritted his teeth, determined not to cry out. But after the third or fourth savage blow, he started yelling in pain. Melanie screamed at The Monster to stop, but he ignored her and kept on punching.

The night air was filled with the dull sickening sounds of fists hitting, the girl screaming, and the goons shouting encouragement to their leader. Billy had stopped yelling. Melanie noticed Monster Mack's fists now glistened in the moonlight; she was horrified when she realized they were covered with Billy's blood.

"Oh, please STOP, STOP, STOP!" she screamed. "You're KILLING him!"

The fists kept hitting.

There was a loud whistling of air, like an incoming bomb, followed by a great crash in the woods near them. The ground actually shook. A tremendous roar split the night air:

"LEAVE THEM ALONE!"

Startled, Monster Mack and his gang froze, then looked around. Great snapping sounds came from the forest, like dozens of tree limbs breaking. The sounds grew closer, louder. Suddenly, the trees at the edge of the woods broke apart as a huge form pushed past them and stomped into view.

"Holy Mother!" yelled a thug. "WhatthehellisTHAT?"

Moonlight shone on an impossible figure: ten feet tall, gigantic chest, arms and legs like tree trunks criss-crossed with corded muscle, untamed dark green hair, a heavily-browed forehead over blazing green eyes and an angry slash of a mouth. The monster raised its huge fists and bellowed in a voice like rolling thunder:

"LET THEM GO! NOW!"

"Great God Almighty!" a goon said, fear in his voice. "Lookit its skin! It's GREEN!"

And so it was. A deep emerald green. A lot of skin was showing, too, as only the remains of a pair of shredded pants covered the beast's loins. Billy would have recognized this creature instantly, but he had passed out from the beating. Melanie stared, eyes wide with shock.

"Impossible," she muttered.

She too recognized the behemoth; she had seen the movies. She barely noticed that the two boys holding her arms had released their grip.

The giant lumbered forward. With each barefoot stride, the ground vibrated under its immense weight of over 1,000 pounds.

THE HERO STONE

Monster Mack realized his mouth was hanging open and with an effort, he shut it. Then he rallied his gang:

"C'mon, guys! Lay into it! It's just some kinda trick! Pile on! Let's beat the bejesus outta it!"

Galvanized despite their awe, the gang swarmed over the emerald giant, their fists flailing. With a great laugh, the behemoth flung them off, effortlessly. One thug was sent flying through the air way out over the lake, hitting the water with a faint splash.

A goon pulled a wicked hunting knife from a leg sheath beneath his jeans, and charged the creature, striking at its huge chest. The blade broke without even penetrating the skin. The green mountain laughed again and swatted the knife-wielder aside. The swat was so strong, the thug crashed into the side of the van and slumped to the ground, unconscious.

Monster Mack smashed off the end of a beer bottle and jumped onto the creature's back, stabbing viciously at its thick corded neck with the jagged end. The glass shattered against the behemoth's skin, and Mack cried out as flying shards cut his own face. The green colossus reached behind and plucked Mack off its back with one massive hand. It held Mack up off the ground, as effortlessly as if he'd been a baby, with his face just inches from its own terrible visage. It said with its great bellows of a voice:

"SO HOW DO YOU LIKE IT WHEN YOU FACE A REAL MONSTER? SEE HOW IT FEELS TO FIGHT SOMEONE BIGGER THAN YOU?"

Mack shrieked curses into the giant's face and received a ghastly grin from that huge mouth for his trouble. Then the creature shook him like a rag doll and flung him to the ground. Laughing in booming gusts, it watched him scuttle off.

Monster Mack regrouped with the two cronies who were still mobile. The behemoth watched them, unblinking, as they whispered among themselves. Then the two cronies ran at the creature, yelling at the top of their lungs. Distracted, the colossus didn't notice Mack slipping away. The onrushing thugs each had knives. Nearing the beast, both boys jumped up, aiming their blades right at its eyes.

The emerald giant jumped too: straight up, its massive leg muscles acting like coiled springs. The men passed beneath it as it leapt, and crashed to the earth with surprised yelps. The creature returned to earth yards away and the ground shook so hard that Melanie stumbled and fell to one knee.

The knife-wielders stood up and charged again. Its huge arms outstretched, the beast waited until the boys were almost upon it. Then it smashed its palms together with tremendous force. There was an ear-splitting *KRAKOW* and a massive shock wave of wind hit the boys, bowling them over backwards. When they stopped rolling, they lay still, blood seeping from their ears.

"HAH!" the creature boomed. *"SO THAT TRICK REALLY DOES WORK IN REAL LIFE!"*

No one had heard the van's engine start or the vehicle drive off down the road. The first the behemoth became aware of the van was when the vehicle was just about to hit it from behind, at high speed. The emerald mountain had a split-second to brace its legs; thigh muscles stood out like huge cables and its bare toes dug deep into the earth. Then the van plowed into it, with Monster Mack howling in triumph behind the wheel.

The creature grunted like a giant elephant at the impact, but didn't move an inch; the strongest legs on Earth anchored it like a granite wall. The van wrapped itself around the beast's legs and buttocks, and came to a shuddering halt in a scream of bending metal. The windshield shattered as Monster Mack came flying through it and hit the broad muscled back of the giant. Over the death throes of the van, Melanie heard a distinct snap as Mack's neck broke. His body fell limp onto the mangled hood.

The jade giant turned and regarded the wreckage of van and man solemnly. Its breathing was stentorian, but it made no other sound.

Melanie ran over to where Billy's battered form lay in the dirt. Falling to her knees, she cradled the boy's bloody head in her lap, heedless of the crimson staining her dress. "Billy! Oh my God! Billy! Are you alright?" She started sobbing. "No, stupid me! Of course you're not alright. Oh, what am I gonna do?"

A huge shadow fell over her, blocking out the moonlight. With a cry, she looked up at the green goliath towering above. She hunched her upper body protectively over her unconscious friend.

"Oh, please don't hurt us! We've been through enough tonight! Please just leave us alone!" she wailed.

Ten feet above her, the beast thundered: *"DON'T BE AFRAID OF ME, MELANIE. I'D NEVER HURT YOU OR BILLY. IS ... IS BILLY GOING TO BE OKAY?"*

Melanie was stunned. This ... thing ... knew their names! "How ... how do you know us? How can you even be here? You're the Hulk! You don't exist!"

"I'M YOUR FRIEND."

Melanie stared, mouth open, brain reeling. The Hulk stepped back and its cavernous voice rumbled: *"I'LL SHOW YOU."*

Two big fingers of a massive green hand squeezed into what was left of a pants pocket. An aura of yellow light appeared around the creature's body, then intensified. The aura became too bright to look at and the girl closed her eyes. When she saw the brightness fade, through her eyelids, she opened her eyes. She gasped.

Michael Johnson was standing in front of her, wearing nothing but a pair of shredded trousers, which he had to hold up with one hand to keep them from falling down. He smiled and said:

"See? Your friend. Now do you believe I can do wonderful things?"

Melanie joined Billy in dreamland, as she fainted dead away.

Chapter 4

Deadly Rage

The bright orange BMW convertible thrummed into Las Vegas, blending right in with the bright lights and gaudy colours of the Strip. But the average-looking man behind the wheel cared nothing for the shows, gambling, outdoor spectacles, or outlandish buildings. He was here to make some cash withdrawals.

He had taken a slight westward detour on his northbound odyssey, in order to hit Vegas. He was tired of supporting himself with the money taken from his victims. It always ran out so fast. He never used any of his prey's credit cards, no matter how tempting. Plastic left a trail. Cash was anonymous. But now he wanted some major dough. So he came to the one town that, thanks to its many casinos, had more available, untraceable cash than a host of banks.

He pulled into the Bellagio, the Strip's most opulent hotel. He gave his car to the uniformed young male valet, who jumped in eagerly and roared off to park it. He strode inside, barely glancing at the million-dollar Dale Chihuly chandelier overhead with its 2,000 hand-blown glass flowers, centerpiece of the lavish lobby. He booked one of their best suites with a view of Lake Bellagio and its dancing water fountains, under Paul Thompson, the name he was using that week. He wrote a false address on the registration card, and paid cash for three nights, aware that it was almost the last of his money. No matter. He'd have more very soon.

As "Paul Thompson" walked through the lobby, following the bellhop carrying his bag, he passed by the newsstand. The cover of *People* magazine caught his eye. The cover headline screamed VANISHED in big yellow type, and the subheading breathlessly informed readers about the dozens of young women who went missing across America each year, never to be seen again. The man grinned. *Yeah, an' since finding The Gift a coupla months ago, I'm responsible for some of them. In fact, I just added two more for them to fret about - twin teenage fillies - who vanished in Arizona. Like the women in the magazine, their bodies will never be found. Love 'em, kill 'em, make 'em disappear. I'm getting quite good at it. Judging from that magazine, other sexual predators like me are out there. But none have what I have.* And his hand drifted to his pocket.

After a shower and a change of clothes, he looked at himself in the mirror and grinned his cold grin. "Time to get to work," he murmured. He pulled on a pair of black cotton gloves that he had bought in a town en route here. His hand went into his pocket and he disappeared,

Moving very carefully, avoiding people who would otherwise crash into him because, after all, they couldn't see him, the invisible man worked his way into the well-guarded main cash room in the belly of the hotel casino, slipping inside as the door closed after an exiting supervisor. There, again moving cautiously, he helped himself to the money on the tables when no one was looking in his direction. He was aware that security cameras watched over the cash room, but he counted on the fact that small bundles of bills, taken quickly from the bottoms of the piles, would not be noticed. The people watching the camera monitors were only alert whenever a person was around the cash, and he was no person at all.

He avoided the stacks of crisp new bills the casino handed out at the tills. He only took from the piles of used cash collected from the customers. He soon had his pockets stuffed with twenties, fifties and hundreds. Then he slowly, carefully, worked his way out of the room and back up to his suite.

He had discovered weeks ago that, when he became invisible, there was a thin aura that surrounded his body. It made his clothes, including anything inside his pockets, as invisible as the rest of him. There was no need to get completely naked, like the famous

Invisible Man authored by H. G. Wells over 100 years ago. This made robbing casinos much easier than pointing a sawed-off shotgun at a terrified teller. Much safer for him, too.

The only inconvenience was that he could only take so much cash at a time, limited to what he could stuff in his pockets or under his shirt. If he picked up anything fat and bulky, like a bag of money, it would stick out of the thin aura enveloping him. People would see the item floating in mid-air. Still, it was an inconvenience he could live with. He just had to make multiple trips, that's all.

To be safe, and to throw the inevitable investigators off the trail, he went to many different casinos along the Strip, stealing packs of cash from each. It was a long and tedious project, as he had to return to his room after each theft, to divest himself of his ill-gotten loot. But, by the end of the third day, he had amassed a very tidy fortune: over three million dollars. All in untraceable, well-used cash.

It pleased him to imagine the consternation at each casino, as their cash count came up significantly, inexplicably short. Some people would likely lose their jobs over this and that thought pleased him even more.

He only had one close call, late the second evening as he was going down the corridor to his room, returning from another foraging expedition with pockets bulging. A besotted overweight conventioneer, wearing an Hawaiian shirt so colourful you needed sunglasses to look at it, came wobbling out of the elevator and headed right for him. "Paul" tried to avoid the lush, but it was impossible to predict where he'd walk, as he tacked from side to side in the corridor like a drunken captain at the tiller of a small sailboat. The drunk plowed right into the invisible man, caromed into the wall, and stopped.

"Jeeesus!" said the conventioneer with a shocked look on his sweaty face. "There's somebody there! I felt a body, but I don' sees nothing! Oh man! Oh man!"

The inebriated delegate wobbled quickly to his room, fumbled for the key card, and managed to let himself in. "Gotta call ... gotta call somebody about this. I ain't *that* drunk! Front desk? Nah. Maybe hotel security? Yeah, that's it!" He let go a thunderous belch, moved to the room phone, and moved right past it as gloved hands grabbed him, propelling him towards his open balcony door. He turned his head, saw no one behind him, and started screaming. He screamed right out to the balcony railing and 17 stories straight down until the pavement silenced him.

As "Paul's" stash grew, he treated himself to lavish meals at the Bellagio's superb restaurants, and bought new clothes from high-end shops like Giorgio Armani and Gucci on the hotel's Via Bellagio. All paid in cash, of course, in a city where someone carrying wads of bills would never be suspicious. People assumed he'd either had good luck at the casinos, or had just arrived and the casinos hadn't separated him from his money yet. Besides the Bellagio, he was careful to patronize other establishments along the Strip, so he wouldn't be "marked" and have unwanted attention drawn to himself.

He ignored the Bellagio's majestic floral displays in the Conservatory and Botanical Gardens, nor did he give the masterpieces in their Gallery of Fine Art a second thought. He had absolutely no interest in the many spectacular shows for which Vegas was famous, not even the renowned Cirque du Soleil shows located at casinos along the Strip, including the aquatic "O" at the Bellagio itself.

He had other entertainment in mind.

Besides his need for money, and the ever-present imperative from The Gift to head north, he had another urge. He'd successfully stifled it while he accumulated his cash stash, but now it was time to address it.

He got directions from the hotel concierge to one of the notorious legal brothels outside the city limits, and drove there early in the evening of the fourth day. He walked in with a swagger, wearing a light jacket to cover his arms. The madam greeted him in the foyer.

"Howdy, Sir," she said. "And what's your pleasure this evening?"

He took his time before replying as he looked her over. Early thirties, with a great figure, especially her tits, which were barely concealed by the tight red evening gown she wore. Her face was sensuous, with a wide mouth and come-on eyes, though she'd overdone it a bit on the make-up, in his opinion. But her most striking feature was her hair: flaming red, cascading over her shoulders in wavy curls.

"You. You'll be my pleasure tonight," he answered finally.

"Why, you flatter me, Sir, but I am your host. We have many lovely girls here, who'll be more than happy to show you a good time."

"No. It's you I want. For the whole night. I'll pay double the going rate."

"Oh, that's quite impossible, honey. I no longer entertain our gentlemen callers; I now own this establishment. But there are many fine ladies who'll - "

"I want you."

The flame-haired woman's smile shrank and an edge crept into her voice. "The answer's no, hon. Now let me get you a nice drink in the lounge here and show you some of my beautiful ladies."

He glowered, but allowed himself to be led into the lounge.

"What's your preference?" she asked.

"Drink or women?" he replied and smiled. She felt a chill travel down her spine at that smile. *If a snake could smile, it would look like that,* she thought.

"Both, hon," she said.

"Single malt Scotch, neat. And women who like it rough."

"We can accommodate you on both, though not too rough with the ladies, I trust." He was shown three sultry women, all in various stages of undress.

"They're fine. I'll take 'em all."

"All? My, but you've quite an appetite. Think you can handle all three?"

"Ah, question is, can they handle me?" And he smiled that smile again, teeth flashing below ice-cold eyes.

He was forcibly ejected from the bawdy house about an

hour later, after the screams and curses of the women brought the security guards crashing into the bedroom. The security men thought they'd seen everything, but what he was doing to the women brought obscenities to their lips. They enjoyed throwing him out.

As he was being dragged away, the madam flung some choice words of her own at him as she comforted her sobbing girls. She yelled a promise to call the sheriff if he ever returned. She made a mental note to phone the other bordellos ringing the city, to warn them about this creature.

The man did not appreciate having his fun cut short. He drove off in his Beemer in a black fury, almost hitting two cars entering the parking lot.

Hours later, around 2 a.m., the brothel had a terrible fire that raged swiftly through the building, killing all of its occupants: prostitutes, johns, and security guards alike.

Next morning, as inspectors from the Fire Marshal's Office combed the smoldering black remains, they discovered that all the exit doors had been sealed shut by some tremendous heat source, fusing them to the door jambs. All they could discover about the fire itself, was that it had started in the basement, and that there had obviously been some type of accelerant, to make it race through the building so fast. No one even had the chance to heave a chair through one of the closed windows.

But the average-looking man with the icy wolf's smile had left Las Vegas by then, heading northeast, toward Colorado by way of Utah. He was driving a new canary-yellow Corvette Z06 convertible, paid for in cash at the Vegas dealership, where the dealer was used to people buying expensive cars in cash after a lucky night at the casino. "Paul" felt it prudent to get a new set of wheels and "legally" this time, instead of stealing it (he'd used another alias and fake address for the paperwork, of course). Before going to the Corvette dealership, he'd abandoned the orange BMW in a hotel parking lot, just in case someone had seen it around that cat house. Besides, he'd been getting tired of it anyway. He'd also been careful to wear a long-sleeved shirt, concealing his distinctive tattoo.

The finely-tuned 625 horsepower 6.2 litre V8 engine hummed as the car flew along the Interstate. It was a beautiful sunny day and traffic was light. He enjoyed the feel of the car, the wind in his hair, the pounding rock music coming from the stereo system.

In the trunk rested two big new duffel bags. One was stuffed with expensive new clothes and the other one with almost three million in cash. Squeezed into the trunk alongside the bags, tightly bound and gagged, was the red-haired madam from the bordello. He had harvested her, before sending everyone else to perdition. Something for the road. For a while anyway. Then she too would vanish.

He cranked up the stereo and gave the road rocket more gas.

Chapter 5

Plastic Revelations

Billy regained consciousness slowly. It was like swimming through thick, white mud towards a shore that always receded. But he finally reached it.

His eyes fluttered open. The first thing he saw was Melanie standing next to him in a too-tight yellow tank top and blue jeans. *When had she changed out of her lovely dress?* She was holding his right hand and tears were streaking her cheeks.

Billy's eyes flicked left and he saw Michael sitting close, a T-shirt straining over his muscled chest. He was holding his left hand and he looked like he'd been crying too. *What was Mike doing here at the dance? It was Friday night; he should be holed up with his new batch of comics.*

He tried to raise his head and pain shot through his skull. He groaned.

"Hey! Billy! He's awake!" shouted Michael. His sad demeanor vanished in an instant and he grinned like a cat left alone with a roomful of canaries.

"Oh, thank God!" said Melanie, quickly swiping away the tears on her face with her free hand and readjusting her thick glasses.

"What ... what's going on?" croaked Billy in a voice that he hardly recognized. He looked down and realized he was lying on a hospital bed.

"You've been sleeping for days. You have a confusion," announced Michael.

Melanie chuckled. "He means concussion. You have a bad concussion and you've been in a coma for three days."

"Three ... *days*?" Billy couldn't believe it. He tried to move, but his body seemed ablaze with all sorts of different pains. "Owww," he muttered, and stopped trying to move.

"Just stay still, Billy," said Mel, concern on her face. "You're pretty banged up. Do you remember what happened?"

"Just ... just the dance ... and the nice time we had ... and how great you looked ... and ... and ... ohmigod ... Monster Mack!" It all came flooding back and the boy winced at the memory. "The last thing I remember ... was that asshole whaling away ... on me. I guess ... I passed out. What happened after? Oh, Melanie, he didn't ... hurt you too, did he?"

"No. We got rescued by a massive ten-foot-tall green creature with muscles on its muscles, before Mack could do anything to me."

"It must be the drugs ... or somethin' that they got ... in me. I thought you said ... ten-foot-tall green creature?"

"She did, she did, Billy," said Michael, nodding his head vigorously. "The Incredible Hulk! Got there just in time, too. Well, too late to keep you from getting so hurted, but I couldn't get the hang of those giant leaps he does. *Thoom!* I was landing in places I didn't want to be, trying to follow the bad guys' van. Once I landed on top of some lady's chicken coop and squished it. I think I hurted a whole bunch of chickens. Boy, I bet she's mad! But I leapeded again before she saw me. *Thoom!*"

Billy closed his eyes and made the mistake of shaking his head. White pain lanced behind his eyes and he groaned.

Melanie said: "It's true, Billy. What Mike has been telling us. He really can change into amazing people."

"Superheroes," said Michael proudly.

"Aw, Melanie! You too? It's mean to pull the leg ... of someone who feels ... like he's dying," reproached Billy.

"I'm not kidding. I saw all of it with my own eyes. Even saw Michael changing back. That part got me as much as the size and fierceness of the Hulk. Then I fainted."

She told Billy about the entire episode, with frequent sound effects and embellishments from Michael. She finished by saying:

"When I came to, Michael was cradling my head in his lap, and I still had your head in my lap. Poor Mike was crying, asking us over and over again to please wake up. The three of us must have looked quite a sight! Anyway, Mike took my place cradling your head, while I looked in the bushes where that bastard had thrown my purse. I finally found it and used my smartphone to call the police. Then I called my parents, who called your parents. They were frantic with worry, since we were very late by then."

"What about ... Mike's folks?"

Mel looked uncomfortable and Michael mumbled something. She said: "Your dad ran over to Mike's house right after my dad hung up. His folks didn't even know Mike was out of the house. They were really angry that he'd snuck out. They told your dad to let the police bring him home and they'd deal with him then."

"That was ... very cold of them. And what did they mean ... deal with him?"

"Punish me for being bad. I didn't stay in the house like I was told," said Michael in a low voice.

"So ... so what'd they do to you ... buddy?"

Michael studied the floor tiles, mumbling: "Same as always. But I can't say. Told me never to say."

Melanie looked at Michael, then cleared her throat. She continued:

"Anyway, my folks picked up yours, and they arrived at the lake at about the same time as the police. You were taken to the hospital here, where they fixed you up as best they could. Besides your concussion, you've got two broken ribs, lots of horrible bruises, your jaw was dislocated, and you've two black eyes. You've been unconscious for three days and we've all been so worried. Your mom's scared sick; they had to give her Valium. We all took turns staying by your bedside. Your folks were here all night. They only left several hours ago when Mike and I arrived to take over."

"What'd the cops say ... about Mike being there?" Billy croaked out. "Especially ... wearing only a pair ... of ripped pants."

"I came up with a story and Mike and I stuck to it. We said Mike had met us walking home from the dance, an' Mack an' his thugs kidnapped all three of us. They roughed up Mike when we got here, which explained his clothes. Anyway, the cops bought it."

Billy asked: "What ... what about Monster Mack and his gang?"

"Oh, the police got his four goons, even the one in the lake. Good thing he knew how to tread water and float. Some of those assholes needed hospitalization and they've all been charged with abduction, forcible confinement, assault, underage drinking, and some other stuff."

"And Mack? What about ... him?"

Melanie looked at Michael, who dropped his eyes and hunched his shoulders. "Well," she said, "turns out he didn't die when his van crashed into that solid green Hulk mountain. He's still alive, amazingly. But he's ... he's ... "

"A paralegal," mumbled Michael.

"A paraplegic," corrected Mel. "Can't even move his head. Needs oxygen piped right into his nostrils just to keep breathing. He's actually just two floors down from here, under police guard. See, he's facing a bunch of charges just like his gang, but worse, since he was the leader and he was the one who almost beat you to death."

"I'm real sorry he's crippled, but he's such a bad guy," said Mike. "Real bad, yes he is. He really hurted you an' you're my best friend. It made me so angry. Besides, he never should've tried to run over the Hulk with his van, 'cause the Hulk's the strongest one there is, yes he is."

"Don't be sorry, buddy," said Billy. "That piece of garbage deserved it."

"Well, Monster Mack won't be able to wiggle off the hook this time, even with his dad pulling strings," said Mel. "Our parents have hired a big Toronto law firm to sue his ass for what he did to us. That'll be a civil suit; 'cause the cops are charging him with all those criminal charges, too. That pond scum won't be tormenting us or any other kids for a long time."

"Oh good," muttered Billy. "Best news I've heard ... since I awoke. But ... but how did Mike come to follow us. That was ... your comic night, buddy."

"Yep, yep, it was," Michael replied. "But last week's batch was not as many as usual. The store only got part of what they ordered. The rest of their order got sended to a store in Newfoundland by mistake. So I finished flipping through 'em near the time the dance ended. I remembered that the dance was supposed to end at 11:00 p.m., 'cause that's when the news always comes on downstairs and my folks always watch the news.

"So I sneakeded out the back door - real quiet, so my folks wouldn't hear - they don't want me out after dark - and went to meet you guys. I wanted to surprise you, 'cause I couldn't wait to tell you, Billy, about this awesome new story in the Justice League comic that I just got. You'll never guess who just came back from the dead - again!

"Anyway, I saw you both from way down the street, just when the bad guys' van pulled up. I saw them surround you and I ran to help you, like you helped me at school the other day. Then I saw you both get throwed into the van. That's when I decided to change into someone real strong so I could stop the van and set you free. I chose the Hulk. But before I finished changing, the van drove off real fast, so all I could do was chase it. Ol' Greenskin can't fly, but he can leap great distances. *Thoom!* He has the strongest leg muscles in Marvel Comics, y'know. *Thoom!* Only, it's real hard to control those leaps, especially where you land. *Crash!*"

Billy looked at Michael. Then he looked at Melanie. Then he said:

"You're both ... serious, huh? It's all true? Mike actually changed ... into the Incredible Hulk?" His two friends nodded. "Okay then, show me, Mike. Please. Change into something ... right now."

Michael frowned. "It's a public place, Billy! I told you before, I gotta be careful of my secret identity."

"It'll be okay, Mike. It's a private room here ... and the door is closed. Just don't change ... into something dangerous, especially not ... the Human Torch, because of all the oxygen ... used around here! Just something simple, so I ... can see for myself, okay?"

Mike sucked a knuckle for several seconds, then said: "Okay." He reached into his pants pocket and closed his eyes. A yellow nimbus surrounded him briefly, then faded. He opened his eyes and smiled.

"Well?" asked Billy. "All I saw was a ... neat little ... light show. You're still you."

"Nope. I changed into one of my favouritest characters; I like him because he's so funny. Look at Melanie's head."

Billy looked and gasped. Two big pink rabbit ears were waving behind Mel's head. She turned her head to look, shouted, "WAAH!", and jumped out of her chair. A long, impossibly-long, arm was moving behind the chair, and the hand at the end of the arm had two fingers that had grown into foot-long rabbit ears.

Mel said: "The ... the arm goes under the chair, under the bed, right up to - " she moved to the other side of the bed " - to Michael! Mike, you stretched your entire left ARM!"

"Heh. Yep. Just like Plastic Man, the original rubber-band man, though of course I can't do his red costume that stretches with him. He can stretch himself like rubber and shape himself into anything. He always makes me laugh, when I read his stories." Mike giggled. "Lookit this."

His arm retracted with a rubbery kind of sound. Then his neck grew. And grew. And grew, until his head was at the ceiling, swaying back and forth like a monstrous cobra. Melanie and Billy gaped.

"As Plastic Man," Mike said, "I can also take the shape of furniture 'n' stuff, like the chairs here, or that cabinet, but I really shouldn't 'cause since I can't do his special costume, I'd haveta get naked first or else I'd rip my clothes."

Michael's long neck slowly returned to normal. "See, Billy? Told you I wasn't lying. Told you." he said.

"Yeah ... yeah, I believe you, Mike. I apologize ... for doubting you. You really can ... do all that amazing stuff. Totally cool! But

... but *how*?"

"With this." Michael brought out something from his pants pocket and held it in the palm of his hand for his two friends to see. It was a very smooth, flat stone coloured in shades of pink and yellow, laced with purple and white streaks with a scattering of gold flecks. The stone was half an inch thick and shaped like a big 'D', with smooth rounded edges, except for the long straight side which had clean right-angles to its edge. It was three inches long along the straight edge of the 'D', and two inches wide.

"It's ... it's beautiful," said Melanie and tentatively touched it with her fingers. "Huh, it's warm. Or is that from being next to your leg?"

"Nope, it's always warm," said Mike. "And it hums too."

"Hums? I don't hear anything." Mel bent down and put her ear next to the stone. "Nothing."

"Well, it hums to me. I can hear it."

"Mike, I've never seen you ... with that rock before, in all the years ... I've known you," said Billy. "How'd you find it?"

"Actually, it founded me," answered Michael, stroking the stone with a thumb. "Yes it did, oh yes."

The big boy saw his two friends looking at him blankly, so he elaborated: "You know I takes a jog each morning, right? Same route, every day: down the street, through Burnham's Woods, around the old Kent place, then back through the Woods to my house. Well, about two months ago, I was running through the Woods when I falled over a big branch in the path. There was a big scary storm the night before and lotsa branches were in the path.

"Anyway, I falled real hard and went down that big hill next to the path and fetched up hard against a big tree at the bottom. Ripped my pants and cut my knee. Anyway, as I was picking myself up, I heard this weird humming sound from a bush next to the tree. I lookeded around under that bush and founded this pretty little rock."

"Then what?" asked Melanie.

"Well, I went home. Mom had to doctor my cut knee. She was real mad, 'cause I'd torn my jeans over the knee. Gave me a few good whacks for that one."

"She ... she hit you ... just for having an accidental fall?" managed Billy weakly.

Michael shrugged. "Yeah. Most times she leaves it to my dad to punish me, but sometimes she can't wait and does it herself. Anyway, I kept the stone with me for days after I founded it. It was always warm and I liked the pretty colours and how it hummed to me. Well, one night after I went to bed holding the stone, I had this awesome dream, just like the comic I'd been reading before bedtime, before Mom screameded at me to shut the light off and go to sleep. In my dream, I was flying, like Superman. Then I bumped into something and that woke me up. It was the ceiling."

"The ceiling," said Billy and Melanie together.

"Yeah! See, I'd bumped into the ceiling 'cause I was floating! I looked down and there was my bed below me. I was so scared, I cried out and covered my eyes with my hands. When I did that, the stone dropped out of my left hand. I fell asleep holding the pretty stone. It landed on my bed and then, so did I. Made a big crash noise, which woke my folks. Which got me yelled at some more."

"So ... so ya gotta, like, hold the rock to change, and if you let go, ya change back?" asked Mel.

"Yeah," replied Mike. "I gotta hold it to change and to change back. But after the change, I just put it in my pocket. I found out that as long as it's right next to me, like in my pocket, the change stays as long as I want."

"Wait, wait ... what about that morning when you first told us about you changing; that time you said you, like, ran so fast your clothes burnt off?" asked Melanie. "You *had* no pockets! So where was the rock?"

"In my hand," said Michael. "I holded it tight in my hand. Same as when I was the Human Torch later that day, at Nosey Tweedle's. I was so scared I'd forget and open my hand by accident and let the stone drop 'cause I was flying so high and knew I'd die if I falled from that high up. But I didn't fall and I controlled the fire so the men could rescue the trapped lady."

Billy's head was spinning and not just from his concussion. He said: "So this rock ... lets you change ... into any superhero character you want?"

"Not any one. Just those with orgasmic powers."

"Orgasmic? Ah, you mean organic, I think," said Billy, as Melanie giggled.

"Yeah, powers that are a part of them, natural powers. Like Flash or Hulk or Plastic Man. Like them. The stone can't create a hero's costume or a hero's technicolour things."

"Technicolour things? Oh, you mean technological?"

"Yeah, like Iron Man's armour or Batman's gadgets. They invented that stuff; it's not a natural ability. See, I can get Spider-Man's orgasmic powers, like climbing walls and his speed and his strength, but I can't create his web-shooters or the web-fluid that goes in 'em. I'm not smart enough to invent that stuff, or Iron Man's armour, or build a Batmobile."

"Hah. Mike, no one ... is that smart, so don't worry ... about it."

"Wait," interrupted Mel. "I don't read comics like you guys, but I saw the first three Spider-Man movies and his webs were orgas ... organic. They came out of his wrists, not from mechanical web-shooter thingies."

"Those first movies had that part wrong, yes they did," said Michael, shaking his head vigorously. "The newer Spidey movies got it right, just like in the comics. His webs and the shooters are arti-fictional."

"Artificial."

"Yeah. Made by him."

Billy shook his head and winced. "Wow. All this is ... absolutely amazing. Mega-cool. Do you have any ... idea where the stone came from?"

"Nope."

"Have you told your folks, or anyone else ... about all this?"

"Oh no! You two are the onliest ones who know. A hero's gotta protect his secret identity, y'know. That's very important.

But I told you 'cause you're my best friends. And best friends have no secrets, right Billy?"

"Yep, right. Listen, guys, I'm really feeling kinda ... funny all of a sudden. Too much all at once ... I guess. My head's really hurting."

"Oh! We're so stupid!" exclaimed Melanie and jumped to her feet. "We should have called a doctor or nurse as soon as you woke up from your coma!" She dashed from the room.

Medical staff soon arrived and shooed Michael and Melanie from the room. Mel called Paul and Janet McDonnell, Billy's parents, and told them the great news. They were ecstatic and said they'd return to the hospital right away.

The two teens took the bus home. During the long ride, Melanie looked sideways at Mike, who was transfixed by the scenery passing by outside the bus window. She thought about his amazing rock and shook her head. It was all, like, totally unbelievable. Except that she'd seen it work with her own eyes.

She walked Mike from the bus stop to his house, saw him safely inside, then trudged homeward herself. She was very happy that Billy was out of his coma and on the mend, but she was tired from her long vigils at his bedside. So she had just two priorities when she got home: bed, sleep.

When she got to her front porch, the screen door burst open. Ashley, her annoying younger sister who was twelve years old going on eighteen and always raiding her clothes and jewellery, charged out, yelling:

"Mel! Billy's dad just called from the hospital! Bad news! Billy's got internal bleeding in his head and has gone back into a coma again! The docs say he's probably gonna DIE!"

Chapter 6

Shadow of Death

The neon sign of the Traveller's Haven Motel flickered in the twilight. Sparse traffic moaned by on the Colorado Interstate and only a handful of cars were parked in front of the motel rooms.

The neon tubes in the sign buzzed fitfully. "Best Motel This Side Of Denver" read the faded words under the Traveller's Haven name. And that was the truth, because it was the only motel this side of Denver.

Al Harwood was behind the front desk, trying to stay awake. It was a slow night; usually most of their 45 rooms would be full up by now. But there were only a few families in, a coupla travelling salesmen, and that rude bastard in Number 27. He took a lot of luggage into his room for a man travelling alone: two duffles and a big bundle wrapped in a blanket from the trunk. Guy sure drove a sweet car, though: brand-new yellow Corvette Z06 convertible.

Al was 21 years old, tall and gangly, with a moon face that never seemed to be clean and a jungle growth atop his head that hadn't seen a comb since grade school. He had the night shift at the motel, which was fine, as that left him free to attend college in Denver during the day. It also gave him and his girl Mary Beth a room to get it on in, whenever she dropped by on her way home from waitressing at the Denny's down the road. Tonight wouldn't be one of those nights though; to Al's horny disappointment, she had to work a double shift.

He was watching a rerun of some dumb comedy show on the TV in the lobby when the thunder started, down the highway a ways. The thunder grew louder and louder, then a horde of motorcycles roared into view. One of Al's worst nightmares came true as the bikes slowed and wheeled into the motel parking lot. There must have been eighteen or twenty of them, huge throbbing beasts of polished chrome and painted metal. Many bikes carried two riders, a male and a female, clad in black leathers accented with silver studs.

"Crap, crap, crap," said Al as one of the bikes pulled up to the office. The biggest, meanest-looking man he'd ever seen climbed off and clomped into the lobby. Well over six feet, the guy looked to be in his late forties. Al wasn't short himself, but this guy was at least a head taller than him. He had a red bandanna on his head, a black eyepatch with a white skull and crossbones over his right eye, and a huge bushy grey-black beard. He was pushing an enormous beer gut in front of him.

"Hey there, kid," the man-mountain growled in a voice that sounded like two rocks scraping together. "Ya got ten rooms for me an' my friends here?"

"Ah ... ah ... ah," said Al.

"That a yes, kid?"

Al nodded dumbly.

"Good," said the biker. "How much?"

Al found his voice, but his throat had suddenly gone dry. He croaked out the rate. The biker scowled down at him and Al quickly dropped the rate by ten dollars a room. The Belly That Walked Like A Man scowled again and Al lowered the rate by another five bucks. With an abrupt smile, the biker agreed and scrawled out the particulars on the registration card.

"Cash OK, kid?" said the biker.

"Cash is fine," squeaked Al. He knew his miserly boss preferred cash; Al suspected he had two sets of books.

The biker thrust a fistful of bills at Al, who gingerly took them. "It should be all there."

Al hurriedly counted the bills, praying fervently that it was the correct amount. It was.

As Al was handing out the keys, he screwed up his courage and stammered: "We ... we have a firm No Noise rule here at the motel, Sir." The man-mountain scowled again and Al said: "Well, actually it's more of a guideline than a rule. We ... we just don't want our other guests disturbed by loud drunken parties, is all."

The biker reached over and ruffled Al's hair with a hand that looked like it could squeeze a watermelon until it popped. "Don' you worry none, kid. We been ridin' all day an' we're tired. Alls we wanna do is kick back, crack open some brews, an' watch cable. No loud drunken parties tonight. Promise."

Within thirty minutes, Al discovered the big biker's promise meant about as much as a politician's after an election. The gang started partying, and it got louder and more rowdy as the night wore on. The switchboard started lighting up with complaints about the noise from the families and the salesmen.

After the first complaint, Al called One-Eye's room, which by amazing coincidence was also Party Central, and politely asked him to quiet down his cohorts. The biker growled agreement and hung up. The noise subsided. For about five minutes. Then it started up again, swelling louder than before.

After more complaints, Al called again. The biker chief swore at him for disturbing his party, using some colourful word combinations Al had never heard before, and slammed the phone down. The noise continued.

More complaints ensued, as all the other guests called the office, except for the guy in Number 27. There was no choice; direct action must be taken. Al wondered if someone age 21 was too young to do a Will, then decided his few possessions weren't worth leaving to anybody.

Swallowing hard all the way, he walked from the office to One-Eye's room and pounded on the door. It finally opened. Al saw a crush of bikers inside, and in the two adjoining rooms whose connecting doors were open. Beer cans were everywhere and the air was thick with the acrid haze of marijuana smoke. Everyone was in T-shirts or muscle shirts above their jeans and leather pants, except for one guy who was down to his jockey shorts. Al's contemplation of his doom was briefly sidetracked when he noticed how nice some of the women looked in those muscle shirts.

Al drew himself up to his full height, coughed from the smoke, then in a voice filled with more authority than he actually felt, demanded to see the leader,. He soon found himself staring into the florid face of One-Eye.

Al cleared his throat, glanced down at the huge belly pressing into his chest, committed his soul to God, and said: "Look you guys, enough is enough. This is your third and last warning. Knock off the noise or I'll call the police. Now I know you don't want that; that's pot I smell. But I'll forget all about that if you please just stop the noise. Okay? Deal?"

"Real purty speech, kid," rumbled the caretaker of the beer gut. Ten seconds later, Al found himself sailing through the air with all the grace of a giraffe suddenly learning to fly. He landed in the motel's outdoor pool, fully clothed, clearing the pool's guard fence by mere inches. He surfaced, coughing and sputtering, to the uproarious laughter of the two bikers who had tossed him there. They returned to the party.

Al returned to the office. The motel owner's rules were clear about what he should do if guests refused to quiet down after three warnings. Dripping wet, he called the state police to come and evict the bikers for causing a disturbance. The desk sergeant said he couldn't send a car over for some time; there'd been a horrific multi-vehicle accident on the Interstate about thirty miles away and all available officers were out there.

Al despaired, as the switchboard lit up again with complaint calls and the bikers cranked up the volume of their music.

The party spilled out onto the parking lot. Chugging contests and arguments were the main entertainment, with one argument degenerating into a fist fight, which One-Eye stopped after several minutes by sitting on one combatant while throttling the other until both agreed to be more sociable. Any guest that stuck his or her head out to yell for some quiet, had a beer can and curses flung at them. Al stayed holed up in the office, with the door locked. Now he was glad Mary Beth wasn't here tonight.

About 45 minutes later, reeling from the effects of beer and pot and needing to piss like a racehorse, One-Eye went to the door of the nearest motel room, Number 27, thinking it belonged to one of his gang. He tried the knob, but the door wouldn't open. Swearing at it for being stuck, the man-mountain heaved his huge bulk against it. The cheap lock broke and the cheaper doorjamb shattered into splinters as the door crashed open.

One-Eye stumbled inside, recovered, and gaped through his fog of inebriation at the scene before him. A naked man was standing next to the bed, on which lay an equally-naked woman with flaming red hair, tied spread-eagled on her back with strips of cloth around her wrists and ankles, her mouth sealed with duct tape.

"Whoa, folks. Wrong room. Sorry I interrupted yore kinky sex game there," said the biker, starting to back out. Then he noticed the blood on the bed sheets, all around the woman. Her eyes were staring at him, unblinking, over the gag. Her chest wasn't moving. He saw the man's hands were dripping red and one hand clutched a knife, also dripping crimson.

"Hey! Jesus, what's going on here? What you do ta that poor thing, ya sick bastard?"

The naked man looked at One-Eye and in a voice cold as a brew pulled from the bottom of an ice cooler said: "Get. Out. Now."

The biker stumbled back outside, but only as long as it took him to holler for his gang. Then he charged back into the room, bellowing like an angry bull. The naked man dove across the room to a pair of trousers draped on a chair, and rammed his hand into a pocket.

As many of the gang that could fit, crowded into the room behind One-Eye. Some stared at the woman on the bed, cursing at the awful wounds marring what had once been a beautiful body. The coppery smell of blood filled the air. Two bikers turned away and retched.

Backed into a corner, the naked man clutched something in one hand. He snarled: "I told you to leave. This is no business of yours, but if you stay one minute longer, I'll make it your business and then you'll sure as hell regret it."

One-Eye swore at him. "Yore a sick, twisted, perv bastard. Ya didn't jest kill her, ya tortured her to death, didn't ya?"

"So? I had her for three days and I got tired of her."

"Sweet Jesus. Yore cold, mister. Real cold. When a biker gets tired of his old lady, he jest tells her ta ride with somebody else. He don' slice her up like Jack the Goddamn Ripper. Well, me and my gang are gonna enjoy whalin' on ya an' there won't be much left for the cops when we're done."

"I warn you, stay back."

"Right. Ya gonna hit us with whatever ya got in yore hand? Ya might have a killer tat on yore arm, but you're really just a wussy tryin' ta look tough. C'mon boys, let's git 'im good!"

The gang advanced on the cornered man. Some had switchblades, others had brass knuckles, and the rest balled their hands into fists. They stopped as a violet glow enveloped the man.

"What th' damn hell?" muttered One-Eye.

The glow faded and thick black shadow filled the corner where the man had stood.

"Hey! Where'd the sicko go?" asked a biker next to One-Eye.

"Holy God in heaven!" another biker shouted. "Am I too stoned or is that shadow moving?"

"It IS!" yelled a third.

Impossibly, the shadow grew upwards and outwards until it reached the ceiling and the walls on either side. Then it seemed to shiver. Just below the ceiling, a head became distinct, atop a thin snakelike neck; a huge dark head with orange eyes and a long narrow snout. The snout towered over the bikers and then it opened, revealing rows of long, pointed, black teeth framing a red mouth.

The apparition *hissed*. The bikers lost their courage at that point, and fought to leave the death room through its single door. Some made it out, spilling onto the parking lot, yelling and swearing. But most couldn't get out in time and were enveloped by the shadow creature. One-Eye was the first to die; the long jaws bit his head clean off. Then it went to work on the rest of its captives. Mingled with their screams were sounds of clashing teeth and ripping flesh and crunching bone. Soon there were no more screams.

The remaining gang members, male and female, gathered outside facing the doorway, holding weapons. Some had fetched guns.

"Should we ... should we go in after it, whatever the hell it is?" asked one.

"Yeah, let's. That was my old man in there," said a woman and cocked her pistol.

In total silence, the shadow erupted from the doorway and surrounded the gang in a heartbeat. Like giant bat wings, the sides of the shadow closed inwards upon the bikers, while the toothed snout waved above on its sinuous neck. The snout opened, black razor-sharp teeth gleamed in the parking lot lights, the head turned upwards and it *hissed* at the moon high above. Then the head plunged down into the centre of the shadowmass. The screaming and tearing and crunching sounds began again.

Wide-eyed behind the office window, Al watched the ... thing ... do its terrible work out on the parking lot. He was so scared that he'd pissed himself, but he scarcely noticed. Long minutes later, he saw the shadow unfold and pull back toward the room, disappearing inside and leaving a pile of twisted, bloody bodies behind. Al left the window and dove behind the front desk counter, curling up into a foetal ball, hoping that those state troopers would arrive soon and praying with all his might that the black thing would not come crashing into the office.

When the police finally did arrive, they found a terrified night clerk huddled behind the office counter, bloody carnage inside and outside room 27, and no sign of the Corvette belonging to the guest who had registered for the room. The name and address he'd put on the registration card turned out to be false, as was the licence number of the car. The desk clerk hadn't checked to see if the plate on the car matched the number the guest wrote on the registration card. Horrified by the vicious deaths, the cops put out an APB on the 'Vette, based on the clerk's description.

The following day, Al Harwood quit as night clerk of the Traveller's Haven Motel and took less stressful employment. As night kennel master for a company that trained attack dogs.

Chapter 7

Miracle Blood

After Ashley's shocking news, Melanie's initial reaction was that her younger sister was playing another one of her sick practical jokes, like the infamous Bra Incident two years ago, when Mel was thirteen. One night after Mel had fallen asleep, Ashley had snuck into her room and replaced the two bras left in her underwear drawer with an identical set, except they were one size smaller. Ashley had saved her allowance for weeks to buy the replacement bras. The next day, a joyful Melanie was convinced that her bust had undergone a sudden grown spurt, and that it was a harbinger of bigger things to come. The deception lasted for several days, with Melanie strutting around, proud of her expanded chest size, and Ashley stifling her laughter all the while. Then Mel's other bras came up from the wash and when she put one on, it fit perfectly. Perplexed, she compared the labels and the jig was up. Ashley had teased her older sister about the gag for months afterwards.

No such luck this time. On threat of instant bloody death if she was lying, Ashley insisted that the call from the hospital was legit. And Mel saw it in her eyes. Annoying Sister was telling the truth. An awful dread filled her; Billy was dying.

Melanie jumped on her bicycle and raced over to Michael's house. She wished Mike's folks were like hers and that they both worked during the week. Then she wouldn't have to encounter Mrs. Johnson. But she was a full-time housewife, though what she did around the house all day was a mystery. Mostly, she drank and watched her game shows and soaps. Still, she was always there when Michael came home from school. You couldn't leave an eight-year-old home alone and, in reality, that's what Mike was, despite his official age of seventeen. However, many times when he came home, Mike found her passed out on the couch - "sleeping" he called it - and was left to his own devices anyway.

She rang the bell. No answer. Rang again. Finally, the door opened and Ruth Johnson stood there, swaying. It was only 10:30 in the morning, but she was already into the hootch.

"Hi, Mrs. J," Mel said. "Can I see Michael right away? It's really urgent."

"Hi yourself, Melanie. He's in the shower. What's so urgent?" said Mrs. Johnson and took a long drink from the glass she carried. She noticed Mel looking at it. "Oh, pardon my manners. It's, ah, Seven-Up. Wouldja like some?"

"No thank you. It's Billy. The hospital just called. He's taken a turn for the worse. They ... they think he's gonna die."

The older woman fixed Melanie with a look. "Really? Die? Huh. Shouldn't'a let hisself get beat up so bad."

Mel was flabbergasted. "What's up with you? It's not like Billy had any choice! Those goons ganged up on him!"

"Too wimpy ta defend hisself, ya ask me. But don't get your panties all in a knot, missy. It's just my opinion, an' nobody cares 'bout my opinion. Wait here an' I'll fetch Mike."

Actually, it turned out that Mel had to go to Michael. His mother blurted out the news about Billy as soon as he stepped out of the bathroom, wearing shorts and a T-shirt, and it devastated the boy. He sat down hard right in the hallway and started crying. His mother yelled at him to stop that and go see his friend who was waiting outside the screen door, but Mike just sat there and bawled. Finally, with a snort of disgust and a snarled remark about him being such a big baby, Ruth Johnson yelled at Melanie to come in. Then she disappeared into the livingroom, where the TV was blaring.

It took some time for Mel to calm Mike down. In fact, his sobs were so heart-breaking that she cried herself for a time. Finally, the two teens stopped their tears.

"Come ... c'mon, Mike. Let's go back to the hospital, okay?"

Melanie snuffled, then blew her nose loudly. "Maybe ... maybe things have changed, y'know?"

"Yeah," said Michael and another elephant trumpeted as he too blew his nose.

Mrs. Johnson was in no shape to drive and Mel didn't know how, so the car in the Johnson driveway was useless to them. Luckily she hadn't spent her allowance yet, so they had enough money for a cab ride. When the teens reached the hospital and went into Billy's room, things had indeed changed. For the worse.

"Kids, the docs say Billy's only chance is an operation on his brain," said Paul McDonnell with a heavy voice. Behind him, sitting on a chair beside her son's bed, Janet was crying with a handkerchief pressed to her mouth. Billy's aunt and uncle were standing on either side of her, trying to comfort her. Mel ached when she saw her friend again lying still and pale on the bed, as he had been for the previous three days.

"What ... what kinda operation, Mr. McDonnell?" Melanie asked.

"A very risky one. The operation might kill him as surely as the bleeding inside his skull. They ... they don't hold out much hope for him, either way."

"The doctors are gonna cut into Billy's head?" asked Michael, horrified, staring at Billy.

"Yes, Mike. They must, to try and save Billy. He's bleeding inside his head and they can't stop it. It's from all those punches and kicks he got from that bastard Monster Mack." said Melanie.

"That's ... that's just not FAIR!" said Michael loudly, and everyone in the room looked at him. "Why, Billy was better when we were here this morning. He was awake and we were talking and laughing and everything!"

"Yes, Mike, it's not fair. Billy took a turn for the worse after we left," Melanie replied, her voice cracking. She sat Michael down on a chair and put her arms around his broad shoulders, hugging him. Quietly, she started crying again. Fat tears chased each other down her cheeks and splashed onto her tank top and Mike's shoulders and she didn't care.

Michael sat there, frowning. Then he started sucking a knuckle noisily, while rocking slowly. Every so often, he'd mutter around the knuckle: "No, not him, no, no." No one spoke to him; everyone was busy dealing with their own grief.

Mike suddenly jerked upright. He rose from the chair and grabbed Mel by her shoulders. She looked at him through watery eyes and said: "What?"

Michael spoke in an excited whisper: "Figured it out! How to save Billy! Yes I did, I surely did!"

Melanie blinked away her tears. "How?"

"Can't say right here. People'll hear. C'mon, lets go outside for a minute. C'mon!"

She followed him down the elevator and outside the hospital. They walked out onto the big lawn in front of the building. Then, with no one around them, Michael spoke:

"Y'know that stone I have and what I can do with it?"

Melanie nodded. "Yeah, but how's that gonna help Billy? Changing into the Hulk or Plastic Man won't do Billy any good."

"Ah, but I can become any superhero I think real hard about and I knows lots an' lots of superheroes from the comics I read. I knows all about what they can do."

Mel looked at him blankly. He went on:

"Well, see, I had to do a lot of thinking. About all the heroes. One after the other, I thought real hard about 'em. Then I thought of just the right one. The one who can save our bestest friend! But ... but I need your help about how to make it work. I can't figure that part out."

"What ... what do you want to do?"

"After I change into this one hero, I gotta get a transformer of my blood into Billy."

"Transformer? Oh, you mean transfusion? *That* what ya mean, getting your blood into Billy?"

Michael nodded. "Yeah. But ... but there's two big problems. See, I don't know how to get a nurse to do it, without giving away my secret. And ... and I *hate* needles. Just hate 'em! But I don't want Billy to die, either!"

"No one wants Billy to die. Mike, exactly what d'you have in mind?"

"Well, see, there's this superhero called Wolverine. Logan's his real name. He's a mutant on this team of mutants called X-Men. He's small and fierce and fast and angry and the best there is at what he does which is killing and he's got these sharp metal claws which I won't be able to do and ... " Michael paused, catching his breath.

Mel cut in: "Yah, I know about Wolverine. I've seen the movies. But - "

Oblivious, Michael rushed on: "AND he has a rapid healing thing in his blood. He can be cut or shot or burneded or beaten and his blood always heals him up again, real fast. See, that's his main mutant power. So, I figure that if I change into Logan and put some of my blood into Billy, then it heals everything that's wrong with him and they won't haveta cut into his head and he won't haveta die!"

Melanie said "Whoof" and sat down on the grass. "Dammit, but this ... this is, like, a helluva lot to take in, Mike."

"You shouldn't use bad words, Melanie. Swearing is bad. That's what Father Walsh says. Anyway, you saw what I can do. You saw with your own eyes, yes you did. So I can do this. I just know I can."

"Are you really sure it'll work?"

"If I really believe I'm the hero when I hold the stone, then I become the hero. All I have to do is really believe. And for Billy, especially, I'll be believing my hardest, yes I will."

Melanie took Mike's hand and squeezed it. "I'll be believing my hardest, too."

She sat there thinking for long moments, while Michael hopped from one foot to the other in his excitement. Finally she said:

"You're right about one thing: How're we gonna get your blood into Billy? No one will believe us if we told the truth about you, and no one'll do a transfusion just because we ask 'em to. We're just kids."

"Well, you sure don't look like a kid. You look like a grown-up."

"Thanks, Mike. But I'm only fifteen."

"Then ... then what do we DO? We can't just let Billy DIE!"

"No, no we won't. I'll just have to figure out how we do this. Now lemme think this out, Mike, please."

Melanie drew her legs up to her chest and rested her chin on her knees, wrapping her arms around her legs. Mike plopped down beside Melanie on the grass and imitated her position. Time passed.

Then Mel gave a laugh and punched Mike in the shoulder. "Got it!" she announced. "And you gave me the answer!"

"I ... I did?"

"Yep! When you said I don't look like a kid! People always say I look a lot older than I really am. That's why senior boys are always hitting on me at school. With the right clothes and the right makeup, I can pass for an adult - like a nurse!" She paused. "But to do this, we both have to be very brave. We can't lose our nerve. Can you be very brave, Michael? For Billy?"

"Of course. For Billy. He's always brave to help me against nasty bullies in the schoolyard calling me the R-word. For Billy, I'll ... I'll even be brave enough to get a needle. I will. If ... if you're there to help me."

"I'll be right there with you. C'mon!"

They re-entered the hospital. Melanie found the staff area and, when no one was looking, marched into the ladies' change room, ignoring the large HOSPITAL STAFF ONLY sign. Michael waited in the corridor outside, under orders to bang on the door if anyone came. Scared and nervous, he shifted from one foot to the other, humming a low plaintive tune.

When Melanie emerged, he almost didn't recognize her. She wore a nurse's scrubs, right down to the shoes. She'd covered her striking blue hair with a green surgical cap and put makeup on her face that made her look more mature.

"Wow," said Mike. "You really look like a grown-up now."

"That's the idea. I got lucky; some of the lockers were unlocked and I found this cap in one of them and these scrubs an' shoes in another. The owner is about my size, too, which was also lucky. I had the right makeup in my purse to do my face sorta like my Mom does hers when she goes to work. I even got this official ID badge, clipped here. See?"

Mike looked at the photo on the card and frowned. "You don't look like this lady. She doesn't even wear glasses."

"True. But I'm counting on nobody looking too close at it."

"But ... but do you know how to do a blood transformer?"

"No, but I'm hoping I can order someone to do one for me. Now change into Wolverine and let's go, before we chicken out."

The tall boy's hand went into his pocket and his brow furrowed as he concentrated. A bright yellow aura surrounded him and when it faded, he was a very hairy man, complete with long sideburns, a thick lion mane crowning his head, and so much hair on his forearms that the skin was hardly visible. He had also shrunk at least six inches; in fact, Mel was now slightly taller.

"Logan, huh?" she asked. He nodded, grinning a roguish grin.

"Wow, ya look just like Hugh Jackman when he plays Wolverine in the movies."

"Nah. Hollywood makes Hugh Jackman look just like me."

"Hah, whatever. Okay then, so I *gotta* see 'em," she said. "C'mon, pop his claws, just like in the movies."

"Melanie! Someone'll see!"

"Nah, we're the only ones in this hallway. So c'mon! Show me!"

Michael straightened both arms, put his hands straight out with fingers curled into fists, and grimaced. Three bony, white claws emerged from each hand above the knuckles and grew until they were a foot long.

"Ow," he said. "It hurts getting them out through the skin."

"Sorry," Mel murmured, staring at the claws. "Wow." Tentatively, she touched one. "They're made of bone!"

"Yeah. That's his natural claws. It's a secret Canadian gov'ment lab that coats 'em an' his whole skeleton in unbreakable metal called ada ... adaman ... oh, I can't say it right."

"That's okay. Wow, this is totally awesome, Michael! Thanks for showing me. Wow. You really *are* Wolverine. Now pull 'em back in an' let's go save our friend."

With another grimace, Mike retracted the claws back into his forearms. The slits in his skin healed almost immediately. Then Melanie took him into the Emergency area. It was busy, with lots of doctors and nurses rushing around. Mel noticed a young nurse, who seemed to be less busy than the others, and looking authoritative (she hoped), strode up to her with Mike in tow. Deliberately speaking slower, like her bank manager mother did, and in a deeper tone than her normal voice, she said:

"Excuse me, but I need you to take a unit of this young man's blood right away. I have to hold his hand - he's scared of needles - so you have to draw the blood. Stat! It's a rare type urgently needed for a serious case upstairs."

Mel wished she'd watched more episodes of hospital dramas on TV, so she could use more medical lingo. But what she'd said apparently worked: The other nurse gave her the briefest of glances, nodded agreement, and whisked them into a cubicle, drawing the curtain. Mel held Mike's hand throughout the procedure, talking to him soothingly, and he squeezed her so hard that she thought her bones would break. The boy whimpered and though his eyes were shut tight, a few tears escaped. But he stayed rigid and didn't cry and then it was done.

"Thank you," Melanie told the nurse. "And you, young man, you were very brave. Now nurse, Dr. Carlstrom asked that this blood be rushed stat to Room 347 and given to the patient there, a young man named William McDonnell. Tell the patient's family that Dr. Carlstrom just ordered this procedure; she instructed me about it as she ran off to an emergency with another patient. I'll stay here with this brave fellow until I'm sure he's alright."

The young nurse assented and left the cubicle with the blood. Mel was thankful she'd remembered the name of Billy's doctor.

"Whew!" she said, wiping sweat from Mike's brow and neck with a wet cloth. "Looks like we pulled it off. You okay?"

"Yeah. But I really feel like smoking a cigar right now, though I'm much too young to smoke, of course." He saw Mel looking at him quizzically and giggled. "Little joke. In the comics, Logan loves a good cigar."

A voice suddenly boomed from beyond the curtain, cutting through the noise in Emerg:

"Where are you going with that blood?"

Melanie stopped breathing.

Another voice answered: "I'm taking it up to 347, stat. Dr. Carlstrom wants it given to a patient there." Melanie recognized the second voice as belonging to the young nurse who had just drawn Mike's blood. The lady challenging her must be the head nurse.

"Really?" said the first voice again, still very loud and now laced with irritation. "Well, I haven't seen any paperwork on it and there's nothing on my screen here."

"Oh, that nurse over there told me to do it. Said the instructions came from Dr.Carlstrom herself."

"What nurse? To whom are you referring?"

Now it was Melanie's turn to sweat, as her mind raced. She couldn't let the head nurse confront her; since she wouldn't recognize Mel's face, she was sure to take a hard look at her ID badge and then they'd be finished.

In desperation, Mel called out from behind the curtain, using the name on the badge she had taken: "She's referring to me: Claire Watkins. I'm still here with the patient, who's not feeling too well yet, after giving blood." She prodded Michael, who understood the cue and gave a loud moan.

"Weak stomach, hates needles," Mel continued. "I'll be giving you the requisition form just as soon as the patient feels better and I can let him go. But that blood must get up to 347 right away; Dr. Carlstrom said it's vital!"

There was a long pause. Melanie and Michael looked at each other, their eyes mirroring panic. Would the ruse work? Or would the head nurse with the foghorn voice walk over to their cubicle and yank open the curtain? She had gambled that the hubbub in the room would mask her voice, in case the head nurse knew the Watkins lady.

Then the booming voice said: "Yeah, okay. Take it on up, Nurse; we don't want to cross Carlstrom. And don't forget that paperwork, Claire, when you're through in there!"

"I won't," Mel answered. She sighed in relief.

"Are we okay now?" whispered Mike anxiously. "Will Billy get the blood?"

"Yes he will, Michael. And I think we're okay. We just have to wait for the right moment to leave this cubicle, so we won't be noticed. If that head nurse sees me, she'll know right away I'm not Nurse Watkins."

Mike nodded, then said: "Thanks for holding my hand when that lady had that needle in me, Nurse Melanie. I hope I didn't hurted you when I squeezed."

"Just a little, but it's worth it if this cures Billy."

Anxious minutes crawled by as the two teens cowered behind the curtain, terrified of imminent discovery. Suddenly Mel gasped.

"Ohmigod! I just remembered: with blood transfusions, you must make sure the blood types match, or it's that universal Type O," she said in a hoarse whisper. "I have no idea what your or Billy's blood type is. If we put in the wrong type, Billy will die."

Michael grew still, thinking hard, sucking a knuckle furiously. Finally he whispered: "Wolverine's blood is very special. It heals. So it should fix any problem with matching Billy's blood. Don't worry, Mel. Everything will be OK."

"Oh, I sure hope so! We didn't really have a choice; we had to risk it 'cause Billy was gonna die anyway if we did nothing."

There was a sudden commotion, with people yelling and the sounds of many feet running. *Great!* Melanie thought. *I hoped I could count on a crisis in here sooner or later. I'm just glad it's sooner.* Cautiously, she peeked around the curtain and saw a knot of people in a glassed-in adjoining room, crowded around two ambulances that had pulled into the enclosed Emergency drive-through. The entrance to their section was deserted; no nurse was standing guard.

"Okay, Mike! Coast is clear! Now let's get outta here! We've had more than enough stress for one day! Let's go back to that change room so I can get into my own clothes again, before we're discovered."

Luck stayed with them. Melanie changed without incident, returning the nurse's clothes to where she found them and scrubbing her face clean of makeup. "Sorry Nurse Watkins," she murmured, as she placed the ID badge back on the shelf in the locker. "I hope I didn't just get you into a lot of trouble."

When she emerged from the change room, Michael had become Michael again. She hugged him and kissed him on the cheek. "Well done, big guy, well done. We pulled it off and I'm real proud of ya," she told him. The boy beamed like he'd just won the lottery.

"How long before that special blood works?" she asked, as they walked to Billy's room.

"Oh, he heals very fast. Within seconds. You saw my hands after I pulled in my claws."

When they reached Billy's room, pandemonium reigned. People were laughing and crying all at the same time. Dr. Carlstrom was there, shaking her head, and one of the two nurses in attendance was crossing herself and muttering something about a miracle.

The two teens gasped. Billy was sitting upright talking to his parents! His skin had a healthy glow and there were no bruises on his face nor black eyes.

"BILLY!" both friends screamed in unison, and they flung themselves at him and gave him a monster hug, oblivious to Janet's cautionary protests. "You're better! You're really better!" Billy said something, but his words were lost behind Michael's massive chest, against which his face was mashed.

This hug was groundbreaking for Mike; normally he avoided physical contact, since it usually meant pain, a lesson he'd learned from his parents' beatings. But here, in his joy, he was initiating the contact, not receiving it, and he discovered that was okay.

"Yes, it's a miracle for sure," said Paul. "Doctor can't explain it. A few minutes after that blood went into him and that nurse from Emerg left, he just woke up and started talking. They're going to take him for a CAT scan soon, just to be sure, but Billy says his head feels fine. No headache and he's not bleeding from his nose. And he says his ribs don't bother him anymore, either. It's just unbelievable."

"Oh yes, yes, it certainly is," gushed Melanie, tears of joy coursing down her cheeks. Michael was crying too, with a fiercely proud look on his face.

"You did it, Mike, you did it!" Melanie whispered into his ear, as they hugged Billy. "You were right, you were right! You saved our Billy."

"You just have to believe," said the big boy.

"What are you two mumbling about?" asked Billy, after finally extricating himself from the hug.

"Just how happy we are to have you back with us," said Mel.

"Yah, and do we gots a story to tell you later, buddy," said Michael. "There was a wolverine in this hospital. Heh. Another little joke. *SNIKT!* Ah, let's hug again."

And they did.

Chapter 8

Detour to Hell

"Are you *sure* you're going the right way?" Delores Stamper asked her husband.

Hunched over the wheel of the van, Ralph Stamper muttered: "Yessss, dear. Sign at the highway said gas was down this road."

"Well, we've been driving down this road for some time now, and I don't see any gas station. Maybe we oughta double-back."

Crammed onto two long seats in the rear were the six teenage girls of Blue Mountain High's hopefully-soon-to-be-award-winning synchronized swimming team. "Will it be much longer?" one asked plaintively. "I really gotta pee. My back molars are floating."

"Won't be long now, Cathy. Hang on. And after, maybe don't drink so much water and pop while we're driving, huh?" said Ralph.

"Now dear, don't be cross," said Delores. "We have been driving a long time this afternoon, after all, and we also need gas."

They were travelling along a two lane country road of cracked and potholed old pavement, with mile after identical mile of corn fields on either side. They had yet to encounter another car, and the occasional farmhouse they passed was set far back from the road. Then the van went around another bend in a series of identical bends and Ralph announced joyfully: "Breathe easier, girls! Here's the gas station."

"This thing?" said his wife doubtfully as they drove up to it. "It looks really crummy."

"Well we don't have much choice, dear. We're running on

fumes and the girls desperately need a bathroom." Still, Ralph privately admitted that his wife was right: this gas station had definitely seen better days. Everything was sagging: roof, walls, the circular sign with GAZ painted on it in faded red. The single pump looked like it was new when Henry Ford was selling Model Ts, and the unpaved ground around the pump had so many dips and cracks that he wondered if the van would bottom out. What paint the station may have once sported had long since faded away; grey weatherbeaten wood was its colour now.

Ralph pulled in and stopped. Even before the wheels ceased rolling, the van's two sliding doors banged open and the girls piled out, racing to see who'd get into the ladies' bathroom first. As it was a room with only a single toilet, the girl who came in second ran into the men's bathroom and slammed the door. Lines immediately formed outside both doors.

Ralph and Delores clambered out and stretched. *Yeah, it had been a long drive,* Ralph thought. *But we're well into Iowa by now and should reach Des Moines by late tonight if all goes well.*

"So where's the gas attendant?" asked Delores, always the impatient one.

"Dunno," said Ralph. He hollered: "Hello? Anyone around? Hellooooo?"

There was a long silence. "Maybe it's a self-serve," offered Delores.

"I don't think so, honey."

A can fell somewhere in the dark cavern of the service bay and rolled lazily out into the afternoon sunlight. It was a beer can. Then four men sauntered out. Two were smoking, one was chewing tobacco, and the fourth was digging into his nose. They were all dressed in heavily-stained jean bib-alls, with T-shirts that had never seen the inside of a washing machine, by the look of them. The men were in their thirties and forties, though the one mining his nostrils looked fresh out of his twenties. They all had the same build and facial characteristics, leading Ralph to suppose they were brothers: medium height, dirty sandy-brown hair, small beer bellies, and brutish faces with almost lipless mouths and small eyes under beetling brows.

Ralph started feeling a bit uneasy, but put on a big smile and said: "Howdy."

One of the men, who looked to be the oldest, moved his cigarette from the left to the right side of his mouth and mumbled: "Howdy yerself."

"Ah, we need a fill-up, please. Super, if you got it."

"Reg'lar. Only reg'lar," said the man, and moved the cigarette back to the left side.

"Ah, okay, regular'll do, thanks."

The older brother went over to the rusted pump and kicked it into life. Somewhere deep in its innards, a tiny bell dinged. He put the nozzle into the van and gas started flowing, lethargically if the cracked yellowed gauge on the pump was any indication. The cigarette still dangled from his lips and Ralph said, somewhat nervously: "Um, shouldn't you put that out while you're pumping gas?"

The man looked at Ralph and his eyes narrowed. "Why?"

The other brothers had noticed the girls lined up at the washroom doors and the one chewing tobacco came over to speak to the one pumping gas. They both smiled and the chewer spat a long brown stream onto the ground, raising a little cloud of dust as it hit.

"Them all yore girls?" asked the pumper.

"Oh, no," said Ralph, watching Delores walk over to join the impatient washroom holding pattern. "Just one, the blonde-haired one there at the end of the first line. She's our daughter, Suzy. She and the others are a synchronized swim team, in the 15-17 year-old category. We're from Minneapolis, on our way to the regional championships in Des Moines. The girls are very good; they might even get into the medals."

"That a fact? Y'know, we don' git many good-lookin' girls like that 'round here. 'Specially dressed like they are, with them l'il short pants an' tight l'il tops. Means they got no shame, y'ask me."

All four men were watching the girls intently and now Ralph

definitely had a bad feeling. They should be on their way and quickly. *C'mon girls, hurry it up! And can't this damn pump go any faster?*

Finally, the tank was filled and Ralph paid cash for the gas. All the girls had visited the facilities by then, and his wife had just gone in. The teens had gathered in a tight group near the front of the van, chattering nervously under the intense stares of the strange men in the bib-alls. The girls' ever-present smartphones had been shoved back into hip pockets after they discovered there was no signal here.

Ralph walked over and said: "Suzy, why don't you and the team get back into the van, huh? I'll just visit the john myself and then we'll be off." They moved to comply and Ralph went into the men's room.

Two of the brothers went back into the station, while the other two watched the team climb back into the van.

"What a bunch of total *creeps*," said one of the girls as she sat down. "See the way they're just *staring* at us?"

"Yeah," the others agreed.

"Look!" said Suzy and pointed. "What's up with that?"

The two men who had gone into the station re-emerged carrying shotguns. They came around to the open sliding doors of the van, one on each side, and levelled the guns right at the girls. "Jest sit tight, there," one mumbled and spat a long stream of tobacco. The girls gasped in shock, eyes wide. Meanwhile, the other two brothers walked to the bathroom doors and jammed long pieces of two-by-fours under the door knobs and into the ground. As the doors opened outward, this effectively trapped the two adults inside.

"What ... what's going on here? What are ... are you doing?" stammered Suzy.

The oldest brother, one of the two holding shotguns, said: "Whall, first we's goin' ta take ya in this fine van fer a l'il drive up to our farmhouse, 'bout a mile away. Then, we'll all git ta know each other."

The girls looked at each other, dumbfounded.

"Ayup," drawled the tobacco-chewer and let fly with another dark brown stream that nailed a big deer fly crawling on the ground. "An' we got four big bedrooms up in that farmhouse, if ya take my meanin'."

"But there's six a' them. With one fer each a' us, whadda we gonna do with the other two?" said the nose miner, clearly the mathematical genius of the foursome.

"Tie 'em up an' lock 'em in the cellar 'till we have need a' them," said the older one. "Or call Fred an' Luke ta come over an' have some fun too. They'd be beholdin' ta us forever for that l'il favour."

"Hah! You bet, bro'."

One girl with black hair jerked forward in the seat. "I just do *not* believe this! You've *got* to be kidding! Look, you guys better knock it off and just let us all go! You can't just kidnap us!"

The tobacco-chewer patted his shotgun. "Oh yes we can, girlie. Do more 'n' kidnap, too."

"Hah!" said the nose miner and leered at the girls.

"What're we gonna do with them parents?" asked the fourth brother, speaking for the first time.

"Ah, we'll figger that out later. Fer now, let's go enjoy ourselves. Been a long time since we had such nice purty gifts dropped right inta our laps," said the oldest man. "Now you girlies jest sit tight there. Jeb, you sit inna front passenger seat an' take my gun an' cover 'em. I'll drive. Tom, you 'n' Hank close up the station an' follow in our truck."

The two men climbed into the van, whereupon three of the girls started crying and whimpering. The other three glared at the men with anger, but the open maw of the long gun barrel pointed at them just inches away caused them to offer no resistance.

Down the road, from the opposite direction to the one the van had travelled, came the sound of a powerful engine. Seconds later, a blood-red SRT Viper convertible, top down, swung into view and stopped on the road beside the gas station.

"Shee-it!" said the tobacco-chewing brother. "Lookit that! That's as fine as any of these young fillies here!"

The dark-haired man driving the Viper silenced the deep growl of its engine and stepped out. He was wearing an expensive-looking golf shirt and sharply-pleated trousers. His leather Gucci shoes cost more than the gas station made in a month. He smiled. "Well, well, well. And what have we here?"

"None a' yore business," said the oldest brother. "Jest drive on, hear?"

"What're you doing way out here anyway, with that fancy car?" asked the one with the wad of tobacco in his mouth.

"Oh, I had to get off the highway and find a nice spot far off the beaten track, in one of these big corn fields," said the stranger, thinking: *I didn't think women hitch-hiked alone any more. Well, she learned her lesson the hard way.*

"Thet ve-hicle new?" asked the chewer.

"Yep. Just bought her several days ago. Had some trouble in Colorado with my other car." *Yeah, like having to drive it off a cliff in case the cops were looking for it in connection with an incident at a certain motel. With luck, they'll figure the driver went up in the explosion.*

"Enough talk. Time fer you ta git, mister," said the older brother. By then, he'd noticed the long nightmare tattoo on the stranger's forearm. A tiny alarm bell started ringing deep in his brain; he ignored it.

"Maybe I need gas. This is a gas station, right? I might need gas before I rejoin the Interstate. But this beast here takes high octane. I don't suppose there's super in that rusty old pump of yours?"

"No, there ain't. Only reg'lar. So move on."

"And leave these lovely damsels in distress? You are in distress, aren't you, girls? I mean, that goon holding a shotgun on you is a clue that's hard to miss."

"Yes!" shouted Suzy. "Help us! These guys are kidnapping us and are gonna rape us! They locked my parents in the washrooms!"

"Aw, ya shouldn't a' tol' him that, girlie," said the oldest brother. "Now we're gonna haveta kill this smartass."

"Yeah, well I git ta drive that there dream machine after, see if I don't," said the chewer. "I'll do that even afore I do one a' these cuties."

Three of the four brothers left the van, and started walking slowly toward the Viper. The fourth one got out of the passenger seat and stood next to the van, keeping his gun levelled at the girls while watching his brothers approach the stranger. The driver of the Viper hadn't moved from beside his car. He stood nonchalantly, one hand in his pocket and the other draped over the windshield.

"What, no more clever talk now, Mister Smartass?" growled the tobacco-chewer, letting fly again.

The new arrival said nothing. As the brothers advanced, the air around the man seemed to shimmer, or perhaps there was a violet glow around him; in the bright sunlight, it was hard to tell. The brother with the other gun stopped walking and cocked the trigger.

Without warning, blue-white jagged bolts of electricity shot from the stranger's eyes right into the four brothers. They shook violently and the guns exploded in the hands of the two carrying them. The girls in the van screamed. Seconds later, charred husks lay on the dusty Iowa ground, smoking in the sunlight. The stench of burnt flesh and gunpowder filled the air.

The man walked over to the van, leaned in the open side door, and looked at the six girls cowering inside. They saw that his eyes were entirely white, and tiny crackles of blue-white electricity danced around them. This close to the man who had done that impossible thing, the teens were too scared to scream again.

"You girls okay?" he asked in a voice like dripping ice.

They were all gawking at him, some with their mouths hanging open. "Y ... yeah," answered one shakily. "How ... how'd you do that?"

The man smiled and there was no warmth whatsoever in that smile. "Magic."

"Thank ... thank you for rescuing us," said Suzy, managing a brief timid smile. Up close, she saw the man's hybrid dragon/snake/scorpion tattoo in detail and the words *Life Ain't Fair.* She shivered.

"Rescuing? Now whatever makes you think I was rescuing you?" The energy around his eyes intensified. "I was just taking you for myself." And he smiled his cold smile again.

The girls shrank back into their seats. "You ... you're not gonna let us go?" said one in a tiny voice.

"Eventually. Maybe."

That got the criers going again, though the others looked desperately at the other sliding door, which was open. Yet no one had the courage to bolt from the van and risk those deadly eyes.

The man leaned in again and said: "Aw, listen, I'm no ogre. Perhaps I spoke too hastily. There's six of you, and that's quite a lot to handle on a cross-country road trip, even for me. Besides, I have a two seater sports car and I sure don't feel like trading it for this boring suburbia-mobile.

"So I tell you what: choose one of you to come with me on my trip, as my date, agreeable to anything I ask of her, and I'll let the rest of you go free. I don't care which one you choose; all you girls have great bods.Sound good?"

The criers stopped and they all regarded him with shocked wide eyes. "WHAT?" said the girl with black hair. "You ... you want us to pick someone to be your ... your ..."

"Date. The word you're looking for is date. And besides, she might enjoy it."

"You're *sick*!" said another girl. "You can just go to hell!"

"Really? Well then, are you all prepared to die? Being fried by electricity is not a pleasant way to go. You've just seen that with your own eyes. Is that what you want to happen to you? Or wouldn't you rather only one of you comes with me, while the rest of you go free, with no harm done to you?"

The girls looked at each other, speechless. "Think about it, my sweets. You got five minutes," said the man and sauntered back to his Viper. He grinned; this was a delicious torment for these teen queens.

Between sobs, the girls talked amongst themselves. Once or twice, voices raised in anger; other times, wails of despair sounded.

After five minutes had elapsed, the man walked back to the van. His eyes were still all white and the girls realized that meant he still had that awful electrical power at his command. "Well? Have you decided? Which one is the lucky lady?"

The girl with black hair, face streaked with tears, answered: "Nuh ... nobody, you monster. We're a team ... we're all in this together."

"Your funeral. You've seen what I can do," said the man. A nimbus of electricity haloed his head, the air filled with the stench of ozone, and the girls' hair stood up with static electricity. Some of the group shrieked in terror.

"No! No! Wait!" shouted the raven-haired one. "Don't do it. I'll ... I'll go. Take me. I'm the oldest. Just ... leave them alone, like you promised."

The other girls protested and one clutched at her arm, but she shook her hand off and stepped out of the van. She tried to put on a brave face, but she was shaking.

"Wise decision, young lady," said the electrical man. "You go sit your pretty little behind in my car." He leaned into the van and said to the others: "I hope you never forget what your friend has done for you here today. Enjoy the rest of your lives."

He climbed into the Viper and started the big engine. It throbbed with the promise of what 640 horsepower would do on the open highway. With his eerie pupil-less eyes, he looked at the teen sitting terrified next to him. "What's your name, sweet thing?"

"Ni ... Nicole," she said in a small voice.

"Well, Ni-Nicole, first things first. Give me your smartphone."

The teen dug it out of a back pocket and handed it over, saying: "There's no signal here. Otherwise we would have texted or called for help when those four assholes started threatening us."

"Well, we'll just make sure there'll be no signal when we drive into another area," the man said. He threw the smartphone out of the car, his white eyes flared, and it landed in the dust a smoking, blackened mess. He turned back to the girl:

"Now, here're the rules: you don't make a sound when we're around other people and you don't ever signal for help or try to run away. Or I'll fry you dead. Understand?"

The girl nodded, trying to keep her eyes from misting with tears. "Who ... what *are* you?"

"Power."

"When ... when will you let me go?"

"Ah, in about three days. I usually get tired of my dates by then. So it's not that long, and then you'll be free. Freer than you've ever been, I promise you. And you oughta feel proud about saving your friends."

"Where are we going?"

A strange look crossed the man's face and she saw his hand slide over his left pocket. "Northeast for now. I've got this ... compulsion ... to travel in that direction and the urge gets stronger with every mile I take."

He put the car in gear and drove down the road, the V10 engine humming. In his rear-view mirror, he saw the other girls leave the van. Two bent over and started vomiting, one stood looking at the departing Viper (*probably memorizing my licence plate,* he thought), while the other two ran to the bathroom doors to free the adults trapped inside.

A short distance away, he stopped the car on a rise in the road. He got out and stood by the gleaming red trunk. He saw that everyone was milling around the van. A faint shout reached him and he saw a pot-bellied older man shaking his fist at him. He chuckled.

As his unwilling passenger watched, horrified, a massive bolt of electricity arced from his eyes down to the gas pump in front of the station. The pump exploded in a small fireball, followed immediately by a gigantic fireball as the underground storage tank ignited. The station disappeared. Seconds later, a massive blast of sound and wind washed over them.

"NOOOO!" screamed the girl in his car. "You PROMISED!"

He got back into the Viper and smiled his wolf smile. "I lied."

Furious, she tried to hit him, but he evaded her fists and slapped her hard across the face, twice. She stared into a face dark with malice, then collapsed into her seat, crying with great wracking hopeless sobs hauled from the depths of her soul.

"That was stupid. Slide forward in your seat and put your hands behind your back," he commanded.

Sobbing, Nicole complied. He fastened her slim wrists together with a plastic zip-tie he took from the Viper's glove box. She gasped at the tightness.

"That'll teach you to try and hit me, Ni-Nicole. Now sit back and behave yourself. Or I'll get nasty. You don't want that." Small electrical arcs danced around his white eyes.

She shrank back into her seat, staring terrified at the monster next to her. He leered at her lithe young body; her tight short-shorts and tank top left little to the imagination.

Her captor laughed as his eyes returned to normal. He slid a CD into the player. The pounding beat of *Born To Be Wild* blared from the speakers; his favourite song. He put the car in gear and drove off laughing.

Chapter 9

The Angel and the Maiden

It was the afternoon following the day of The Miracle of William McDonnell (as the local media were calling it), and Melanie was sitting at her desk in her room, engrossed in her computer. It was another warm spring day: all the windows in the house were open and she was wearing shorts and a T-shirt. Sipping at a Coke, she was searching the Internet for any information about mystical stones, legendary stones, weird stones, space stones, meteor rocks, whatever. She was trying to find an explanation for the amazing things Mike could do and where that odd warm stone of his might have come from.

Billy was still stuck in the hospital and, according to his frequent texts, anxious to get home. They were running every test they could think of on him, and the results were all coming back negative: he was completely cured. Strangely, even his blood work came back normal. To the joy of his parents and friends, Billy would be released tomorrow.

Mel had been web-surfing for over an hour, and had read a lot of stuff about stones. There was the Philosopher's Stone, of course: that famous mythical artifact that was the Holy Grail of ancient alchemists since it could turn base metals into gold (and do other things, according to the first *Harry Potter* book and movie). There were many other legendary stone talismans of antiquity; almost every civilization on every continent had them. Wearers believed that these talismans endowed them with magical abilities, like protection from disease, or injury in battle, or death in childbirth, or bad luck. She learned that some of our modern superstitions arose from these ancient legends, like carrying a lucky rabbit's foot.

She accessed some way-out sites full of stuff about UFOs, alien abductions, glowing rocks that turned you into awful creatures or gave you superhuman mental powers, radioactive meteors, and more. All stoutly denied by the government, of course.

She was getting tired of reading and was just about to quit looking, when her search engine brought her to a site about the myth of Atlantis and its "power stones". She sat up straighter, interest piqued. Supposedly created by Atlantean magicians, these stones enabled the user to do amazing things by will-power alone. But there was a cost, a dire price to pay - the site had no details - so the stones were used sparingly. When Atlantis disappeared beneath the waves and into legend, so too did the stones.

The site had some colour drawings of these "power stones", based on ancient myths that had survived the cataclysm that sank Atlantis. "Hel-lo," murmured Melanie as she stared at her screen. One of the stones looked almost like the one Michael had, except the colours were a little different and it was bigger and oval-shaped.

"But how would a stone from Atlantis end up here in Ontario?" she murmured.

Then she saw the box at the bottom of the page, which proclaimed: "Now YOU can have your own Atlantis Power Stone! Guaranteed to work! Just $89.95! Click HERE for ordering information! And for a hot-link to genuine Atlantean psychics, direct descendants of the ancient race, click HERE. For magical Atlantis Bath Salts, guaranteed to cure any body aches, click HERE. For an ancient Atlantis Elixir guaranteed to make you lose weight in just 30 days, click HERE. Major credit cards only. No coupons accepted. Allow six to eight weeks for delivery."

"Oh brother," sighed Melanie and clicked off the site in irritation.

She was deep in a site about moon rocks brought back to Earth by Apollo astronauts, when a voice at her open window said: "Hi Melanie." Normally, this would not in itself be strange, except that her bedroom was on the second story! Startled, she jerked her head around to look.

An angel was hovering outside her window, huge white wings flapping slowly in the bright afternoon sunlight.

"Holy God!" Melanie shouted, and sprang to her feet, knocking over her chair. Then she got a good look at the angel's face. It was Michael. He was grinning like a Cheshire cat.

She ran to the window. "Michael, what are you *doing?* You scared me half to death!"

"Aw, I'm sorry, Melanie," said the angel. "I thought it'd be fun to surprise you."

"You sure did! I almost peed myself! Now you better get in here right away, before someone sees you!"

Michael landed on the window sill, crouched low, folded his huge wings tight against his back, and eased into her room. Once inside, he straightened up and allowed the wings to half-open, careful not to hit any of Mel's things. He wore sneakers and blue jeans, and was naked from the waist up. She knew he'd been weight-lifting for four years; his chest and arm muscles were magnificent.

"Wow, you're ... ah, these wings ... are amazing!" breathed Melanie. "Can I touch you - the wings, I mean?"

"Sure," said Michael. He extended one wing around his body toward her. She ran her hand along it and was surprised to find it was composed of real feathers. Each wing was as tall as Michael and nearly half as wide. She thought they were beautiful.

"Wow," she said again. "It's so soft!" She walked behind the boy, staring. "They come right out of your back, by your shoulder blades! I can't believe I'm seeing this. Doesn't it, y'know, hurt?"

"Nope. Well, it hurted when they first came out, and I did knock my head a few times learning to fly with them, but I learneded real quick and I'm a real good flier now."

"And you're, what? Another superhero?"

"Yep, one of Wolverine's teammates. An X-Man called Angel."

"Yeah, I can see how he got his name. But why?"

"Why what, Mel?"

"Why'd you, y'know, turn into this Angel character and come over here?"

"To give you a ride."

Melanie stared. "What, like, go flying with you? Out there? You're kidding, right?"

"Nope. I feeled so happy that Billy's OK now, that I feeled like flying. And I thought you'd feel the same way. You don't have to worry about me dropping you. I'm real strong."

"Yeah, I can see that. But ... but right now? In broad daylight? Someone'll see us! You're hard to miss, with those big wings!"

"Oh, you'd be surprised how few people take the time to look up at the sky. Hardly anybody, really. No one sawed me fly over here. And we'd fly out over the countryside, where there's hardly anybody. C'mon! It'll be lotsa fun!"

Melanie Van Heusen was never one to pass up a challenge. She led Michael into her parents' bedroom, where they had a walk-out balcony. Her folks were at work, and brat sister Ashley was safely at school. Mel and Mike had been excused from school for several days, in view of their recent ordeal.

Out on the balcony, Mike scooped her up in his big arms and hugged her close to his chest. He looked at her and smiled: "You're gonna like this." Then the big wings spread wide and he launched himself into the sky.

Involuntarily, Mel closed her eyes. Wind buffeted her face, pulling her blue hair straight behind her. There was a deep, rhythmic *thrumming* sound. Long seconds later, satisfied that the ground had not greeted them in a fatal embrace, she opened her eyes and gasped.

They were really flying! The streets and houses and yards of their neighbourhood spread out below them, like a giant diorama. They were soaring high above it all, and gaining altitude with each mighty *thrum* beat of the wings. She laughed with joy.

"Neat, eh?" said Michael. "Toldja you'd like it!"

"Wah-HAAA! It's completely AWESOME!" exclaimed Mel, laughing again. "This is, like, totally unbelievable! Beats any carnival ride or plane ride I've ever been on!"

"I guess so. I never been on any. My mom and dad never take me anywhere. "

"Aw, that's so sad. Well, you're certainly going somewhere now! WHOOO!"

Then they were out over the countryside and her joy turned to rapture. Angel Michael swooped over rolling hills, sparkling lakes, placid farms, and winding roads. The warm spring air flowed past their faces in a constant caress, the *thrum* of the mighty wings adding a backbeat to the music of the wind in their ears.

Michael changed altitude on a whim, soaring high one minute, then the next, diving down and flashing low under a bridge or along a lake. Once, they came up behind two fishermen standing in their boat and swept past them mere feet above their heads. The men were so startled, they fell overboard. The teens laughed, then Mike worried that the men might drown until Mel said she'd seen them wearing life-jackets. Still, Mike vowed not to do that again.

Twisting, turning, soaring, swooping, diving, darting - the magic of flight engulfed them. The sun beat down on the modern-day Icarus, but no matter how high Michael flew, his wings would never melt. And sometimes he flew quite high; once Mel could barely make out the tiny speck that was Clearwater.

It was one of the most intense experiences of Melanie's young life. She felt completely safe cocooned in Mike's strong arms, pressed against the warm flesh of his chest, feeling his hard shoulder muscles move in sync with the beating of his wings.

After about an hour, Michael announced he needed to rest. He swooped down to an isolated grassy hillock overlooking a lake, back-stroked his great wings at the last moment, then touched down as light as a feather. He released Mel, who promptly sat down, then stretched flat on her back in the grass. She breathed in deeply, exhaled in a long sigh, and said: "Wow."

Mike grinned. Then he sat next to her, his long wings flowing out behind him, feathers ruffling in the breeze. Wordless, the teens relaxed in the late afternoon sun.

After a while, Mel said: "Y'know Michael, I was thinking. Do you think we should, like, cure Monster Mack the same way you cured Billy? I know he's a very bad person, and he almost killed poor Billy and then he would've ... ah, hurt me, and he'd never do the same for us if he had your stone, but still, I dunno, it's an awful way to spend the rest of your life paralysed like that, and Wolverine's strange blood would heal him, and he'd still go to jail for a long long time, and I know I'm babbling a lot, but I've been thinking about this since this morning. Whaddya think?"

Mike stared at her, frowning. He sucked on a knuckle, then shook his head. "No, no, no, Melanie. He is a very bad mean person and he deserveded what he got. Remember, he did it to himself when he tried to run me over when I was the Hulk. How could you even say what you just said?"

"Yeah, you're right. And we were really really lucky that we got away with what we did at the hospital, with the blood transfusion and all. But still, I dunno, I just wonder if, like, we should use your gift to heal him. Maybe only because it's the right thing to do, y'know?"

"No, I don't know," Mike said stubbornly. "If I went through that again, an' remember I *hate* needles, well, then shouldn't I heal good people that deserve it much more than Monster Mack? Like a little kid or a mom or a dad who's dying of something horrible, like cancer?"

Melanie raised up on her elbows and stared at her friend. "Y'know Michael Johnson, sometimes you're very wise. I bet that special blood could cure cancer, or Parkinson's, or diabetes, or heart conditions, or polio, or ... or just about anything!"

She thought for several minutes, then looked at Michael. "That's what we should do. Get some of that Wolverine blood to top researchers to analyse. If they can discover what makes it work - what Logan's mutant 'healing factor' is - then they could mass-produce cures for many diseases that we have no cures for."

Michael regarded her dubiously. "But that means I'll haveta get stuck with needles again. I only managed to get through it last time 'cause I like Billy so much; he's my bestest friend. And it means I'll haveta give up my secret identity an' the secret of my stone."

Suddenly he grabbed her shoulders. "Mel! They could take my stone away from me, once they know about it!" He released her and started rocking back and forth. His great wings swept forward, enveloping him protectively so that just his head showed.

The girl saw the panic in her friend's eyes. "No, no Michael! Don't worry, we'd never risk you losing your stone. If we did anything like that, it would haveta be very carefully planned out, to make sure you and your stone were protected."

He stared up at the sky and his wings returned to their usual position behind him. "I dunno. I dunno. Needles. Losing my stone. I don't think I wanna do anything like that at all. Grown-ups often say one thing an' do another. Ya can't trust 'em."

Mel repeated: "You're very wise, Michael."

"Aw, thanks. My mom and dad always say I'm a slow thickhead."

"Really? Well, they're quite wrong. And it's mean of them to put you down like that. You never asked to be the way you are."

"And what way's that?"

Suddenly flustered, Mel said: "Well, I mean, like, um, how you're special, how you're different from other kids your age, y'know?"

"Yeah, I know. I'm ineffectually disabled." He hung his head and stared at the grass. Behind him, his wings drooped.

Melanie got to her knees and gave him a big hug. Involuntarily, Michael flinched at her touch. "No, Michael Johnson. Not like being intellectually disabled. You are who you are, a very special boy who has two friends who love you very much. There's lots you can do as good or better than anybody else. Like how you always whup Billy's ass in chess or checkers. Like how you know more about comic book superheroes than any other kid in school. And like how you're the only person in the whole world who found that amazing stone that lets you do amazing things!"

Mike brightened, said "yeah!" and hugged Melanie back. His hug was so strong, the breath whooshed right out of her.

After the hug, when she regained her breath, she asked: "Y'know, Mike, I was wondering: in your head, you don't see life as a comic book, do you?"

Michael stared at her. "Eh? What do you mean?"

"Well, like in panels with word balloons when people speak? I know your love of comics lets your wonderful imagination create superheroes in real life with your stone, so I was just wondering."

Michael laughed. "No, Melanie. I do not see life that way. What a question."

They sat silent for another long while, watching the sky and the clouds. Then Mel spoke again:

"Mike, do ya think I could try that stone of yours? Y'know, to see what it's like?"

"Oh, well, I dunno," the boy replied doubtfully. "I know you're supposed to share with your friends, and I don't mind sharing stuff with you and Billy, like my comics whenever Billy wants to read some, an' I'd lend you my comics too if ever you wanted to read them, but my stone is so very special to me. It's the most specialist thing I got. It hums to me, y'know."

"Oh, I wouldn't keep it long. You'd be right here with me and I'd give it right back."

"Now? You wanna try it now? But if I give it to you now, I'll lose the wings. The stone has to stay next to my body to keep me from changing back, y'know. I toldja that in the hospital. An' if I haveta regrow these wings, well, they do hurt coming out, yes they do."

Melanie smiled and touched Mike's hand. "It's cool, I understand. I don't wanna hurt you or stress you out. Some other time, maybe?"

"Yeah." He patted his jeans pocket, and she saw the outline of the stone under the cloth. She touched it and said:

"Wow, it's much warmer than when I touched it in Billy's hospital room! It's almost hot! It that ... normal?"

"Yep, when I'm using it to be someone else, like now. It only gets cooler after I change back, when it's not being used."

"Huh." Mel had the strongest urge to touch it again, through the jeans, so she did. She felt a tingle in her fingertips and withdrew her hand quickly. "Huh," she repeated.

They went back to watching the sky, pointing out shapes in the big fluffy white clouds.

"There! See that one?" asked Melanie. "That looks just like Goofy's head."

"Yeah," said Mike. "But look at that cloud over there. It's a big sailboat!"

"Uh-huh. And there's an alligator! See?"

"Yep, and there's two elephants, a mommy and her baby."

"Oh! Here comes the best one yet, Mike! It's a train! See?"

"Yep. That is an awesome one, yes it is. Hey, wanna go ride it?"

Mel giggled and said yes and then they were airborne again, soaring high into the sky toward the train cloud. Long minutes later, they reached it and burst through it just past the engine, shrieking with glee. They zoomed in and out of the train cars. Then they dive-bombed a huge rhinoceros, crashing through its immense horned head. The wings *thrummed,* the teens laughed, and wisps of disturbed cloud streamed past them, eddying in their wake.

Then the sun was setting and Michael started to tire again, so they headed home with great beats of the wings as the sky turned crimson, then purple, and the clouds, now shadowy, continued their majestic parade.

The next day, the local paper, *The Clearwater Expositor and Farmers' Chronicle,* had a small article buried on page 23, squeezed next to the results of the retirement home's weekly Euchre tournament, about an amateur birdwatcher, one Phyllis Henderson, who swore that she saw a giant condor in the skies over nearby Harvey Township. Her birdwatching club, with a collective sniff heard in the next county, promptly revoked her membership.

Chapter 10

Visitors Strange and Wicked

The room was dark, except for the pale, eerie glow of seven computer monitors. The monitors were on tables banked against the walls in a big U-shape. Beneath the tables were the powerful computer towers. In the centre of the U, keeping watch over the different scenes on each screen, was an ambulatory scarecrow.

The word "eccentric" did not begin to describe Ethan Delperdang. The way he looked didn't help. Well over six feet tall, he had a physique that made a broom handle look well-fed. There was not a bit of fat on his body; if you were unfortunate enough to see his naked chest, you'd see a sunken cavity with every rib clearly outlined. It looked like he was on a starvation diet, though he ate three hearty meals a day.

His skin was pasty-white, not from some disease, but because he rarely left his computers in the shadowed confines of his home. His long narrow face had perpetual razor-stubble; Ethan only shaved at irregular intervals. Atop his head was an unruly mass of reddish-blond hair that would terrify a barber into quitting if its owner ever thought to get it cut. Instead, he tamed most of it by tying it in a big pony-tail.

He had spread the story that he was an American from California, where he had worked in Silicon Valley. He now lived alone in an isolated, rambling old farmhouse in a sparsely-populated region of New Zealand. The locals called him "The Yank", and thought he was a harmless eccentric. Until that morning about seven months ago when he had come running into the village screaming that everyone must hide in their cellars because nuclear Armageddon would be unleashed at noon. By

1:00 p.m., when it was apparent that life still proceeded as usual, the word "harmless" was removed from Ethan's descriptor and replaced with "stupid" which, in the local dialect, was pronounced "stew-pid".

Ethan was a "conspiracy nut". He saw hidden conspiracies everywhere; that was one of the reasons he rarely left his house. He was convinced governments covered up alien landings, that a mind-control drug lurked in the "secret sauce" put into every Big Mac, that the Apollo moon landings had actually been done in a Hollywood special effects studio, that several gunmen had assassinated President Kennedy, that Elvis was alive and well and living in Topeka, and that covert government agencies had spy-cams in elevators and washrooms of large corporations. And those were just the conspiracies he was prepared to discuss; he kept many more to himself.

He was also a genius software programmer; according to his carefully-manicured local legend, he had become a multi-millionaire by age 25.

Now looking like he was in his thirties, he had devoted considerable time and effort to ensuring his real name and identity did not exist anywhere in the world's records. "Ethan Delperdang" was not even his real name, though he maintained a valid American passport in "Ethan's" name, for those rare occasions when he had to travel abroad. He had created online records for "Ethan", in case anybody did a background check on him. In reality, however, he was a ghost, a citizen of nowhere.

There was a soft "ping" from one of the computers. Like a hawk diving on its prey, Ethan was at the machine in an instant.

"A-hah," he murmured. "Someone's accessed my Atlantis site. God bless my little 'cookies' for collecting data without the user knowing it."

His long thin fingers danced over the keyboard. Specialized software, created for the CIA and modified by Ethan, went to work. In minutes, he had the street address of the computer used to access the site, geographic location of the town, names and ages of everyone in the family, credit and employment history of the parents, schools the two girls attended and their test scores, traffic tickets (the mother liked to drive fast), past year's credit card purchases, health records of the family members, magazine subscriptions, and more.

"Okay, now let's correlate. It could be an innocent hit on the Atlantis site; a fan, or a kid researching a school project. So let's see if anything unusual has been happening in or around the little town of Clearwater, Ontario, Canada," he said to the roomful of high-tech machinery. He fingers flew over the keyboard again, and he was soon skimming through recent online editions of the *Clearwater Expositor & Farmers' Chronicle.* Where he found stories about The Miracle of William McDonnell following the abduction of he and his female friend by an obviously-drunk gang, who swore they'd been attacked by the Jolly Green Giant with attitude.

"Gotcha."

Using the Internet, he booked a plane ticket to Toronto, Canada - economy class, of course - and the cheapest rental car available to drive from Toronto to Clearwater. Then he started packing. There was nothing orderly or careful about how Ethan Delperdang packed for a trip: whatever he laid his hands on that was (mostly) clean, got shoved unfolded into a large soft-sided sports bag. If the zipper succeeded in closing, he was packed.

One hour later, in an ancient Land Rover that had no need of air conditioning due to the many rust holes throughout the body, he rattled off towards the regional airport, a three-hour drive. There he would board a small prop plane to take him to Auckland International Airport to catch his flight next morning to Canada by way of Hawaii. He'd be in the air for almost 24 hours before he finally arrived.

He could hardly wait.

ॐ ॐ ॐ ॐ ॐ ॐ

Another strange visitor entered Canada around the same time as Ethan Delperdang was arranging his trip. One infinitely more dangerous.

The blood-red SRT Viper pulled up to the Canadian border station at Windsor, Ontario, just before noon on a bright sunny morning. The border guard keyed the car's license plate into her computer, then motioned for the car to advance to the inspection window. Her computer showed everything was in order; there were no alerts or outstanding warrants on the car. A few perfunctory questions, and he'd be on his way.

"Are you an American citizen?" she asked the sole occupant of the Viper.

My citizenship is irrelevant, now that I have The Gift, he thought, but said aloud: "Yes ma'am, born and raised in New Mexico. Here's my passport."

"Purpose of visit to Canada?"

Death and general mayhem. "Pleasure trip, just touring around your beautiful country."

"How long will you be staying?"

As long as it takes to find what I'm meant to find. "Oh, just a week, two at the most."

"Are you personally aware of everything you're carrying in your car, including the contents of your trunk?"

Yeah, don't worry, there's no kidnap victim in my trunk. I already took care of her. "Yes ma'am. Only a coupla bags in there. Can't fit much in a Viper's trunk."

He smiled a long toothy grin, meant to be warm and friendly, but coming off as cold and predatory, like that of a shark getting ready to separate you from your leg. The border guard decided the man's oily smile gave her the creeps, but you couldn't deny entrance to someone just because of his smile. She returned his passport. "All right, proceed. Enjoy your visit."

Oh, I intend to. "Thanks, ma'am." Another plastic grin. The worst sexual predator and serial killer in years was waved into Canada.

The Viper roared off, heading east on the 401 Highway toward Toronto, four hours away. The man with the cold smile didn't know exactly where he was going yet, but The Gift would tell him. It had led him this far.

And the trail of death and destruction he'd left in his wake as he'd travelled through the United States had never caught up with him. He'd been oh-so-clever in covering his tracks. He believed in the old pirate saying: "Dead men (and women) tell no tales".

Actually, to his great surprise, he had broken his no-survivors rule today. He had let Ni-Nicole live. He didn't know why; he certainly had no conscience with which to feel remorse, or heart to which she might appeal. It was, he finally decided, to honour her bravery in sacrificing herself to him to save her friends. A thought struck him: *am I going soft?*

Of course, leaving her alive did not mean letting her go free. She had seen too much and could describe him to the authorities, and he couldn't allow that. So he had chained her, nude and definitely worse for wear, to a thick support pole in an old, but solid, windowless woodshed behind the cabin in upstate Michigan he'd rented for one month, though they had only stayed there for three nights. Then he'd padlocked the shed door. Even if Ni-Nicole could somehow work herself free of the chains in the inky blackness of her prison, she still had to contend with the sturdy locked door. And screaming for help wouldn't do her any good; the cabin was very isolated. But just to be on the safe side, he'd sealed her mouth with several layers of duct tape, wrapping the tape right around her head in an unbroken band. She didn't squirm in protest; after what he'd done to her in the past three days, her mind had retreated into its own haven, oblivious to what happened to her body.

He buried her clothes, shoes, and purse in the woods beyond the shed, then scattered dead leaves and brush over the fresh-dug earth.

Actually, the more he thought about it, the more he realized that leaving her in that predicament was a diabolical torture more satisfying than killing her outright. It was highly unlikely she could free herself, much less being able to escape the shed. Which meant she faced a lingering painful death by starvation, alone and naked in the dark.

And hoping for rescue, because the last thing he had said to her before closing the shed door was: "Now don't you worry, sweet thing. You've been fairly cooperative with me, so I'm gonna do you a favour. I'll contact the cops and tell 'em where you are as soon as I'm in the next state."

Which he had absolutely no intention of doing, of course. But he had seen the hope flare in her tear-filled eyes.

His lips peeled back in an icy grin of blackest malice. Delicious.

No, I'm not going soft.

As he sped down the freeway, the wind tugging at his coal-black hair, he brayed a laugh of chilling delight and wondered if Canadian girls would be as much fun to play with.

Chapter 11

Death Comes to Clearwater

Whack!

The sick sound of wood against flesh. Michael choked back a cry - if he cried out, he knew he'd be hit all the harder - and squeezed his eyes shut against the tears.

Whack!

"This'll teach you to be late for supper and not tell us where you were! Ya coulda used that damn cellphone we gave ya, to call us!" snarled Bert Johnson, standing over Michael, who was curled into a ball in the corner of the basement rec room. In his right hand, Bert held a ping-pong paddle. A bottle of beer filled his left hand. He took a long swig of brew, then delivered another vicious strike against the boy's bare buttocks.

Whack!

Michael knew it was useless to protest or - worse - beg his father to stop. And he also knew he'd get no help from Ruth, his mother; she was sitting in a nearby chair, drink in hand, encouraging her husband:

"C'mon, Bert! More! Give the inconsiderate bastard some more! That'll teach him to worry us by coming home late! Make sure he won't be able to sit for a week!"

Whack! Whack! Whack!

The wooden paddle had blood on it by the time Bert Johnson decided Mike had enough. The boy was crying openly by then, in great heaving sobs.

"Aw, shaddup, ya big baby," growled Bert, flinging away the paddle. "Now pull up your pants and go to your room. An' don't you *dare* come out until we tells ya! There'll be no supper for you tonight!"

Michael did as he was told. His rump was a white-hot blaze of pain. He'd felt that pain before. Many times. Whenever his father commanded him to go into the basement, he knew what was coming. None of the neighbours could hear anything that went on in the basement.

He had seen the fury in his parents' eyes as soon as he got home after that wonderful flight with Melanie, and terror had gripped his stomach with icy claws. He knew he was in for a beating. But he certainly couldn't tell them what he'd been doing, because that meant he'd have to tell them about his special stone and he'd never, ever do that. Not to those two.

So he'd taken his beating - which seemed to hurt more than the last one. In fact, since about a year, each beating seemed worse than the previous one. He knew he could use the stone to turn into something big and fierce and powerful to make his father stop and even hurt him back, but he didn't. It wouldn't have been right. He had broken a rule, so he must be punished. That was the way of things. But he really wished his father wouldn't hit him so hard, or so often. And, as usual, he couldn't say anything about this to anyone, not his best friends Billy and Melanie, or Miss Sarah, his teacher. That was another rule.

Michael cried himself to sleep. Not all of the tears were because of the pain in his backside.

ം ം ം ം ം ം

Mid-morning the following day, Saturday, found Billy McDonnell pacing impatiently in his private room at Clearwater General Hospital. Today was the day he was to be released, but no one could give him a clear answer as to exactly what time. He was anxious to leave. No just because he was bored bored bored stuck in here, but because he wanted to ask Mike a zillion questions about that stone of his.

Like a caged jungle cat, his pacing followed a numbing pattern: window-bed-door-window. The window overlooked the parking lot, and he had just reached it for the fiftieth time when a red

Viper convertible entered. Billy stopped abruptly and exclaimed: "Whoa, coool!" You didn't usually see a car like that in this town. He watched it circle the lot slowly, then park. A man with black hair and awesome-looking wraparound sunglasses got out, dressed in golf shirt and slacks. Then Billy's parents burst into the room, joyfully announcing that the paperwork was all done and he was free to go, and Billy forgot all about the red Viper.

ఇ ఇ ఇ ఏ ఏ ఏ

Several floors below the happy McDonnells, the person responsible for Billy's hospital stay prayed for death. But God wasn't listening, and the machines around his bed continued to keep him alive, so all Monster Mack could do was just lie there on his back and curse. For an all-star sports jock, now unable to move his paralysed body, this was a living hell. He'd clench his fists and beat the bed in rage, but he could not. He prayed for death again.

His prayers were answered.

Movement caught his attention. He flicked his eyes to the door, and saw an ordinary-looking man standing there, watching him. Mack knew he wasn't a cop; his police guard had been withdrawn when the doctors had confirmed he'd be paralyzed for life. Though he still faced a host of criminal charges, it was obvious he wasn't going anywhere.

The man entered the room and came to stand at the foot of Monster Mack's bed. Dark emotionless eyes looked him over, then the stranger gave a cold predatory smile.

"So you're really a crip now, huh?" he said and smiled again. "Local paper says you're a paraplegic. Says you rammed your van into the back of a green mountain that walked. That so?"

"Who ... who are you?" croaked Monster Mack.

"Just a guy lookin' for something. Something that you encountered, according to a little ... hunch ... of mine, y'might say. A hunch that's led me here to you. There's kind of an ... energy trail ... that I'm following, and there's a residue of that energy on you."

"You're nuts," wheezed Monster Mack.

The cold smile vanished in an instant and the man's face darkened.

"Now you better treat me with more respect than that, boy," he said in a low chilling tone. "You don't want to get me angry, I promise you."

"Get ... out," breathed the Monster.

"When I'm damn good and ready. I need information from you, first. I need you to tell me everything that happened that night, so's I can find what I'm supposed to find."

"You ... some kinda lawyer ... my dad hired?"

"Nah. But trust me, ya wanna tell me everything."

"Reporter, then?"

"Wrong again." The stranger moved to stand beside Monster Mack, and leaned over the supine boy. His face was inches from Mack's. "Talk. To. Me. Now."

For the second time in a week, fear swept over the Monster and he didn't like it one bit. Fear was something that he caused in other, weaker people. It was not something he himself experienced. He looked into the man's unblinking eyes and quailed at the malice he saw there.

So he talked. In slow, halting sentences, Monster Mack told the stranger everything that had happened. The stranger was particularly interested in the two younger teens that the green monster had come to rescue, and made him repeat their names.

"Billy McDonnell and Melanie Van Heusen, huh? Okay, they're my next stops. In fact, the paper says McDonnell is in this very hospital somewhere, courtesy of you." The stranger smiled his wolf smile. "Thanks, kid. You were very helpful. Sounds like you're a nasty son-of-a-bitch after my own heart. I'm sorry your punch-up and planned gang rape got interrupted."

"Oh, me too," whispered the paralysed boy.

Monster Mack watched as the man walked over and switched off the heart-monitoring and oxygen machines. *Now, why'd he do that?* flitted through his mind, then the answer came to him and he felt strangely calm, not frightened or angry at all. The man closed the door to Mack's private hospital room, then stood next to his bed again.

"Y'know, kid, since you're so much like me, I'm gonna do ya a real big favour. I know I couldn't live with myself if I ended up like you, all crippled and unable to move, unable to act upon the ... desires ... I got inside me. That'd drive me crazy."

Gently, the stranger lifted Monster Mack's head and removed the pillow beneath it. Gently, he laid the boy's head onto the bed. Gently, he placed the pillow over the boy's face. The last thing Mack saw was the nightmare tattoo on the man's forearm, before blackness filled his vision. *Yeah, life ain't fair* was his final thought.

The stranger held the pillow over the boy's face for a long time, long after Monster Mack's chest stopped moving.

Then the stranger left the room, closing the door behind him. He paused, as if listening, then followed the silent urging of The Gift up several floors to Billy McDonnell's room.

He arrived to find the kid gone. A cute candy-striper changing the bed told him he'd left with his family about 40 or 45 minutes ago. She went to the same high school as Billy, and in a bubbly voice, told him where he lived and how to get there from here. She looked to be about 16, with blonde hair and a slightly plump figure straining against her uniform. The stranger briefly considered locking the door and raping the girl, then silencing her cheerful voice forever, but the *insistence* of the thing in his pocket was too strong, now that he was so close to whatever it wanted. So he just smiled, thanked her and left.

༄ ༄ ༄ ༄ ༄ ༄

At the McDonnell household, pandemonium reigned. Friends, relatives, and neighbours were there to welcome Billy home. There was much hugging, back-slapping, hand-shaking, and a few tears. Billy was completely overwhelmed by it all. He smiled and looked brave and said what he hoped were the right things, but what he wanted to do most of all was to slip away with Mike and Mel and find out more about that stone. He hoped maybe Mike would even let him try it.

It seemed like an eternity later that the three friends were able to extricate themselves from the mob and go out onto the front lawn. Billy noticed that Mike moved stiffly and seemed subdued, though he was happy to see his buddy back home. They plopped down under the big maple tree - except for Mike who remained standing - and Melanie breathlessly updated him on what had been going on at school since the incident, as related by her girlfriends. Billy groaned inwardly; he'd have to wait a while longer before asking Mike about his miracle stone.

None of them noticed the red Viper parked down the street.

About ten minutes later, as Mel paused for breath, Billy said: "C'mon, Mike, sit down here with us. We won't bite. I'm sure Mel's got lots more gossip to tell me, and I wanna ask you about stuff."

The big teen shuffled his feet and looked uneasy. "Naw, it's okay. I likes to stand."

Billy looked at his friend closely and saw the pain in his face. "Something wrong, Mike? You look like you're hurting."

"Yeah, I am. I ... kinda hurted my bum."

"What? Get out! How'd ya do that? Sit on a nail or something?"

Michael laughed. "Naw, it wasn't that. But I can't say."

Melanie piped up: "But we're friends, Michael. Best friends. Friends can, like, tell each other anything."

A stubborn frown clouded Mike's face. "No, not this. I just can't, okay?"

Billy and Mel looked at each other. Billy said: "Well, that's okay, buddy. If ya don't wanna, ya don't haveta. It's probably embarrassing for you." A sudden thought struck him. "Hey listen! Why don't you just change into Wolverine and let his healing factor fix whatever's hurting you, like you did to cure me in the hospital?"

Michael shrugged and looked at his feet. "Yeah, Billy, I did thinked of that, but it would not be a good idea. My parents would get superstitious."

"Super - ? Oh! You must mean suspicious, right?" asked

Melanie.

"Right," mumbled Mike. "Look, can we talk about other stuff, now?"

Billy still had misgivings; he felt there was something bad about this. But he went along with Mike's wishes and changed the topic: "So then. Tell me more about what you can do with that awesome stone of yours. I know we talked about it when I was in the hospital, just before I almost died, but I was pretty drugged up that day an' my memory's fuzzy on some stuff."

Mike brightened instantly. "Well, like I told you before, it gives me superheroes' powers. But I can only turn into those with natural powers, powers they don't get from gadgets an' stuff, an' you'd be surprised how few of those there really are in comics, when you think about it."

"Yah, I remember you saying that Batman and Iron Man were out. So someone like Green Lantern is also out?" said Billy.

"Yep. He gets his powers from a ring."

"Thor?"

"Needs his mystic hammer."

"The Atom?"

"Piece of white dwarf star in his belt."

"Hawkman?"

"Artificial wings."

"Oh, but that guy you were yesterday; he had wings," interjected Melanie.

"Angel. His wings are part of his body; he's a mutant."

"Ah!" yelped Billy. "Speaking of Angel, I got one: Cyclops of the X-Men!"

"Yeah, but that'd be real dangerous 'cause he needs his special ruby-quartz visor to control his optic blasts an' I can't create that."

"Well, how about Storm of the X-Men?"

"She's a girl."

"So? Her powers are all natural. She controls weather and she doesn't need a hammer like Thor to do it."

Michael looked at Billy like his friend had just suggested

he go play in traffic. "Bil-ly! I don't wanna change into a *girl!* Ewww! Come on!"

Melanie said: "And what's wrong with girls?"

"Well, nuthin'. It's just ... just that they're ... girls."

"So? I'm a girl; does that mean there's somethin' wrong with me?" Mel asked.

"No, 'course not! You're my friend! But boys is boys, an' girls is girls. You're just different."

"And Amen to that difference!" said Billy.

Michael looked down at his two friends, frowned, then laughed when he saw Mel wink at Billy. "Aw, you're teasing me! Stop teasing, you two!"

"Okay, okay, what about Magneto, or the Lizard, or Clayface, or the Parasite? Their powers are natural," asked Billy.

With a shocked look, Mike said: "No way! That's worse than girls! They're bad guys! Vanillas!"

"Villains, you mean."

"Yeah, what I said! No way I'd ever turn into one of those! They're evil, not heroes at all."

"Well I'm no comic geek like you guys," said Mel, "but it seems to me that if you became one of them, it doesn't mean you'd be evil too. Like, you'd just get their powers, but you'd still be you, right?"

"Well, maybe. I dunno. An' I'll never know 'cause I'll never turn into one of 'em. It's just not right!" And Mike set his jaw in the way that told his friends that his mind was made up.

"Hey, what about the world's first superhero," Billy said, getting up on his knees. "The one who started it all way back in 1938, co-created by a Canadian teenaged artist, the one with all organic powers and no gadgets: Superman! Damn, he can fly, is invulnerable, has half-a-dozen different visions in his eyes, super-speed, super-strength - he can do everything!"

"Yeah, an' that's the problem with him," replied Mike. "He's way too complicated. I tried already. I can't do him. I even tried to do just one or two of his powers, but it didn't work. Too complicated, yes he is."

"Speaking of trying, Mike, wouldya let me try that stone sometime, when we're alone?"

Michael looked uncomfortable. Mel said: "Oh, I asked him that yesterday. I'd like to try it too. But he's kinda reluctant."

Billy pouted: "Huh. C'mon, I thought friends shared stuff."

"They do," Michael said. "I share all my comics with you whenever you wanna read 'em. An' I always share my after-school snack with you. Look, I'll lets you try it - both of you - honest. But not just yet. I'm still getting used to it; I've only had it for a little while, y'know. Just thinkin' about lendin' it to someone else makes me feel real funny, yes it does. Just gimme a little more time, okay?"

Billy and Melanie looked at each other, disappointment evident on their faces, then Billy said: "Yeah, okay." There was an uncomfortable silence and Melanie took this as her cue to launch into more school gossip.

The man in the Viper lowered his binoculars. There were two boys and a girl. The girl had crazy blue hair and glasses, but she had a killer bod, and the man felt the familiar urge stirring in him; the urge that pre-dated his discovery of The Gift. He swallowed hard and forced his thoughts back to the matter at hand.

The ... energy ... surrounding those three teens matched what he was looking for. In fact, it was quite strong. The girl was obviously not the McDonnell kid, but which of the two boys was Billy? The tall muscular one or the short fat one? Did the energy signature come from all three kids, or just whoever was Billy? He couldn't tell, with them all bunched together like that. And he couldn't just change into something and wade into them and discover what he needed to know. It was way too public with far too many people around.

Frustrated, he had no choice but to sit and watch. He ground his teeth; he was not used to being patient.

Sometime later, he saw an adult step onto the porch and holler something to the teens. They split up. The fat boy waddled back into the house - so that must be Billy since that was the address the candy-striper had given him - and the other boy went towards the house next door, while the blue-haired girl jumped on her bike and pedalled off. He groaned; each teen had an energy signature! So which one should he follow?

No brainer, really. He'd follow the girl. Oh yeah. He laughed and started the Viper.

ఞ ఞ ఞ ఞ ఞ ఞ

Michael sucked a knuckle walking over to his house. Steps from his front door, he stopped, spun on his heel and returned to Billy's house. He rang the bell and asked Billy's mother if he could see Billy. Surprised to see him back so soon, Janet bellowed for her son.

Billy, hauling down a new shirt, clumped down the stairs.

"Mike? What's up? It's only been a couple minutes; I'm not even finished changing yet."

"Come with me," said the tall teen. "Around the side of your house."

There was a narrow strip of lawn on one side of the McDonnell house, bordered by a high hedge on one side and the house on the other. The house had no windows on this side. When they were halfway down the strip, Michael stopped and thrust his hand out to his friend, saying:

"Here. Try it."

It was Michael's shiny, colourful stone. Billy looked up at Michael. "Seriously?"

"Yah. We're bestest friends. Bestest friends share. Try it."

Almost reverently, Billy took the stone. It felt warm in his palm. "So, whadda I do?"

"Imagine a superhero. Think real hard that ya wanna become that superhero. *Believe* that ya wanna."

Billy closed his eyes and gripped the stone hard. He concentrated. Nothing happened. He opened his eyes and stared down at his bulging stomach; disappointment flooded through him.

"Try again, Billy. *Believe.*"

Billy concentrated harder than he'd ever concentrated on

anything in his life, even an algebra exam.

When he open his eyes and looked down, he was still shaped like the Michelin Man.

"Aw, forget it," he said mournfully, handing back the stone. "I'm still Billy the Whale."

"I dunno why it doesn't work for ya," Michael said. "Who were ya tryin' to become?"

"The most perfect physical shape I could think of: Captain America. Either in the comics, or as Chris Evans portrays him in the movies; either body would be totally awesome. What I wouldn't give for a body like Cap's."

He looked up at Mike and patted his broad shoulder. "Thanks anyway for lettin' me try your stone, buddy. I really appreciate it."

"You're very welcome. Sorry it didn't work for ya. I really dunno why, Billy,"

"Oh well, story of my life, eh? Anyway, I gotta finish gettin' changed. See ya soon, okay?"

"Okay."

Both teens returned to their respective homes, Michael sucking his knuckle as he fretted about why his special stone didn't work when his best friend had tried it.

༄ ༄ ༄ ༄ ༄ ༄

Melanie reached her house, flung her bike down on the lawn, charged up the steps two at a time and tore open the front door. She was ecstatic. Billy was cured, he was back home, and now they were all going out for a huge celebration dinner. She had raced to her house to change, then Billy's folks would collect Michael and come pick her up in their station wagon. She scribbled a quick note to her parents, who were out this afternoon watching Annoying Sister playing goalie and throwing tantrums at a soccer game. Leaving the note on the kitchen table, she pounded up the stairs and started tearing her clothes off as soon as she entered her room.

She was down to her underwear and rooting through her

closet, trying to make up her mind about what to wear, when she heard a soft *scuff* at her bedroom door. She turned. A strange man was standing there leaning against the doorjamb, staring at her.

"AAAH!" she yelped. She yanked the sheet off her bed and wrapped herself in it. "Who the hell are you? What are you doing here?"

"Enjoying the view," the stranger replied. "Ya got a killer bod there, four-eyes." He took a step inside her room.

"GET OUT!" she screamed, backing away. "I MEAN it, I'll call the cops!"

The man laughed, without a trace of humour. Mel saw a thin violet aura shimmer around his body then, impossibly, amazingly, he disappeared.

"What the hell ...! Hey, where'd you go, you creep?" she exclaimed. Then something had her around the throat, squeezing, squeezing, and there was no one for her to kick, and no matter how hard she struggled, she couldn't break free, and then everything went black.

ഗ ഗ ഗ ಳ ಳ ಳ

Melanie slowly regained consciousness, groaned and tried to raise her hands to her head. They wouldn't move. Her legs were also stuck.

Full awareness flooded in. She looked down. She was tied to her desk chair, her ankles bound to the front chair legs and her wrists lashed to the arms of the chair. Her bedsheet wrap was gone. Her mind screamed: *oh my GAWD! I'm in my underwear!* She swallowed hard, looked down again and saw that pairs of her own knee socks had been used to bind her wrists and ankles.

She looked up and saw the intruder standing to one side, eyes fixated on her. Specifically on her chest, which, despite the bra she wore, seemed completely exposed the way he stared at it. *Aw hell, what IS it with guys and boobs? Life was so much simpler before I grew these things; before my body turned into a damn sex object!*

"What's ... what's going on? Are ... are you here to rob us? There's not much money in the house."

"I'm not here to rob," said the man. "I'm here for you."

"Me? Who *are* you and what do you want with me?" she said in what she hoped was a strong voice.

"Right now? Information," said the man. "Then, later, we'll have some fun together. You're Melanie Van Heusen, right?"

"Yeah, and you ... you better just let me go, right now!" She tugged at her bonds. "My folks are due back any minute!"

"What a cute little liar. I read the note you left for them in the kitchen; they won't be back until after dinner. I'm afraid it's just me and thee, sweet thing."

Melanie shrank back against the chair as the man came to stand next to her. She suddenly realized how vulnerable she was. She froze as he placed his hands on her breasts and kneaded them through the soft fabric of her bra. Shock gave way to anger: "HEY! Let GO! Stop that, you perv bastard!"

With a final hard squeeze, he did so, stepping back with a chuckle that left her cold. *That's the second time in a week that I've been pawed! This sucks!* She had had a close-up view of the monstrous black tattoo on his left forearm and the image chilled her.

"You're right, sweets. Time for pleasure later. Now, it's time for business. I want you to tell me everything that happened the night you and the McDonnell kid were kidnapped, especially about the green monster that rescued you."

"No! Why should I?"

"If you don't want to get hurt, you'd damn well better."

Mel looked into his eyes and shivered as she saw only grim intent. She realized this was a man who made good on his threats.

So she told him everything, except the part when the monster changed into Michael because of that wonderful stone. But the stranger sensed she was holding something back. He leaned close to her ear and said in a sibilant whisper:

"There's more, isn't there? Something that you're not telling me. C'mon, babe, spill it."

"No .. that's it. That's everything. Honest."

The man stepped back and regarded her. "You're lying to me again. And you're in no position to do that, are you?"

Mel shifted in her chair, straining against her bonds. *Oh, if I could just get free! Then I'd show him!* "Really, that's all I know. Honest, Mister."

"I don't believe you. It appears you need a little persuasion."

He shut her bedroom window, muting the snarl of lawnmowers and the whine of weedwhackers that filled the spring air outside. He went to a shadowed corner of her room. Violet limned his body, then he disappeared again. As Mel watched, transfixed, the shadow in the corner grew. Taller, broader. Then it reached out towards her and she realized in horror that it was a long black neck ending in a large triangular slab of a head with orange eyes and a huge mouth filled with jagged black teeth.

Her brain reeled at the impossible sight and she screamed. The black thing *hissed*.

She screamed again as those awful jaws delicately gripped her left leg below her knee. The jaws tightened, ever so slightly. Black needlesharp teeth cut into her flesh, and tiny red rivulets started coursing lazily down her calf. She screamed a third time.

"AAAA! Okay! Stop! Stop! I'll tell you everything! Just *stop!*" she cried.

The thing released her and rose up, towering above her. It *hissed* again. Then it flowed backwards into the corner. Seconds later, the stranger stood there, smiling at her. Melanie sobbed, not caring that she was crying in front of this creep, because the pain in her leg was intense, far worse than the time she'd fallen out of Jimmy Cuthbert's treehouse and broken her leg. And that shadow thing terrified her; she had thought it was going to bite her leg clean off.

"So you're more cooperative now, huh?" The man stepped closer. "Tell me the rest."

And she did, between snuffles. She told him all about Michael and the stone he had found and how it let him change into comic book superheroes and - she stopped. She just realized that this man did much the same thing.

"Yeah, me too, babe. Thanks to The Gift, which I found in the New Mexican desert a coupla months ago, I can change into powerful things, though they come out of my own imagination, not some stupid comic books." The man reached into his pocket and brought something out. He held it up to her and she saw it was a colourful D-shaped stone just like the one Mike had. "Does that kid's stone look like this?"

She nodded.

The stranger whistled softly and replaced the stone in his pocket. "Well I'll be Goddamned. So that's what I'm meant to find. That's what's drawn me clear across the continent. Another stone like mine! Except that it's being used by some dumb retard!"

He stood there for long minutes, thinking. Mel stopped crying. She looked at her leg and was relieved to see the bleeding had mostly stopped. She squirmed again, anxious to be free of her restraints.

"This Michael retard, he the other boy with you and McDonnell this afternoon at the McDonnell house, the one who went into the house next door?" asked the man.

"N-no. Mike lives across town. We know him through school. And stop calling him a retard. That's a horrible label! He's a wonderful, exceptional boy despite his disability."

"Awww, my bleedin' heart's gonna break. Real touchin', sweet cheeks. Now, tell me exactly where I can find him."

"I'll do better than that. Just untie me and lemme get dressed and I'm take you right to him myself."

The intruder regarded her, then grinned his mirthless grin. "That's a deal, cutie. And don't try any funny stuff; you've seen what I can do."

He pulled something out of another pocket, thumbed it, and a wicked switchblade flicked open. He sliced off the socks binding her and stepped back as she stood, massaging her wrists. She saw him ogling her crotch, seeming to stare right through her panties, then his eyes travelled upwards to stare at her chest again, then she kicked him hard right between his legs.

"AOW! You little BITCH!" he howled, doubling over. But

she was already spinning in a perfect roundhouse kick that caught him square in the jaw. His head snapped back and he collapsed to the floor and lay still.

She stood over him, breathing heavily. "Take that, you bastard! Now you've seen what *I* can do! I'm not some helpless girl! I've been taking kickboxing since I was ten! I have a brown belt! So screw you!" She kicked him twice more, in his side. "Bastard sicko pervert!"

She grabbed some clothes from her closet and yanked them on. She was just tying her sneakers when the man on the floor groaned and stirred. She smashed her chair over his head. He stopped stirring.

She snagged her purse and ran out of the house. Then a thought hit her and she spun around and raced back to her room. She looked at the unconscious intruder. She didn't want to get close to him, much less touch him, but she gritted her teeth and shoved her hand into the creep's pocket and took his stone. It was warm, just like Michael's. She jammed it into her jeans pocket and charged back outside. Jumping on her bike, she pedalled furiously down the street. She had to get away from that evil creature and she had to warn Mike.

She reached Mike's house just as he was climbing into the McDonnell's blue Volvo station wagon with Billy and his family. They gawked as Mel skidded to a stop and blurted out her story, leaving out the part about the stone. When she had finished, she looked at a sea of faces showing various degrees of disbelief and surprise.

"But it's TRUE!" she cried. "This man tied me up in my own bedroom and turned into some kinda shadow MONSTER that BIT me and forced me to tell him all about Michael!"

"What about Michael?" asked Paul McDonnell, with the stern look he used as vice-principal of Clearwater High.

"Never mind that for now," said Janet. "Melanie, you said you were bit? Show me."

Mel rolled up her jeans leg and everyone gasped at the ring of teeth marks leaking blood; the wounds had reopened with her exertions in riding over there.

"That needs tending to right now," announced Janet decisively. She turned to her husband. "Paul, hospital."

"No, not now! We gotta call the police and send them to my house!" protested Melanie. "They gotta arrest that pervert!"

Janet gave an exasperated sigh and went into her house to fetch some bandages, while her husband called the police on his smartphone. Minutes later, Billy helped his mother wrap a gauze bandage around Mel's leg. Michael sat still, sucking a knuckle and watching, great concern on his face. Then they drove over to Melanie's to meet the police. Mel gave a little cry as they came up to her house.

The red Viper was gone.

As her stomach churned, her hand shot to the pocket of her jeans where she had put the stone. She sighed with relief as she felt its hard bulge beneath the cloth; she still had it - it was *hers* now.

She could hardly wait until she was alone to try it.

The cops soon arrived, and everyone trooped upstairs to Melanie's room, where they saw the evidence of the broken chair, the cut knee socks and drops of her blood on the carpet. And no intruder.

With some skepticism, the officers wrote down Melanie's statement about the assault, including her description of the man and his awful tattoo. They couldn't deny that something had bitten her leg, which was still bleeding through the gauze. Then Janet insisted they get Mel to the hospital. They left; en route, Mel texted her parents with her smartphone. Frantic with worry, her parents arrived at the hospital soon after the McDonnell's car pulled into the drive-in Emergency door.

The doctor dressed Mel's wounds and gave her pills for the pain and a shot to ward off infection. "Now, if the authorities catch the animal that bit you, young lady, and it proves to be rabid, then you have to return here for a rabies shot, understand?"

Melanie nodded and thought *but it wasn't an animal.*

With everything that had just happened, plans for Billy's

celebratory dinner were postponed. Mel also had no chance to get Mike alone to tell him she'd been forced to spill his secret and that she had a stone that was just like his. The families returned to their homes, with Mel getting drowsy from the medication en route. Her dad prevailed upon the police to post an officer at the house for a few days, in case the attacker returned. Then Mel went to bed. She was asleep before her head hit the pillow.

She dreamt of a giant ebony snake trapping her in its coils, its huge head swaying above her, laughing. Once she even woke up, terrified and covered in sweat, convinced that something was lurking in the dark, watching her. Then the drug in her system reclaimed her, hauling her back down to unconsciousness.

She awoke to sunlight and birdsong. She heard the clatter of dishes and the voices of her family downstairs. She fumbled for her glasses on the night table, slipped them on and glanced at the bedside clock. She was shocked to see it was lunchtime. She swung her legs over the side of the bed, sat up and groaned. Her injured leg throbbed with pain. Gingerly, she stood and stifled a yelp. The pain increased when she put weight on it.

Then she remembered the stone, that warm and pretty rock with the magic power, and shuffled to the corner where she'd flung her jeans last night. Picking them up, she put her hand in the pocket where she'd put the stone.

It was gone.

She gave a small cry, and frantically checked the other pockets.

Empty.

Despair flooded her. Did she lose it when she went to the hospital? Or when she got undressed last night? She searched the floor of her room which, like most teenagers' floors, actually served as a gigantic shelf for all manner of clothes and stuff.

Nothing.

A horrible realization hit her. Maybe that awful creep had returned, had stood right here as she slept, and retrieved his stone! She suddenly felt nauseous.

She pulled on a dressing gown over her PJs and staggered

downstairs. Sharp pain lanced through her injured leg each time she put weight on it. She endured the attention of her parents and sister hugging her, asking how she felt and how was her leg and did she feel like eating, then she asked if the police officer guarding the house had seen or heard anything last night. He hadn't.

In the post-medication-waking-up-in-mid-day haze that suffused her senses, Melanie wondered if what happened yesterday had maybe been just a bad dream.

She might have succeeded in convincing herself of it, too, if it weren't for the throbbing pain in her leg.

After breakfast, and a visit to the bathroom to swallow more of the painkillers, she hobbled painfully back to her room. That's when she noticed her favourite stuffed animal: Pooh Bear, a beloved souvenir of a family trip to Walt Disney World when she was eight. It was sitting in its usual spot on her dresser. With both eyes ripped out and its rotund stomach sliced open cleanly, as if with a sharp blade. Like a switchblade. Pooh stuffing had spilled out over its chubby legs.

But the mutilated bear of little brain was not what set her screaming, so loud that it brought her family running, along with the cop posted outside. It was the note she found in Pooh's soft paws, written on a scrap of paper in a messy cramped style:

This aint over bitch. Yore fancy kickin days are done.

Chapter 12

When Titans Clash

Michael flowed through the water, marvelling at the scenery. Clumps of boulders, from small to so massive that even he wouldn't be able to lift them. Piles of logs, felled over a hundred years ago when the timber trade thrived in this area, escaped from their log booms and now scattered in drowned repose. A snowmobile, snout buried deep in the muck, whose driver wanted to be "the first across the lake this winter" and who had discovered that the ice wasn't thick enough yet. The odd refrigerator and car tire and bed spring. Shoes. Bottles. An old Evinrude. All covered in a thick brown film of mud, algae and sand; looking like some post-apocalyptic wasteland in the grey light filtering down from the surface.

The schools of fish excited Michael the most. He'd be cruising over the silent landscape, skimming past tracts of seaweed, when suddenly he'd be in the midst of a bunch of bass, or trout, or pickerel. They were as surprised to see him as he was to see them. A big human down here amongst them, breathing water as they did. After a moment of shocked surprise, the fish always scattered in panic, leaving Michael in their wake hooting laughter in a flurry of big air bubbles.

Being Aquaman is a real cool power, thought Michael as he swam effortlessly along the lake bottom. It had felt totally weird just after the change; he had a moment of panic when he first started breathing water. *You're gonna DROWN,* his brain screamed. But he didn't, and breathing water soon felt as natural as if he'd been born to it. His eyes had become light-sensitive, allowing him to see quite well in the dim underwater world. His skin was harder and thicker, insulating him from the cold water, especially when he passed the thermocline at 10 feet and went deeper. And his swimming, always jerky at best, had become sublimely graceful; he was a human dolphin, knifing through water as a bird soars through air.

But what he really revelled in was the *quiet*. Except for a few clicks and grunts from the fish, he moved through a silent world. And that was just what he needed, after everything that had happeed in the past three days.

There was quite an uproar the day after Melanie had been attacked, when she awoke to discover her attacker had returned during the night, slipping past the police guard and entering her room while she slept and stealing back his stone and cutting up her Pooh Bear. Her parents had gone ballistic, the police had tripled the guard, and Michael had spent as much time as he could at her house, ready to help protect her if the nasty man returned.

But he did not. Everyone was so relieved. Then, yesterday, Mel's leg wound became infected; so fast and so bad that she was rushed to the hospital, stifling cries of pain. That's where she was still, pumped full of antibiotics that really didn't seem to be working, with the doctors suspecting it was some kind of new flesh-eating disease. It got worse overnight and today the doctors were talking about having to amputate her leg if the mysterious infection continued to spread. When Billy told Michael that news, the big teen had cried in anguish.

"You're not as grown-up-looking as Melanie, Billy," Michael had said, snuffling. "If those anti-bionics don't work, you can't pass as a man nurse so I can get a transformer of my Wolverine blood into her to heal her like I healeded you."

"That's right," said Billy miserably. "Nobody'd listen to me ordering them around."

Then Billy went back to the hospital with his folks, to stand vigil with Melanie's family. Michael had begged off, saying he had a lot of thinking to do. He had pedalled his bike to Half-Moon Lake, stripped down to his underwear after first making sure no one was around, gave himself the powers of Aquaman, and slipped beneath the waves.

At least he didn't have to think about Monster Mack anymore, and whether he should use Wolverine's blood to heal the bully who had almost killed his best friend. The Monster had died the very same day that Melanie was attacked. Hospital officials hadn't quite figured out how he'd died yet, though "likely of natural causes" was printed in the local paper. That hadn't stopped Mack's father, furious in his grief, from vowing to sue the hospital for gross negligence.

Michael surfaced hours later, having made a significant decision. If Melanie was going to lose her leg, then to heck with his secret. No secret was worth having his friend crippled for life. He would march into that hospital, show the doctors what he could do, change into Wolverine again, and have them put his blood into her so she could be healed.

But he had a more immediate problem. He had lost track of time while underwater. It was now dusk, well past dinner time, and that meant he was in for another beating.

"Oh no, oh no, oh no," he muttered, standing there dripping as he watched the setting sun. He became the Flash for several seconds, spinning himself around in a whirlwind blur. He reverted back to Michael, now completely dry, and hurriedly hauled on his clothes. He dug out the basic cellphone from his pocket, which he rarely used, and carefully pressed the two buttons to speed-dial his home. Maybe the beating wouldn't be so bad if he told them where he was and that he was on his way home now.

The phone rang and rang. Finally, his mother answered. "Hel ... hello?" Her voice sounded strained.

"Hi Mom, it's Michael. Look, I'm really, really sorry I'm late for dinner. I'm down at the lake an' I was thinking a lot about Melanie an' I forgot the time an' I'm sorry, but I'm coming home right now honest."

"That's okay, honey. We appreciate you calling to tell us where you are; we were worried about you. Now you just come straight home, all right?

"Uh ... yeah, okay. Be there soon. 'Bye." Michael hung up,

puzzled. She hadn't screeched at him. Even more amazing, she called him "honey". She hardly ever did that.

He rode home as fast as he could pedal, elated that she wasn't mad at him and hoping that maybe it meant he wasn't in for a beating. He was so excited that he didn't notice the stone in his pocket getting warmer, the closer he came to his house.

As he approached his house, he saw that the McDonnell's car was not in the driveway. Billy and his parents must still be at the hospital with Mel's family. He made a quick wish that Mel's leg had gotten better. If not, then he knew what he had to do.

Michael leaned his bike carefully against a tree, then charged into the house and knew immediately that something was very wrong. Apart from the loud *BANG* of the screen door behind him (he always forgot to hold that door), the house was eerily quiet. No dinner sounds. No omnipresent TV sounds. No voices.

"Hello? Mom? Dad?" he called.

His mother's voice came from upstairs. "Up here, honey. C'mon up."

She called me 'honey' again, he thought and smiled as he ran up the stairs, two at a time. In his pocket, the stone was now beyond warm. It was hot. He didn't notice.

"Where are ya?" he said.

"In here, honey," came his mother's voice from her bedroom.

He entered his parents' bedroom, saw his father's face, and screamed. Bert Johnson's head was on his dresser, sitting in a pool of blood that slowly dripped down the closed drawers. His face, frozen in terror, stared at his headless body crumpled in a gory heap in a corner across the room.

His mother, wearing the stained pale blue track suit she usually *schlumped* around the house in, was crucified upside down on the wall at the head of their bed with what looked like black spikes through her hands and feet. Her track suit was even more stained today. With blood. As Michael screamed in the doorway, she turned her head and said to the man sitting in shadow in the chair next to the bed:

"There. I got the bastard here for you. Now lemme go, like

you promised."

"Yes ma'am and I always keep my promises," said the man. The black spikes oozed out of Ruth's hands and feet and flowed into the shadow around the chair. She crashed to the bed and curled into a ball, cradling her bloody extremities, sobbing quietly.

Michael saw the design on the man's left forearm. In an awful moment of truth, he realized this was the man who had attacked Melanie.

"Well, well. So you're Michael Johnson," said the stranger in a cold voice. He had a funny accent. He stood, stretched, and smiled the nastiest smile Michael had ever seen, even nastier than the bullies who taunted him at school. "I woulda been here sooner, boy, but that bitch friend of yours clocked me so hard that I've had a headache for days. I can't concentrate to use The Gift if my head's splitting. Y'know, I just can't believe your stone picked a kid to bond with, and a retard kid at that."

Michael was speechless. The stranger took a step toward him, and the boy backed away.

"Now, don't you run off, boy," said the man. "You got something I want. You don't want me to do to your maw what I did to your paw here."

Mike stopped, and his mother said angrily: "You promised not to hurt me anymore if I brought the bastard to you. Well, I did! So you do what ya want to him, you take whatever it is that he's got, but just leave me alone! I gotta get to the hospital."

Michael gawped: "Mom?"

The stranger laughed. "Hah! And she's your mother! Well, boy, you just hand it over an' I'll be on my way."

"Hand ... hand what over?" Michael croaked, suddenly knowing the answer and dreading it.

"Something that looks like this." The man took an object from his pocket and showed it to the boy. Michael gasped. It was a stone just like his! His hand drifted to his pocket and he finally realized how hot his own stone was. It was almost burning his skin through the fabric. There was also a deep hum in his mind.

The man's eyes had followed Mike's hand and he said: "So.

You feel it too, huh? The stones are calling to each other. That's what's been pulling me all this time, across all that distance. C'mon, boy, let's see yours."

In a daze, Michael pulled out his stone, holding it in his palm. The man said: "Well, I'll be Goddamned! It's a duplicate of mine! No, wait. Well hell, it looks like we both got half of what used to be a larger rock! Look at the pattern of the colours in yours; they continue on in mine perfectly. Hot damn! Just imagine how powerful the complete stone would be if the two halves were put together!"

The teenager looked at both rocks and saw the man was right; they were a matching pair. He looked up and saw an unholy *need* in the man's eyes. He had also edged closer.

"C'mon, boy. The stones belong together; can't you *feel* it? Just give me your stone and we'll call it quits. Then you can call an ambulance for your maw."

"NO!" yelled Michael, and backed away again until he was standing just outside the bedroom door.

The stranger swore. "I don't wanna fight you 'less I haveta, what with you having that stone. I know the power it gives. Besides, there's an easier way."

The man moved back into the shadows next to the bed and suddenly, horribly, a large wedge-shaped head snaked out and grabbed his mother's arm just above the elbow in a terrible mouth full of black needle teeth. The jaws closed slightly and Ruth screamed:

"STOP! STOP! Michael, you Goddamn bastard, give him the damn stone! NOW, before this thing takes my arm off!"

Michael stood frozen in shock and fear. The creature's jaws tightened some more. Blood soaked the sleeve of his mother's sweatshirt and she yelled in agony:

"GIVE HIM THE STONE! AAAAA! Oh, why did we ever take you in, you stupid ungrateful retard! We should have just let you go to an orphanage, an' ta hell with the trust fund! Oh GOD, this hurts!"

"Orf-nage? Trust fund?" stammered Michael, trying to grasp

what his mother was saying.

"Aaaaa! Yes, stupid, stupid boy! Orphanage! You never knew this, but you're not really our son; we couldn't have children! You're my younger sister's illegitimate dumb bastard! She gave you up for adoption, an' your rich grandmother set up a trust fund for any relative who'd take you in, 'cause she felt so sorry for you, an' Bert 'n' I needed the money, so we adopted ya an' raised ya as our own, even though we always HATED you an' I'm DYIN' of pain here! HELP ME!"

Michael couldn't believe his ears. "You ... you're not really my mommy? You don't ... don't love me?"

"No! Of course not! How could we love a retard? Even your real mother rejected you! We just wanted the money that came with you! Aaaaa, Jesus, it hurrrrts!"

"But ... but ... "

"GIVE HIM THE STONE!"

But Michael just stood there, brain reeling with the bombshell of his mother's words, hands pressed to his face in shock. With an awful *KLACK,* the monster's jaws came together. His mother's severed arm fell to the floor with a ghastly *thunk* and blood geysered sideways from the stump that was left. Ruth shrieked, staring at the crimson stream spurting in time to her heartbeat. Then she fainted.

The creature regarded its handiwork with baleful orange eyes, then looked at Michael staring open-mouthed in the doorway, and *hissed*. Michael gave a cry and jumped back. The black thing flowed back into the shadows, and then the stranger stood there, smiling his arctic smile.

"Well, boy, that was quite the story, huh? Ain't you surprised! No wonder she was agreeable to leading you right to me. A mama usually protects her kids, no matter what. Now just give me that damn stone, and you can call 9-1-1 before she bleeds to death."

Michael knew the man was lying. If he gave up the stone, he'd be killed out of spite, just like his father ... or the man he always thought was his father. He forced himself to concentrate and a yellow aura limmed him briefly.

"No, no, no, this is *my* stone and you are an evil, nasty man," he said with more courage than he felt. "I'll run to the police fast as the Flash and they'll come and arrest you and save my ... my mommy ... that lady."

He turned and raced in a blur down the stairs towards the door. And slammed into a thick black wall that suddenly appeared just in front of the door. With a cry of pain, he ricocheted backwards and crashed hard against the floor. His head bounced on the varnished hardwood.

A voice from somewhere within the blackness said: "You ain't the only one who can move fast, boy. Well, you had your chance to do this peaceably. Now it's gonna hurt."

The black wall suddenly became the huge creature with the snake neck, big head and awful jaws. It lashed out at Michael, still too stunned to react even with the Flash's super-speed, and swallowed him whole!

The monster reared back and *hissed* its triumph.

The hiss ended as a fireball exploded from the creature's belly, melting away the blackness. With a terrible wail, the shadow-thing fled into the living room as Michael, now the Human Torch, stood blazing in the hallway. The hardwood floor started smoking beneath his feet and the Torch quickly became Michael again before he set the house ablaze. The boy was naked; the flames had incinerated his clothes and cellphone. He gripped his stone tightly in his left hand.

There was a crackle of electricity from the living room and Michael had just enough time to transform into the invulnerable green-skinned Hulk before he was hit with a massive electrical discharge, so strong that it propelled the thousand-pound-plus Hulk through the wall and out into the front yard. The Hulk tried to stand, bellowing its rage, but was hit again with a terrific dose of voltage. Then a third time.

Struggling to his feet against the effects of enough electrical shocks to kill a herd of elephants, Michael roared in the Hulk's stentorian voice: *"THE MADDER HULK GETS, THE STRONGER HULK GETS!"* It was one of the Hulk's favourite sayings.

"Oh, please," said the electrical man and blasted Michael with another massive jolt. Then another. Then two more.

Shocked almost senseless, Michael collapsed in the smoldering crater formed by the electrical attacks. The air was thick with the reek of ozone. Mister Buttons, Nosey Tweedle's cat that Michael had been feeding while the old lady recovered in hospital, fled squalling for parts unknown with every hair on its body standing straight up due to the static electricity.

The stranger stepped from the house, a blue-white electrical nimbus dancing around his eyes. He looked at the still form of the naked green behemoth and laughed.

"Well, boy, the best man won. Easier than I thought, too."

As he approached, intent on prying the stone from the jade giant's hand, the Hulk shimmered and disappeared.

"Hey, what the hell!" the electrical man yelped, then heard bare feet running down the driveway, away from him. "Hah! Got ya! I do that invisible trick too!" he crowed and sent a wide-arc electrical blast down the driveway. Michael flung himself aside onto the lawn as the deadly jolt whizzed by; he was not invulnerable as the Invisible Kid, one of the Legion of Super-Heroes. The electrical force hit Mansoor Mitha's car parked in his driveway across the street, next to the charred skeleton of the Tweedle house. The car blew up. The air shook with the roar of the explosion. Michael thought *surely that'll bring the police. I just haveta hang on for a little longer.*

Then the electrical man walked around the side of the house and Michael could tell he was preparing to unleash another blast in his general direction. Invisible or not, it would kill him if it hit him. He didn't want to turn into the Hulk again; the lumbering mountain was an easy target, and Michael ached from the electrical punishment he'd already taken. He concentrated, then with the strength and agility of a very visible and very naked Spider-Man, he leapt high into a big oak tree just as the man sent another zap of electricity across the lawn. Seconds later, Mike leaped onto the roof of his house as a narrow blast singed the tree limb he'd been crouching on.

"Hold still, damn you!" yelled the stranger. He sent another blast at Michael, but his Spider-sense, which alerted him to danger, and Spider-speed, enabled him to evade it easily. He ran over the roof to the other side and, being Spider-Man, had no problem crawling down the two-storey wall to the ground.

He stopped, trying to decide what to do. He couldn't think clearly; his mind was roiling with what he had learned in that bedroom. He couldn't keep fighting like this, he had to call for help for that lady ... his ... mom. But he had to defeat this Nastyman, too. Who should he become, to do all that? *Why was it so hard to think?* A thick blue-white bolt hit him square in the back, flinging him clear across the backyard face-first into a thick tree. If it wasn't for Spider-Man's strength, Michael would have been killed instantly. As it was, he collapsed in a heap, unconscious.

Spider-Man's power caused Michael to regain consciousness quickly. Pain shot through his face; when he touched his nose, his hand came away bloody and he realized it was broken. Then he also realized that the Nastyman was kneeling next to him, about to pry his stone from his fingers.

"Y'know boy, maybe you got somethin' there, reading them comic books. I just change into a few things with my Gift, but you can change into a crap-load of powerful characters. Seems like I should expand my imagination. After I kill a few more people that've pissed me off first. Starting with you and your blue-haired bitch friend."

With a cry of defiance, Mike used Spider-Man's muscles to swat the man away from him. He went soaring through the air for twenty feet and fell to earth with a yelp of pain.

Michael decided to change into the Flash again, to race away and get help. Suddenly a mighty blast of electricity arced towards him. He leaped nimbly aside, one of Spidey's trade-marked quips rising to his lips, then realized too late that the blast had not been aimed at him this time. With an ear-splitting *CRACK,* the big tree next to him broke in two halfway up, and the entire upper portion fell squarely on Michael. Spider-Man was strong, but not as strong as the Hulk, and Michael yelled in agony as he was crushed to the ground and bones snapped inside him.

It was more pain than Michael had ever felt in his life, far worse than his dad's beatings. It felt like at least two ribs were broken, plus his left arm, and his left thigh blazed white-hot where a tree limb had slashed deeply down one side. Through a haze of tears, coughing blood, he saw the man limping toward him. Mike felt some pride; at least he had been able to hurt him too.

"You ... you Goddamned retard," the man gritted as he hobbled closer. "You hurt me. Me! I ain't never been hurt since I got The Gift and now some half-wit manages to wreck my ankle. Hell, I think it's broken! You just wait, boy. Pain you're in now's nothin' like what you got comin' to ya."

Michael forced himself to concentrate through the pain and he turned into something that had no bones, broken or otherwise. Plastic Man flattened himself wafer-thin and slid out from underneath the tree. Then, inspired by the comic book antics of his favourite hero, Mike formed a giant slingshot with his body, anchoring his arms and legs around the limbs of the fallen tree and stretching his body backwards. As the stranger came around the tree, trying to see in the darkness, Michael released his elastic body. With a loud *sproing,* he hit the stranger squarely in the chest and sent him soaring away, far into the night sky. He lost sight of him disappearing over the roof of Billy's house, still gaining altitude.

Michael changed into Wolverine, and cried out in torment as the mutant's healing factor repaired his broken body. He heard sirens, then the squeal of tires as cop cars slammed to a stop in front of his house.

Luckily today had been wash day. Michael plucked some jeans and a shirt off the line, drew them on, placed his precious stone deep in the jeans pocket, and padded barefoot around the house to try and explain all this to the police. Somehow.

And he tried not to think about the fact that his parents were not really his parents at all, and that they had never ever loved him. It didn't work. He was crying when he reached the cops.

Chapter 13

The Price of Power

"In jail? Mike's in JAIL?" Billy could not believe what his father had just told him. Father and son were in the corridor outside Melanie's hospital room, where doctors and nurses still worked desperately to reverse the unknown infection ravaging her left leg.

Paul McDonnell regarded his son with sympathy. "Yes, it's true. I just got off the phone with Chief Arnott; that was the call the hospital paged me for. Something terrible's happened at Michael's house and he's asking for us."

"Something terrible? Like, what happened, Dad?"

"Michael's parents have been brutally murdered and the police think he did it."

"WHAT!? That's INSANE! Mike wouldn't hurt a fly!"

"Well, Billy, we may know that, but consider how the police see it. The boy is quite strong - you've seen his muscles - and he does, after all, have an intellectual disability, and Arnott says his story about what happened is completely unbelievable, so the police reached a natural conclusion."

"No way! Not Mike! C'mon, Dad, we gotta get over to the police station! Poor Mike's probably going nuts, being thrown in jail just after his parents get killed! He's a guy who needs his routines an' now his life's been shot to hell! Goddamn it! We gotta help him!"

"We'll leave immediately. And I'll call our lawyer en route, to meet us there. Don't worry, son; we'll sort this out. And you don't have to swear."

༄ ༄ ༄ ༄ ༄ ༄

Chief of Police Frank Arnott had been born and raised in Clearwater, and had been a cop since graduating high school. A stubby man who wore high-heeled cowboy boots to compensate and worked hard at keeping his figure trim, he had a weatherbeaten face and steel grey eyes that missed nothing. Born to do police work, he had applied himself conscientiously to carve out a mostly-blameless career (except for that one early incident with Widow Wentworth's two twentysomething daughters). Now, decades later, as Chief, he'd thought he'd seen it all, as far as small-town crime was concerned. But what he saw at the Johnson house broke new ground.

The carnage was something to make one puke, which was what two of his younger officers promptly did after seeing the bodies of Bert and Ruth Johnson. It was quite obvious how Bert had died, and Ruth had bled to death from that amputated arm. And the story their son babbled out, standing there barefoot and teary-eyed, was absolutely crazy: A man wielding supernatural powers had killed his parents and almost killed him. There was no evidence left behind of this mystery killer, and the killer himself had vanished from the scene - last seen arcing over the McDonnell house, according to the Johnson boy, who refused to say how the man had become airborne. A police manhunt of the neighbourhood around where the man must have landed turned up nothing, beyond barking dogs and citizens irritated by cops tramping unannounced around their yards. A check of the hospital's Emergency ward, and the town's two walk-in clinics, to see if a male had come in with an injured ankle, had also proved fruitless.

So of course they had to lock the kid up; he was known to have an intellectual disability. Until they found something to back up his nutbar story. Which was what Arnott was trying to explain to Vice-Principal McDonnell, who wasn't having any of it.

"Come on, Frank," said Paul. "We've known Michael for years; we're next-door neighbours. And you've seen him around town many times. How can you even suspect him of doing these awful murders?"

"Well, I'd like to think he didn't do it, Paul. Really. But what choice do I have? His story's obviously pure fantasy, he's strong as an ox, meaning he's strong enough to have done the killings, and maybe he's off his meds tonight an' he snapped. Could be; you never know with these types."

"These types? Nice to see you have an open mind. Look, Michael Johnson isn't on any medication."

"Well, maybe that's the problem right there."

"Frank, he's never needed medication. And he loved his parents. This makes no sense at all!"

"A-yep. An' that's why I'm locking him up until it does."

"Well, my lawyer's on his way over, and we'll see about all this when he gets here. And I trust you've notified the Community Living association to send a case worker over?"

While the men waited and continued to argue, Billy slipped away and obtained permission to visit Mike in his cell. There, he found his big friend quite distraught, pacing back and forth in the confines of his cage like a restless tiger. He stopped pacing and ran to the bars as soon as he saw Billy.

"Billy! Oh, am I happy to see you!" he exclaimed joyfully. The boys hugged exch other through the bars separating them.

"How ya doin', Mike?" Billy asked.

"Not good, not good, no, not good at all. My ... my parents - or who I always thought were my parents - are dead, I fought the Nastyman, the one who hurted Mel, but what's the worstest of all is: they took my stone!"

"What?"

"They took my stone, they took my stone! The police! I was always told the police are my friends! But they're not! Before they put me in here, they wanted everything from my pockets an' the only thing I had was my special stone! I told them I needed it, but they took it anyway! Billy, ya gotta get it back!"

"I will, Mike. Calm down. It's what the police always do; they take a prisoner's things before putting 'em in jail, but they keep the stuff safe until you get out. So don't worry, you'll get it back."

"Really?"

"Really. An' I'm sure you'll be gettin' out soon; my dad's here an' he's got his lawyer comin' to get you released. Now while we're waiting, tell me everything that happened tonight. The whole story. I bet you didn't tell the cops about a large part of the fight, an' I bet it's the part about how you changed into superheroes. Right?"

Michael nodded and launched into a detailed retelling of the evening, laced with many sound effects. And tears, when he got to the part where he discovered he was adopted, and that the people who he had always thought were his parents really didn't love him at all.

"Adopted? Man, buddy, I never knew. But that's not so bad; lotsa folks are adopted, an' they're cherished just as if they were natural offspring. No, what's awful is your mom saying that they never loved you, that they only wanted you for this trust fund money that came with you. That's cold, man, awful cold. You sure about that?"

"That's what she said. She was very, very clear," said Mike softly.

Billy reached in and gave his friend another hug. "Hey, at least you still have me. An' Mel. We love ya, an' we'll stand by ya. Don't worry. An' when my dad's lawyer gets down here, he'll have you outta jail soon."

Michael brightened, but still fretted about getting his stone back.

Billy had a sudden horrible thought: "Aw cripes! This man, the one with a stone like yours, he obviously knows all about us by now - the three of us. He must have been watching us, asking folks about us. And *that* means he probably knows where you are right now! Stuck in here, helpless!"

Michael frowned and said: "And if he knows about police stuff like you do, then he'll figure out I don't have my stone with me while I'm in jail."

"Yeah! An' you said your stone kinda, like, calls to him, so he could be after it right now, wherever the cops have it in this station!"

Mike got all agitated again: "An' if he comes after me, I'll be a sitting goose without my special stone!"

"Buddy, you're absolutely right! We gotta get you that stone back right now! Lemme go talk with Chief Arnott."

"Please hurry, Billy. I gotta bad feeling about all this. An' I still gotta get to the hospital to save Melanie's leg!"

જ જ જ ત ત ત

Chief Arnott wouldn't budge. Billy tried every reason he could think of, short of telling the truth, such as the stone had a soothing influence on Mike, keeping him calm. Or that it was a special gift from his real mother. Or it was essential for a school project due tomorrow. Arnott wasn't buying any of it.

"That stone stays put in the desk sergeant's cabinet until that kid is either booked or released. Period. If he's booked, it goes into evidence. If he's released, it goes back to him."

Billy opened his mouth to protest some more, when the lights went out.

Pandemonium reigned as the whole station was plunged into darkness for about fifteen seconds. Then the emergency generators kicked in and lights came on again. Arnott left them to check on the cause of the power failure. Billy took advantage of the confusion to sidle over to the big desk in the station lobby where the desk sergeant usually presided. The officer wasn't there; he was one of those cops running around making sure everything was okay.

Heart pounding, sweating, fearful he'd be caught at any moment, Billy yanked open the doors to the big cabinet behind the desk marked "Prisoner Possessions". Luckily it was unlocked. That was because there was hardly anything inside - there was only one other prisoner in the cells tonight. He quickly saw that Mike's stone was not there.

A sick feeling gripping his stomach, Billy frantically searched through the dimly-lit, almost-empty cabinet, checking all the corners.

No stone.

He looked up and saw the burly sergeant striding down the

hall back towards his desk. The boy closed the cabinet doors and slunk away, unseen.

No! Stone!

Did that mean the killer had turned invisible as Mel said he could, caused the brief power failure, ran in, and grabbed the stone? And was he even now approaching -

"Michael!" Billy yelled, and broke into a run toward the holding cells.

The guard again let him pass, and he pounded up to Mike's cell. The big teen was there, face pressed anxiously against the bars.

"Didya get it?" he asked as Billy skidded to a stop in front of him, gasping for breath.

"No. It's ... it's gone!"

"Gone?" Michael said, then a look of intense sorrow clouded his face. He sat down heavily on the floor and began to cry. Nothing Billy could say would make him stop.

He made quite a ruckus. Fortunately, the only other prisoner in the cells was Broken Nose Coyle, the town drunk, passed out on his cot. A pride of roaring lions would not wake him up. The door guard came in to see what was the matter, then he left, shaking his head. He returned with a woman Billy hadn't seen before: tall, thin, with lined face and skin like parchment, and short black hair streaked with grey. She introduced herself as Pamela, a social worker from Clearwater's Community Living association, and instructed the guard to open Mike's cell door at once.

She went inside, knelt, and soothed the sobbing boy. "Now there's no need to cry any longer. I was on my way back here to see you, y'know, but I had to clear some paperwork with the desk sergeant first. Power failure delayed things. Anyway, I'm here now and I got something for you, something they said you wanted desperately. I got it just before the lights went out. Here."

And she held out something colourful that sparkled in the dim emergency lighting: Michael's stone. With a cry of joy, the teen grabbed it.

"Oh, thankyouthankyouthankyou, nice lady!" he gushed,

swiping away the tears from his eyes.

"Do they know what caused the power to go out?" asked Billy, as a huge weight lifted from his heart.

"Yeah, some car hit a pole with a transformer about a block away. Drunk driver, I gather. The entire area has lost power," replied the woman.

"Can I go now?" Michael said.

"Not just yet, dear," she said. "But I want to take you from this cell into a nice room where we can have a chat. I want to hear your story. And I'm confident we can get you out of here by tomorrow." She looked at Billy. "Especially when your dad's lawyer gets here."

Both boys chorused in anguish: "Tomorrow? But that'll be way too late!"

"Why?"

"Because ... because Mike doesn't like staying in a strange place. He has to get out tonight," said Billy, as Michael nodded eagerly.

"Oh, I doubt that'll happen. I know you're a minor, but the police think you may have done some terrible things tonight, and so this lawyer and I will have considerable talking to do. And his parents' house is now a crime scene, so Michael can't go back there when he's released."

"But that's not FAIR!" protested Mike. "I didn't do those bad things!"

"Well, that's what we have to convince them of," said the woman. "After that, we've got to get you to a trauma counsellor."

"Why do I have to go to a counsellor in Tarrana? I live here in Clearwater."

"Not Toronto, trauma. Someone who helps people cope with terrible grief, like what you experienced tonight seeing your parents murdered."

"Oh."

She led Michael away to an interview room, while Billy rejoined his father. While waiting for the lawyer, Billy couldn't help staring at every shadowed corner, thinking he saw movement there. And at every man who entered the station, to see if they matched the description of the attacker Michael and Melanie had described.

The lawyer finally arrived, just as the social worker finished with Mike. The teen was returned to his cell, while the lawyer and the social worker joined the McDonnells in arguing with Chief Arnott.

Twenty minutes into the argument, with neither side able to claim victory yet, an officer came into the room waving a sheet of paper. "Sorry to barge in, Chief," she said, "but you wanna see this right away. We got a match on the guy those kids described."

"What? This guy really exists? I'll be damned. Give it here," barked Arnott. He read the paper and gave a low whistle. "Well, looks like I owe the Johnson kid an apology. We got us a break. Just to see if there was any truth to Johnson's story, we sent a description of the assailant he described out over the wire. It also matched the description given by the Van Heusen girl of her attacker, by the way. RCMP picked it up and found a match with a guy wanted by the FBI in the States for kidnapping and multiple murders. The suspect has a distinctive tattoo on his left forearm, which perfectly matches the one Johnson and Van Heusen saw. FBI just posted the warrant, which is why our inquiry came back negative several days ago when we first sent it out after the attack on Van Heusen."

Arnott looked at a sea of expectant faces, and elaborated: "This mysterious killer has a name: Robert Moses Brack. Real careful about covering his tracks; usually keeps himself under the radar. And none of his victims survive to talk. Slipped up, though, lucky for us. He rented a cabin in upstate Michigan for a month. Several days later, the real estate agent who rented it to him remembered some things she forgot to tell him. Cabin has no phone, so she drove on out. It's pretty isolated. No sign of Brack when she got there. She walked around the place and noticed a shiny new padlock on the old woodshed out back. When she went up to the shed door and rattled the lock, she heard faint moaning from inside. She fetched a tire iron from her car, broke open the lock, and found this naked teenage girl chained up inside, gagged with tape. Name of Nicole Drabinsky, 17 years old. Girl was half-dead, she'd been there for several days and it still gets quite cold at night this time of year.

"Anyway, state police and EMS arrived and cut her loose. Nicole had quite the story to tell. Seems she was part of a synchro swim team that had died in a massive explosion at a remote gas station in Illinois the previous week. Everyone thought the whole team had died, so no one was even looking for this girl. Well, she gave a full description of the bastard who'd caused the explosion - and how he'd caused it - and what he'd done to her for three days afterwards."

"Good Lord," murmured Paul. "How's the poor girl?"

"Well, says here that after some surgery to repair what the kidnapper did to her, she's expected to make a full recovery, physically. But I bet she's gonna need years of therapy. An' the sicko that did all this needs his own special kind of therapy, y'ask me: bullet, right between the eyes."

Arnott paused and his audience could see the anger in his piercing grey eyes. He went on: "Her description of the suspect matched that of a man the New Mexico state police have on file as a nuisance pervert: one Robert Moses Brack, a repeat offender charged with several stalking and Peeping Tom incidents. No convictions, though, so officially he's got no criminal record. And there's nothing in his file about kidnapping, rape and murder, attempted or otherwise."

That's probably because he's never had a power stone before, thought Billy.

"Anyway, appears that Brack crossed into Canada a few days ago, at the Windsor border. We let him right in, 'cause he had no convictions, not even a DUI. So it's highly likely he's here in Clearwater, based on what our two teens say. An' the electrical trick he does, that the Johnson boy reported, matches what Nicole Drabinsky said he did to that gas station. Though how the hell he does it, is quite beyond me."

All sorts of questions flew at the Chief, but it was Billy who shouted over the din: "Does this mean Mike's free to go now?"

Arnott gave Billy a flinty stare, then smiled and said: "A-yep. Guess it does."

He instructed an officer to release Michael immediately. Billy gave a whoop of joy, and accompanied the officer to Mike's cell.

Behind the locked door, the cell was empty.

Consternation erupted. No one could figure out how the boy had escaped. But Billy knew *(changed into the Flash and vibrated right through the wall)*, and he also knew why.

"Dad!" he said urgently. "We gotta get to the hospital! That's where Michael went! To save Melanie's leg!"

His father put on his sternest vice-principal look and demanded a full explanation, but Billy insisted on leaving *now* with explanations to come later.

A squad car brought them to the hospital, siren wailing. The small posse charged inside, Billy puffing in the lead, moving surprisingly fast for his bulk. Ignoring nurses who commanded them to stop running and be quiet because it is a damn hospital you know, the group raced to Melanie's room.

They found an empty bed. The arms of Brianna Van Heusen, Mel's mother, were around the shoulders of Michael and Ashley, Mel's younger sister. All three were crying. Her father, Gord, sat in a chair, head buried in his hands.

"Mike! Here you are!" Billy yelled. "You shouldn't have broken out, buddy! We were on our way to release you! Hey, what's going on? Why all the tears? An' where's Mel?"

Michael looked at his friend and his face was a portrait of utter anguish. Billy's heart went cold.

"It's Melanie," the big teen said in a broken voice. "I was too late, too late, too late." He started crying again.

"Too late? Oh. My. God. She's ... she's not *dead*, is she?"

Gord Van Heusen lifted his head, his face aged beyond his years, and answered in an pitiful burnt-out voice: "They amputated our little girl's leg an hour ago, just above the knee."

Chapter 14

Three No More

Two days after her traumatic operation, Melanie was allowed to have visitors besides her immediate family. She was still heavily medicated, though that didn't stop her from crying whenever she lost her resolve *not to look*, and glanced down at the shape of her legs under the blanket. Instead of seeing two long mounds, she now saw only one on the right and a short stump on the left.

She wept for hours.

Her first two non-family visitors were Michael and Billy. As she had expected. Mel's parents and sister left the room with Billy's father, who had driven the boys over, leaving the teens alone. That suited her fine; she had a few things to say.

The two boys tried mightily to look cheerful, but their thin facade collapsed as soon as they saw the mismatched shape of her legs under the blanket. They stood there, staring wide-eyed at the stump, not knowing what to say.

Melanie said: "Michael Johnson, where *were* you?"

The big teen blinked and stammered: "H-huh?"

"Where *were* you? You *knew* about the terrible infection eating away at my leg because of the black monster that bit me, an' how they couldn't cure it; you *knew* they were thinking of cutting it off before it spread further; so why in God's name didn't you come and do that miracle blood thing like we did for Billy, an' save my leg? *Why?*"

"But, Melanie, I tried to come! I really did! But all sortsa stuff happened! My ... pretend-parents got killed; then I got into a big fight with the Nastyman, the same one that bit you; then I got put in jail without my stone; then as soon as I got it back, I escaped as the Flash and zoomed right here, though not so fast that my clothes burneded off; but when I got here, it was too late."

Mel shot a look at Billy, who nodded miserably. "Yeah, it's true. He tried, he really did, but he couldn't get here in time. He's been feeling just awful about it ever since; me too."

Michael looked like a boy who'd just seen his beloved new puppy get run over by a car. Melanie didn't care. Her next words hit him with almost physical force:

"Awww, so you feel just awful, eh? Like, how the *hell* do you think *I* feel? Eh? I LOST MY LEG! And *you*, Michael Johnson, could have saved it! We went through a lot to save Billy, but you just couldn't manage to save ME!"

Big fat tears started rolling down Mike's face and he hung his head. Billy gaped at Melanie: "Mel! C'mon! You're not being fair! Mike almost died fighting that scumbag - the bastard has a power stone too as you very well know - and still he tried his hardest to get to you. He'd even decided to reveal his secret as soon as he got here, so the docs would put his Logan blood into you."

"Well, he didn't try hard enough, did he?" Melanie blazed. "Like, just *look* at my legs! Look! Not exactly a matched set anymore, are they?"

"You're not being fair, Mel."

"Don't tell *me* what's fair, William Butler McDonnell! I've been made into a victim! A damn victim! I'm the one who's now a cripple for the rest of her life! And I'm only fifteen! Quite the thing to happen to an active girl like me, eh? How am I ever gonna dance with you again, Billy? Huh? And won't I be just *great* at soccer now? Or skiing? Or kickboxing; I'll *never* get my black belt now! Or even riding my damn *bike*?"

Billy knew that, with training and special equipment, disabled people could actually do all those things, but he didn't think she wanted to hear that just now. "Melanie - "

"Don't 'Melanie' me! It's condescending! You both - and especially *you* Michael - simply weren't there for me like I was there for you, Billy! And because of that, I'm a cripple now!"

Billy cleared his throat and said: "Ah, the correct word is 'disabled' or 'mobility impaired', not crip-"

"Oh SHUT UP with the politically-correct words, Billy! I'm in no mood for that crap! Cripple describes perfectly what I am now! So tell me, comic book *geeks*, can the Wolverine's blood regrow a leg? Well, can it?"

Both boys shook their heads mournfully.

"I didn't think so! Are there any of your stupid superheroes that can regrow my leg?"

"N-no," admitted Michael, in a tiny voice. "I been thinking my hardest about that for two days, an' I can't think of one hero that can do that. Billy neither. There's a Spider-Man villain that can - the Lizard - but you don't want the side effects of his ability, oh no."

"Yeah, I saw the movie. Well, I know what can. That stone of yours. It lets you change into different things, altering your body, so why wouldn't it let me regrow my leg?"

"Oh, I dunno, Mel," said Billy. "I dunno if it works like that. I think the stone changes you as you are; it works with the body you got. I think - "

"You think too damn much sometimes, Billy! I saw him with a pair of six foot wings sticking out of his back! Michael, just gimme the damn stone an' let me *try* it, f'God's sake!"

Michael fished in his pocket and brought out the colourful rock, saying: "Now you gotta wish real hard an' you gotta really really *believe* in what you're wishing for."

"I assure you that ever since I woke up from the operation, I've wished really really hard that I had two legs again. Gimme!" Melanie grabbed the stone from Mike's outstretched hand. He gulped nervously; his first instinct was to grab it back, but he mastered his emotions and stepped back.

The girl gripped the stone tightly in both hands, so tightly that veins stood out on the backs of her hands. She closed her eyes and concentrated.

Nothing happened.

She opened her eyes and looked accusingly at Michael. "Well?

What's the matter?"

"I dunno. Think harder. You gotta really focus, really believe!"

"There's nothing I want more right now than to get this leg back. So, yeah, I'm really focussed! Like, duh!"

She tried again, eyes screwed shut, brow furrowed. Nothing. Not even a flicker of the tell-tale yellow aura around her body. She concentrated a third time, then a fourth. Nothing.

"Ah, I couldn't get it to work either, when Mike let me try it the other day," said Billy.

"Is ... is it at least humming to you?" asked Michael.

"NO. It's just being a stupid cold hunk of rock!"

"Cold? That's wrong; it's usually always warm. Once it got real hot, when I got close to that other stone held by the Nastyman."

"Well, it's cold now! And it's *not* working! And that means I'm *stuck* being a cripple! I so do not like being made into a victim!" With a gut-wrenching wail of anguish, she flung the stone away. It smashed into the opposite wall, then thudded to the floor. With a small cry, Michael dashed over and picked it up. He examined it carefully. Relieved to find no damage, he replaced it protectively in his pocket.

"So, there's no way at *all* you can get that thing to work for me?" Melanie blazed.

"It should have worked. Honest. I don't know why it won't work for you, or Billy either. It works fine for me. See?"

Yellow outlined the teen, then he stretched his neck upwards until his head touched the ceiling. He returned to normal with a rubbery sound as Melanie gave a disgusted snort.

"Well, there goes my last hope! I really can't count on you when I need you the most, can I?"

"Aw, c'mon Mel, calm down, okay?" said Billy. "You're upset, I get that, but Mike an' I are your friends. We'll help you through this. We'll help you cope - "

"Cope? *Cope?* I don't wanna cope! I WANT MY LEG BACK, you ... *you big, fat jerk!*"

It was the first time she had ever made a derogatory comment about his size. Stung, Billy stammered: "We ... we can't help you with that, but we can help - "

"Then get OUT! Both of you! Just leave me alone! I don't *ever* want to see either of you again! Some friends *you* are! You failed me! When I needed you the most!"

She turned from them and stared out the window, determined not to show them the hot tears springing to her eyes. Like whipped dogs, the boys slunk out of the room.

"She ... she really hates me now, eh?" asked Mike.

"She hates both of us, buddy. But I'm sure she didn't really mean those things she said. She just has to calm down. She needs time to get used to ... it. And she's on meds, maybe that clouded her mind," said Billy.

"Oh, she seemed pretty clear to me, yes she did. She really really hates me - and us. An' so she should. I faileded her. She's my onliest friend beside you, Billy, an' I faileded her."

Everyone was quiet on the way home. In the back seat of the McDonnell's car, Michael stared out the side window, seeing nothing, while fat tears crawled down his cheeks, leaving glistening slug-trails.

ೞ ೞ ೞ ಎ ಎ ಎ

Back in her hospital room, alone, Melanie's tears of anger evolved into tears of pity at her situation. "It's just not *fair*," she muttered, fists clenched, pounding the mattress. "I don't deserve *this*. Life's *so* unfair."

The far corner of her room, between the dresser and the wall, was in shadow. Sometime after the boys had left, as Mel continued to rage and weep with self-pity, a sliver of that shadow *moved*. Unnoticed by the girl, it slunk along the floorboards toward the open window, stretched up to merge with the shadow beneath the curtains, then slipped out the window. It travelled sideways a short distance along the bricks to a drainpipe, then flowed to the ground in the shadow cast by the pipe. Once on the ground, it slithered from bush to tree to hedge, until it was well away from the hospital.

He had learned a few things, back in that hospital room. The Three Misfit Musketeers had broken up. The retard's stone didn't work for everybody. And his hatred for Michael Johnson had grown. He ached for a rematch. But not yet; he was still too weak, still healing. How had the kid, his prey, healed himself so fast?

And he had almost got the other half of the stone just now! When the girl threw the rock away, it landed across the room from where the shadow lurked. The creature immediately started sliding toward it along the baseboards, electric with anticipation, except the retard had got there first. Damn!

His time haunting the shadows inside the police station last night had also paid off. He was shocked to learn that he had been identified; that there was now an all-points-bulletin out on him in the U.S. and Canada ("Consider him armed and extremely dangerous"); that they'd found and impounded his red Viper along with his duffel bag of cash in the trunk; and that they were slowly discovering the string of rapes, murders and mayhem he'd caused on his way up here to Jerkwater, Canada.

No matter. They hadn't believed what the teens had said about his powers, meaning they still had no clue about The Gift, and what he could do with it. It was a bloody nuisance that they had his money stash, though. Now he'd have to go through the trouble of stealing it back, or stealing a whole new stash. Damn cops.

The shadow-thing reached a large thicket, flowed deep inside, and rested. Buried within the shadow, the man refused to transform back to human. If he did, his broken ankle would still be broken, and the pain would be severe. He couldn't go to a hospital or clinic to get it set; he figured the police had alerted these places to be on the lookout for him. No, he'd stay a shadow-thing for now; there was no pain in this form, because there were no bones or organs. It was just *blackness*.

He knew the shadow-force was healing his broken ankle somehow, and faster than it would heal if he were human. Soon, maybe in a couple days, he'd be fit again. Until that time, he'd continue to watch, wait and plan. Then, watch out.

Next time, no more Mister Nice Guy.

Chapter 15

Looking for Love

Over a week had passed and Melanie had healed well enough from her amputation operation to be released from hospital. She was now recuperating at home. If there were no post-operation complications and her stump continued to heal properly, she would soon be scheduled for physiotherapy and the fitting of an interim "training" prosthetic leg. Which only served to depress her more.

She was still angry at Michael and Billy. She had ignored all of Billy's texts, and he texted her almost every hour during the day. She had ignored his pleading Facebook messages. Both boys had tried to see her, to talk with her, several times during the past week. She refused to see them, sending them away with sharp, furious words. Michael took this especially hard; nothing Billy said could alleviate the dark guilt Mel had heaped on him. Not even Mike's beloved comic books could shake his mood; for the second week in a row, he had not gone to the comic shop on Friday afternoon to pick up that week's new batch. He had never missed a week of comics before, much less two.

֍ ֍ ֍ ֍ ֍ ֍

Clearwater Chief of Police Frank Arnott used to think he'd seen it all, at this stage of his career, but the horror show at the Johnson place last week had taught him otherwise. Today, he learned another new thing: scarecrows can walk. And talk.

One had eloped from a cornfield and was doing just that right now, in his office, right in front of his desk.

"C'mon, Chief. I've travelled from the other side of the world to get here; least you can do is tell me what happened," spoke the apparition.

Arnott regarded the tall, impossibly-thin man with the riot of tangled hair crowning a narrow face, and said: "Have a seat. What'd you say your name was, again?"

"Delperdang, Ethan Delperdang. Finally arrived from New Zealand. Took me forever to get here, too. First plane I was on developed engine trouble and had to divert to a Godforsaken airstrip of World War Two vintage on some Godforsaken South Pacific island, where the biting No-No bugs outnumber humans a million to one. Ate us alive. Finally took off from there two days later, only to have a terrorist threat hit LAX just as we landed, trapping us in the plane on the tarmac for hours, then in the terminal for hours more, then the whole terminal was shut down and we spent the night in a hotel. Took two days to get another flight out. Then, on the flight from Los Angles to Toronto, a corporate suit had the Big One - massive cardiac - and we had to make an emergency landing in Armpit, Nebraska, where we skidded off the too-short runway into a field which damaged our landing gear, which stranded us for another day until a smaller plane arrived to shuttle us out in groups. And THEN - "

"Wait, that's enough," interrupted Arnott. "More than enough. I get it: was hell getting here."

"Yes, it was hell. But it was arranged that way! You see, it was a Goddamned conspiracy - I'm totally convinced of it - engineered so I would just give up and go home. The Powers That Be didn't want me coming here!"

"Uh-huh. The Powers That Be. And you're here, why exactly?"

"Because of what's been happening in your town these past couple weeks! I think I know why; I've done a lot of research on this. But to be sure, I need more information: from you and from the three teenagers who were involved."

Frank Arnott fixed the scarecrow with a cold look from his steel-grey eyes. "You a reporter?"

"Yeah, kinda. I publish a blog for a very select list of online subscribers."

"I hate reporters."

"Well, of *course* you do. And I'm not really a reporter. I'm like a scientist."

"What kinda scientist?"

"A researcher into paranormal phenomena, investigating certain types of unexplained occurrences."

"Ah. A crackpot."

Delperdang bristled: "I am not a crackpot. I have scientific proof of things that would give you nightmares during the *day*."

"Uh huh." Arnott made a move to get up, signalling the interview was over.

"Wait!" squawked the scarecrow. "I noticed a poster in your lobby; you're raising money to build a Ronald McDonald House here in Clearwater, a place to stay for families of kids in the hospital, right?"

"A-yep."

"Well, if you tell me everything that's been going on here - and I mean *everything*, not just what I read in the paper - then I'll contribute $1,000 to your fundraiser. Cash. Right here, right now."

"Seriously?"

"Seriously."

Arnott stared at him, unblinking, then grunted: "Okay, you're on, bub." He settled back in his chair and recounted the events of the past week in minute detail, starting with Monster Mack and his gang kidnapping the three teens and encountering the green giant, and ending with the unfortunate amputation of the Van Heusen girl's left leg. Delperdang listened closely, interjecting a question now and then to clarify details, and scribbling furiously in a large dog-eared notebook. To Arnott, the man's handwriting looked totally incomprehensible: like short black stick figures clashing in epic battle, or leafless trees quivering in a November gale. Nothing remotely resembling writing. (The Chief was wrong; it was indeed writing. 700-year-old writing.)

"Huh. I figgered someone like you'd be typing his notes into a tablet or laptop," said Arnott.

"Nope. I prefer paper. Electronic records can be hacked. I

oughta know; I do it all the time."

When Arnott was done, Delperdang whistled. "Wow. Some story. And those three teens: poor devils."

"Yeah. So, you got your story. Happy now?"

"Yes sir. And I'll give you your $1,000 right away." He pulled out a huge wad from one of the many pockets on the faded cargo pants he wore, counted off ten crisp Canadian hundred dollar bills, and plopped the money on Arnott's desk with a flourish. "There. I'm a man of my word."

"That's a lotta money to be carrying around, buddy. Safer using a debit card."

"No, no! Those leave electronic trails. Then *they* can track you. Cash is anonymous."

"Uh-huh."

"Y'know, this Robert Moses Brack that attacked the two teens, you said there may be more to him than first appeared?"

"A-yep. Just got more info last night. An FBI profiler in Washington's been working on it for a coupla days, an' thinks Brack may be behind several abductions and unexplained incidents. Now that we got a name an' a face, FBI has been re-tracing his journey across the USA. Awful truth could turn out to be that this Brack sicko may be a serial rapist an' murderer, someone as bad as their John Wayne Gacy or our own Paul Bernardo. Sexual predator/killer; real nasty piece a' goods."

Delperdang sat back in his chair, brow furrowed. "Then what brought him all the way to Clearwater? And why's he targeting these kids?"

"Dunno. But we'll sure find out when we catch him," Arnott growled.

"No luck, yet?"

"Nope. But it's only a matter of time. We'll get 'im, make no mistake about that, Mr. Paranormal Researcher. If that's really what you are."

The thin man smiled at the police chief. "Oh, it is. Trust me. You're welcome to check out my background."

"Uh-huh. We will."

"Well, thanks for the information, Chief. Now I'm off to check into a hotel or motel and flake out to get over my jet lag. Then tomorrow, I want to have a word with this Michael Johnson and his friends." He unfolded his lanky frame from the chair, stood, and mashed a worn poorboy hat onto his jungle of hair, trying to tame it. The jungle fought back and won; the poorboy popped off and Delperdang caught it as it fell.

"Now you listen here: you better make sure you don't mess around with our police investigation," Arnott warned. "Stay out of the way of my officers."

"Don't worry, Chief. I'll be very careful."

"And anything you happen to turn up, that has bearing on this case, you be sure you inform us right away."

"I will. Promise."

"Well then, just a final word of advice, bub," said Arnott, rising to shake hands. "This is a farming community, so be mighty careful if you leave the city and go tramping about the countryside. Some farmer gets a look at you, he's like to have a heart attack, thinking one of his scarecrows has come to life."

"Oh, hah hah. Canadian country humour."

"Seriously, Delperdang, do be careful. Brack's still out there somewhere."

"Yeah, an' that raises two disturbing questions: where the hell *has* Brack been since the Johnson murders and, more importantly, what has he been up to?"

ତ୍ଵ ତ୍ଵ ତ୍ଵ ଵ୍ତ ଵ୍ତ ଵ୍ତ

The following day, Janet McDonnell gave the scrambled eggs a critical look: ready in about two minutes. *Good,* she thought. *Time to Move the Mountains.* She left the kitchen, went to the foot of the stairs leading up to the second floor, and bellowed: "Boys! Up! Breakfast!"

She returned to the kitchen, sipping the molten lava she called tea while stirring the scrambled eggs. She heard the slow shuffle of her husband's footsteps descending the stairs. *Well, that's one up.*

"'Morning, hon," Paul mumbled as he entered. He kissed her, sat down, and promptly inhaled a cup of coffee. Vice-Principal McDonnell was not a morning person.

"You hear the boys stirring, dear?"

"Nope."

"Huh. Gonna be one of those mornings, I see." Janet strode from the kitchen and thumped up the stairs, face set in grim determination. *This ought to be a damn Olympic event: Getting teenagers up for school in the morning. Too bad I couldn't use an electric cattle prod. Or dynamite.*

She reached her son's closed bedroom door and pounded on it with gusto. "Bil-ly! Up boy! School today! Come on, shake a leg!"

A deep guttural sound, like that of some ancient dragon irritably awakening from a long slumber, came from behind the door.

"UP! Breakfast!"

The sound came again, and she deciphered the word "'kay" in it. *Good. One to go.*

She padded to the closed door of the guest bedroom. Since the awful deaths of his adoptive parents, Michael Johnson had been staying with them, while the authorities searched for any relatives, to see if they would take him in. She couldn't understand why that nasty Johnson couple, who everyone had thought were his real parents, had secretly hated the boy so much. She'd always found him to be a charming lad. It was a pleasure to have him as a guest, even in the depressed state he was currently in.

The McDonnells had comforted Michael since that terrible ordeal at his house. The murders of Bert and Ruth had been bad enough, something that would shake anybody up, but poor Michael had received a double shock: being told he had been adopted and only because of the money that came with him. That really hurt. During the emotional sessions, as they helped Michael adjust to the new realities of his life, the fact that Bert Johnson had regularly and harshly beat him came to light. The McDonnells were horrified to learn of this.

"Well, I deserved it," Michael had mumbled. "I was a bad boy."

"No, you were not a bad boy," said Paul firmly. "You must never blame yourself. No one deserves such beatings. That's child abuse and that's a crime. If we had known about this, we would have gone immediately to the police."

Billy echoed agreement. Michael had just shrugged.

And now, as if all that had happened to the lad hadn't been enough, Melanie Van Heusen had gone berserk and announced she never wanted to see the boys again. Astonishingly, through some twisted logic, she blamed Mike for her misfortune. What nerve! As if there was anything the boy could have done for her. Michael had been devastated at the collapse of his friendship with the girl; the three teens had been inseparable.

She knew, from the sounds behind his closed bedroom door, that Michael cried himself to sleep each night.

Janet gave Melanie some allowances because of the awful trauma of losing a leg, but still: she had no right to take it out on Mike. Well, if that girl didn't come to her senses soon, Janet would have a very blunt talk with her.

She played a staccato rap on the guestroom door. "Michael! Breakfast! C'mon, get up! Race Billy to see who'll get into the bathroom first!"

No answer, not even a dragon's guttural growl. *Well, I always wanted a second child. Now I suddenly have two impossible-to-awake teenagers. As the Chinese say: Be careful what you wish for.*

She pounded on the door, both fists.

Silence from within.

"I don't have *time* for this, the eggs'll burn," she muttered. She opened the door and yelled at the mass of rumpled sheets piled on the bed:

"Come. On. RiseandShine! Up, up, up! Eggs to be eaten!"
No movement.

"Hello? Ground Control to Major Tom: wakey-wakey!"
Nothing.

With a great sigh of exasperation, Janet strode to the bed and grabbed at the bedclothes, intending to rock the body mummified within.

Except there was nothing within.

She spun around and sped to the bathroom. Empty. Returning to the guestroom, she noticed Mike's big knapsack was gone. She flung open the dresser drawers; most of his clothes were missing.

A horrible realization hit Janet McDonnell: Michael had run away!

෴ ෴ ෴ ෴ ෴ ෴

The scarecrow unfolded his lanky frame from the dirt-cheap sub-compact rental, and stared at the scene in front of the McDonnell house. Two police cars, a crowd of curious busybody neighbours, and Chief of Police Frank Arnott talking to three very distraught people on the verandah, who he took to be the McDonnells.

The impossibly-thin man ambled over and put on his best innocent smile. "What's up, officer?" he asked of the cop who moved to block his advance up the walk.

"Who the hell are you?" replied the lawman in a tone that said he had had his fill of nosey neighbours and was itching to shoot the next one that bothered him.

"Ethan Delperdang. Your Chief there knows me; we had a nice long chat yesterday."

The cop turned to call out to his boss, and Ethan smoothly slipped by him and continued up the path, waving and calling out: "Hey Frank! Good to see ya again!"

"Now you just get your bony ass back here, Mister!" squawked the cop in his wake. Arnott looked over at the noise, grimaced when he saw Delperdang bearing down on him with a big fake grin plastered on his cadaverous face, then motioned to his officer that it was alright.

"You again," Arnott growled. "No time to shoot the breeze today. This is a police investigation, y'know."

"I can see that. And may I say it looks like you're doing a fine job."

"Cut the smooth talk; you're not fooling me. You got something that's important to this investigation, spill it pronto. Otherwise, I'll have my officer there evict you. I've no time for games; we've got a missing kid to find and every hour counts with missing kids."

"Well, I believe I can certainly help you, Chief." He turned to the McDonnells. "Hello, I'm Ethan Delperdang, special investigator all the way from New Zealand." They shook his hand, warily.

"Special investigator of what?" asked Paul.

"Special things. Unusual things. Your son would know what I'm talking about."

His parents and the Chief looked at Billy, who reddened and stammered: "N-no, I don't, Mister."

"Well, we'll talk later. Now, what happened?"

"Excuse me, but it doesn't look like you're with the police, so why should we tell you anything?" said Paul.

"Because I asked nicely?" replied Ethan, and widened his smile even further, until it looked like it would split his thin skull horizontally in two.

The McDonnells looked at Chief Arnott, who ground his teeth in irritation. "It's okay, folks. I had a talk with him yesterday and we've since checked him out. He's flaky, but harmless."

Whatever you say, Chief, thought the scarecrow.

Paul and Janet looked at Ethan, then at each other. Janet nodded. So they told him of Michael Johnson running away. Billy finished by saying: "We're really, totally surprised he did that. Mike is a creature of routine; he's got an intellectual disability, y'know. Routines are very important to him. To just leave everything that's so familiar to him and take off, well, it's, like, totally unbelievable."

"But he did it anyway," said Ethan, stroking the wispy beard on his chin. "Must have been a powerful motivator to make him do that. And all by himself, too. His mind's like that of an eight-year-old, right?"

The McDonnells nodded.

"Well, that sure took guts," Ethan mused. "Anyone have any idea of where he went?"

"We were just getting to that when you butted in!" barked Arnott. "Billy here said he might have something. C'mon boy, spill."

Billy cleared his throat. "Well, it doesn't make much sense, but he said to me a couple nights ago that one day he was going to go find his real mom, the one who gave him up for adoption. He said she lived in a place called Fred MacMurray."

"Fred MacMurray?" said Paul. "There's no such place. That's the name of a famous American actor from years ago; he's dead now."

"Gibberish," grunted Arnott. "Figures."

"Yeah, could be," replied Billy. "But Mike doesn't usually talk gibberish. Just stuff we don't understand yet, sometimes."

"What put that name in his head?"

"I dunno."

"So it appears he took off on a wild-goose chase. Could be heading anywhere; who knows what's in his head. Well, how's he travelling? What's he doing for money?" asked Arnott.

"We have no idea how he's travelling, Frank," said Paul. "As for money, Billy says Michael took his entire comic book fund, the money his adoptive parents gave him at the start of the month to buy comics each week. It was the one indulgence they allowed him. Billy says he hadn't been to the store in the past two weeks, and he bought a lot of comics every Friday, so I gather he has over 200 dollars with him."

"Two hundred bucks?" gasped Arnott. "That's a helluva lot of dough for funny books!"

"Comics are expensive these days, Chief," said Billy. "Most comics cost $3.99 U.S., plus a surcharge for the Canadian dollar exchange, plus our 13% federal and provincial tax. And most comics aren't funny books anymore. They're very intense dramas."

"Geez, I remember when they only cost 12 cents," muttered

the Chief.

"Careful, Frank. You're dating yourself," admonished Paul, smiling.

"Ya mean back in the days of no colour TV, no computers, no rock music even?" said Billy in his most innocent voice.

"Smartass," growled Arnott.

The Chief gave instructions to have officers check the bus and train stations, and get an APB to all patrol cars as well as an announcement on all radio and TV news broadcasts. "Also get it out to the Ontario Provincial Police and the RCMP; if the kid is hitching his way along a highway, maybe they'll spot him." Then Arnott grilled the McDonnells about Michael's disappearance for another twenty minutes. Finally satisfied he had drained them of information, he left to coordinate the search.

The scarecrow from New Zealand made no move to leave, but just stood there with his beaming smile. Flustered, Janet invited him to join them for a belated breakfast, which he readily accepted, and they all went inside.

The shadow cast by the tall juniper bush near the verandah *moved.* And kept moving until it flowed around the corner of the house, out of sight.

ൟ ൟ ൟ ൟ ൟ ൟ

By the end of breakfast, the McDonnells had learned a lot about Ethan Delperdang. Or at least what he allowed them to learn.

Ethan helped himself to another slice of toast, drowned it with Janet's home-made jam - he had already eaten enough for two people - and smiled his ghastly smile. "So, no one's seen hide nor hair of this Robert Moses Brack since that night he killed the Johnsons, despite the police looking everywhere for him. That's real worrisome."

"Ah!" said Billy with a start. "Maybe Mike didn't run away at all! Maybe this Brack guy kidnapped him!"

"Yeah, that went through my head when you first told me about it," said Ethan. "But both you and the cops say there were no signs of violence in his room. And a guy as strong as you say Mike is; well, he'd put up a struggle with any kidnapper."

"Unless he was drugged," murmured Billy.

"Listen here," interjected his father. "You went to all this effort and expense just because of some kind of unusual stone?"

"Yeah. I'm retired and quite wealthy ... " Ethan saw Paul eyeball his scruffy clothes, glance out the window at the cheap rental car and raise his eyebrows ... "And unusual rocks that come with a history are a hobby, actually an obsession, of mine. I travel the world tracking them down."

The tall man turned to Billy and smiled a death's-head smile. "You'll agree that your pal Mike has a very unusual stone, doesn't he?"

Billy was thunderstruck. *He knew!* "Yeah, maybe," he managed.

"Well then. So here I am. Unfortunately, just in time for Mike to become a runaway."

☙ ☙ ☙ ❧ ❧ ❧

Bob McCurdy had been hauling frozen meats all across Ontario for 21 years. He owned his own tractor-trailer rig and it was all paid off too. He had a clean record: no traffic violations or safety infractions. And he was always on time with his deliveries. Sure he sometimes wore pantyhose under his Levis when he drove, but so what? Who did it harm? Besides, everybody's got a secret.

He finished the last of his Clearwater deliveries around 2:00 that afternoon, slammed shut and latched the doors on the refrigerated trailer, checked that the cooling unit was operating okay, and went inside the supermarket to finish the paperwork. Ten minutes later, he emerged, climbed into the big Peterbilt's cab, and started the diesel engine. As the motor rumbled into life, Bob slid a Country 'n' Western CD into the player and shifted the rig into gear. Next stop: Orillia. Then Bracebridge. Then more small towns westward across Ontario's North, as he headed for Thunder Bay, his last stop. It was a good run, with lots of great scenery that he never got tired of, no matter how often he saw it.

Beautiful country, Canada.

As he expertly marshalled his extra-long rig through what passed for Clearwater traffic toward the open highway, Bob never suspected he had an uninvited passenger back in the trailer. Of course, he would never consider it; nobody could survive for long in that sub-zero compartment stacked high with frozen specialty meats.

But it was an ideal climate for the Iceman. Colder it was, better he liked it.

The Iceman, another mutant member of the X-Men, lay flat on his stomach high atop some boxes at the front of the trailer. His clothes were covered with a thick layer of frost that crackled when he moved. Under his clothes, from his head to his toes, his gleaming blue-white body was a perfect ice sculpture of the human form. Even his hair resembled intricately carved strands of ice. Next to him lay Michael Johnson's black knapsack, also frost-encrusted.

The Iceman cradled his head in his arms and tried hard not to think of anything sad. He wasn't sure if a person made of ice could cry, but he didn't want to find out. The tears would instantly turn to ice, and icicle tears would probably be very painful.

Besides, after he had made up his mind to run away, Michael had also resolved not to cry any more. He was all of 17 years old, and other boys his age didn't cry like little kids whenever things went bad. Anyway, he'd had enough of crying these last few weeks.

He still couldn't believe he had done it: left the people he knew and the familiar surroundings and even his precious comics, and headed off all on his own. He'd never done *anything* like this before. He should feel excited, starting off on a big adventure all by himself. Instead, he felt awful: scared, worried, fretful.

But he had to do it, and alone, too. The Nastyman could track him somehow, through the stone he carried in his pocket. Michael didn't want to expose his friends to danger again. Look what had happened to poor Melanie.

He knew this truck was headed west - he'd overheard the driver talking while hiding in the bushes - and that suited him fine. He had to get to Alberta, to that town where Aunt Julia lived. Now that he knew he'd been adopted, a memory had surfaced; something that lady he'd always thought was his mother ... Ruth ... had said to him, years ago. She'd said he looked almost exactly like Aunt Julia, who lived in Alberta, in a place called Fred MacMurray. So maybe this Aunt Julia, whom he'd never seen a picture of, much less met, was his real mother. It was worth a shot. If she was his real mother, then maybe she'd take him back and love him like a mother should.

Right now, it was Michael's fondest hope.

He didn't know how he'd find her, once he finally arrived. Maybe he'd ask the police. He grimaced, causing fine lines to spider-web across the ice at the sides of his mouth. He hoped the police there were nicer than the ones in Clearwater. Imagine thinking he'd been lying, that he'd actually caused all that death and destruction! And that wasn't the worst of it; putting him in jail and taking his stone away had prevented him from reaching Mel in time, and that had cost her a leg. And now she hated him.

The trailer swayed rhythmically as the truck sped westward. Despite his best efforts, Michael's thoughts kept returning to the awful events of last week: the Nastyman; his parents not really being his parents and - worse - not loving him; one of his best friends being mutilated and declaring she wanted nothing more to do with him, ever. Shock after shock.

As the miles wore on, Michael discovered the Iceman could cry after all. Big icicle tears crinkled down his cheeks, breaking off and crashing to the floor. And it was indeed very painful.

Chapter 16

The Black Widows

Twenty-four hours had passed since Michael had gone missing, with still no word. The police had found no trace of him whatsoever. With fatalistic grimness, Chief Arnott had ordered his officers to start checking morgues across Ontario. Billy was beside himself with worry. His mind conjured up all kinds of nasty scenarios that could befall a teen with the mind of an eight-year-old travelling alone for the first time; even someone who could access superpowers. Powers or not, he was still Michael, still a naive trusting person who would be so easy to prey upon.

Billy paced restlessly around the house. His parents had allowed him to stay home from school; he was too distraught to concentrate on schoolwork. They had gone down to the police station to see if there were any new developments, while he waited at home in case Mike called.

When the doorbell rang, Billy jumped.

He dashed to the door, flung it open, and was disappointed to see the tall beanpole figure of that strange American from New Zealand.

"Hello, Billy. Can I come in?"

"Ah, I dunno. My folks aren't home," he replied.

"That's okay. It's you I want to talk to."

"Me? About ... about what?"

"Oh, ships and sails and sealing wax and power stones that let you become almost anything you wish. And I have some intel about your friend Mike, too."

Billy let him in and they went into the living room. Ethan was carrying a sturdy leather shoulder bag that showed considerable wear. From it, he pulled out the most impressive-looking laptop Billy had ever seen. He placed the computer on the coffee table and turned it on. Billy was amazed to see it booted up almost instantly.

"Cool, huh?" said Ethan. "Assembled it myself. Besides the keyboard, it has cutting-edge touch-screen tech."

"Yeah, it looks awesome all right," said Billy, eyeing the sleek, thin machine. "But, c'mon man. *Everybody* uses a tablet or smartphone these days. Laptops are so yesterday."

Ethan fixed the rotund teen with a cold look. "Look kid, I grant you that tablets an' smartphones have come a long way. But they're still not powerful enough for my specialized needs. I could run the space shuttle - if it was still flying - with the power of this slim laptop."

Billy gulped. Ethan went on:

"Now I did some digging last night, once I found a hotel in this burg that had high-speed cable Internet access. I discovered who Mike's birth mother is."

"What? How? I thought adoption records were sealed unless you got special permission."

"They are, Billy, me lad, they are. But I've got some very powerful specialized software, stuff that only outfits like MI6 and the CIA have. I found and hacked into Mike's adoption records."

"How ... how'd you get hold of a software program like that?"

"It's easy when you're the one who created it."

"Wow! You musta made a million on that."

"Many millions, actually. Though it took forever to get paid. Damn bureaucratic red tape."

"Well, I don't mean to be rude, but with that kinda money, why do you dress so grungy and drive such a crummy beater?"

Ethan looked at Billy. "Because, young man, I mean to keep those millions. There's nothing wrong with being frugal. I only spend money when necessary and, unless it's an emergency, I take pains to get the biggest bang for my hard-earned buck. Savvy?"

The boy nodded.

THE HERO STONE

"Good lad. Now look here: Mike was put up for adoption when he was three years old, soon after he was diagnosed as being developmentally-delayed. His real last name is Gilmour. His father is listed as 'unknown', but his birth mother is Julia Gilmour. She was married to a Fred Gilmour, but divorced about a year before Mike's birth. It was only after she gave Mike up for adoption that she reverted back to using her maiden name: Chartrand. It's French-Canadian; her folks were originally from Quebec. And look where she was living 14 years ago: Fort McMurray, Alberta."

"Fort ... ah, so *that's* the 'Fred MacMurray' Mike was talking about! He has a knack for mangling English sometimes. He meant Fort McMurray. That place with the huge oil sands project."

"Correctamundo, Sherlock. That must be where Mike's heading, hoping his mum is still living there."

"That's great work, Ethan! We gotta tell Chief Arnott, so he can alert the Fort McMurray cops to watch out for Mike."

"Cool your jets, fella. That might not be a good idea, given that wonderful rock Mike has and the psycho that's most likely still chasing him. Cops might make matters worse, might even make it easier for the psycho to grab Mike's rock. Remember how they took it from him the night they arrested him?"

"Oh yeah. So then, what do we do? We can't just sit here and do nothing! That's my best buddy out there!"

"Before I tell you what we're gonna do, I need you to tell me everything - and I mean everything - you know about Mike and his stone. How he found it, how he uses it, what he can do with it. Everything."

Billy regarded the thin man for a long time before speaking. "Why? So you can steal it from him? That really why you came here from the other side of the world?"

"No. I came to save your friend. He has no idea what he's got ahold of. It's a wonderful thing, yes, but it's also a deadly thing. Power always has its price."

"I'm sure it does," said Billy, suspiciously. "So, like, now you're gonna offer me money to betray my buddy?"

Ethan made an exasperated sound and deftly fingered the keys on his laptop. "Here, Doubting William. Look at this."

It was a photo of an very old man lying in an ornate casket, obviously at a funeral home.

"Who's that old fossil?" asked Billy.

"My younger brother, Dave. Step-brother, actually. Born and raised in Oz; that's Australia to you. He was 28 years old when he died. For eight months, he had the stone that your friend now has. Take a good look. That there is the price of power."

Billy stared at the withered old man in the photo, nausea gripping his stomach.

೯ೂ ೯ೂ ೯ೂ ೪ ೪ ೪

It was 5:30 a.m. and Brad Melnyk was driving his pride and joy down the Trans-Canada Highway, heading west from Thunder Bay, anxious to be home. There was no one on the road this early in the morning, and he revelled in the power of the 305 horsepower V6 engine. Lakehead University was done for another year and he was looking forward to seeing his folks again, working at the family farm for the summer, and getting in some fishing. The fact that Mary Jo, his long-time sweetheart, would also be home from college for the summer, was a definite bonus.

He rounded a curve, saw the accident, and immediately braked. His new black Mustang convertible slowed to a stop and Brad was out the door almost before the wheels ceased rolling, eager to offer assistance. An old clunker of a pickup truck had gone into a ditch, and four people were sprawled on the ground beside it.

"Is everybody alright?" he called as he ran up. "Can I help you?"

"Why, you sure can, bud," said one of the people, a man in his late thirties with matted black hair, wearing dirty jeans and T-shirt. He rolled onto his back, uncovering a long something beneath him, and sat up. "You can help by giving me the keys to that fine automobile you're driving."

Brad jerked to a halt just steps from the man, and found himself looking down the barrel of an immense shotgun. The other "victims" leapt to their feet and quickly surrounded the student.

"Hey, hey come on, guys!" Brad protested. "I thought you were hurt."

"We just got better," sneered the man with the elephant gun. "Keys, bud. My trigger finger's gettin' itchy."

"Aw, no, no! C'mon! Not my 'Stang! I worked my ass off for three years to buy her, and to pay the yearly insurance premiums. She's - "

"Ours now, college boy. 'Less you want to die for her."

Brad looked like he wanted to cry, but bit his lower lip and fished in his pocket for the keys. He had no choice. His life was worth more than his new car.

The thug holding the huge gun cried out. Brad looked up and blurted: "What the hell ..." The gun was floating in mid-air, pointing at its owner!

The would-be carjackers used much more colourful language. As their leader gaped into the maw of his own gun, the three others jerked out their own weapons: revolver, knives, and a short iron pipe.

All of which were wrenched out of their hands and sent sailing high overhead toward the lake on the other side of the road. The weapons hit the water bunched together with a large splash, followed seconds later by the elephant gun.

The carjackers slowly backed away from their intended victim. "You some kinda freak magician?" asked the leader, eyes wide. "Pullin' a Yoda on us, somehow?"

Brad shook his head. Metal groaned as the old truck stirred from its resting place in the ditch, rose into the air until it was four feet off the ground, turned until its battered grill faced the gang, then silently bore down on them. That did it. With wild yells, the thugs turned and ran down the highway, closely pursued by their floating truck.

Brad just stared. Then he ran to his Mustang, gunned the engine, and roared off down the T-Can in the opposite direction, the direction he'd been heading in before he stopped to play Good Samaritan. And he vowed to never again party until four a.m. before leaving on a long road trip.

Laughing so hard that tears streamed down his face, Michael Johnson stepped out from behind the roadside bushes that had concealed him. He was channelling the awesome magnetic powers of Cosmic Boy of the Legion of Super-Heroes. But even those powers had limits; he could not let the truck get too far ahead of him or it would crash to the ground. It sure felt good to use his stone to help folks, and as a bonus, this rescue had turned out to be very funny.

He used a fraction of his power to push against Earth's magnetic field, levitating his body a foot off the ground. Then he sent himself down the road in the direction the thugs had taken, eastward back to Thunder Bay, floating effortlessly and with increasing speed. He intended to have the carjackers' pickup chase them all the way into the city and right up to the first police station he saw. Then he had to find a McDonald's; he was starving.

An hour later, his belly full of breakfast burritos and hash browns, Mike sipped his third cup of orange juice and took stock. He knew he was about a day's drive from the Manitoba border; he had carefully studied the large wall map outside the tourist bureau next to the McDonald's. *Man, it took forever to drive out of Northern Ontario; the province seemed to go on forever.* Too bad he had to leave that nice refrigerated trailer, but Thunder Bay was its last stop before it swung around and, empty, started its return trip.

He hated to give up being the Iceman. He'd discovered he didn't get hungry as a being of living ice, which certainly saved his limited supply of money. *But man, was I hungry when I changed back to me.*

And now he needed another ride. He couldn't magnetically propel himself westward; there were too many cars on the highway now and he'd be quite obvious. For the same reason, he couldn't become the Angel and fly. Someone would eventually notice a flying man with a 12-foot wingspan soaring high above. And he got so hungry every time he became the Flash. He had to follow this highway marked by the small green and white signs of the maple leaf with the "1" in the centre of the leaf and the words

"Trans Canada" and "West", because it was the only thing he knew for sure that led west.

He couldn't afford a bus ticket; he figured he had just enough money to eat at fast food joints. He couldn't spare any for transportation or accommodation. That wasn't a problem while he had travelled in the refrigerated trailer; he simply slept in the trailer between stops. But it was a problem now.

He didn't want to hitch-hike. It had been drummed into him that hitching was dangerous. Maybe he should find a truck stop, and access a power that would let him slip inside a trailer headed west. It had worked once, why not again? Should he ask the nice older lady behind the McDonald's counter for directions to the nearest truck stop?

He cupped his chin in his hands and groaned. *Why was it so hard to think about what to do?* He also had to fight down how anxious and scared he felt without the familiar routines of his life. *Maybe this wasn't such a good idea, going off on my own to find my real mommy.*

"Hey there."

Michael looked around. There were three women at a table several feet away; they'd been eyeing him the whole time he'd been eating, though he'd tried not to notice. They were older than teenagers, but not as old as many of his teachers. He thought they were very pretty. They wore clothes that celebrated this glorious spring day - shorts and T-Shirts and sandals - though the clothes looked much too tight. Two of the women were blondes, the third had red hair. They were all smiling at him. It was the redhead who had spoken.

"Yeah, it's you I'm talkin' to," she said. "You alone?"

Mike nodded.

"Just travellin' through here?"

He nodded again.

"Got your own wheels?"

"Y-yeah, but not with me. I left my bicycle at home."

The women laughed.

"Cute! You made a funny! So where ya headed?"

It had also been drummed into him not to talk to strangers and here he was talking with three of them, but they seemed so nice and they had such charming smiles. "West. Along the Trans-Canadian."

The redhead chuckled. "Really? Well, what a coincidence. So are we, right girls?" The others nodded and giggled.

"Listen, ya need a lift?"

"Y-yeah, but I been told ... I shouldn't ... couldn't ..."

"Nonsense! Why, we're real friendly - can't ya tell? An' we'd love to give a lift to a studly hunk like you. Got lots of room in our motor home. What's your name?"

"Michael Johnson. And I'm 17 years old."

"Ach! Jailbait," whispered one blonde to the other, too low for Mike to hear. "An' I think he's simple, too."

"Shaddup," hissed the other blonde, speaking even lower. "As if age ever bothered us before. An' lookit the bod on him! If he really is simple, it's a bonus. Who needs a man with brains?"

Almost before he realized what was happening, Mike found himself in the living room of a 27-foot motor home with one of the blondes, who said she was Kirsten. He sat in a wing-back chair that was bolted to the floor, but, to his joy, swivelled. Kirsten sprawled on a couch across from him and never took her eyes off him. Victoria, the redhead, drove and the other blonde, who had introduced herself as Sally, sat in the passenger seat, swivelling it half-around to talk.

The motor home was very similar to the one the McDonnells had, though larger, and Mike found that comforting because he'd been camping in it with Billy many times.

They headed west on the T-Can. As soon as they cleared the city limits and were surrounded by magnificent Canadian Shield wilderness again, Kirsten pulled a strangely-shaped cigarette out of her purse and lit it. She sucked at it, inhaling the smoke deeply. It gave off a smell unlike any cigarette the boy had ever smelled, and his pretend-parents had been heavy smokers.

"Want a hit?" she asked, offering it to him.

"No, thank you," he replied firmly. "Those are not good for

you, no way, nope."

"Ah, that's where you're wrong, young Michael. Still, your loss." She shrugged, and passed the joint to Sally in the front passenger seat, who took a long drag, then shared it with Victoria. The air soon filled with acrid-sweet marijuana smoke, making Mike feel a little dizzy.

The women chattered constantly, asking Mike many questions. He tried hard to be careful with his answers; it wouldn't do to let them know he was a runaway with no family or friends within hundreds of miles from here. Which is exactly what they found out.

The miles wore on. The warm sun beamed through the window where Mike was sitting, the rhythm of the wheels and swaying of the RV was soothing, and the women's voices became a musical backbeat. He started nodding off.

"Tired, Michael?" Kirsten asked.

"Uh huh."

"Well, we have a nice Queen-size bed at the rear of this RV. Why don't you go lay down on it? Be much more comfy for you to sleep."

Michael nodded. He was soon lying on top of the bedspread, fully clothed except for his shoes, head snuggled into the first pillow he had felt in days, the swaying movement of the vehicle lulling him. His last thought as he fell into deep slumber: *Yeah, I'm very lucky: they're real nice ladies.*

༄ ༄ ༄ ༄ ༄ ༄

Ethan gave a long, low whistle. It sounded like a tea kettle being strangled, if such a thing was possible. Billy had just finished telling him everything about Mike and his stone, including what Mike had told him about his battle with the Nastyman.

"Jeezus. So Brack has a stone too!"

Billy nodded. Scratching at the scraggly beard that clung to his chin, Ethan said: "An' worse than a monster like Brack havin' his own stone, is that it's my brother's old stone broken in half! That should not have been possible! The rock is supposed to be virtually indestructible. But you say that Mike saw how the pattern of his half led into the pattern on Brack's half, so both halves would flow together as one pattern, right?"

Another nod from Billy.

"An' Mike's stone, as you described it to me, is shaped like a big 'D' and it's about half the size of what my brother Dave had. The original stone was oval, about four inches long by three inches wide, with no straight sides. By Jeezus. One stone broken into two, an' both parts still work! I'll be damned."

"Now I have questions for you," said Billy. "How do you know so much about these stones, and what exactly are they? Are they from outer space, or created by some ancient wizard? What?"

Ethan gave Billy a shrewd look. "I know lots about that rock because I made it my business to find out, after my damn-fool brother got his hands on it and started doing miraculous things. I spent months researching it, and only discovered the cost of using it at the end, too late to save Dave. He found out about the cost the hard way; you saw his picture.

"As for what that stone - stones now, it seems - really is, well, Billy me lad, that's a long story for another day. For right now, let's just say it - they - are older than you could imagine."

"And one half attached itself to Michael," mused Billy. "Called to him, as it lay near the trail he was running on."

"Yeah. The stone seeks a suitable host - er, user. As I imagine the other half, which ended up down in the Southwestern States, called out to a completely different personality: this Brack fella," said Ethan.

"Hey, that's another mystery! How'd the stone halves get from Australia to North America, with one half appearing in Canada an' the other in the USA?"

"Aw, Billy, you read comics, huh? Bet you're a *Star Trek* fan, too. So that'd be easy for you to imagine. It's a type of teleporting. Something that powerful, that taps into people's wishes an' makes them a reality, could easily have the ability to teleport itself anywhere it wished."

"Anywhere *it* wished? An' you also said *it* seeks a suitable host. What, is it alive?"

"In a way. Mike said it spoke to him?"

"Hummed, he said."

"Right. Close enough. It's semi-sentient, an' reacts to certain types of people."

"What types? It wouldn't work for me, or for poor Melanie when she tried to regrow her leg in the hospital."

"Well, it's not as easy to use as it seems. This Melanie was very angry when she tried to use it, right? See, that affected her focus. Your mind must be clear, totally focussed, to access the power."

"That explains how Mike can use it so easily. His mind is not like ours."

"Exactamundo. He's blessed with the simple unbroken focus of a child; a wonderful ability that we lose as we get older. What he's focussing on at the moment, becomes his entire reality, with no distractions. An' you tell me he's totally into comic books, right? Well, a richer fantasy world than that would be hard to come by. Comics give him bold colourful visuals, to augment the fantasy. Perfect for using the stone."

"But Mike said Brack told him he didn't read comics."

"Well, judging by his crimes, Robert Moses Brack has a twisted fantasy world all his own to tap into." Ethan shivered.

"Did your late brother read comics?"

"Nope. But he read fantasy and science fiction novels like crazy. Had quite the imagination, did Dave. More ways than one, according to his girlfriends."

"But if your brother's mind was normal, how come the stone worked for him?"

"Who said he had a normal mind, Billy? He wrote scripts for children's cartoon shows on TV. Dave was a guy still tapped into his childhood; he never grew up. An' besides that, my bro was totally into Zen Buddhism. He could meditate an' clear his mind of all its clutter, allowing him to focus on one thing without distractions."

Billy frowned. "Y'know, one thing still bothers me. Mike is

a creature of habit. He depends on his routines, and gets really flustered when any routine is disturbed or changed. So, why the hell would he just up and run away? You'd think that after what happened, he'd want to stay around here more than ever, to hang onto the remaining things that are familiar to him. Like me."

"Well, I'm no shrink, but perhaps it's because of what happened that he left. His safe familiar world had been destroyed: parents, home, the certainty of his parents' love. Something everyone should be able to count on is the love of their parents, no matter what. Especially the love of a mother for her child; they say that's the strongest emotion."

Billy nodded miserably. Ethan continued:

An' you said you three kids were inseparable, right? Well, Melanie shattered that friendship."

"Yeah, but *I'm* still here for him!"

"Maybe every time he looked at you, Billy, he was reminded of how it used to be a happy threesome."

"Huh. Yeah, maybe."

"So, with everything in shambles around him, he grasped at the one straw left to him - to find his birth mother - in the hopes she'd restore the security in his life."

"Well, I miss him, an' I'm worried sick about him bein' on the road alone."

"Ah, don' fret too much, lad. I did a fair bit of hitchin' when I was younger; the myth of vicious predators roaming the highways lookin' for prey is largely just that: a myth. This Brack monster is a rare exception. Most folks are happy to help out a hitcher. So don' worry. I'm sure your friend's fine."

ஒ ஒ ஒ ஐ ஐ ஐ

Michael awoke groggily. The motor home had stopped. His shirt was off. He was on his back. Hands were touching him. All over.

"Hey!" Michael came fully awake and struggled to sit up. But couldn't. His wrists were tied tightly together behind him. Two bodies pressed into him, one on each side: the blondes. A third woman - the redhead - was standing at the foot of the bed, staring down at him.

"Why am I tied up? What are you do-" One of the blondes, Kirsten, kissed him, smothering his question and filling his mouth with her tongue. *GROSS!* his brain screamed. He grunted in protest, and tried to disengage his lips, but she pressed into him hungrily. He finally wrenched his head away, yelling:

"Stop that! All of you! Just stop!"

"Oh, no way, stud. No way at all." It was Victoria, and her voice sounded different, more husky. Mike suddenly realized that the three women were completely naked. He had never seen live naked women before.

Conflicting emotions flooded him: shock, fear, anger, and - excitement. *Oh, this is wrongwrongwrong. They shouldn't be touching me like this.*

"Now you just relax and enjoy the ride. We're gonna give you the treat of a lifetime," cooed Kirsten. "You're livin' every male's fantasy, right here. So just relax and enjoy."

Mike opened his mouth to protest, but Sally suddenly filled it with her tongue, mashing her lips against his. The boy kept his eyes open, staring wildly. "I'm next after you, honey," Kirsten murmured to Victoria. "Make sure you leave some for the rest of us."

"Oh, don't worry," Victoria replied. "We won't even have to force a Viagra into this one. I'm sure stud here has lots to give. He's a virgin, I'll bet."

"My God, he's got awesome muscles," breathed Sally, running her hands over his chest and shoulders.

"He's only got one muscle I'm interested in right now," said Victoria, climbing on the bed and sitting astride his legs.

Michael started twisting his body, using his considerable strength. But the redhead had his legs hammerlocked between her strong thighs, and the blondes just pressed against his upper body even more. Try as he might, he couldn't dislodge them.

Victoria suddenly leaned forward and slapped his face, hard. Michael cried out at the pain, and tears sprang unbidden into his eyes.

"Kirsten said *relax*, stud," she said, her voice hard, mean. "Keep squirming and we'll get rough. Real rough. You won't like it that way, I promise you."

Mike froze at the menace in her voice. He saw that the eyes of all three women had grown cold, predatory, like old Nosey Tweedle's cat just before it pounced on a bird.

"That's better," muttered Victoria.

"Oh, get it on, girfriend," said Kirsten petulantly. "We're hungry for it too, y'know."

Victoria murmured agreement. She started unbuckling his belt. The enormity of what she was about to do hit him. *Oh no! Nonono! That's completely GROSS!*

With strength born of desperation, bile rising in his throat, Michael heaved his body sideways. Victoria fell off, landing hard on Sally, their heads hitting together with a loud *crack*. He jerked his body in the other direction, sending Kirsten sprawling. With a squeal, she fell off the bed and crashed onto the floor. The air was fill with vicious curses. Victoria dislodged herself from Sally, holding her forehead. Blood seeped through her fingers. In a voice filled with malice, she grated:

"You Goddamned *stupid* fool! And we were being so gentle with you, too! GodDAMNIT but you're in for it now! We'll do you just like all the others! More rope, girls! Let's tie him up so tight, all he'll be able to do is bat his eyelashes! We'll screw his brains out, then drag him outside into the woods an' get the knives an' start slicing off body parts!"

But Michael was still moving, twisting around. His fingers fumbled into a jeans pocket and found the warm hard object deep inside. A happy humming filled his head.

The two women left on the bed flung themselves at him, pulling him flat on his back again, then holding him down by lying crosswise atop him. The third woman, Kirsten, rubbing a long scrape on her hip courtesy of a cabinet she had hit as she fell, fished out a coil of thick rope from a drawer under the bed. She started to wind it around Mike's ankles, saying:

"You're a real dumb-ass, boy. Fightin' something most guys'd give their right arm for. You'll soon wish you'd never been born, we get through with you. What's left'll be buried in a hole deep in the woods, where no one'll ever find ya. We're real good at hidin' bodies."

"Less talk, more tying," gritted Victoria lying atop his chest. "Double-loop everything; he's strong."

"Don't worry. No guy's ever snapped this rope or slipped my knots before. He's ours."

"He's dead, is what he is. Just like the rest. We'll - AIOWW! What's with his skin? It's gettin' hard an' coarse!"

"And orange! What the hell?"

The women pulled away from Michael, staring. The boy's skin, now like coarse sandpaper, increased in texture. What started as faint outlines of small rocks deepened into jutting hard rock-like orange scales. They appeared all over his body. And his body grew, not in height but in breadth. Shoulders became massive, arms bulged with muscle, legs turned into tree trunks, hands and feet each lost a digit while the remaining four grew wide and thick. His face mutated most of all: wide lipless slash of a mouth, small pug nose, eyebrows joined into a thick ledge over deep-set eyes, all topped by a bald head covered with the same rocky scales as the rest of his body. And the creature was heavy; the bed sagged under its weight, the wooden foundation box started splintering.

The Thing had arrived.

Two of the would-be rapist/murderers screamed. The third, Sally, backed out of the bedroom, eyes wide as goose eggs.

The stout ropes around his wrists and ankles had snapped like straw as his limbs thickened and hardened. The orange, rocky and quite naked Thing leaned forward and, with his free hand, gave each of the screaming women the merest flick of his big forefinger on her chin. Their heads snapped back and they collapsed, unconscious. Mike kept the Thing's other hand balled into a fist around the stone.

Sally decided she very much wanted to be elsewhere. She ran to the side door of the motor home, fumbled with the lock, and finally managed to get it open. She scampered outside and ran toward the rear of the motor home. She was just passing the rear corner, eyes set on the road beyond, when the metal wall of the vehicle split like paper and a giant orange paw grabbed her shoulder and hauled her back inside through the hole. Another flick of a rocky forefinger, and she joined her cohorts in oblivion.

Effortlessly, the Thing tore down the entire rear wall of the RV. He scooped up the three limp women and carried them outside. He dropped them in a heap several feet from the vehicle, not caring how hard they landed on the ground. He looked around. The motor home was parked in a small grassy clearing off a narrow forest road in what looked like the middle of nowhere. Dense woodland surrounded them; the only sounds were wind and birdsong.

"Well, ladies - an' you're definitely not - seems like ya really wanted ta get off th' beaten track ta do yore nasty business. So I figger ya might as well stay here." He spoke like the Thing would and his voice sounded like crushed stone turning slowly in a hopper.

The Thing removed Michael's shoes and knapsack from the motor home. Then he demolished the vehicle. Slowly, methodically, his super-human strength crumpled metal, wood and fibreglass as if it all were paper, with no damage to his rock-hard skin. Within five minutes, 27 feet of carefully-designed RV had been transformed into a giant ball, leaking various fluids onto the grass of the meadow.

The Thing surveyed his handiwork and laughed: a coarse gravel rumble that sent every bird within 100 yards winging away.

The strongest member of the Fantastic Four lumbered over to the three unconscious women and stood over them, watching as they breathed softly. They looked so innocent now, but the Thing knew that was just a sham. They were vicious killers.

It would be so easy to end their lives. A massive orange foot pressing down on each skull would do it. Quick and clean. Evil erased. No courts, posturing lawyers, endless appeals.

No more victims.

The Thing sighed. It sounded like the air brakes of a big tractor-trailer. He couldn't just kill them, not in cold blood, no matter how evil they were. *I'm a good guy. Whatta revoltin' development dis is!*

What to do?

Michael squatted on massive orange haunches and thought. After long minutes, he got an inspiration. He moved his stuff to the road, then had the Thing terraform the meadow. Thick arms worked like steam shovels, chunky legs like pistons. Fifteen minutes later, the Thing again stood in the road and gazed at a high wall of earth, rock and uprooted trees that completely surrounded the clearing on all four sides. The inner angles of the walls were too steep to climb, at least for ordinary humans. The women were trapped inside, naked and helpless.

Now they would know how their victims felt.

When they regained consciousness, they'd find a note in carefully-printed block letters, on paper from Michael's knapsack, stuck to the large ball that had once been their vehicle:

CONFES TO POLIC OR I BE BACK. AND VERY ANGRY.

The orange man-monster lumbered up the dirt road, toward what he hoped was the main highway. *It looks like fresh tire tracks, so I'm prolly okay walkin' this way. If not, well, there's always the Angel to fly high an' figure out which way to go, an' then there's the Flash to run there at super-speed, if I can find food. Gots to be careful not to get dressed if I do the Flash.*

He'd change back to Michael before reaching the highway, then get dressed. He'd have to pull a spare set of clothes out of the knapsack; the women had cut off his shirt as he slept and his pants had been shredded when he transformed. Then he'd walk to the nearest phone, and make an anonymous call to 9-1-1, telling the police where to find the women.

The women. Michael refused to think about what they had wanted to do with him. And what would happen to him after that.

He knew he'd get violently ill if he did.

Chuff, chuff, chuff. The rough sound of a pair of stony bare feet - more like big flat shovels - as the Thing walked along the road. His breathing, while calm, sounded like a bull moose in heat. Small forest animals scattered at his approach. Unseen in the bushes, an adult male black bear regarded the passage of this strange orange biped, wondered if it should attack, decided that flesh covered in small rocks wouldn't be that tasty, and wisely stayed put.

Springtime in the North woods meant there was more than love in the air. There were also black flies. Thick clouds of them. Voraciously hungry.

But they didn't bother naked Michael at all as he trudged along the road; their bites couldn't even begin to penetrate the Thing's thick rocky hide. In fact, Michael didn't even feel them, so he never even noticed them.

Which is why he never thought about what those biting bugs would do to three completely-exposed human bodies.

Chapter 17

Inn-cidents

As the Flash, Michael had run from Northwestern Ontario into Manitoba and then almost clear across that province, following the Trans-Canada Highway. It was now late evening, and the sun was setting over the vast prairie ocean of flat fields, their crops of wheat, barley, oats and canola undulating in the breeze, a sea of grain waves.

Wearing only his sturdy Kodiak boots (not running shoes; he'd remembered how the soles of those had melted the first time he became the Flash), the boy had been racing along the shoulder of the highway at super-speed, so any onlooker saw only a faint blur. He enjoyed how straight the highway was and how easily he was able to pass the cars. To the Flash, it seemed as if the cars were crawling.

But running at that speed for so long had a price, and now Mike paid it: he was suddenly starving. He'd burned up so many calories, his stomach was hurting in its hunger, his blood sugar was dangerously low, and he became dizzy. He stumbled, which is something you do not want to do at super-speed. With a cry, the boy tumbled headfirst onto the pavement, and rolled out of control for hundreds of yards before coming to a stop upside-down against a signpost. The soles of his boots were smoking from the high-speed run.

"Ow, ow, ow!" he yelped, shaking his head groggily. Though the Flash's speed aura had protected him from serious harm, his naked body was still covered with hundreds of bleeding scratches. Worse, he had dropped his special stone as he fell!

Wincing at the pain from his lacerations, heedless of his

nudity, Michael searched frantically along the roadside for the colourful rock. Luckily, no cars passed him, or else he'd have to deal with awkward questions from motorists who would have jammed on their brakes at the sight of a buck-naked young man with a knapsack on his back looking for something.

With a whoop of joy, Mike found his colourful stone and grabbed it like a drunk latching onto a new bottle. He became Wolverine, healed his injuries, then scampered down a ditch and loped across a field, away from the highway. Stopping, he turned back into Michael, pulled some clothes from his knapsack, and hurriedly dressed. Then he fished out three slightly-mangled sub sandwiches - he'd bought them before his run because he knew how hungry the Flash would get - and wolfed them all down.

He sighed deeply when he finished eating; the intense hunger pains were subsiding. He walked back to the highway, now almost devoid of cars. Reaching the T-Can, he trudged westward again, admiring the rich red and purple hues of the prairie sunset. A roadside sign stated that he would soon reach a city called Brandon. A hawk circled lazily overhead and Michael considered morphing into Angel and soaring up to play with it, but decided against it.

Then, in the distance, he saw the welcoming lit sign of a roadside motel and he quickened his pace. He could use a good shower and a warm comfy bed, even though his funds were limited.

He came to a modest country motel of 15 rooms, set back from the highway. It was in good repair, though needing a fresh coat of paint. The neon sign, humming softly and flickering, proclaimed: "Sometimes Sno'd Inn". The youth walked into the small building attached to one end of the motel, marked "Office". A bell chimed as he entered.

Nervously, he looked around the tiny reception area. He had never done this by himself before. He had just decided that this was too risky and turned to leave, when a soft voice behind him said:

"Yes? Can I help you?"

THE HERO STONE

Mike swung around. He saw a small man standing behind the counter, staring at him. The man was about the same age as Billy's late adoptive father, balding, with a lively face dominated by high cheekbones and a generous mouth.

"Sure, ah, I need a room for the night, please, sir," the youth said.

"Well, I have just one room left, at this hour. Is it just you?"

Mike nodded.

"Is it just you?" the man repeated.

Mike blinked. Didn't the man just see him nod? He nodded again, harder.

"You'll have to talk to me, fella. I can't see you," said the motelier, with a touch of annoyance.

Mike was confused. *I'm standing right in front of you.* "Yes, sir," he said.

"Okay. Just fill out this registration card." He pushed a card and a pen across the desk at Michael. "Room rate is $65."

The boy swallowed. That was half of what he had left in his pocket. "That's ... that's, um, a lot."

"Oh, it's quite reasonable compared to what others are charging. Say, are you a teenager? Sounds like you are."

"Yes sir. I'm 17."

"Really? Well, I don't rent rooms to minors. Can't risk it, seeing as how underage kids can't be bound to a contract, which means you can't be held responsible for any room damages or theft. Sorry, son." The man's hands felt along the desk top, located the registration card, and pulled it back, away from Mike.

Though it was a lot of money, Mike had really been looking forward to the comforts of a motel room for the night. "Oh, well, okay," he said, disappointment evident in his voice.

The man stared hard at Mike, with eyes of palest grey, almost opaque. "You travelling alone, son?"

"Yes."

"Well, that isn't too safe. Not nowadays. Lotta strange people prowling the roads. Where you headed?"

"Fred MacMurray. Going to find my real mommy, yes I am."

"Uh-huh. What's your name, son?"

"Michael Johnson, sir."

"Well, my name's George. George Sparrow. Pleased to meetcha." The man stuck out his hand, and as Mike shook it, he continued: "Look, I think you better stay the night after all. You promise not to damage the room, or take anything from it?"

"Oh, yes, sir!"

"All right. Fill out the card. I'll give you a special rate of just $35. Sound okay to you?"

"Oh, yes! Thank you!"

Using his best printing, Michael laboriously filled out the registration card, using Billy's address. Then he carefully counted out 35 dollars, and handed the bills to the innkeeper. The man just stood there, staring.

"Um, here's the money," Mike said, waving the bills.

The man held out a hand, saying: "Place it in my hand, please."

Mike did so, frowning. The man turned and fed the bills into a small rectangular machine, one at a time. As each bill disappeared inside, a tinny mechanical voice announced its denomination.

Mike watched, wide-eyed. "Wow, a talking money thingy," he said.

"Yep, it sure comes in handy," said the man. He pulled out a room key, ran his fingers over a small group of bumps on the tag attached to the key, and held it out to Mike, saying: "Room Eight, son. Now you need anything, just call the front desk here and let me know."

The boy beamed a big smile. "Thank you, sir. You've been very kind." On impulse, he stuck out his hand. The innkeeper made no move to shake it. Frowning, Mike kept his hand in the air, finally saying: "Don't you want to shake? You did just a few minutes ago, yes you did."

The man held out his own hand and said: "You have to put your hand in mine, son. I can't see; I'm blind."

Astonished, Mike did so and they shook hands again.

"Blind?" said Michael. "Geez, I ... I didn't know."

"Yep, blind as a bat. Oh, I know the politically-correct words nowadays are 'visually-impaired', but blind is what I am and politically-correct words won't change it. Been this way for 37 years now."

"Ah, that's why you have the talking money thingy."

"Yep, and a talking computer that scans printed material and reads it back to me and reads me my emails, and a talking clock, and so forth. Helps me run my business despite my disability."

"Oh, I knows about that. I gots a dis-ab-ility too, sir. Yes I do. I'm departmentally-delayed."

"Depart - ? Oh, you mean developmentally-delayed. Ah, I understand now. That explains why you say you're 17, but you speak like my young nephew."

Mike nodded, then remembered the man couldn't see, so he said: "Yes, sir."

"And your folks let you travel all by yourself, eh?"

The boy looked down at his feet, coughed and said: "Ah, my ... pretend-parents are ... are deaded now. So I'm off to find my real mommy, yes I am."

"Really. Huh. Well, you run along to your room now. And come talk to me first thing in the morning, okay?"

Mike agreed and went to his room.

After a long hot shower and a very restful night of deep, dreamless sleep, Mike presented himself at the office early next morning, as requested. George greeted him heartily, then led him into a small apartment behind the front desk, hand travelling along the walls as he did so. The smell of bacon and eggs filled the air, and Mike realized he was famished again.

Entering the kitchen, Mike was introduced to Beatrice, George's sighted wife, a tall, prim woman with a Scottish accent that promptly made the boy laugh.

"Why are you laughing, young man?" asked Beatrice, eyeing him.

"Oh, you sound just like a lady Shrek," giggled Mike. "You know, that big green ogre in the movies. They're some of my favouritist movies."

Beatrice stared, then shook her head, chuckling. "Oh aye? Well, I've never heard that said about me before." She sat Mike down and served him a hearty breakfast, the first home-cooked meal he'd had since hitting the road. It was delicious.

Over breakfast, Michael learned about his hosts. A childhood disease had gradually robbed George of his sight; by the time he was 21, he was completely blind. Beatrice was the physical therapist who had trained him to live without sight. During his months of rehabilitation, they had fallen in love and got married.

Refusing to sit in a chair at home and collect disability cheques from the government, George had purchased this motel. It was an ideal business for the couple. He ran the front desk, while Beatrice and a local girl from the nearby city cleaned the rooms. George did the motel laundry in a carefully-organized laundry room. He even took care of the couple's large vegetable garden out back. Once Beatrice planted the produce each Spring, in ordered rows, George painstakingly memorized each section, then kept it weed-free and watered for the rest of the summer.

"It was rough for the first two years with George in that garden," laughed Beatrice. "Until he got the system down pat, he kept pulling up the vegetables and letting the weeds grow!" Mike laughed too.

The couple made Mike an offer: he could stay for free for a week, and get three meals a day, if he painted the exterior of the motel. The youth was reluctant to delay his westward trip for so long, and frowned so fiercely that his eyebrows looked welded together while he noisily sucked a knuckle. Then his face suddenly cleared and he agreed.

After breakfast, Beatrice found some coveralls that fit him and instructed Mike how to apply the paint, then watched as he started on an end wall. The youth worked carefully, anxious to do a good job for the couple who were being so nice to him. Nodding her approval, Beatrice left to see to her housekeeping chores.

When she returned several hours later to announce lunch, she was amazed to find the entire back of the motel painted. "My God, but you certainly work fast, laddie!" she exclaimed. Mike just grinned at her, then stated he was starving and he hoped she had prepared a big lunch.

By dinnertime, Mike had finished the entire motel, although he wore as much paint as the walls. *The Flash sure comes in handy at times,* he thought as he cleaned up and showered for dinner. *Though I didn't use full speed, so's the clothes wouldn't get burneded off. Besides, if I painted too fast, they'd get superstitious.*

George and Beatrice couldn't believe the young man worked so fast, though they certainly weren't complaining. Mike just grinned.

The next morning, arriving for breakfast, Mike found Beatrice in tears and George looking furious. They had just discovered that the four walls in Room 12 had been coated in pungent Worcestershire sauce! The room had been rented to four college kids, on a road trip across Canada now that classes were over. They had sounded like nice lads when George registered them yesterday, polite and well-spoken, and Beatrice said they drove an expensive blue Mercedes convertible. But after their early morning check-out, the damaged room had been discovered.

Upon hearing the story, Michael blurted: "Why, that's so mean!"

"Yes," said George grimly. "And when we reported it to the police, they discovered that the license plate number those bastards had put on the registration card was false. Since they paid cash for the room, we have no way of tracking those miserable SOBs."

"It'll take us at least two days to scrub that room clean," sobbed Beatrice. "Plus losing two days' rent. With a small motel like ours, that lost income hurts."

Michael frowned and sucked his knuckle furiously. "Not two days," he finally announced. "Just leave me alone in the room today, and I'll have it done by supper. Promise. You saw how fasted I painted your motel. You just do your usual stuff."

The Sparrows were too distraught to argue. When Mike was left alone in the damaged room, armed with cleaning supplies and almost gagging at the pungent smell, he discovered that several bottles of unopened Worcestershire sauce had been left in a corner. The boy suddenly smiled a smug kind of smile, like that of a lawyer preparing for a divorce case.

Stripping off his clothes except for his Kodiaks, he became the Flash, grabbed the bottles, and raced westward along the Trans-Canada. After 200 kilometres, not seeing a blue convertible carrying four young men, he turned and raced in the opposite direction, increasing his speed to make up for lost time and causing a sonic boom that rattled windows and birds.

He found the car parked outside a roadside diner. The distinctive symbol on the hood matched the one described to him by Beatrice at breakfast. Through the large window, he saw four young men frozen - to him - in the act of chowing down on a huge breakfast.

Still moving at a super-speed blur, he let the air out of all four Michelin tires, then smeared the strong-smelling sauce from the bottles all over the car's expensive leather interior. Then he shot into the restaurant and ate everything off the plates of the four vandals - all that running had made him ravenous - in the time it took the men to blink. He finished by dashing into a nearby phone booth, where he dialled 9-1-1, reporting that the bad men who had damaged the Sometimes Sno'd Inn were at this diner and gave the name he read from the exterior sign.

Smiling in satisfaction, Michael raced back to the motel and, deliberately slowing down, had the Flash clean the odious room for the rest of the day. He needed three helpings of supper that night.

The next day, he gave a second coat of paint to the exterior of the inn, again slowing his speed so that it took him all day (and left his clothes intact), which was amazing enough to George and Beatrice. The Sparrows' mood was much better; the police had called with news that the four culprits who had sauced Number 12 had been caught. The owner of the car was demanding the authorities move heaven and earth to find the bastard who'd ruined his upholstery.

Late that night, as Mike lay in bed waiting for sleep to come, a wild party started in the adjoining room. Like a growing hurricane, it soon spread until four roomfuls of guests were doing their best to make a lie of the motel's "Quiet Time After 11" policy. It was now almost midnight.

Soon after the disturbance had started, Beatrice pounded on the doors, commanding the rowdies to tone it down. It worked. For five minutes. Then the noise started up again, even louder.

George then called the police, who eventually came and gave the offending guests a stern warning. That worked too. For a whole 15 minutes after the cops left. Then the noise started once more, ratcheted up by several decibels.

George called the police again, trying to convince them to return. This time, the cops were uncooperative; they had better things to do than quiet down unruly tourists.

Outside the rooms where the party raged, several guys were drinking and chucking empty beer cans at a scarecrow they'd uprooted from the garden out back and impaled on a picnic table off the parking lot in front. Since the men had personally drained their ammunition, they missed the target as often as they hit it. The night rang with their laughter and the clatter of cans on table and pavement.

Running out of ammo, they disappeared back inside their room to harvest more. They soon returned. One of them heaved back and let fly with a vicious overhand at the hapless scarecrow. Who deftly caught it in one hand and flung it right back at the man, hitting him in the chest, saying:

"Stop that! I'm not a target! How do you like it when cans are thrown at you?"

The men gawped at each other: were they all having the same drunken hallucination? The scarecrow reached down with spindly arms that seemed to grow, grabbed more empty cans off the ground, and commenced a furious barrage at the men. As a group, yelling in disbelief, the guys unanimously decided to call it a night and promptly went to bed - fully dressed - with the covers pulled over their heads. One even started praying for the first time in over two decades.

The drunks never noticed the dark vines that had grown up the back of the scarecrow and then into the back of its head and along the back of its arms. After the men had fled, the vines retracted back into the earth, leaving the scarecrow lifeless again.

Soon after, in the room that had become Party Central, couples were gyrating to a pounding beat coming from the radio. One guy reached down, grabbed a fresh beer from the cooler beside him, raised the brew to his lips, and blinked. A small pot of geraniums next to the radio - one of the innkeepers' homey touches in each room - had a twig sticking up in front of the flowers. The twig, which had a bulbous head and small spindly arms, was swaying in time to the music.

"Hey!" hollered the guy above the music. "Which one of ya brought the Dancing Baby Groot toy, from that *Guardians of the Galaxy* movie?"

The dancers stopped dancing and gathered around the small, swaying twig.

"Aww, he is *so* cute!" gushed one lady, bending down. "C'mon, who brought it? I wanna get one for myself. It's such a cute toy!"

"Ah, y'know, come ta think of it, I thought the toy came in its own pot," said the man who had first noticed it.

Suddenly, the twig stopped moving. In the centre of its bulbous head, black eyes snapped open and a black slash of a mouth said loudly:

"I. Am. Groot. I. Am. *PISSED* at all the noise you are making! People around you are trying to sleep! So knock it off!"

The geraniums behind the talking stick suddenly developed mouths and, in unison, stuck out their tongues and gave furious raspberries to the partiers.

The lady said "AI-YAI!" and stepped back in shock. She collided with her dance partner and they both fell onto a bed in a tangle of limbs and half-dressed bodies. Soon after, the couple discovered they had no further interest in upright dancing and a great interest in the much-quieter horizontal mambo.

The man said "WAAAH!" and dropped his beer bottle. Killing the radio, he decided he'd had quite enough to drink, wobbled to his adjoining room, and passed out on his bed.

The rest of the dancers fled. Two needed a change of underwear.

In the last party room, the potted geraniums impossibly grew four feet tall and began lecturing to a man on the couch who'd been singing off-key at the top of his voice to the two women snuggled on each side of him. The flowers, speaking in turn with mouths in their petal-fringed centres, decried the dangers of booze and loose women, causing the man to swear off both then and there. He joined the priesthood the next day.

Blessed peace returned to the Sometimes Sno'd Inn.

In Michael's room, the massive, green, moss-and-root-encrusted figure sitting on the bed grinned a slash-mouthed grin, then shimmered yellow. Mike slipped back under his covers, tired but happy with another job well done. *I sure do love the tricks I can do as Swamp Thing,* he thought. *I can send my mind into any plant, an' make it do what I want, an' even talk from it.* Smiling, sleep overcame him.

The next day, after breakfast, Beatrice presented Mike with an envelope.

"There's $200 cash in there, laddie. I know our agreement was room and board in return for your work, but you did extra for us and you worked so fast too, so we feel you deserve this. Besides, I think you can use some extra cash, aye?"

Michael said: "Yes, ma'am!" He jumped up and gave each of the Sparrows a big bear hug and announced he really, really had to go now. He turned, grabbed his knapsack and ran out the door.

"Damn!" said George, who'd been hoping the lad would stay longer while they checked with the authorities to see if he might be a runaway.

Dashing to the front door in pursuit of the boy, Beatrice looked out over the parking lot. Michael was nowhere in sight. In fact, the only movement was a big tractor-trailer moving van leaving the gas station across the road, heading west with a belch of black smoke and horrible grinding of gears. With a hidden stowaway, still giggling over what Swamp Thing had done the night before.

Chapter 18

Deadly Shadow, Desperate Quest

Amy Harrison drove her white Porsche 918 Spyder just at the speed limit, which for her was agonizingly slow in a car with 887 horsepower under the hood. She had to be careful not to call any attention to herself. She had to get home without delay. Or it would be the end of her daughters.

On the passenger seat was her designer gym bag filled with $700,000 in cash. All she could get her hands on in such short notice. The pencil-necks at the bank had balked at giving it to her, asking all sorts of inane questions, until she'd finally threatened to yank the rest of her investments and take them to another bank. She got her money real quick after that.

She had done exactly what that bastard demanded. Not a word to the cops, no secret notes to the bank teller, no commotion, just $700,000 in cash. So when she returned home, she expected him to live up to his end of the bargain and release her daughters. A deal's a deal. And Amy Harrison understood deals.

Twenty years ago, she had invented those flashing red lights that went into the backs of running shoes. Selling the patent to Nike had netted her millions in upfront cash, plus royalties in perpetuity. Even after the messy divorce with her parasite husband, who claimed he'd helped her invent it and who had pictures of her and their landscaper in positions that would have made a gymnast wince, she still ended up with over 25 million dollars. Which made her the richest lady in Clearwater.

And she acted like it. Extravagant parties. Luxury sports cars (six so far, including the $900,000 Porsche). Private school for her teenage daughters. Designer clothes. Exotic vacations. And lots of

... landscaping ... around the house.

All of which came crashing down around her ears when the intruder had arrived. She still didn't understand how he had slipped past her state-of-the-art security system. But when she awoke this morning, there he was: standing at the foot of her bed, dressed in jacket and slacks, grinning the coldest smile she had ever seen. Even in her mirror.

She had never seen him before (and she knew everybody worth knowing in Clearwater). Average height, slim build, sandy-blond hair, face reminiscent of a young Robert Redford. She watched the nightly news and he certainly looked nothing like that criminal suspect the police were searching for; the one who'd killed that couple in the North End and attacked those two teens.

He had said, in a voice colder than his smile, that her maid and cook were locked up in a basement closet. Her phones were dead. As was Brutus, the family German Shepard. Then, with a tight grip on her arm, he had yanked her out of bed and down the hall to see her daughters. (She was thankful she hadn't slept naked that night.)

The girls had adjoining bedrooms and Amy was relieved when the intruder assured her that her daughters were in their beds and he hadn't touched them. Then she saw them.

Both girls lay on their backs, under a black blanket. *But they don't have black blankets,* Amy's mind had said. She looked closer. And realized it wasn't a blanket at all, but a *shadow* that completely enveloped the girls from head to toe, leaving only their noses showing. Amy could hear their quick panicky breathing. The ebony material gripped them firmly; Amy saw just the merest of twitches beneath the black. The girls were helpless. And in great danger: the intruder said the *shadow* that covered their faces made them mute, deaf, and blind, and prevented any air from reaching their mouths.

When Amy had finished screaming and threatening, which was immediately after the man placed a wicked switchblade at her throat, he told her what he wanted. He had finished by saying if he even suspected the presence of police, he'd have the *shadow* flow over the girls' noses, leaving them unable to breathe. Slow death by suffocation.

So Amy had done exactly as she was told, after hurriedly dressing in full view of the leering bastard. The intruder stayed in the house. With his hostages.

She guided the Porsche up her long driveway and parked it by the front door. She lugged the gym bag inside. The man was waiting at the top of the stairs leading to the bedrooms. He motioned and Amy carried the bag up to him. She unzipped it, displaying the bills.

"Very good, darlin'. An' no sign of cops. Good girl," said the intruder with another icy smile.

"Now you'll let my daughters go?" Amy asked.

"Yup. I always keep my promises. Go see."

She ran to her daughters' bedrooms, and saw the black shrouds slowly, almost regretfully, melt away from their bodies. Laura, 13, was dressed in loose cotton PJs, for which Amy thanked God, because Laura had blossomed into quite the young woman this past year. However, Ashleigh, 16, wore a bare-midriff two-piece silk outfit consisting of a top that barely reached below her breasts and a bottom that redefined the word "briefs". Both girls ran to their mother and started crying.

"Aw, ain't this a real purty family moment." It was the man, behind them. They all turned and stared at him, the girls still snuffling.

"What ... what was that awful black stuff?" Laura demanded. "We couldn't move or see or hear or speak or anything! We couldn't even breathe through our mouths!"

"A little something I can do," replied the man. Amy noticed his eyes fixed on Ashleigh, and moved in front of her daughter to block his view. *Dammit Ash, why don't you wear a sensible PJ like your sister?*

"So ... so now you'll leave, right? You got what you wanted," Amy said.

"Not everything I wanted. Not yet," he said.

"Ah, car. Right? You want one of my cars? Take the Porsche

outside; it's not even a year old. Keys're still in it. Or take one of the others in the garage. There's even a limited edition gold Prowler down there. Help yourself. Just go and leave us alone."

"Yeah, an' you'll go to the cops as soon as I'm gone, huh?"

"No! We won't! Promise! Just leave. Please."

"Sorry, I don't believe you. I think I'd better lock you up downstairs with your house staff. Time you break out of that closet, I'll be long gone."

He herded them downstairs, oblivious to their protests. Down in the basement, he unlocked the door to the big walk-in closet, opened it, and flicked on the light. The maid and cook were sitting quietly on the floor. Holding their severed heads in their laps. Blood was everywhere.

The three Harrisons started screaming. Amy and Laura were shoved inside with the corpses, then the door slammed shut behind them and locked. Amy shrieked in horror as she realized the man had kept Ashleigh outside with him:

"Ashleigh! NO! Leave her alone, you monster! Don't you DARE touch her!"

There was an awful male laugh, then Amy heard Ashleigh's screams change in pitch, becoming louder and more frantic. Then her screams became guttural, as if they were being muffled somehow. Those sounds went on for some time. Then there were no sounds at all.

It was quiet inside the closet, except for the wracking gasps of the women's sobs. Mother and daughter hugged each other close, standing as far away from the bodies of their servants as the closet would allow. The copper stench of blood was overpowering.

The door to the closet suddenly snapped open, banging hard against the wall. Amy screamed and clutched Laura tighter. A solid wall of black swept in. A *shadow* cocoon enveloped Amy, leaving only her eyes and nose free. The ebony straightjacket held her motionless. Another cocoon shrouded Laura, but this time, just her eyes were left exposed. Powerless, screaming deep in her throat, Amy watched her youngest daughter suffocate to death just inches away from her, blue eyes pleading for help before bulging and then staring into nothingness.

Then slowly, almost lovingly, Amy's cocoon closed in over her own nose. Five minutes passed. The black rolled back out of the closet, like some odious nightmare tide, leaving the bodies of Amy and Laura in the company of their dead servants.

The *shadow* became human and the black-haired ordinary-looking features of Robert Moses Brack surveyed his handiwork with satisfaction. It had been a good morning. He had lots of ready cash again, his choice of fine automobiles, and some long-overdue sex fun, too. *That young filly had been mighty fine. While she lasted. Wonder if her momma knew she wasn't a virgin?*

He went into the basement bathroom to relieve himself and caught sight of his face in the mirror. *Have to remember to change my looks again before I go out; my normal face is everywhere now.* He was proud of his newly-discovered ability to use The Gift to change his appearance; the days of practice had paid off. *Necessity is the mother of invention.*

Ah well. Time to hit the road and get after that Goddamned retard. Brack knew the boy had left town; his Gift was again urging him to follow it.

"Yeah, yeah," he muttered, as he walked past the inert bloody mass that had been Ashleigh Harrison and climbed the stairs out of the basement. "I'm going. But I'm gonna shower an' change first. Then I've one more stop to make in this town. A little insurance. Heh."

I'm being so much cleverer this time. That stone won't get away from me again.

୨୦ ୨୦ ୨୦ ୧୧ ୧୧ ୧୧

Billy McDonnell was terrified. He was going to do something unthinkable, totally out of character: chase after his best friend in the company of some guy he hardly knew and without asking his parents' permission first.

"But ... but I *have* to ask them!" he protested to Ethan Delperdang. "I can't just take off!"

"You can and you must," replied the human walkingstick.

"Cleaner, simpler that way. No messy goodbyes, no tedious questions. Let's just go an' you can call 'em from the road, telling 'em you're okay. But you tell 'em we're looking for Mike on the East Coast, in your Atlantic Canada. Don't say where we're really goin' in case they call the cops an' report you as a missing child. Which, from what I've seen of your folks, they prolly will."

"But they'll freak out with worry!"

"Yeah. But that's the price of being parents. They always worry. Your first bike ride without training wheels. Your first date. Your first solo drive. Your first long trip without them. When you're away at college. Even when you're an adult an' livin' your own life miles away, they worry. Comes with the territory."

"But ..."

"But nothin', Billy me lad. Every hour we delay, is another hour that Mike's on his own, likely with that Brack monster on his trail. I've made all the arrangements, so let's go."

The teen looked hard at Ethan. "Why are you doing this? Chasing after Mike at your expense, an' you bein' such a skinflint. Why do you care?"

Ethan grimaced. "I could lie to you an' say 'cause it's the right thing to do. But I won't. It's 'cause that stone is too powerful to leave in the wrong hands. Don't get me wrong; I'm not sayin' your pal Mike is the wrong hands, but Brack sure as hell is, now that I know the stone is split in two. My self-appointed mission is to get that rock away from that evil bastard. So when we find Mike, then Brack won't be far behind."

Then the stick man grinned: "Besides, you're leaving on a Quest an' I'm the wise mentor! Every Quest has a wise mentor. It's tradition! I'm your Gandalf!"

The teen looked at Ethan. "Yeah, right."

They were in Billy's room. Billy finished packing a suitcase, managed to seal the lid, and gave a heavy sigh. "Okay. Let's go. But I wanna make a stop first. Got somethin' to get off my chest with Mel."

"Aargh," said Ethan.

༄ ༄ ༄ ༄ ༄ ༄

God, I look awful. Melanie Van Heusen looked at herself in her bedroom's full-length mirror. She had on her favourite jeans and past her left thigh, the cloth hung flat and limp. *SO obvious I'm missing a leg!*

Supporting herself with crutches, she turned away from the mirror and sat on the edge of her bed. Bending, she pinned up the left leg of the jeans. *Well, I won't be like this forever. That healing sock over my stump continues to do its job, then another week or so, I can get an artificial training leg. With more physio, I'll get the hang of walking with it soon.*

Her heart quickened. That's right! Physio! Her third physiotherapist appointment was today. That meant Jonathan would be coming to pick her up soon.

She looked at herself critically in the mirror again, decided she didn't like her top and shucked it off. Using crutches, she went to her closet and yanked out five more tops, flinging them onto the bed one at a time. Sitting on the bed again, she tried one on. Then another. Then three more.

The only good thing about losing her leg was that she had met this absolutely awesome guy who volunteered his time to drive disabled patients and the elderly around town for hospital, doctor and physio appointments, errands, and the like. Jonathan Stewart was his name, and he looked almost exactly like a younger Leonardo DiCaprio, when the hunky movie star had starred in James Cameron's *Titanic*. Several years ago, when she had been 12 desperately going on 20, she had rented the DVD and had developed such a crush on DiCaprio. She and her friends had seen *Titanic* 11 times that summer because of him. Her sleep had been filled with dreams of him.

Then she got over him, like teenage girls do. Though she still kept Leo's poster on her bedroom wall, as she matured she developed new crushes on new hunks. Subject to - frequent - changes without notice. "The flavour of the week," her Mom said wryly.

Until now, when this volunteer guy had showed up to take her to physio while her folks were at work, and he looked so like

Leonardo that her first infatuation came roaring back and she started crushing on him so bad. *Gawd, if he ever wanted to kiss me, I would NOT say no.*

She finally settled on a top and started slowly down the stairs using her crutches. The doorbell rang as she reached bottom. She winced as she hurried to the front door; her stump still throbbed sometimes beneath its protective medical sheath. She paused for one last critical check of her hair in the hall mirror.

With her most blinding smile, she flung open the door with a cheery: "Hi Jonathan!"

It wasn't a handsome twentysomething hunk at all.

"Hi Mel," Billy said.

"Go away," she ordered and started closing the door. But Billy stuck his body between the door and the door-frame, and nothing was going to move that 280-lb mass. Certainly not Melanie.

"No, I will not go away. Not this time. Not until you hear me out," he said.

She glared at him, made an exasperated snort, and retreated. "Okay, talk. But I may not listen."

"Michael's run away, y'know."

She shrugged. "I heard."

"It's partly your fault that he did. Those nasty things you said to him."

"So?"

"So? C'mon, Mel! Don't you see by now that you're being totally unfair? We were friends for years! Don't you believe Mike - both of us - were trying our best to get to you, to help you, that night?"

She shrugged again. "I don't regret a thing I said. You realize that if I hadn't been hanging around Michael Johnson and his stone, that awful man wouldn't have assaulted me, an' I'd still have my left leg today?"

"Yeah, that's right, sure. But do *you* realize that if it wasn't for Mike and his stone, that you'd have been gang-raped by Monster Mack and his four goons, and I'd probably be *dead* right now?"

Melanie stared at Billy. She opened her mouth for a sharp

retort, but none came. She lowered her head, shifted her weight on the crutches, and eyed the carpet.

"Look, Mel, the three of us were always outsiders. Kids picked on me 'cause I'm whale-sized; they hassled Mike 'cause he's developmentally-delayed; and they taunted you 'cause of your thick glasses. But we managed to put up with all the teasing an' bullying 'cause we always had each other. We were a *team*. An' now we're not, an' it's tearing me apart."

For a moment, Melanie felt remorse. Then the hollow *ache* of her missing leg swept over her and the moment passed.

"William Butler McDonnell, don't you *dare* preach to me! You weren't the one to become a cripple; both *your* legs are still under you! When people look at me now, all they see is a cripple - a victim - an' all I see is the pity in their eyes! Even annoying Ashley looks at me with pity, an' I can't *stand* it!"

"Mel, c'mon. You're only a cripple if you allow yourself to think that way. You're a survivor, a winner, if you overcome your disability and get on with your life! Many disabled people are stronger now than before they became disabled: in goals, outlooks, accomplishments."

She looked at him and that radiant smile of hers slowly emerged. Billy's spirits rose. *She looks so beautiful when she smiles.*

Melanie said: "Where'd you hear that crap? Some self-help TV show?"

Stunned, Billy said: "No. I was talkin' with my folks. Mom works with a guy whose brother lost both his legs in a car accident when he was 23. Now he's VP of the company where he works. What they said makes sense to me; I agree with them."

"Well, I *don't*. Now, will you please leave?"

"Melanie, don't destroy years of friendship over this."

"Leave."

Billy gave her one last anguished look, turned, and walked slowly away. He said, over his shoulder: "I'm going to search for Mike. He's out there somewhere, all alone, lookin' for his real mom. I'm real worried about him an' I'm gonna find him."

He stopped, swung around, and looked right at Mel. "Because that's what friends do."

She answered him by slamming the door.

Billy shuffled to the rented wreck that Ethan drove, and slowly eased his bulk onto the passenger seat. The car groaned like it was afflicted with severe arthritis, and somewhere underneath a piece of metal clunked to the street..

"I saw," the scarecrow said sympathetically. "I don' wanna say 'told ya', but, well, I'm sorry she's still pissed at ya."

"Just drive, please," said Billy miserably.

ॐ ॐ ॐ ॐ ॐ ॐ

The doorbell rang again and Melanie flung open the door, expecting to see Billy, back for yet another try. Angry words died on her lips when she saw the smiling face of Jonathan Stewart. *Gawd, he's SO gorgeous!* Once again, he wore a crisp, pressed long-sleeved shirt tucked into crisp, pressed slacks. Today, his clothes were in shades of blue. His light brown leather belt perfectly matched his leather shoes. *His trim body makes that outfit look SO awesome.*

"Hi, Mel. Ready to leave for your physio?" he asked.

"You bet. Just lemme grab my purse."

With Jonathan hovering next to her protectively, she slowly descended the stairs and travelled down the path. When they reached his car - a too-cool silver-blue Audi TT convertible that moved like the wind thanks to a modified engine - Jonathan took her arm and helped her sit in the passenger seat. Her heart skipped a beat. She loved his touch; it was gentle yet firm. She could feel his arm muscles under his shirt, and had a sudden urge to rip his shirt off and run her hands all over his skin. *Control yourself, girl! Don't be slutty.*

Jonathan closed the door, stowed her crutches in the trunk, and went around to the driver's side. She ogled him as he slid lithely into the leather driver's seat and buckled up. He pressed the keyless-start button on the dash, awakening the Audi's turbocharged engine, and they powered away from the curb.

"So, what shall we talk about today?" he asked with a beautiful smile.

"Oh, whatever you want," she replied with a giggle. She found him so easy to talk to; she had told him all sorts of things, as if he were an old friend. *I just can't seem to shut up around him!*

"Well then, tell me more about how this Michael guy uses his stone. That's quite fascinating. If it's true, that is."

"Oh, it is, it is." She had already told him a lot about Mike and his stone; it started when he'd asked how she lost her leg, and it snowballed from there as she told him the whole story. She didn't see why she had to keep anything secret - Mike certainly was no friend of hers anymore - and Jonathan was so sympathetic when he'd learned how she'd been disabled.

So Melanie went into great detail about the wonderful beings Mike could turn into, while Jonathan smiled that beautiful smile of his, and a small voice deep in her brain wondered how it would feel to have his arms around her and his lips on hers.

☙ ☙ ☙ ❧ ❧ ❧

A noxious smokescreen of blue smoke in their wake, engine sounding like it would explode at any moment, Ethan coaxed the rented wreck onto the highway leading away from Clearwater, heading west. The speedometer inched up to 45 kilometres an hour and stayed there, even with the pedal pressed to the floor.

"Y'know, I don't wanna say anything rude, but there's no way we're gonna catch up to Mike in this rust bucket," said Billy. "We could travel faster riding bicycles!"

"Right you are, my lad. That's why I've chartered a private jet to fly us there."

"What? *You* spending money on a charter flight?"

Ethan looked hurt. "Hey, remember I told you that while I'm usually careful about my money, I have no problem spending it for emergencies. Well, this is an emergency."

He swung the car onto the road leading to Clearwater's small municipal airport. There was a loud *KLANG* behind them as another piece of the vehicle jettisoned itself. Billy had a horrible thought: *what kind of plane had this skinflint rented? Something flown by the Red Baron in World War One?*

"Are we flying direct to Fort McMurray?"

"Not at first. We'll try and intercept your friend before; the sooner we link up with him, the better, so we can help protect him from Brack."

"Yeah, but how will we find him?"

"Oh, Mike's leaving a good trail, if you know how to look. I've been tracking him on the Internet. I've got a keyword search program running 24/7, scanning media reports for strange and unusual occurrences between here and Alberta. There's been a few."

"Really?"

"Yep. Grocery store clerk unloading frozen meat in Sault Ste. Marie who swears he glimpsed a man made entirely of ice sitting atop the cargo at the front of the trailer; gang of carjackers chased into Thunder Bay by their own truck - floating four feet off the ground; and three naked women found trapped in the woods east of Kenora driven almost insane by black fly bites, who said an orange rock monster had corralled them, and who then confessed to a slew of unsolved rapes and murders of male hitchhikers. Sounds like Michael's been busy, huh?"

"Yeah."

"So, estimating how far he travels in a day based on the dates of these stories, I figure he's in Manitoba by now, likely past Winnipeg on the way to Brandon. He seems to be religiously following your Trans-Canada Highway westward. So we'll land in Brandon and try to connect with him there."

They pulled into the airport parking lot, and Billy whistled at the plane he saw on the tarmac. It was nothing like this car.

Gleaming in the sunlight was a white-and-tan luxury executive Challenger jet, engine already warming and uniformed female flight attendant waiting by the stairs.

"That's ... that's for us?" gasped Billy, who had only been on a plane once before, when he was 12, crammed into economy class on a flight to Florida.

"Yessir. We'll catch up to Mike in no time."

Ethan parked the car, but before he could switch off the engine, it chose that moment to defiantly commit suicide. An awful high-pitched whine sounded, the car started shaking violently, then the engine died with a horrible metallic screech accompanied by a huge backfire, which belched a giant black cloud from the tailpipe. Oil and radiator fluid started leaking from beneath the car almost immediately.

"Welp, looks like I won't be gettin' my damage deposit back," observed Ethan mournfully.

Chapter 19

The Eagle Flies Again

Michael knew he was in trouble as soon as he came out of the tractor-trailer. They were at a small diner off a narrow two-lane highway. They had left the Trans-Canada! He looked around frantically; there were no roadside signs identifying the famous east-west national highway. Except for this secondary road, almost devoid of traffic, they were surrounded by fields of parched earth and stunted crops. The sighing wind raised miniature dust devils that chased each other across fields starved for moisture like children let out for recess.

At the gas station across from the Sometimes Sno'd Inn outside Brandon, Mike had gotten lucky - or so he'd thought. He'd found a big tractor-trailer moving van headed west, with Alberta plates. The words painted on the cab said it came from Edmonton, and Mike knew from studying a map that Edmonton was in the northern part of Alberta, and Fred MacMurray was north of that.

So he'd slipped into the trailer as the Invisible Kid when the drivers opened the doors to check the load. After the big doors were closed and locked again, he had become visible, clambered over the stacked furniture until he found a comfy couch near the front of the trailer, and settled into it as the vehicle lumbered westward. He had quickly fallen into a deep sleep.

He slept the sleep of utter exhaustion for a long time; he had no idea how long. In fact, it was an entire day and night. The next morning, after the drivers finished their breakfast 'n' bathroom break at a roadside diner, they had opened the trailer doors to check the load again. The clang of the door latch had awakened Mike. As sunlight flooded in, he quickly disappeared. When the

Invisible Kid had stepped outside, he discovered to his horror that they were no longer on the highway with the maple leaf signposts. He dashed back inside, grabbed his knapsack, held it close to his body so it became invisible too, and barely escaped from the trailer before the men slammed the doors shut.

Michael watched as the big rig rumbled off down the highway. The silence of the Canadian prairies enveloped him. He felt lost, abandoned, but resisted the urge to cry.

Becoming visible, he went into the coffee shop: a small tired building of indifferent design with faded peeling paint. It reeked of cigarette smoke and grease. The diners looked him over with mild interest. Trying his hardest to act as old as he looked, he ordered breakfast. He was starving. After he had eaten, he mustered his courage and asked the bored-looking waitress where he was. She gave him a funny look, mumbled the name of a place Mike didn't recognize, and said it was two hours northwest of Saskatoon. He asked if Sasktoontown was on the Trans-Canadian.

"It's the Yellowhead Highway that runs through Saskatoon," the waitress said around the wad of gum she was pulverizing in her mouth. "That's what we call the secondary Trans-Canada 'round here."

Michael gulped. "Does this Yellow Highway have a green-and-white maple leaf sign with a number one in the middle?"

"Yer almost right, fella. But the Yellowhead's maple leaf has a 16 in it, not a one. The main Trans-Canada is much further south an' goes through Regina."

Michael felt sick to his stomach and it wasn't the greasy sludge he'd just eaten. His worst fear had been realized: he was lost.

"Where ... where does the Yellow Highway lead, please?" he quavered.

"Well, follow it westward long enough, you'll reach Edmonton in Alberta, then it takes you through the Rockies alla way to Prince Rupert in B.C. on the Pacific Ocean."

Edmonton! She'd said Edmonton! Aloud, Mike said: "So I just haveta go back to Sasktoontown an' then follow the maple leaf with the 16 to Edmonton, right?"

"Right. 'Course, it might be quicker if ya follow Highway 40 west to North Battleford an' pick up the Yellowhead there. Ah, but I hear there's major re-construction of Highway 40 with lotsa traffic delays, so mebbe Saskatoon's yer best bet. Lissen, order's up for Table 15; I gotta dash."

He left the diner and started walking south in the direction the waitress had pointed when she talked about Saskatoon and the Yellowhead Trans-Canada 16 Highway. He decided he would wait until dark, then change into the Angel and fly; Angel's keen eyes could follow the road in the moonlight. If he became the Flash and ran at super-speed, that meant he'd be very hungry after the run, which meant another hit to his limited cash supply.

He trudged along, dejected, in the blazing sun, for over a hour. The afternoon heat was intense: a stifling thick mass that pressed down inexorably. He'd have to find some shade to hole up in soon. Michael sweated profusely and wished he'd thought to buy a bottle of water at the diner.

The land all around him also ached for water. Farmers' fields were full of pale-brown withered crops; copses of trees drooped with shrivelled leaves of palest green or brown curled inwards, leeched of life. Bone-dry stream beds were everywhere. He crossed one bridge over what used to be a wide river; only dust devils flowed down it now.

Desolation. It matched his mood.

A horn honked behind him. Startled, he hastily stepped onto the shoulder of the road as a battered old pickup came up to him. Whatever colour it had originally received at the factory had been replaced by a thick coat of another colour that was all the rage in that region: Prairie Dust. The truck stopped and a middle-aged lady with bright green ayes and a cheery voice called out of the passenger window:

"You lost? Need a lift?"

Michael shook his head forcefully. He'd learned his lesson about accepting rides from strangers.

"You sure? Looks like a dust storm's brewin'. You don't want to be caught outdoors when it hits."

Michael looked and saw the sky to his left had gone an ominous brown. A wind had started. He swallowed hard; *what should I do?*

The man driving the pickup leaned forward so Mike could see his face clearly, and said:

"C'mon, son. Hop in here with us, an' we'll take you into town. Got a bus depot there, you can get yourself a ticket to wherever you're goin'. Be better than sloggin' along this road with that storm comin'. Wind-whipped dirt can peel the skin right off ya."

Mike still hesitated.

"Oh c'mon, dear," said the lady and smiled. "We won't bite you."

Nervous, one hand in his pocket gripping his stone tightly, Michael said "Okay" and climbed into the cab as the woman scootched over closer to the driver. The man put the pickup in gear and they rattled off down the highway.

Mike glanced sideways at the couple. The cheerful woman was small and rotund, with reddish hair invaded by occasional wisps of grey. She had an easy smile, a perky upwards tilt to her head, and eyes that were questing, inquisitive. She reminded Michael of Mrs. Nesbitt three doors down from where he'd lived in Clearwater; she had always been nice to him, unlike other neighbours who either ignored him or, worse, were very condescending because of his disability.

Another sideways glance, this time at the middle-aged driver, and Mike saw that the man was her direct opposite: tall, thin, almost bald, severe face with leathered skin from a lifetime of outdoor work, deep-set gloomy eyes and a downturned mouth to match. He reminded Mike of Eeyore, the pessimistic donkey from *Winnie The Pooh*.

The woman noticed Mike looking at them and said: "My name's Meredith Birski and this is my husband Jesse. We own a farm near here. What's your name, dear?"

"Michael Johnson, ma'am."

"Travelling alone?"

Mike nodded, nervousness increasing.

"Well good gosh, what're you doing way out here?"

"Ah ... um ... took the wrong bus. Now I'm losted. Need to get back to the Yellow Trans-Canadian in Sasktoontown, an' follow it west."

"Really? Saskatoon? Why, that's hours away by car," said Jesse. "Were you figurin' on just walkin' there, son?"

"Uh, sorta."

Jesse snorted and Meredith laughed, saying:

"Well, not today you won't, dear. That dust storm'll hit soon, and you won't be able to see your hand in front of your face, much less walk anywhere. And you'd hardly be able to breathe, to say nothing of what'd happen to your eyes and skin. You'd be in a terrible pickle."

She looked at Jesse and an unspoken agreement passed between them. She said: "Michael, why don't you come home with us? We'll put you up for the night, then tomorrow, when the storm's gone, we'll drive you into town an' put you on a bus."

Mike looked out the window at the approaching wall of brown sky. Over the chuckling of the truck engine, the wind was now a keening wail. He swallowed and nodded:

"Okay. Thank you."

"Wonderful! It's settled, then," said Meredith. Jesse muttered something about picking up another stray, but his wife shushed him.

"Excuse me, but where exactly are we?" asked Mike. "Like I said, I'm kinda losted."

"Why, we're near the little town of Albatross Narrows, dear," said Meredith.

"Yep, if there's such a thing as a thriving centre in Saskatchewan, this place is the farthest from it," added Jesse gloomily.

Michael frowned, sucked a knuckle, then said: "But ... but this part of Canada is miles an' miles from the sea. I know this 'cause I lookeded at a map. So why is your town called Albatross Narrows? An albatross is a big sea bird."

Meredith laughed. "Oh, that's a story! Early European explorers that passed through this area, thought they would soon reach the Pacific Ocean - hah! as if! - and they saw some big birds circling in the distance which, to their sun-baked eyes, looked like albatross. The explorers were following a river that got very narrow near where the town is today; so they named it Albatross Narrows."

"Huh. Well, it's still a funny name for a town that's nowhere near the ocean."

"A-yep. Funny town, too."

By the time the old truck shuddered down a dusty track masquerading as a road and turned into the Birski farm, Meredith and Jesse had found out that Michael was 17, travelling from Clearwater, Ontario all the way to Alberta to find a mother whom he'd never seen, that it was his first time travelling by himself and he really didn't like it, and that he missed his friends and comic books terribly. As Mike gaped at the scenery outside the window, the couple exchanged glances.

The farmstead was modest: a small house, adjacent barn, several livestock pens with pigs and chickens lethargic in the heat, tractor of the same vintage and colour as the pickup truck, all surrounded by fields of plant life gasping for water. The farmhouse was in good repair, but careworn, in need of fresh paint.

The pickup wheezed to a stop in a cloud of dust. As its occupants exited, an energetic Golden Retriever bounded up, barking a welcome. Michael drew back timidly as the big dog checked him out.

"Oh, don't mind him, dear," said Meredith. "That's Lucky an' he's friendly as can be."

"Really?" asked Mike. "Can I pet him?"

"Why sure. He loves attention."

The teen crouched and petted the dog, who thumped his tail vigorously. Lucky licked Michael's face, and the boy shouted with joyful surprise. Then the Birskis herded them inside as the dust storm descended.

Inside the rambling farmhouse, Mike was introduced to the fourth member of the family: Grandpa Kenny. Meredith's father, Kenny was a frail man of 92, now confined to a wheelchair. His body was thin, his skin almost transparent, and an impossibly-narrow neck supported an angular head with a great beak of a nose and strands of pure white hair stubbornly sticking to his scalp. Though his body was infirm, his mind was still sharp and his grey-blue eyes missed nothing. He eyed Mike, cataloguing details, then announced that he seemed like a fine lad and did he perhaps play Monopoly?

"Oh yes, sir," Michael replied. "That's one of my favouritist games!"

"That's good. It's a pleasant surprise to find a youngster nowadays who likes board games. Most kids - an' many adults - are wired into video games, often on the Internet."

"Well, I can play some video games, yes, and I do like them. But I really really like board games better, especially chess an' checkers an' Monopoly."

"That's wonderful to hear, son. We'll play after supper. Probably by candlelight; this storm'll likely knock out the power. Again. You can always count on Saskatchewan Light & Power."

Meredith took the teenager upstairs and settled him into the spare bedroom - it had been their son's room, but he was grown and off working on the other side of the world - then left him to shower and change before dinner. She returned to the kitchen, saying:

"Well, he seems like a nice, well-mannered boy."

"Yep, but he also seems simple. Retarded, like," said Grandpa Kenny.

"Now Dad, nowadays they say intellectual disability or developmentally-delayed."

"Yeah," said Jesse, going to the fridge and extracting a beer. "So then, what's he doing travelling all by himself?"

They all enjoyed a challenging game of Monopoly after dinner, lit by two fat emergency candles. (The old man had predicted accurately; they lost power ten minutes into the game.) The timeless game really broke the ice, and by the end of the game, Michael felt like one of the family. Later, after a huge piece of home-made peach pie and a glass of milk, he went upstairs and fell asleep with a smile on his face, cherishing the crisp sheets, soft pillow and mattress.

The dust storm howled throughout the next day, making travel impossible. Michael insisted on helping out with some chores in the house and in the barn. He also played with Lucky and the house rang with the teen's happy child-like shouts. Growing up, Mike had always wanted a dog, but had never been allowed one. Finally, completely worn out, Lucky escaped to his favourite spot beneath the china cabinet and slept.

Then Mike spent time with Grandpa Kenny. The elderly man called himself "Captain Kenny, RCAF, retired". He had been a fighter pilot in World War Two, where he'd been nicknamed "The Eagle" because of his prominent nose and large premature bald spot. Mike listened with rapt attention to his war tales.

"Well, Dad's found a new audience," chuckled Meredith, assembling a stew in the kitchen.

"Yep," said Jesse, struggling to fix a leaky faucet. "Two of 'em have really hit it off. Lucky's taken to him, too."

The following day dawned clear and bright. But everything outside was covered with inches of dirt, and the wind had peeled off part of the barn roof. While Jesse and Meredith drove into town to buy supplies to repair it, Michael carefully wheeled Grandpa Kenny onto the verandah, which he had broomed clear of dirt beforehand. Then the teen sat cross-legged on the porch deck, with Lucky laying by his side, and listened to more war stories.

Finishing one harrowing tale, the old man leaned back and looked at the sky. He sighed: "Ah, I sure do miss it."

"War?" asked Mike.

"Certainly not, son. War's a terrible thing. Flying. I miss flying. I'd give anything to soar among the clouds again, before I die."

"Oh, you're not gonna die, Captain Kenny, RCAF, retired."

"Son, everybody dies. But flying's something I'd sure like to do again, before my time comes."

"Well, why don't Jesse and Meredith buy you a plane ticket to somewhere?"

"Oh no, I'm not interested in a big cattle-car commercial flight, travelling at over 30,000 feet. That's not flying, least not as far as any self-respecting pilot's concerned. That's just mass-transit. People haulage. No, I'd like to be closer to the ground, in a small agile private plane, travelling wherever the whim takes me."

"Well, why don't they just rent a pirate plane with a pilot for you?"

"Private plane, son. Oh they would if I asked 'em, but I don't want to. An' you better not breathe a word of this to 'em either, young man! The farm is on hard times, Mike. You can see around you that nuthin' is growin'. Last year was bad, an' this year, we haven't had a decent rain in months, so the ground's very dry. So money's very tight; much too tight to waste on a charter flight just to please a silly old man. No, The Eagle is grounded."

Grandpa Kenny had a sudden coughing fit that lasted almost a minute. When it was over, he continued:

"Besides, Meredith an' Jesse have been very good to me in my old age. By rights, they could have stuck me in a retirement home after I had my stroke an' could no longer fend for myself; in fact I insisted they do so, but they flat-out refused. Said I was to move in with them, an' that was that. So I certainly don't want to take advantage of them. That means, Mike, that this wish of mine to fly one last time, stays just between us two. Our special secret. Okay?"

Michael nodded. They watched fluffy white clouds scud across the deep blue sky for a while. Mike's brow was furrowed and he sucked a knuckle. Finally, he said:

"You really really wanna fly again?"

"Oh yes. But remember that's our secret."

"Well, you trusted me with your secret, so can I trust you with mine?"

The old man stared at the boy, then grinned and said: "Sure, kid. You bet."

"Promise?"

"You have my word as an officer."

Mike peeled off his T-shirt. "Okay. Brace yourself; here it is."

Grandpa Kenny saw the boy put his hand in his pocket, then saw his face furrow in intense concentration, then a yellow aura outlined his body, then the old man's world fell apart. He saw a pair of gleaming white wings sprout next to the teen's shoulder blades; small at first, then slowly growing until each was an immense six feet long. Michael's face grimaced in pain throughout this procedure. Lucky took one look at this strange apparition and took off for a refuge under the porch, howling in dismay.

Transformation complete, the Angel stepped off the verandah and flexed his magnificent wings. He rose high in the air and did a perfect loop-the-loop, then descended and hovered about five feet above the ground, wings flapping lazily, the downdraft raising tiny dust-devils. He had a huge Cheshire Cat grin.

"Jesus! What ... what *are* you, boy?"

"Right now I'm the Angel, but I'm also still Michael. Don't worry, Captain Kenny, RCAF, retired."

The Angel touched down and walked up to the elderly war vet. He seemed very light; his feet barely made an impression in the dirt. "So, you still wanna go for a ride?"

"You ... you mean it? With you? Up there?"

"Yep. That's why I'm trusting you with my secret. You really wanna fly again, well, I can make it happen. So let's do it!"

Grandpa Kenny gawped at Mike, speechless.

"Now don't worry, I won't drop you. I'm very strong and I've flown as Angel before. It's awesome! So c'mon, can I give you a ride, sir?"

The old man nodded, still speechless. Mike scooped him up from the wheelchair, holding his frail body effortlessly. He weighed less than Melanie. "Now, you're sure you won't tell anyone about this?"

Grandpa Kenny stared into the Angel's piercing blue eyes, then chuckled. "Hah! You better believe it, son. If I said anything about this, they'd lock me up in the old folks' home for sure, convinced I had senile dementia!"

Michael laughed too, though he had no idea what seasonal demerita was. "Ready?" he asked.

"Let's fly."

The Angel's legs flexed, then he sprang into the air in time with a strong downbeat of his wings. They gained altitude quickly, each powerful beat of the great wings pulling them higher and higher into the mid-morning sky.

The wings *thrummed* and the warm air whistled past their faces as the Angel flew high over the farm, then out over the surrounding countryside. The old Captain gasped with awe and wonder.

"You doing okay, sir?" Mike asked.

"Yes, son. By God, this is amazing! I thought heaven was flying my Spitfire, doing barrel rolls and tight loops and power dives. She was a wonderful kite, very responsive. But this! *This!* It's absolutely amazing!"

Michael laughed, happy that his new friend was enjoying himself. Then he noticed tears on Grandpa Kenny's cheeks.

"Oh! Are you crying, sir?"

The vet swiped a hand across his eyes. "Nah, not at all, young man. It's just the wind against these old eyes, causing 'em to water. That's what it is."

"I'm happy you're happy, sir."

"Thank you. You're a real gem, you know, to do this for me."

"My pleasure."

"So how on earth can you change into a winged man like that?"

"Oh, I can be more than just the Angel. I have a very special stone that lets me become almost any superhero I want."

"Superhero? Like in comic books and movies?"

"Yep. I'm a big fan; I read lotsa comics."

"Huh. Y'know, I used to read comics during the war - 'all in colour for a dime' they used to say - stuff like Superman, Captain America, Green Lantern, Sub-Mariner, Batman, Human Torch, the Flash, Dr. Fate, the All-Winners Squad, the Justice Society.

Man, I can still see 'em clear as day in my mind, as if I just read 'em yesterday."

"Well, those heroes are still around today, Captain. But comics sure don't cost just a dime anymore! No sir, they don't."

They stopped talking then, enjoying the soft sounds of wind and wing as they soared over miles and miles of rural Saskatchewan countryside. The Angel had keen far-seeing eyes, and saw only a few people scattered across the vast landscape, none of whom looked skyward.

The only incident was when a small red and white single-engine Cessna 172 came into view, and Michael banked gracefully and headed for some clouds, to conceal themselves. Grandpa Kenny protested, urging the boy to fly right past the plane, "to make the pilot piss his pants". So Mike did, flashing past the plane and soaring up and away as the pilot, a middle-aged man with bushy salt-and-pepper beard, reacted with open-mouthed shock.

"Haw!" Grandpa Kenny cackled. "You see the look on that guy's face? He can't believe what he just saw! An' no one'll ever believe *him* when he talks about it!"

Mike laughed too, though he worried about exposing himself so openly.

Inside the Cessna, the shaken pilot thumbed his radio transmitter into life. "Ah, Air ... Air Traffic Control, this is Charlie Foxtrot Lima Uniform Bravo. Um, you're not gonna believe what just buzzed me."

The twosome flew to the north, to where the prairies turned into lakes and woodlands. There was evidence of drought here, too, though not as bad as the farmlands. They swooped low over clear lakes, shrunken to half their usual size, and once-frothing rapids now reduced to languorous trickles. Occasional herds of grazing deer scattered in panic as they shot by overhead. They both laughed whenever that happened. Once, they surprised a big bear scrounging for grubs under a log by a lake; the bruin leaped up in shock and jumped into the water with an outraged bellow.

They were airborne for about an hour, before Grandpa Kenny asked Mike to return home. "I'm startin' to get chilly - all this wind on me - and we want to be back before Jesse and Meredith return."

"Yes sir. I'm gettin' tired too."

Dutifully, the Angel swung around and powered back to the Birski farm. They both sighed in relief when they saw the driveway was empty. The boy landed featherlight, and placed the old man gently back in his wheelchair.

"My God, my God, but that was wonderful! I still can't believe it happened," Grandpa Kenny said. "Thank you, Michael, thank you. The Eagle flew again, thanks to an Angel. Heh, heh. You've made an old war vet very, very happy."

"Aw, it was my pleasure. I just wanted to make your secret wish come true. Hey, are you crying again?"

"Nah. It's a speck of dust in my eye this time, that's all. Lotta dust 'round here."

When Jesse and Meredith drove up about 20 minutes later, they found Grandpa Kenny asleep under a blanket in his wheelchair and Mike asleep on the porch swing with Lucky snuggled next to him, also in dreamland.

"Well, doesn't that look sweet?" said Meredith.

"Huh. Must be nice to be able to sleep all day," muttered Jesse.

ം ം ം ೞ ೞ ೞ

The gleaming white Porsche 918 Spyder left Kenora, Ontario, accelerating powerfully down the beckoning Trans-Canada Highway, heading west. The driver touched the hard object in his pocket, and grinned a cold wolfish grin.

"Yeah, you must be usin' your stone, retard boy. Well, you just keep on usin' it; it only leads me right to ya all the easier."

ം ം ം ೞ ೞ ೞ

That evening over dinner, during which Meredith marvelled at how animated and happy her dad was, Jesse remarked that if they didn't get rain soon, the spring crop would be beyond saving, if it wasn't already.

"The land's so dry, even the weeds won't grow. Since a year now, we've only had half the rainfall we useta get. Many farmers an' ranchers across the northern prairies are losin' valuable topsoil. If only we had an irrigation system, like the bigger, richer farms have, drawing from deep wells. But we just can't afford it."

"An immigration system costs a lot?" asked Michael.

"Irrigation, yeah. So we're totally dependent on the weather, an' there hasn't been a decent rainfall in months. But y'know, we wouldn't even need the rains if that ol' river hadn't dried up several years ago; the one that used to go down the middle of our land. We had all the water we wanted; we simply pumped it from the river into the fields."

"What happened to the river?" Mike said.

"Ah, we don't rightly know. It was fed by a big lake far to the north of here - Lake Wakimac it was called, an old Indian name mangled by the European pioneers that meant either 'great for skinnydipping' or 'always full', dependin' who you talked to - anyway, the lake simply dried up. Was a spring-fed lake. Geologists an' such are still arguing about it. Most common theory is that some underground quake shifted something far below, cutting off the spring that filled the lake. An' it must be really deep underground, 'cause a bunch of us farmers pooled our money an' hired well drillers to drill deep down in hopes of findin' the spring again. Went down three hundred feet before we gave up. No water at all."

"Really? So if, like, the spring was founded again, the lake would fill up an' the water would come back into the river?"

"Why sure, but I reckon we'd have to wait for another quake to do that, an' we'll be bankrupt long before, at this rate. Our banker has held off as long as she can, but she can't let us go much longer. Business is business, an' we're way overdue on our mortgage an' our credit line's maxed out an' then some. We lose this year's crop - an' it appears we will - then she'll have no choice but to foreclose an' take away our farm. We can't even sell it to pay off our debts; no one wants to buy land in a dust bowl. Be a bitter pill to swallow, losin' this land; it's been in my family for generations."

"What about government assistance? They usually help out farmers during disastrous times," asked Grandpa Kenny.

Jesse snorted. "Yeah, sure they do, but only after an eternity of talkin' an' arguin'. We've talked about this before, Kenny. Ottawa has announced a multi-billion-dollar federal-provincial farm aid program to provide drought assistance and cash, but here in Saskatchewan, our government is squabblin' with the feds an' haven't signed onta the agreement. They want the feds to pay the whole shot with no provincial funding, 'cause they don't wanna take Saskatchewan inta debt. Time those well-fed politicians get around to actually makin' a decision that helps us farmers, much less gettin' any money into our hands, we'll have been kicked off our land by the bank.

"This drought is just makin' a bad situation worse. It's just not economical to operate a small farm anymore. Each year, more an' more small farmers like us are bein' forced to abandon their land an' move to Regina, or Saskatoon, or inta Alberta to find work. So small-town rural life is dryin' up, just like our land. Local small businesses are closin', schools an' churches are closin', medical facilities, you name it."

"I don't understand all of what you're sayin' Mr. Jesse, but would most of your problems be solved if that river had water again?" said Michael.

"Yep, son, that's right. But it's wishful thinkin'."

Much later, lying in bed after another hours-long Monopoly marathon, Michael thought about Jesse's words. He murmured softly: "These are real nice people, an' they're real nice to me. It's so sad that they'll lose this farm. I gotta do somethin' to help them - but what?"

He went through his mental catalogue of superheroes, once again discarding female heroes, villains, and those with artificial powers or gadgets. Nothing applied in this instance. He reviewed the catalogue again, focussing on lesser-known heroes.

Then it came to him.

He got out of bed, dressed except for his shirt, and slipped outside. Around back of the barn, out of sight of the house, he became the Angel and rejoined the sky. The Angel's keen vision worked very well in the pale light cast by the three-quarter moon. He flew over the Birski land until he spotted what was obviously a dry river bed, then banked and followed the sinuous depression northward.

After a time, he alighted by the shore of a large dry lake bed. It was obvious it hadn't known the touch of water in years.

"Well, I'll fix that," he muttered.

Yellow shone around his body, and the angel's great wings disappeared, to be replaced by an ordinary-looking man. But it wasn't a man at all. While it looked human, its body was a silicon-based life form that could turn itself into sand or stone, phase through earth, glass or bricks, and had the ability to manipulate sand and stone with its mind, even causing earthquakes if it wished. Michael had become the being known as Sand.

The hero concentrated, sending his mind deep into the earth, casting left and right, reading the strata and geologic forces like a sailor reads wind and waves. Sand encountered mineral deposits, a huge pocket of natural gas, a thick strata filled with dinosaur bones, but not a hint of water.

He cast his mind deeper, ever deeper, sifting through the underground layers. Time passed. Finally, he found it, almost 400 feet below the surface: a big underground stream. Now the real work began; he had to free it and send it upwards again. There was incredible geologic pressure and giant rock slabs above the stream, and the rocks stubbornly resisted Sand's attempts to shift them. The hero concentrated until a pounding headache developed, but still the subterranean forces refused to move at his command.

"Wow, that hurts!" exclaimed Michael as he gave up and sat down heavily in the dust of the lake bed, holding his throbbing head. He sat there for some time, moaning. Then he swallowed hard and gritted his teeth. He leaned forward and placed his palms flat against the earth, saying:

"I"m *not* gonna give up. The hero Sand can command stone, and by gosh that's what I'm gonna do. Rocks, you *will* obey me, you hear?"

He sent his mind down again, to the slabs of rock sealing off the underground stream, and *pushed* once more. His temples felt like they would explode. Still he *pushed*. The pounding in his head became white-hot agony. He kept *pushing*. Grey fluid seeped from his nose - it would be blood if he were human - falling in fat drops onto the cracked ground.

Long minutes later, slowly and grudgingly, the geologic pressure lessened just a fraction and the giant rock slabs moved sideways. The stream eagerly found its former channel and started its long journey upwards. Sand stayed with the rising water, removing any small obstacles it encountered on its journey. Finally, with a harsh cough, water started pouring into the lake bed, slowly at first, then in a gush.

"YAY!" Michael shouted, then immediately regretted it as it made his headache worse. "Ow, ow, ow. How can a sandman get a headache anyway? Ow."

Over the next hour, the silicon being sat by the lake bed, nursing his headache and watching the basin slowly fill with cold, clear water. Finally, satisfied that nothing was impeding the flow, and realizing it would take quite some time for the entire lake-bed to refill, he stood up.

"Whew," said Sand. His headache had retreated to a dull throb, but it was manageable, far less than the blinding pain of before. At least now he could concentrate enough to use his stone.

The weary boy exchanged Sand for the Angel and flew back to the Birski farm in a wobbly flight path. While he was happy with what he had accomplished, his overriding urge was to collapse into bed and sleep. Which is exactly what he did, after alighting by his bedroom window, folding his giant white pinons against his back, entering, and flopping face down onto the bed, still dressed, wings and all.

Chapter 20

Oh My Goddess!

Robert Moses Brack was pissed; so angry he could hardly see straight. He'd been stalking two women last night - office worker types, late-twenties, toned bods, snooty attitudes - whom he'd followed as they left a roadside bar 'n' grill near Winnipeg, Manitoba. He had just been getting ready to attack them, when his Gift awoke with a vengeance. He had been *compelled* with an urge so powerful, so insistent, that everything else had to become secondary. Even satisfying his other, older urge, the one that made him do the terrible things he did to women.

His thoughts seethed: *God, those bitches sure deserved it, the way they snubbed me in the bar. As if I was nothin'. As usual. Well, I ain't nothin' no more.* He groaned in frustrated anger; their outfits had been so tight they looked sprayed on and it was quite obvious there was no underwear beneath. *Yeah, they were askin' for it.*

And. He. Had. To. Let. Them. Go.

Damnation!

The retard must've used his stone for a helluva intense time last night, to cause my Gift to react so strong that it forced me to drop everything - NOW - and git back to my journey towards the other half of the stone. Christ!

Brack detested having to suppress his sexual urges.

Just one more reason to hate you, boy. One more reason to do what I plan to do to you next time we meet. And to anyone who's with you.

Well, he was getting close. His Gift felt it. *Won't be long now.*

Brack gave the 887 horsepower engine more gas and the Porsche shot down the highway westward, the morning sun glaring in his rear-view mirrors. He gritted his teeth; woe to any Mountie who had the bad luck to stop him for speeding. He had a lot of frustration to unleash.

※ ※ ※ ※ ※ ※

Ethan Delperdang was frustrated too, but for a different reason. He and Billy had missed Michael Johnson in Brandon, and had failed to pick up his trail anywhere west of that city along the Trans-Canada Highway. Ethan had his chartered jet land at municipal airports at regular distances along the highway, then he and Billy rented a car and scouted around, asking the locals if any unusual things had occurred and showing a picture of Mike on Billy's smartphone, but no Mike. Not a hint. They were now in Regina, Saskatchewan, scouting along the T-Can in diners and gas stations, and still drawing blanks.

"We're never gonna find him," muttered Billy with characteristic pessimism. Ethan didn't know if he should agree with the kid, or heave a shoe at him.

Then they caught a break. Ethan's keyword computer search program picked up a report by a civilian pilot who'd been solo flying his Cessna 172, call letters C-FLUB, northwest of Saskatoon yesterday, who swore he'd been buzzed by a half-naked angel carrying an old man up to heaven. Aviation authorities were currently testing the pilot for drugs, alcohol and mental stability.

Ethan looked at Billy and grinned: "Bingo! We got him! That's gotta be Mike; you told me he turned into this Angel character once back in Clearwater, to give Melanie a ride."

"Yeah!" said Billy, actually becoming excited. "So let's get up there!"

"Up there indeed. For some reason, Mike has left the main T-Can and trekked way north. Strange. Wonder why?"

They hustled the crew to get the Challenger jet refuelled and prepped. Forty minutes later, they took off and headed north. Overflying Saskatoon, the sleek plane continued northwest, toward the area where the civilian pilot reported he'd encountered the angel. Ethan and Billy could hardly sit still, anticipating an imminent end to their search.

Then the Challenger ran into the dense smoke and superheated air of the worst forest fire in years.

ఞ ఞ ఞ ఞ ఞ ఞ

The Birskis never discovered the angel sleeping in their son's old bedroom the next morning, because of The Miracle. Jesse and Meredith were just trudging in from before-breakfast chores, when the phone rang. It was one of their friends north of them, babbling that he had just heard from a friend even further north that ol' dried-up Lake Wackimac was filling with water again for the first time in years. Cold, clear water. The underground spring had returned!

The Birskis couldn't believe their ears.

"My God, Jesse," gasped Meredith. "It's a miracle, a blessed miracle."

"Seems like," allowed Jesse, frowning. "Musta had another underground quake or somethin', last night."

They woke Grandpa Kenny in his ground-floor bedroom and told him the wonderful news. But they didn't disturb Michael. Meredith had tip-toed up to his closed door and listened; she heard loud snoring, guttural, wrenching, sounding like a pack of hogs with strep throats. The boy was obviously exhausted, so she let him be.

After breakfast, Jesse and Meredith drove out to the dry river bed that bisected their land, to see if any water had started flowing down it yet. Jesse was anxious to dust off their pumping equipment so they could take water from the river and irrigate their arid fields. "Mebbe we can still save the crop after all," he mused.

About an hour later, Mike rolled over onto his back - or tried to. A pair of massive wings stopped him. He awoke with a start, shocked to realize that he was still the Angel. He quickly became Michael again, got up, shuffled to the bathroom, then shuffled downstairs.

Grandpa Kenny was in his wheelchair, reading the paper. He greeted Mike cheerily and told him about The Miracle.

"Gee, that's really awesome!" the youth exclaimed. He had a big smile and to the sharp-eyed war vet, it seemed like a very self-satisfied smile. A sudden thought struck him:

"Say there, son. Did you perhaps have anything to do with this miracle? Did you maybe change into some kinda superhero that got us our water back?"

Michael blushed and looked away, becoming very interested in the cereal box on the kitchen table and announcing he was quite hungry.

"Uh-huh," murmured Grandpa Kenny. He watched the youth wolf down two bowls of cereal. Each time Mike caught the old man's eye, he'd smile (causing milk to leak from his lips), blush, then quickly lower his head to concentrate on the bowl again.

Guilty as sin, concluded the former pilot.

Soon after, Jesse and Meredith returned, effervescent with excitement. Mike had never seen Jesse so animated - he was even smiling - and Meredith fairly glowed with happiness.

"There's just the tiniest of trickles coming down that river bed," she said. "But it's slowly getting bigger. By tomorrow, we should have our river back!"

Jesse nodded vigorously. "Yep, this afternoon we'll roust out our irrigation pumps an' make sure they're in workin' order. We'll be needin' 'em tomorrow, for the first time in years!"

The couple hugged each other, then sandwiched Grandpa Kenny in another hug. Before Michael knew it, he became the filling in their next hug sandwich. His first instinct was to flinch as the hug started - hugs had been non-existent at his former home, where physical contact from his adoptive parents usually meant pain - but he resolutely ignored that instinct. He discovered it was a great feeling, being hugged like that.

The teen was overjoyed at seeing his new friends so happy and was bursting with pride that he had been the cause of it. He longed to blurt out his secret to Jesse and Meredith, to tell them all how Sand had restored Lake WackiBigMac. But he stifled himself - with great difficulty - because, after all, secret identities were just that: secret.

After lunch, with Grandpa taking his nap, they trooped outside to see to the pumping equipment. A strong wind had come up and the air was filled with a yellowish haze. Mike sniffed. "Is somethin' burning?"

The Birskis sniffed the air. "B'God, the lad's right. Definite smell of burnin'," opined Jesse. "An' this haze is everywhere, far as the eye can see. It's so thick, you can barely see the woods across our east field."

Meredith went back into the house to listen to the radio, while Jesse and Michael continued into the barn. Minutes later, she ran into the barn, breathless, gasping:

"Forest fire - big one - huge - over 370,000 hectares already - started two nights ago - far to the northeast of here - caused by a lightning strike during a brief thunderstorm - now it's out of control thanks to strong winds - and everything being so dry - fire's being fanned by winds of over 80 kilometres an hour - spreading rapidly - they've evacuated three towns northeast of us already!"

Jesse and Michael, mouths agape, stared at Meredith.

"Radio say anything about our area?" asked Jesse.

"Yes! We're right in the fire's path! And the radio announcer said because the blaze is so huge, the water bombers and choppers with Bambi buckets aren't having much luck controlling the flames! It's a huge wildfire that's completely out of control, burnin' up forests and farms and villages alike!"

"Well, if that don't beat all," muttered Jesse. "We finally get a miracle an' get our river back so we can water our crops, then this fire comes along to burn 'em to the ground!" He walked over to a bucket, kicked it upside-down and sat down on it, hard. Michael just stood, stunned.

"Jesse, this ain't no time to mope. Radio says we gotta evacuate. There's a wall of fire coming at us fast. It'll be here in about an hour!"

Mike found his voice: "Can ... can anything stop this fire?"

"That fire's become a monster; fire crews are pret' near helpless," said Meredith. "Radio says the only thing that could help would be rain: lots of it and soon. But there's no rain forecast at all. We're in a drought."

Jesse stood up. "Well, you're right, Mother. No use talkin' about it, or crying in our cups. You wake your dad an' get him ready. Then pack some clothes for us an' gather some precious keepsakes, like our old photo albums. Mike, fetch your things. I'll set the animals loose, so's they have a fightin' chance to run away. Then let's get the truck loaded an' get out, while we can."

They all ran into the house through the front door. Michael ran right through the house and out the back door. The others were too busy to notice. He sprinted into the middle of the east field and stopped. His heart was pounding and not from his run, but from what he was planning.

The Human Torch could control fire - he had done it to save Nosey Tweedle - but Mike doubted the Torch could control a conflagration as big as this one. And because he doubted, then he would never be able to do it.

So if controlling the fire was impossible, then it had to be quenched. He needed Thor, God of Thunder, but Thor needed his mystic hammer, Mjolnir, to call the storm, and Michael's stone couldn't create artificial objects. There was only one other hero he could think of right away, who had the natural ability to create a big rain storm. But it was a FEMALE.

AAAH! I can't change into a girl! It's just so WRONG! I'm a boy! He pressed his hands to his temples, trying to drown out the clamour in his head. *But I gotta, I gotta! She's the only hope of saving this farm, and everyone else's farm too! I gots NO choice!*

With a stifled sob, the teen gripped his stone. *Wrongwrongwrong! ShutupshutupSHUT UP!*

The yellow aura outlined his body. His skin darkened to a rich chocolate brown, his thick mop of dark brown hair lengthened until it reached down to his shoulder blades and turned a dazzling white, even though the hero was only twentysomething.

Since discovering his wonderful stone, Michael had transformed into many fantastic beings. But this was the most fantastic transformation of all.

This time, he changed genders.

Beneath his clothes, his sculpted muscular body became more rounded, lithe instead of bulky. His breasts grew, becoming two firm mounds pushing against his T-shirt. His waist shrank, becoming the centre of his new body's hourglass shape.

Regal, imposing, Storm of the X-Men drew breath. And immediately coughed in the smoke-filled air.

But Mike didn't care about any of that; he was horrified at what had happened in his crotch.

His hand flew downwards, diving beneath the waistband of his suddenly-too-large jeans. He gave an anguished cry. His Willie had disappeared! Gone! In its place was - nothing! He wailed:

"Where's my junk!?"

His other hand still clutched his stone and the traumatized youth almost willed his body back to Michael again. *No! I can't! I have to put that fire out first!* He gritted his teeth and fought down the panic at the totally alien body he now wore. Then he noticed the constant burning smell blown by the wind had become stronger, more acrid. Mike spun around to face the wind - and almost fell over. His sense of balance had changed; he wasn't used to moving with two large breasts. He looked down: *Ah! I can't even see my feet with Storm's boobies!*

He looked up and realized why the burning smell had gotten worse. In the distance, barely visible through the haze, an awful wall of orange flame danced high above even the tallest trees. Michael quailed. *The fire! It's almost here!* It had obviously moved a lot faster than the radio report had estimated. It was a relentless tidal wave of blast-furnace destruction, pushed by the strong wind and fed by tinder-dry forest and fields. The flames roared their supremacy; a nightmare sound that chilled his blood despite the heat.

There was no time to lose. She had work to do.

The wind blew Storm's snow-white tresses straight out behind

THE HERO STONE

her as she planted her feet firmly and faced the onrushing firewall. The awful *crackle* of burning wood could now be heard, and the yellow haze in the air had been replaced by a dark grey pall.

The tall African-born weather goddess lifted her head to the sky and accessed her mutant ability. Her eyes went completely white as her brown pupils disappeared. She lifted her arms and concentrated. Sweat broke out on her brow, to be whipped away by the wind that was driving the fire straight at her. She continued to focus her awesome power, commanding the elements to do her bidding, ignoring the wind, the *crackle,* the heat, the acrid air.

The fire was approaching the edge of the Birskis' farthest field now. Tendrils of flame snaked out into the withered crops, hungry.

Storm refused to panic, concentrating even harder. The immense effort bathed her in sweat, constricted her breathing, and her heart felt like bursting. The fire, a solid terrible wall of loud superheated destruction, stood poised to charge across the field. Its fire-tendrils slithered closer.

Then the heavens responded. There was a *sha-rakk* of lightning, a *WHABLAMM* of thunder, and it started to rain. Hard. Massive sheets of water. An ark-floating Biblical Deluge.

The weather goddess smiled.

In the midst of frantically loading the truck, the Birskis barely had time to register the horror of the sudden closeness of the fire, before the torrential rain started. Standing frozen at first, they started whooping with joy when they realized what was happening.

In his wheelchair on the verandah, peering through the watery veil, Grandpa Kenny squinted. He could barely see the lone figure in the middle of the east field, standing with arms outstretched and hair - white hair! - blowing wildly. *Damn, but it looks like a woman's out there,* he thought, then shook his head. *Rain's playing tricks with my old eyes. That's gotta be it. It's the boy who's out there; one helluva brave boy.*

The white-haired young woman kept the rain sheeting down: a wall of water that warred with the wall of fire for supremacy. The conflagration roared and hissed its defiance at this brazen attempt to extinguish it; the rain fell all the harder. Storm increased her already-intense concentration and expanded her weather system eastward and northward, until it covered tens of thousands of hectares. She was trying to douse the entire fire that raged across northern Saskatchewan.

With the rains extended to the absolute limit of her mutant ability, she could lessen her concentration and take a breather as the deluge continued. *Whew, that took a lot out of me!* Michael thought and put a hand to his chest - and snatched it away immediately at the strange feeling of Storm's breasts, covered only by the thin wet T-shirt. *Yuck!*

Mike noticed the Birskis talking with Grandpa Kenny on the verandah, and the three of them trying to see him - her - through the downpour. *Uh-oh! That won't do!* Storm concentrated again, mentally commanding the wind currents. She was lifted gently off the ground and carried above a grove of trees a half-mile away where no-one would see her.

The master of the tempest sent her mind back into the rain storm, surfing the system, checking this, adjusting that, to ensure that the heavenly Niagara would continue for several hours. *That oughta kill the forest fire!*

Satisfied, she bade the winds to gently lower her to the ground, where she slumped against a tree. She was exhausted; creating that weather system had taxed her power to the utmost. As her breathing returned to normal, she became aware of an urgent need to pee.

Michael stepped back from the tree, and turned to face it as he unzipped his pants. Absently following a habit ingrained by 17 years of maleness, he reached in to grab his Willy, found nothing to grab, and suddenly remembered his plumbing had changed. He groaned. *I can't pee like this! I gotta pee like a girl now!*

He had no idea how girls peed, especially in the woods.

And decided he really didn't want to find out.

Storm mentally checked her weather system one last time. Then woman became man. *Whoa! I'm never EVER becoming a GIRL again.* Michael took hold of his Willie with relief, and urinated with even greater relief.

During the long slog back to the farmhouse in the rain, Mike checked his crotch several times. Just to be sure he was still a he.

Chapter 21

Comes a Killer

Ethan and Billy were so anxious, they sat on the edge of their seats as their rental car sped towards Albatross Narrows. *Thank God he's been renting decent cars since this trip started,* thought Billy. They stared eagerly ahead - as if doing so would pull their destination closer to them by force of will - as Ethan drove at precisely the speed limit - maddeningly slow to them, but they'd been warned about the Mounties' zero-tolerance for speeding out here. It was galling that the only direct route to the town was along secondary highways and country roads, full of undulations and blind corners. Each bend they came around, they held their breath, hoping to see their journey's end, though the logical part of their brain insisted they must be only half-way.

The forest fire had forced their Challenger jet to turn back to Saskatoon. They arrived in late afternoon. On landing, Ethan had grabbed a rented car and they started driving northwest to Albatross Narrows. Ethan fretted about whether they'd be able to argue their way past the inevitable road blocks, which were always set up to keep people away from a fire zone. He needn't have worried.

They drove right into a massive downpour. The rain was so intense, they were forced to reduce speed to almost a crawl; sheets of water prevented them from seeing much past the front of their car.

"Yeesh! What rain! Hey, you think this is Mike's doing?" asked Ethan. "It's just what's needed to douse that huge forest fire this whole state - er - province is talkin' about."

"Dunno. Could be, I guess, but I don't see how," Billy replied.

"Turning into Thor wouldn't help him, 'cause he can't create the guy's hammer which he uses to summon storms. An' he'd never become Storm, the X-Men's African weather goddess, 'cause he can't turn into women."

"Can't or won't?"

"Won't. Definitely won't. The thought of turning into a female totally freaks him out."

"Hah! That'd freak out most males, Billy me lad. Though there's some that'd find it right kinky."

They had just passed a sign informing them that Albatross Narrows was still all of 230 kilometres away, when a white Porsche shot by their slow-moving car, disappearing into the grey downpour as quickly as it had appeared.

"Damn fool!" exclaimed Ethan. "Going way too fast for these conditions! He'll end up in a ditch somewhere."

"Hope so. He deserves it, whoever he is," groused Billy.

Ethan shot him a glance. "Compassion, me lad. Let's have some compassion. That driver is a fellow human being."

"Humpf."

୨୦ ୨୦ ୨୦ ୧୧ ୧୧ ୧୧

Michael awoke with a start. His stone, which he always kept under his pillow while he slept, was humming to him. His hand found it and discovered it was very warm.

Now when have I felt it like that before?

He sat bolt upright, stifling a cry. In Clearwater! As he had pedalled from the lake to his house! Then the stone had become quite hot when he raced up the stairs to his pretend-parents' bedroom - just before the Nastyman had attacked him.

It meant the Nastyman was getting close! He had to leave! Now!

Mike remembered vividly what the Nastyman had done to him and to those around him. Poor Melanie would still have her leg and his pretend-parents would still be alive.

I gotta get out of here so the Nastyman won't find me with these nice farmer people! I don't want them hurted!

He swung out of bed and squinted at the glowing numbers of the clock-radio on the night stand: 4:20 a.m. He hurriedly dressed and packed his few possessions into his knapsack. In mounting panic, he eased out of his room and silently descended the stairs, sucking a knuckle as he started thinking about what hero he could turn into to get away quickly.

"Well, well, well. Going somewhere?"

Michael froze at the bottom of the stairs, heart pounding. Faint moonlight fell on him from the foyer window. He gripped his stone so fiercely that it bit into his palm. The voice had come out of the curtained blackness of the living room.

"Yes, I see you," said the voice. It sounded closer.

There was a soft rubbing sound, coming right toward him. Mike tensed, not breathing, wondering whether he should flee or fight.

The rubbing sound was now almost upon him!

AAAH! He's here! The Nastyman! What do I DO? his brain screamed. He sucked the knuckle savagely.

A few feet from where Michael crouched, Grandpa Kenny wheeled into the pale moonlight.

Mike's lungs *whooshed* in relief. "Oh! It's just you, Captain Kenny, RCAF, retired!"

"Yep, just me. Couldn't sleep either. Didn't mean to scare ya, son."

"Well, you sure did! I thought you were the Nastyman!"

"Eh? Who's the Nastyman?"

"A very evil person who's trying to take my stone away from me. He has a stone too, just like mine. In fact, his stone was broken off from mine an' he wants to get the two halves together again. My stone woked me up - it's getting real warm an' that means the Nastyman is almost here. So I gotta get away before he arrives 'cause I don't want him to hurt you people. He can turn into horrible things. He killeded both my pretend-parents an' he bit poor Melanie's leg an' inflicted it so bad that the doctors hadda cut it off!"

The old man looked closely at the teen, then nodded. "Okay, I

THE HERO STONE

believe you. It's not a bad dream that's got you imagining things. You're damn scared and dead serious. Look, let's wake Jesse an' Meredith up - they'd be rising soon for chores anyway - an' get ready to face down this thug. Jesse's got a shotgun an' Meredith's got a revolver she uses for target shooting an' scaring off Jehovah's Witnesses who come calling. We'll also ring up the local RCMP detachment, an' have 'em send some officers right over."

Michael shook his head vigorously. "No, no, no! Won't work! Not against the Nastyman. The creatures he can turn into are much too powerful. He'll kill Jesse an' Meredith an' you an' the policemen real easy. I'm the only one who stands a chance against him 'cause of my stone - I did beat him the first time we fought, but just barely - but I'm worried that he'll kill you folks during our fight. So it's bestest if I just get away from here so he'll follow me an' leave all of you alone."

"Now see here, young man. We're not about to let you face this freak by yourself. We're gonna stand by you. Besides it bein' the right thing to do, it's also the least we can do considerin' all you done for us. An' you know what I mean: I'm talkin' about the river an' the rain storm."

"No, no, NO!" Mike was hopping from foot to foot in great agitation. His eyes looked all around him wildly, as if he expected his nemesis to pop out of the shadows at any second. "You guys will get killeded! I know what the Nastyman can do! I've fought him, I've seen him kill, as quick an' easy as you please! Bullets won't work against him! To save you, I gotta go! Now! It's the only way!"

Grandpa Kenny regarded the upset youth, then sighed. "Okay, son. If that's the way it's gotta be, though I still think we should stand our ground. You don't fight a bully by running away. We didn't treat the Jerries that way in World War Two. But it appears this ain't no ordinary bully. So I'll get Jesse an' Meredith to drive you into town pronto. There's a bus leaving for Edmonton, Alberta at 5:30, about an hour from now. We looked up the bus schedule couple days ago, when you first arrived. From Edmonton, you can get a bus to this 'Fred MacMurray' of yours. That oughta shake him from your trail."

Greatly relieved, Michael said "thank you," though he still looked as nervous as a politician facing a lie detector test.

The Birskis were awakened. Without mentioning Michael's stone or what he could do, Grandpa Kenny soon convinced them that the teen had to leave immediately to catch the 5:30 interprovincial bus, that it was an emergency, and that all their questions would be answered later. The couple looked at each other, then at Michael, in shocked surprise, then saw that the war vet had a firm set to his jaw and his eyes glittered with resolve. Jesse, normally inclined to complain about any disruption to his routine, stifled his questions. Meredith had her fearsome "there's no way this is gonna happen" look, but her fortitude vanished when she saw the determined mien of her father; she knew better than to argue with him when he was like that.

Soon after, Mike found himself sitting to the right of Jesse and Meredith in their battered old pickup as it swayed and thumped and splashed towards town along the rutted road half-drowned with numerous puddles from yesterday's deluge. No-one spoke. Mike had an enormous sub sandwich crammed into his knapsack, made with lightning speed by Meredith before they left.

Michael had had an emotional leave-taking of Captain Kenny, RCAF, retired. His cheek was still wet with his tears, and the old man had got something caught in his eye again. But he had given Mike a firm handshake, saying in a low voice: "A million thanks for everything you done, son. I'll never forget it. Especially that flight."

Lucky, their Golden Retriever, had also seemed sad to see Mike go. The dog hadn't had so much exercise in years, since the teen's arrival.

They reached the bus depot at Albatross Narrows, located in the town's sole restaurant and convenience store. Jesse bought Michael a ticket to Fort McMurray, by way of Edmonton. He carefully explained:

"Now Mike, you have to change buses at the main terminal in Edmonton. There's no bus that goes direct from here to Fort

McMurray. So when you get to Edmonton, you ask the driver to show you where you get the Fort McMurray bus, then you get on it an' show them your ticket." He repeated the instructions, making sure Mike comprehended.

"Okay," said Mike. The enormity of what was about to happen suddenly hit him: he'd be leaving - perhaps forever - this couple who'd been so kind to him, kinder than his pretend-parents had ever been. *I don't wanna go, but I gotta! I don't want them hurted by the Nastyman!* He choked out: "Thanks for everything. I'm ... I'm really gonna miss all of ya."

"Oh, we'll miss you too, son," Meredith said and tears suddenly coursed down her cheeks. She gave Michael a fierce hug, with a strength belying her diminutive stature. She planted a very wet kiss on his cheek, then released him, saying:

"Look, Michael, Jesse an' I have been talkin'. If ... if things don't work out in Fort McMurray, an' if you don't want to return to Clearwater, you're very welcome to come live with us," she said in a voice heavy with emotion. "You'll always have a place with us."

"Really?" gasped Mike.

"Really." That was Jesse, and he stuck out a big callused hand that gripped Mike's strongly. "I dunno how, but I have a powerful feeling that you had something to do with our river returning an' even yesterday's rain that snuffed the wildfire. Our luck turned around the day we brung ya home. Even Grandpa Kenny says you're a very special lad."

The teen blushed and stammered his thanks.

A garbled announcement, sounding like a drunken auctioneer, came over the speakers and Meredith said Mike's bus was arriving and he had to go. The two farmers sandwiched Michael in a monster hug, then watched him board the mud-splattered motor coach.

"Thanks again for everything!" Mike called out as he disappeared inside the big Greyhound.

The Birskis watched as the bus pulled out and rumbled off into the pre-dawn gloom, resuming its westward journey. And just like that, Michael Johnson was gone.

"Oh, I do hope he finds what he's looking for in Fort McMurray an' that it works out for him," said Meredith, crying again. "He deserves it. He's such a nice boy."

"A-yep," murmured Jesse. "An' a very unusual boy, too, judging by the hints your dad's been dropping. Very unusual."

ço ço ço ço ço ço

Twenty minutes later, the Birskis pulled into their yard to the sounds of Lucky's raucous welcome. Emotionally weary, Meredith still snuffling, they trooped into the kitchen for breakfast, the big dog leading the way.

On the narrow dirt road that passed the entrance to the Birski farm, a mud-camouflaged Porsche stopped. The driver read the faded name on the battered tin mailbox standing crookedly at the start of the rutted laneway: Birski.

"Ready or not, here I come," said the driver in a voice colder than a banker foreclosing a widow's mortgage.

The formerly-white Porsche 918 Spyder swung onto the rutted track and drove towards the cluster of farm buildings in the distance. Many times, the car's low undercarriage scraped the ground, thanks to the deep ruts. More mud, a byproduct of yesterday's downpour, spewed onto the car. The driver didn't care. He was smiling broadly.

There was no warmth in that smile at all.

Chapter 22

Communion

Michael's bus ride was tiring and seemingly endless. After awhile, vistas of prairie and forest, no matter how beautiful, became identical; a scenic rotoscope playing by his window. But he admitted sitting in an air-conditioned motor coach was far better than riding in the back of moving vans or frozen meat delivery trucks.

Those poor farmer people were real nice to buy me this bus ticket, he thought. Then sadness welled up inside him as he remembered he probably would never see them again. *Well, at least I saved them from the Nastyman.*

He had no illusions that he'd permanently given his nemesis the slip. He knew that somehow the Nastyman's half of the stone drew him irresistibly to his own half. All he'd done was delay the inevitable conflict that must occur when they finally met again.

So maybe I should just get off this bus an' wait for him in a big empty field somewhere. Then there'd be no danger of anyone else getting hurted when we fight.

Sucking his knuckle, Mike thought a lot about that as the miles rolled by, and finally decided that he really wanted to find his real mom first. *I'll just haveta make sure I stay far enough ahead of the Nastyman, that's all.*

The long trip passed mostly without incident. Two young women travelling together, then one older man travelling alone, had expressed a lot of curiosity about his body, marvelling at how "buff" he was, whatever that meant. But after talking with him for awhile, they had lost interest and left him alone.

Michael found himself nodding off for long stretches of

highway.

He was real proud of himself about one thing on this bus trip: At the main terminal in Edmonton, he had carefully followed his bus driver's directions and successfully navigated through the crowds and confusion to the motor coach bound for Fort McMurray.

And his stone was still only slightly warm, its usual temperature. So the Nastyman was far behind him. For now.

An announcement over the coach's PA system awoke him from another nap. They were entering Fred MacMurray! Mike hastily rubbed sleep from his eyes and stared eagerly out the window. He saw a billboard proclaiming this was the home of the Athabasca Oil Sands and urging tourists to visit the award-winning Oil Sands Discovery Centre. He frowned; he couldn't imagine why any place would brag about having oily sand. Another sign stated that the Oil Sands contained more oil than all the known reserves in the Middle East and currently produced two million barrels daily.

The bus disgorged its passengers into the terminal, where most of them were met by relatives or friends. The air rang with cheerful shouts and greetings; there were lots of hugs and kisses. Michael stood to one side near a wall, alone.

So here I am, I made it!

His elation at having successfully completed his cross-Canada journey all by himself suddenly vanished, replaced by a great loneliness. And something else: confusion.

Now what?

He realized he had no idea how to go about finding his mom. He didn't even know her last name! All his energy and thought had been devoted to surviving the challenges of the road and reaching this place.

Now what?

Nobody was watching him, but he knew he couldn't stand there forever before a grown-up approached him and asked if he was lost, or needed help, or something. He had to get going.

But where?

He started sucking a knuckle. He considered going to the police and asking them to find the woman he knew as "Aunt

Julia". After all, how many Julias could there be in this town? He had always been told by his teachers and the McDonnells that the police were his friends if he ever needed help. But then he remembered his experience with the Clearwater police: not only had they not believed his story, but they had put him in jail and taken his precious stone away. And that delay had cost Melanie her left leg.

No, not the police.

What about teachers? They had always been kind and helpful to him. Why couldn't he just find a school and go inside and ask a teacher to help him find "Aunt Julia"? They knew all about computers an' stuff, just like Billy and Melanie. Surely computers could find his real mom. Computers could do anything.

No, I can't just walk into a strange school. They'd get too superstitious about me. Would probably call the police. Same thing would happen if I walked into the local Community Living office.

Michael's frustration grew. To trek clear across the country, to have all those adventures (some of them quite scary), to finally make it here - and now to be stuck!

Oh, this is stupid, stupid, stupid! Why can't I think clearly?

The big teen decided to go outside, find a park, and sit on a bench or under a tree. He shouldered his knapsack and headed for the door. He had to think this out. Maybe there was some superhero he could become, who could figure out a solution.

Yeah, Reed Richards of the Fantastic Four, or Tony Stark who is Iron Man, are two of the smartest heroes in the Marvel Universe. Or what about Bruce Wayne - Batman - the world's greatest detective in the DC Universe? Batman could find out anything.

With a heavy sigh, Michael discounted all three heroes. He knew that whomever he became, however much his body changed, his mind would still be the same. While he'd look like Reed Richards or Tony Stark or Bruce Wayne, he'd be no smarter than Michael Johnson.

Phooey!

A heavy hand grabbed his shoulder and a voice boomed in his ear: "GOTCHA!"

Without benefit of any superpowers whatsoever, and sloughing off the hand holding him, Michael jumped three feet in the air. Straight up.

"WHAAAH!" he screeched.

Michael knew that Alberta had grizzly bears. But he was sure they did not frequent bus terminals. So he was further surprised when he returned to earth and was immediately grabbed in a mighty hug by what could only be a grizzly.

Except this grizzly talked.

"MIKE! Mike, Mike, Mike! Oh wow, we found you at last, buddy!"

It was Billy McDonnell, his best pal, all the way out here!

"Billy? Oh, Billy! Geez, what are *you* doing here!"

"Finding you, ya big lug! We've been chasing you all across Canada."

"You *have*? But ... but why?"

"To help you find your mom, an' to help you in case Brack attacked you again."

"Who's Brack?"

"Oh, you call him the Nastyman. Robert Moses Brack, a real evil piece of crap."

"With a power stone just like yours, Michael. Except he uses his to do awful things," said Ethan Delperdang, stepping out from behind Billy.

"Who are you, mister?" asked Mike, drawing back. "An' how do you know about the special stones? Billy! Did you tell? It was supposed to be *secret*." Unconsciously, his hand slipped into his right pants pocket and touched his stone.

Ethan noticed the movement, then put on a big grin and stuck out his hand. "Ethan Delperdang, traveller from New Zealand, computer genius and expert on stones of wonderment, at your service, Michael Johnson. And I knew all about the stone before I even met your friend Billy."

"It's okay, Mike. He's a friend. He's here to help you," said

Billy. "He arranged an' paid for both of us to travel across Canada searching for you."

Hesitantly, Mike shook Ethan's hand, saying: "I don't wanna be rude, but are you okay, mister? You're ... you're so *thin*. Like a scarecrow."

Ethan laughed. "Well, I've been called worse. I'm fine and, yep, I'm thin. An' you look like an over-muscled Olympic weightlifter an' Billy looks quite chubby. So what? As long as life is good an' we're happy, who cares what we look like? An' if other people have a problem with it, well, that's their problem, isn't it?"

Billy and Michael looked at the thin man, then Billy said: "Right on! As my Dad's fond of saying."

Mike had a million questions, but Ethan forestalled them by announcing: "I'm starving! An' I bet you guys are too. Mike, I've got a rental car outside, so let's get outta here an' find a Denny's or something, okay?"

The boys nodded agreement. As they trooped out, Ethan said: "Of course, I read up on Fort McMurrray on the 'Net as we flew in. This place has the world's largest mining machines, y'know. The scoops on the power shovels are as big as a two-car garage. They have the world's largest trucks here too - the Caterpillar 797 - with 12-foot wheels that haul loads up to 400 tons. So let's see if they have the world's largest breakfasts to match!"

They piled into the car, and went in search of a restaurant.

Over a huge breakfast that completely met Ethan's approval, stories were exchanged. Mike told of his experiences on the road, to the amazement of Billy and Ethan. Billy outlined what he and Ethan had gone through, trying to find him. Ethan gave his background (the parts he was willing to share, anyway), and updated Mike on what the police had discovered about the murderous sexual predator, Brack.

Michael shook his head when Ethan had finished talking about Brack, and said: "Geez, he really is the Nastyman."

"You better believe it, bud," said Ethan, helping himself to another order of flapjacks smothered in maple syrup. The teens watched him in astonishment; the thin man ate more than Mike and Billy put together.

"But, how'd you know how to find me at the bus terminal here?" asked Michael.

"Well, when we finally got to Albatross Narrows, we stopped at the restaurant an' convenience store which, happily, was also the bus depot. When we gave the store clerk your description, she remembered selling a ticket to a local farmer named Jesse Birski, who she then saw give the ticket to you. She also saw you get a group hug from Jesse an' his wife Meredith, before boarding the bus. She told us the final destination and arrival date on your ticket, so we simply flew here an' waited for you to show up."

"Yeah, the farmer people were super-nice to me," said Michael. "But I had to leave them real fast 'cause my stone heated up, which meant the Nastyman was getting near. I didn't want them to get hurted. But I sure miss them. Hey! Didja call 'em or drive out to see 'em?"

"We tried calling them," said Ethan. "But their phone just rang an' rang. Guess they musta been out in the fields or barn, doin' farmer stuff."

Mike frowned. "Yeah, maybe. But Captain Kenny, RCAF, retired - he lives with them - should have answered. He's in a wheelchair, so he doesn't leave the house much."

"Well, nobody answered. Which was too bad, 'cause we wanted to ask them about how you were," said Billy. "They don't have a cell phone?"

"No, just a regular land line phone, like in olden days," said Michael. "Mister Jesse doesn't believe in cell phones; calls 'em a nuisance."

"Oh. Anyway, we didn't want to take the time to drive all the way out to their farm; we wanted to meet your bus at this terminal so we wouldn't miss you again."

Michael shifted uneasily in his chair. "Oh, I sure hope the Nastyman didn't go there. Geez, suppose he did?"

"I'm sure the Birskis are fine," said Ethan. "But if it'll ease your mind, I'll access the local paper an' police blotter later with my laptop, an' see if anything's amiss."

"Thank you. Oh, I sure hope they're okay," Mike fretted.

"Don't worry. Now listen, what about what you came all this way to do?" asked Ethan. "What about your mother?"

Mike shrugged helplessly, looking like he was about to cry. "I dunno how to find her in this place. I only know her first name: Aunt Julia."

"Don't worry about that," said Billy excitedly. "Ethan here found out all about her: last name an' current address an' everything! After all these years, she's still here!"

With eyes big as saucers and elation building inside him, Mike looked at the scarecrow. "Really, Mister Ethan? For true?"

Ethan nodded. "We can drive over there right now, if you wish. She's prolly home 'cause it's a Saturday."

"LET'S!"

Twenty minutes later, they pulled up to a small clapboard house in a neighbourhood of identical small clapboard houses, each with its own tidy little front lawn. The house seemed to be in good repair, with a pleasing coat of white paint and red shutters. A big pale-blue Crown Victoria sedan, almost 30 years old but still in good shape, dominated the narrow driveway; the huge boat of a car seeming out of place next to the small house.

"Huh," murmured Ethan. "I read that housing's super-expensive up here, 'cause of the oil boom. Costs a fortune just to rent a small bedroom in a shared mobile home. So this modest l'il house must be worth a bundle."

As they mounted the porch, Ethan noticed Michael sweating and his eyes twitching slightly.

"Nervous, kid?" the scarecrow asked.

Mike nodded. "Very."

"Well, relax. You'll be fine." He gave Michael a sudden hug. "Just lemme do the talking."

Billy rang the bell. Long minutes passed. Michael hopped from one foot to the other in nervous excitement. Then the solid inner door opened and a small rotund woman in her late fifties stood there, staring at them through the closed screen door. Barely five feet in height, she had a round moon face, narrow mouth which seemed disposed to turn downwards at the edges, and a handsome pair of double chins. Carefully-coiffed steel-grey hair framed her face.

"Yes?" she asked, making no move to open the screen door. "Can I help you?"

Ethan cleared his throat: "You are Julia Chartrand, formerly Mrs. Julia Gilmour?"

"Why?" answered the woman suspiciously. "Who's askin'?"

"Oh, don't worry, we're not cops or lawyers or anything like that. Seventeen years ago, did you give birth to an intellectually-disabled son and then gave him up for adoption when he was three years old?"

The woman grimaced. "Intellectually-disabled. Is that what they're calling it now? No, that ... that was my sister. Wasn't me."

"Your sister?"

"What I said."

"Well, where can we find her?"

"You ... can't. She's dead."

"Dead? How, when?"

"Ah, hit by a truck. Almost eight years ago now."

'Oh, that's awful!" said Billy.

"Yep. She was drivin' home late one night an' the driver of the truck was drunk," said the woman. "Listen, just who the hell are you people, anyway?"

Ethan ignored her question. Clearing his throat, he said: "Now see here ma'am, pardon my language, but I think you're jerking us around. I've checked the adoption records with my computer, and they state that Michael Johnson's birth mother was called Julia Gilmour, nee Chartrand."

"Yep. My sister, God rest her."

"But my computer search showed Julia Chartrand as currently livin' here an' payin' taxes at this address. *You're Julia Chartrand!*"

"I am now. I took my sister's name. Not that it's any of your business whatsoever, I went through a nasty divorce some years back. My rat of a husband was very abusive, so after my divorce, well, I assumed my late sister's identity so he wouldn't be able to track me down."

"And it was your sister who gave her son up for adoption, after her own divorce?"

"Yep."

"Why?"

"Well, he was retarded, wasn't he?"

"Intellectually-disabled, yes, but that's no reason to shunt him aside."

"Was all the reason in the world, as she saw it. I certainly agreed. Who wants to raise some dumb retard? Shoulda been put down like a dog - we treat our damaged pets better, y'know. When pets are born crippled or come down with cancer, we put 'em right outta their misery. That kid wouldn't ever have amounted to anything 'cept bein' a drain on her, pullin' her down, keepin' her from doing what she wanted in life."

For the first time, Mike spoke: "I am *not* dumb an' I am *not* a dog! I am Michael an' I am a *person.*"

The woman stared at Mike and a strange emotion flickered across her face. Then it became impassive once more. She said: "Well, well. So that's him? The retard my sister gave up?"

"Yes, this is my friend and he is 17 years old and I'd appreciate it if you stopped calling him a retard," said Billy icily.

"It's what he is, ain't it? Well anyway, why are you here?"

"He is looking for his birth mother."

"Why?"

Mike blurted out: "So she can love me like a real mommy should!"

The woman barked a short laugh. "Not bloody likely, kid. You're damaged goods. My sister, God rest her, wanted a normal child. Can't blame her."

"God, that's cold," said Ethan. "And so are you."

"So sue me. Now you tell me how you found out about his real mother. I thought adoption records were sealed."

"They are. I unsealed 'em."

"Well, that seems to me to be against the law. Maybe I should report you to the RCMP, eh?"

"You can try, lady. For now, though, you can tell us where your sister's buried, so Michael here can pay his respects an' get some kind of closure."

"Ah, she wasn't buried. Was cremated."

"Then where's her urn being kept?"

"Uh, no urn. She wanted her ashes scattered over her backyard garden, so that's what I did. She loved that garden, 'cept for the damn squirrels that always dug holes an' ate up her corn an'such."

"Huh. Well, where was her backyard, where'd she live? We'll go there."

"Oh, house is gone. It's a shopping mall now."

"So this is a complete dead end," said Billy, reverting back to his characteristic gloominess. "Poor Mike came right across Canada all by himself for nothin'. Figures."

Mike looked like he was about to cry.

"Yep, complete dead end, kid," the woman muttered. "That door shut years ago."

"C'mon, boys, let's get outta here," said Ethan in disgust, adding sarcastically: "Thanks for all your help, ma'am."

The woman snorted and slammed the inner door.

They returned to the car in a daze. Michael sat numb all the way back to the motel where Ethan and Billy were staying.

"Sorry, buddy," said Billy during the drive, putting his arm around Mike's broad shoulders. "I know how much you were lookin' forward to findin' her, but she's long dead."

His words only made Mike look sadder.

"Now look, Mike. You still have folks that love you, that care about you. There's me an' my parents an' even this Birski family, from what you told us. So c'mon. It's not all that bad; you're not alone."

"Oh, you're right, Billy," said the big teen. "It's just that you an' Melanie have real parents that love you, an' I don't. And, well, ah, I really really wanted to get to know my real mommy an' ask her why she gave me up for adaptation."

"Adoption," said Billy. "Well, what can I say, buddy? Life is unfair."

"Got that right," muttered Ethan. "I been around long enough to know."

Ethan had rented two adjoining rooms at the motel. The boys went into one room, Mike still morose, while Ethan disappeared into the other. He connected his laptop to the room's dataport, booted it up, cracked his skeletal fingers and sat down. He bent over the keyboard, long bony fingers flying over the keys. He accessed death records, and found no record of a Julia Chartrand within the age parameters of Mike's mother, in any province in Canada.

"Strange," he murmured. On a hunch, he accessed a genealogical database. Long minutes passed. Then he swore, jerked to his feet, switched off his laptop, and stormed out of the room.

"Going out for a bit," he hollered at the boys through their closed door. "Stay put; I'll be back soon." There was no sound of acknowledgement from inside the boys' room.

Twenty minutes later, he was banging on the screen door of the small clapboard house again. The rotund grey-haired woman opened the inner door, and scowled when she saw that a scarecrow had planted itself on her stoop once more.

"Thought you was gone for good," she growled.

"Thought you were telling the truth," Ethan growled back. "I checked. Your parents, the Chartrands, had three kids: a boy an' two girls. The oldest girl was named Ruth an' she married Bert Johnson an' they produced no natural offspring. Your parents named their second girl Julia an' she married Fred Gilmour. That's you. You're really Julia Chartrand an' Michael's really your son. It was the recently-deceased Ruth, your real sister, an' her equally-recently-deceased husband Bert, who adopted Michael. Your story about your sister an' how she died an' you taking her name was complete garbage. In fact, it was your brother an' his partner who died eight years ago in a car accident because of a drunk driver. So why'd you lie to us?"

The woman stared at Ethan for a long moment, then snorted: "Look, Mr. Busybody, I had two completely normal kids before that one was born: a son an' a daughter. Both grew up normal an' healthy. I love both of 'em an' they love me an' both are in my Will. As far as I am concerned, those are my only two kids. Period."

"It shows you know nothing about intellectually-disabled children in general and your son Michael in particular. Despite growing up in an abusive household - which I'm sure you couldn't care less about either - he turned out to be a warm and loving person, and he's made a positive difference on many people's lives. Especially over the past several weeks."

"So you say. So what? I do *not* consider him my son. And legally he is *not* my son. Period. End of story."

"Don't you even want to get to know him, to give him a chance? You saw him; he's become a fine young man."

"A fine retarded young man."

"That doesn't matter! You have to get past that! He has a right to life and love and happiness too, just like everyone else. And, not that it should make any difference, but he's only mildly disabled."

"You can refer to him by any current politically-correct term you want; the fact remains that he's still retarded. Damaged goods."

"Look, lady, on top of years of hidden parental abuse, Michael has just survived a very traumatic experience at his home in Clearwater. His adoptive parents - *your sister an' her husband* - were brutally murdered, basically right in front of him, an' he suffered added mental anguish when he discovered he had been adopted, after years of believing the Johnsons were his true parents. Emotionally, he's in shock. All he wants now is to meet his real mother, get to know her, an' maybe - just maybe - know a mother's love."

The woman regarded Ethan through the screen. He thought he saw that strange emotion flit across her face again, but he couldn't be sure as it disappeared as quickly as it came. Then she stepped close to the screen and said in a low, hard voice:

"A nice sob story, mister. Now go peddle it somewhere else. I have two children, an' that boy you brought here earlier is *not* one of them. I deny that child. I refuse to acknowledge that child. He does not exist as far as I'm concerned and he has not since I gave him up for adoption 14 years ago. I never wanted to see him again and you, Mr. Busybody, have done both him and me a great disservice by bringing him here.

"An' another thing: I was never close with either of my two siblings or their spouses, so Ruth an' Bert's deaths mean nothing to me. Didn't even go to their funerals in Ontario."

She made to close the inner door, but Ethan said urgently: "Wait! What about Michael's biological father? He's not listed on the birth certificate, so I couldn't track him down. But if you at least tell me his name, then I'll probably be able to find him. If Mike can't get to know his real mother, then he should have the chance to meet his father."

The woman regarded him with small glittering eyes. Her narrow mouth compressed even more and she gritted: "If that miserable bastard ain't dead by now, he should be, by God. That part of my past is also closed. I've no idea where he is, and I certainly have no intention of telling you his name."

"So I take it Mike's pop is not the Fred Gilmour you were married to, the one who fathered your other two kids, whom you later divorced before Mike was conceived?"

"Correct. And that is also none of your business."

"Why'd you dump Mike's biological pop?"

"He had his faults, not least of which was that he fathered a retarded child."

"Oh, for Chrissakes! You're putting all the blame on *him* for Michael? It takes two to provide the ingredients, lady! Don't you realize that a case like Mike's happens randomly, at the whim of fate? Whether the father's an astronaut, banker, teacher, truck driver, or ditch-digger, developmentally-delayed offspring can occur. You can't *blame* someone for it!"

"I can and I do. Before I changed partners, I produced normal kids. So obviously the fault wasn't mine."

"Lady, your logic is *nuts!*"

She glared, drew herself up to her full height, all five feet of it, and said, double chins quivering: "Your business with me is over. You will leave an' you will not come back. If you bother me again, I will call the police." And she slammed the door.

"Well, hell," said Ethan.

He drove back to the motel, cursing that miserable cold-hearted woman in English and Maori and a third language that had been dead for 700 years. He considered using another of his special computer programs to wreak havoc with her life, in revenge.

"Oh, the things I could do to her credit record, her bank balance, her phone bill, her tax returns, her house deed, even her Book-of-the-Month Club membership if she's got one," he muttered. "Christ! What a horrible way to treat her own flesh and blood! She never even gave the poor kid a chance."

He resolved not to tell Michael that his mother was still alive and stewing in hatred inside her small clapboard house. *Better for him to keep thinkin' she's dead. That bitch would only cause him more pain an' heartbreak by rejectin' him to his face.*

He also resolved to hack into that odious woman's savings accounts and donate half of what he found there to the Canadian Association for Community Living and the Canadian Mental Health Association, split into equal amounts, in her name. *I'd love to see her face when she gets the thank-you letters from CACL and CMHA after those donations!*

He pulled into the motel parking lot and stopped before a carnival of red and blue flashing lights atop a sea of police cars, with many people shouting, screaming, and gawking.

Ethan sprang from his car, suddenly filled with dread, and slipped his bony frame through the press of people towards his two adjoining rooms. The door to the boys' room had been shattered - outwards. Debris lay scattered over the sidewalk and pavement. There was no sign of Michael and Billy.

Ethan groaned. *Damn! I shouldn't have left them alone!*

Chapter 23

Confrontation

Ever since he was ten years old, Billy McDonnell had been in a constant war with his clothes. They always got too tight, too fast. And being tight, they graphically advertised how fat he was, adding embarrassment to his discomfort. No matter how loose the clothes were when they were bought, they soon became constricting.

Like now. So constricting, he couldn't move.

Billy slowly regained consciousness; he felt like he was swimming up through thick black molasses that slowly became grey, then pale grey, then white. He opened his eyes. He was in a large bare room with walls of unfinished drywall, exposed ceiling beams, and dirty cement floor. Pale light filtered in through papered-up windows. Thick floor-to-ceiling pillars marched down the room at regular intervals, like soldiers standing sentry. Piles of building materials lay here and there on the floor, including rolls of coaxial cable and electrical wire. The air was stale, musty. It was obviously a big office under construction, but the job had been abandoned for some reason, he concluded.

As full awareness came to him, Billy realized the reason he couldn't move was not because of his clothes. Something hard pressed cruelly into his back and his arms were stretched painfully behind him around it. He looked down and was shocked to discover he was tied to one of those big pillars. From his shoulders to his ankles, it seemed like miles of white coaxial cable were wrapped around his body, disappearing into his soft flesh, hurting in their tightness. Flesh? He was mortified to realize that someone had stripped him down to his underwear. And he couldn't even voice his protest; his mouth was packed full of cloth and sealed by a cloth gag so tight that it dug deep into his cheeks and the back of his neck. Near his feet were the ruins of his T-shirt and he knew where the material used to gag him had come from.

What the hell? he thought. He tried to move, to even twist his arms and legs, but the cables biting cruelly into his body held him fast. He'd been tied by an expert, someone who really enjoyed his work.

It occurred to Billy that maybe he should feel totally embarrassed at being on display wearing just his undies. *Same thing happened to poor Melanie.* He quickly decided that this was certainly not the time for modesty. Rather, it was an excellent time for panic.

There was a horrible groan off to his left. Billy twisted his head to look and immediately wished he hadn't. It was Michael, likewise clad only in his underwear, bound to the next pillar about 15 feet away with lots of white cable, but without a gag. His eyes were swollen almost shut, blood dripped from a nose which now looked misshapen, his mouth was a horrible red mass, and his beautifully-muscled body bled freely from dozens of cuts. As Billy watched, a hand holding a switchblade, with the deadly long blade extended, came around the far side of the pillar and made a long slow cut into Mike's chest, causing the teen to groan piteously again.

Billy screamed into his gag and strained against the cables pinioning him, which didn't give at all.

The holder of the knife stepped out from behind the pillar and Billy screamed again. *HIM! HERE!* He recognized the face from the police pictures. The grotesque black chimera tattooed on his left forearm clinched it.

Robert Moses Brack.

And we're helpless before him!

"Ah, finally awake, are ya, fat boy?" said Brack in a voice that chilled Billy to the core. "You're missin' the show here. I'm tryin' ta convince your stupid retard friend ta tell me where he hid his stone, but he ain't willin' ta tell me. Even after all the special attention I've given him."

"I ... I told you ... already ... many times," Michael choked out through puffy bloody lips, which had obviously been on the receiving end of vicious punches. "I don' ... know where my ... special stone is. I musta ... losted it."

"Oh, stop lying ta me, boy. You take me for a fool? You'd never lose something precious like that, something that lets you change into all those wonderful things. Now all ya gotta do is tell me an' this hurtin' will stop." Brack flicked his wrist, the knife blade flashed deadly silver, and another cut opened up on Michael's body. This time, the teen screamed. Echoes of his anguished cry bounced around the empty office.

"Look, retard," continued Brack, walking slowly around Mike's bound form, "I searched all through your clothes an' even all through the clothes of your whale friend here, an' there was no stone. I'd already searched your motel room, while I was waitin' for ya to return, so I know it's not hidden there either. SO WHERE IS IT?" And he slashed his captive again, eliciting another scream.

STOP IT! Billy shrieked deep in his throat, but only a guttural growl sounded. Brack took no notice.

"See, Mikey boy, normally I wouldn't haveta do this, y'know, 'cause my Gift is drawn to your stone, somehow," said Brack, taking a long swig from a beer can. "Most times, the pull is clear. Like when it drew me right across the USA into Canada an' then on to Clearwater, or when I was drawn to that Birski farm in Nowheresville, Saskatchewan. Man, *that* was a strong urgin'."

Mike jerked his head up. "You ... went ... to ... the ... nice ... farmer ... people?"

"Yup. Was all fired up to trash the place an' everyone in it, ta get to you. But just as I drove up to the front door, an' that big stupid dog came out barkin' an' growlin' like crazy - dogs never seem ta like me for some reason - my Gift sensed you'd moved on, westward, an' were travellin' fast. That really ticked me off - I thought I finally had you. An' when I get ticked off, I gotta do somethin' about it."

"Did ... you ... hurted ... them?"

The predator laughed; an icy heartless sound. "Now wouldn't you like ta know? Mebbe I'll tell ya, just before I kill ya."

He took another swallow of beer. "Anyways, after I left, the damn Porsche blew a tire, an' there was no spare, so I had a long delay in Armpit Narrows while the tire was fixed. An' that brings me to my present predicament. See, you been using your stone so much, you've had it with you so long, that there's a strong aura of it all around ya. So strong, it's confusin' my Gift, so's it can't tell me where its other half is, now that it's this close to you. That's why ya gotta talk to me, boy."

"I ... don' ... have ... it. I ... don' ... know ... where ... it ... is." Michael coughed, spitting blood. Brack cursed, flung his beer can across the room, and opened up another bloody cut on Mike's body.

As his friend screamed again, Billy knew he was telling the truth. After Ethan had left, shouting something at them through the closed door, one of the shadows in their motel room *moved.* The shadow grew and had swiftly enveloped Billy in a tight unbreakable cocoon. As the blackness stretched out towards Michael, Billy had seen his friend quickly shove his hand into his right pocket, where he always kept his stone, then look at him with an expression of pure shock and incredulity. Then the shadow had swallowed Mike, too. Another part of the shadow became a huge battering ram, smashing out through the motel door, then both boys' cocoons had grown over their heads, blinding and suffocating them.

As Billy had slipped into unconsciousness, his last thought was: *Mike! What happened to your stone?*

Another slash, more blood, another scream. Billy ground his teeth into the cloth wad filling his mouth and fought the cables biting into his flesh. To no avail. All he could move was his head. Even his fingers were immobile now; numb from the tight bindings.

Brack stepped away from Michael and swore again. His victim sagged limply against his bonds, head lolling on his chest. The floor around Mike was slick with blood and the musty air was heavy with its copper tang.

Brack slapped his thigh in frustration. "Passed out. Damnation! Well, I was gettin' real tired of askin' him anyway. Stubborn son-of-a-bitch! Unbelievable! Mebbe I need to try somethin' different."

Brack grabbed another beer from a bag on the floor, popped the tab, then walked over and stopped in front of Billy. Taking a long swig, he leaned close to the wide-eyed, terrified youth and said: " Well, one of the old sayings my daddy used to parrot, when he wasn't blind drunk or beatin' the crap outta me an' my ma, was 'waste not want not'. So here I am with not one, but two helpless sacks of meat to play with. Now I wonder what your pain threshold is, fat boy. Shall we find out? It occurs to me that mebbe you know where retard hid his stone. If not, then mebbe your screams will convince your buddy to tell me. Worth a try, either way."

Brack slid his knife along Billy's cheek and sliced off his gag. As the cloth strip floated to the floor, the predator reached into Billy's mouth and yanked out the cloth wadding, flinging the soaking mass away.

"Wait ... wait, mister," Billy gasped, struggling to make his dry aching mouth work. "Mike ... Mike was telling you ... the truth. He really doesn't know ... where his stone is. He really did lose it, sometime between when we left the bus depot an' when you attacked us at the motel. Honest!"

Brack stood back and eyed Billy coldly. "Really? Well, that's not what I wanted to hear, fat boy. Not at all. Unless you're a real good liar, which you might be, come to think of it."

He finished his beer and flung the can away. It clattered against the concrete floor and rolled to a stop against the far wall. He walked slowly around Billy, admiring his handiwork.

"Yep, gotta admit, I sure do truss up a body real good. A work of art. Y'know tubbo, I'm real disappointed your pretty l'il girlfriend didn't come with you on this trip. I'd sure have loved to tie her naked body to one of these poles an' have some fun with her. Damn, does she ever have a nice rack."

"You've hurt Melanie enough, you Goddamned bastard,"

Billy rasped. "She lost her left leg after you bit it an' a nasty infection set in that the docs couldn't cure!"

"Yeah. I know. I'm so mean, huh? Serves the bitch right though; she kicked me like a mule on steroids."

Brack spit, then fetched a bottle of water from his bag and poured it over Michael's head. The unconscious boy stirred, groaning. Brack slapped his face harshly - twice - and Mike slowly regained consciousness.

"I want ya awake ta watch this, retard," gritted the killer. "See what I do to your whale friend. You can stop me anytime - just tell me where your stone is."

Brack turned and came back to Billy. As fear rampaged through him, the teen thought: *Wonder if I'll last as long as Mike did, before I start screaming? But I gotta be strong. For Mike's sake. Gotta live up to Mike's example.*

Ah, who'm I kiddin'? I'll scream like a baby with the first cut.

Brack stepped close and Billy felt the cold blade against his ample belly. "How 'bout we start here, hmmm?" said Brack with Arctic smoothness. "Got lots ta work with here. How 'bout I do ya a favour an' slice off a few pounds? Bet ya'd like that, huh?"

To Billy's surprise, it wasn't really painful as the sharp blade cut into him. The pain hit him only after the cut was made: an agonizing piercing jolt far worse than having his wisdom tooth pulled last year. He felt wetness flow down his skin: first blood. He opened his mouth to scream.

A booming amplified voice sounded from outside the front door: "ROBERT BRACK. THIS IS THE POLICE. RCMP. WE KNOW YOU'RE IN THERE. COME OUT SLOWLY WITH YOUR HANDS IN THE AIR."

The effect on the predator was immediate. He dropped his knife and reached into his pocket; a brief violet glow outlined his body and he disappeared. Billy heard the thud of his footsteps as he raced for the back door. Then the footsteps stopped. They started up again, this time coming closer. Brack reappeared, standing near Michael. Crimson fury twisted his face.

"No. I ain't gonna run," Brack gritted. "Not when I'm so close to gettin' my hands on that stone. So pardon me, boys, while I go teach these Mounties a lesson. I'm gonna fry me some Canuck bacon. Don't y'all go anywhere while I'm gone, y'hear? Haw!"

Violet limned his body, then Brack strode forward with blue-white electrical arcs dancing around his eyes. He unlocked the front door and stepped outside, blinded by the bright sunlight and calling: "Don't shoot, officers! Here I am! I won't give ya no trouble!" The door swung shut behind him.

"Hsst! Michael! I found your stone! Here! C'mon, grab it!"

At the sound of the loud whisper, Billy jerked his head around and saw Ethan Delperdang crouching behind Mike's pillar. He was pressing something into Mike's hand. But Mike couldn't grab it; his hand was slick with blood and completely numb from the bindings cutting off the circulation for so long. The power stone fell to the floor, clattering on the cement.

Ethan swore, picked up the stone, and again pressed it into Mike's palm. "C'mon, kid! Brack won't be gone long! There's no cops out there; it was just me, usin' a megaphone I swiped from a cruiser in all the confusion at the motel. I snuck in here through the back door as Brack went out the front. But we've only got several seconds! C'mon!"

Realizing Michael couldn't take hold of the stone, Ethan held it in the youth's hand with his own hand. "C'mon, change into something! Fast, f'God's sake, or we're all dead when Brack returns!"

"Can't," choked Mike, so low Billy could barely hear him. "Hurts ... too much. Can't concentrate ... with such pain."

"But ya gotta concentrate, kid! Ya gotta reach down deep an' block out the pain an' do whatever it is ya do to change. Or we're all finished!"

Michael only groaned.

"C'mon Mike!" Billy urged, trying to keep his voice low. The fire across his stomach was intense and he could only imagine the agony his friend was in, with his multiple cuts. "Mike! Do just like Batman does! Focus past the pain - put the pain in a tiny box in your head an' lock it away! Change into Wolverine an' heal yourself, then change into somethin' else, somethin' strong, an' get us the hell outta here. C'mon, buddy!"

The front door crashed open. Robert Moses Brack stood there, a dark figure against the bright daylight behind him. Its closing mechanism broken, the door stayed open against the wall.

"What is going on?" Brack asked in a quiet voice, as his eyes started adjusting to the gloom inside the building.

Desperate to focus the killer's attention on himself to buy Mike some precious time, Billy yelled:

"Hey! Tough guy! I have some questions for you!"

Brack walked over to Billy with a sneer on his lips. "Oh yeah? Like what? Where's the nearest food truck?"

Ignoring the taunt, Billy said: "To get into our motel room, did you become that shadow creature an' slip through the space at the top or bottom of our door?"

"Yeah, tubbo. I can slip through the narrowest of cracks. What of it?"

"Well then, what happens to your stone when you're that shadow thing? Especially when you get super-thin? With Mike, he has to always hold his stone in his hand or keep it in his pocket. I don't think your shadow has pockets, an' I'm sure your stone doesn't get thin."

The sneer on Brack's face vanished. "Well hell, fat boy, come to think of it, I dunno. It's in my pocket when I change into my shadow form, then when I change back, I'm wearin' my clothes again an' my stone is still in my pocket."

Billy's delaying tactic worked: Brack did not see Ethan crouching behind Michael's pillar, or the yellow aura that briefly outlined the bleeding teen. Ethan watched in astonishment as the hideous cuts all over Mike's mutilated body quickly healed, as did the split lips, black eyes and broken nose. Then yellow limned the teen's body again.

It was the snapping sounds that caught Brack's attention. He turned in time to see strands of coaxial cable flying in all directions. Then the air was split with a thunderous roar:

"REMEMBER ME, PUNY HUMAN? YOU HURT MICHAEL BAD. YOU HURT FRIEND BILLY. MAYBE EVEN NICE FARMERS. NOW YOU GET HURT."

"Oh Christ!" yelled Brack, and his eyes unleashed a fierce bolt of electricity right at Michael. Except that Michael wasn't there any more. Ten feet and over one thousand pounds of almost-naked emerald green fury had taken his place. The Hulk had returned. And he was pissed.

Brack's electrical discharge would have fried an ordinary man. It bounced off the huge green-skinned chest of the Hulk, only causing him to roar again in rage. Brack swiftly changed tactics, firing a bolt straight at Billy. Moving at a speed that belied his massive size, the Hulk stuck a huge hand in front of the blast and deflected it into a wall, where it punched a smoking hole.

Snarling like an angry tiger, Brack launched another jolt at the emerald behemoth. It hit the Hulk square in the crotch. The creature looked down, wide-eyed, then his giant mouth split into an awful grin. Bellowing, the Hulk moved toward Brack with ponderous steps.

"Goddamn, Goddamn!" said Brack, grabbing hold of his Gift in his pocket. "The bastard surprised me! Where the hell did he get his stone all of a sudden? Need a minute ta regroup!"

The violet aura had just started to appear around the predator's body, when a tree trunk of an arm smashed into him, sending him flying through the air. He crashed into a wall and slid to the floor in a heap, unmoving.

"HAH! NO ONE BEATS HULK!"

The emerald man-mountain scooped up the unconscious Brack in one hand, turned and lumbered outside. He drew back one mighty arm, and flung the man high into the sky, arcing far away, northward over the miles of convoluted steel pipes and massive buildings, storage tanks, and smokestacks of the Oil Sands extraction plants along the Athabasca River, in the general direction of Fort MacKay upriver.

"YAAY!" shouted Billy, who had seen it through the open door.

"NO!" yelled Ethan, who had followed the Hulk outside. "Mike, you fool! He was out cold! We coulda easily taken his power stone away from him!"

The Hulk swung around, glaring at the skinny man who stood in front of him with bony fists clenched on his hips. The Hulk's broad Neanderthal face twisted into a horrible snarl. He lowered his head until it was mere inches from Ethan's face. The force of the creature's stentorian breath threatened to knock Ethan to the ground.

"YOU NO LIKE HULK'S DECISIONS, SCARECROW?"

"Ah, no, no of course not. Just, just voicing an opinion, that's all. Minor opinion, really. Don't give it another thought."

The Hulk snorted. The brief gust blew Ethan's long hair straight back.

Ethan ran back inside and retrieved the switchblade that Brack had dropped. He went to Billy and sawed through the cables binding him. Freed, Billy sat down in a rush, his useless arms and legs splayed around him. He grimaced in agony at the sharp pins 'n' needles pain of returning circulation.

The Hulk approached, elephantine footfalls echoing in the cavernous building. He grabbed Ethan around the waist, lifting him under one arm. He tucked Billy under his other arm, carrying the portly youth effortlessly, as if he weighed nothing. The emerald giant stomped outside again, heedless of the protests of his passengers.

The Hulk faced south, the opposite direction to where he'd thrown Brack, and crouched.

"Oh man! Brace yourself, Ethan! He's gonna jump!" yelled Billy.

The strongest legs on Earth straightened abruptly, like thick coiled springs suddenly released, sending the Hulk and his cargo soaring a thousand feet into the air in a long arc that covered over a mile on the ground.

"EEYAHH!" screamed Ethan. The Hulk looked down and grinned his awful grin.

"THANK YOU FOR FLYING AIR HULK."

Chapter 24

Confession

After about an hour, the Hulk had enough of *THOOMING* all over the countryside. Carrying his two passengers, the jade giant had covered hundreds of miles with his incredible leaps, leaving dozens of mini-impact craters in his wake. His final leap brought them to a small lake, surrounded by meadow and miles of forest, in the exact middle of nowhere. Which suited the Hulk just fine; he hated civilization.

As soon as his massive slabs of bare feet smashed down for the final *THOOM*, his huge thigh muscles absorbing the shock, the Hulk gently lowered Ethan and Billy to the ground. Whereupon, they both threw up with gusto. After watching them dispassionately, the emerald beast turned and lumbered to the lake, where he drank enough for a herd of thirsty camels.

"Oh, man!" gasped Ethan, between retches. "All that bouncing, that shooting through the air, then coming down, then rocketing upwards again! Over an' over! Christ!"

"Yeah," agreed Billy, face ashen and the remains of his last meal displayed on the ground in front of him. "And the wind! Let's not travel that way ever again!"

"Amen to that, kid."

When they had finished vomiting, they looked around for the Hulk and instead found Michael asleep by the shore of the lake, snoring loudly. His right hand still gripped his colourful stone.

"Well, I reckon he's earned the right to flake out, considerin' the horrible things he suffered through at the hands of Brack, an' then his exertions as that monstrous green fella," said Ethan. He noticed Billy examining the long livid cut on his stomach, which thankfully had stopped bleeding sometime during their bouncing journey. "Speakin' of Brack, I bet that hurts like hell, huh? Luckily, it's not deep. Go wash it in the lake; that'll help. It looks worse than it really is, but we should get some disinfectant on it, just to be sure. An' we gotta get you two some clothes; all you're wearin' are your gauchies, an' Mike doesn't even have much of that left after the Hulk's big butt stretched an' ripped 'em. All your other clothes an' stuff - mine too - includin' your smartphone, are back at that motel in Fort McMurray."

"Any idea where we are?" asked Billy.

"Nope. I kept my eyes closed during most of the time that the Hulk played hopscotch across the countryside with us under his arms. Hopefully we're very far from Brack, assumin' he survived the Hulk's long pitch. Which he prolly did, knowin' our luck. Lemme use my cell."

Ethan pulled a smartphone from one of the many zippered pockets on his jacket. He made a disgusted face. "No signal. Damn! That confirms it: we're far off the beaten path. Wish I'd thought to bring my satellite phone, but it's back in the plane."

Billy said: "I think I saw a small town in the distance, just before we landed. That way." He pointed.

"Well, why don't I go hike to it an' you stay here with Sleeping Beauty. It'll be dark soon, an' we don't wanna spend the night in the open with no food or shelter an' no clothes for you guys. Seems to be a path through the woods in the direction you pointed, so I'll just follow that. I'll come back with some clothes, food, bug juice, an' first aid supplies for your cut. Okay?"

Billy nodded and Ethan left. He watched until the tall, thin figure was swallowed by the deep green of the forest.

"And we never saw him again," he muttered melodramatically. The shadows were lengthening; it was late afternoon. He hoped Ethan would return before dark; he was hungry and already a little chilly. Thankfully, not too many biting bugs were out - yet.

He went to wash his cut in the lake. He yelped as the cold clear water stung the slash. Then he walked to where his friend lay processing cords of wood with each snore, curled up on the ground near him, and immediately opened his own sawmill for business.

❧ ❧ ❧ ☙ ☙ ☙

The teens were awakened by the cheerful *crackle pop* of a campfire and the *hiss* of a propane camping lantern. It was full dark and the air was heavy with a chill mist, but they found themselves each covered with a blanket. Rubbing sleep from their eyes, they squinted into the light.

"Just me, boys!" came a familiar voice. "Ethan of the North, returned with supplies."

"I'll say," marvelled Billy as he got up and looked around. A four-person nylon tent had been pitched in the meadow; three sleeping bags were visible inside through the closed screen door. There was a cardboard box of supplies and another box of food. A bag of clothing lay next to Ethan. A red four-wheeled ATV with wide fore-and-aft carry racks was parked nearby. Typical of teens, the boys had slept through its arrival and the noise of Ethan erecting the tent, only to be awakened by the softer sounds of fire and lantern.

"Wow, you really went to town," said Billy.

"Literally," chuckled Ethan. "Took me almost three hours walkin' before I reached it, too. Anyway, here's some clothes for ya both. I got sweatshirts an' track pants, stuff I didn't haveta know your exact sizes for. Got running shoes too; one size larger than I figgered you'd need, just to be safe. Besides bug spray, I also got food: six subs packed with a variety of meats. Plus stuff for breakfast."

"Thank you very much, Mister Ethan," said Michael and Billy echoed agreement. Gratefully, the boys hauled on the clothes. Ethan opened a first aid kit and treated the long thin gash on Billy's stomach, pretending not to notice as the youth hissed in pain when the disinfectant touched it. He covered the cut with several long bandages. Then all three of them attacked the food.

"So where'd you get all this?" asked Billy between mouthfuls.

"From the General Store in the little town of La Corey, which is about 25 miles west of Cold Lake, Alberta, which is almost at the Saskatchewan border. The Hulk really travelled; we're hundreds of miles from Fort McMurray to the north."

Mike blushed and mumbled something the others couldn't hear.

"Cold Lake. There's a big military base near there. Air Force," said Billy.

"So I understand. Anyway," Ethan continued, "I got a signal in town, so I used my cell to contact my plane crew in Fort McMurray. They'll go clear out our stuff from our motel rooms, then fly to Cold Lake tomorrow an' rent a car an' come get us in La Corey. There's no airport in La Corey. We'll trek into town after breakfast tomorrow, or rather, you two will; I call dibs on the ATV. I did my share of walkin' today. The owner of the General Store loaned me that machine, once I gave him a hefty security deposit. Good thing I always carry lots of cash."

"Then what?" asked Billy.

"Well, then we take to the air an' put some serious distance between us an' that Brack psycho. But as to where we go, that part I wanna to discuss with you guys. See, we haveta make a stand somewhere; we can't keep runnin' from him. Evil must be faced."

"Where'd you find my stone?" asked Michael quietly.

"Huh? Oh, when I went back to see Julia, after you guys went into your room. I saw it, ah, by the path leading to her door; you musta dropped it and never noticed, what with all the emotion you were feelin' at the time."

Michael looked puzzled. "First time I ever dropped it; I'm always real careful of it."

Ethan smiled: "Well, nobody's perfect, Mike. First time for everything."

"Why'd you go back to that awful lady?" Billy said, watching Ethan closely.

"To ... to ask her some more questions. About that sister of hers: Mike's birth mother. Just to make sure that she, um, wasn't really buried somewhere. Y'know, so we could bring Mike to her grave site to pay his respects an' get some closure."

Billy stared hard at the scarecrow, then put down the second sub he'd been eating. "Ethan, we really appreciate all you've done for us, y'know, but I've been travelling with you for almost a week now and I've come to some conclusions. One: you know a lot more about the power stones than you let on. Two: there's a lot more about yourself that you're not telling. And three: you're a terrible liar."

Ethan stopped chewing and said: "Excuse me? Liar?"

"Yeah," said Billy. "Don't think just because I'm fat, that I'm stupid or gullible. After years of listening to nice words from relatives an' teachers an' coaches about my weight, an' knowing that they really scorned or pitied me because of how I look, I know when I'm being hosed. So I know you're lyin' about how you found Mike's stone, an' about Julia too."

"Now wait just a Goddamn minute!" Ethan shouted, jerking to his feet.

Billy also stood, shouting louder: "No, *you* wait! Tell us the truth: did you really 'find' Mike's stone? Or did you steal it from him, eh?"

The thin man glared at the large teen, then looked at Michael, who had also stood and was staring intently at him, arms folded, corded muscles standing out. Neither Ethan nor Billy had seen the brief flash of yellow surround Mike.

"You've got some nerve, accusing me of lying," said Ethan in a small, hard voice. "After all I've done for you, includin' those new clothes on your back an' the food in your first-aided belly."

"Billy's right: you are lying," Michael announced. "I hear your heartbeat, which is racing, and I smell your sweat. You're sweating, yet it's very chilly tonight."

"What the hell are you on about? How could you tell that?" barked the scarecrow. "An' what's wrong with your eyes? Ya look blind."

"I am blind," said the youth. "I'm Matt Murdock, also known as Daredevil. Though I can't see, my other senses are superhuman.

I can hear heartbeats, I can smell better than any animal, so I can be a walking lie detector. Rapid heartbeat combined with sweating means you're lying. Daredevil often uses his super-senses to find that out about people, yes he does."

Ethan looked at both teens, sighed and said:

"All right. No secrets between friends, huh? Okay, Mike didn't lose his stone. You're right, Billy: I took it. Picked his pocket as I hugged him while we waited on Chartrand's stoop."

"WHAT?" both boys exclaimed together.

"WHY?" demanded Billy.

"It's too powerful to use for long periods of time. Billy, you saw what it did to my younger step-brother. I wanted to spare Mike from that fate, yet I knew he'd never give it up willingly. One of my hidden talents is ... well, picking pockets, to put it bluntly ... so I took it, figgerin' Mike would simply think he lost it. But I swear I had no idea Brack was so close, that he was actually waitin' inside your motel room as that shadow thing. I didn't have the stone next to my body in a pocket; I'd placed it on the floor under my car seat when we returned to the car. So if it became very hot because Brack was near, as Mike says it does, I wasn't even aware of it. As soon as I returned from my second visit to Chartrand's place an' realized what had happened to you guys, I raced to where Brack was holdin' you an' gave Mike his stone back so he could defend himself. You saw that! I rescued you!"

Billy was furious: "Oh, you think you did us a favour? Don't you realize that you were responsible for the awful torture that poor Mike suffered through? Brack was torturin' him to tell where he'd hid his stone, an' kept at him even though Mike insisted he lost it! An' then Brack started on me with his knife! If he'd had his stone, Mike coulda stopped Brack from kidnapping us in the first place! Maybe even defeated him then an' there!"

"Yeah, I'm real sorry about what Brack did to you guys, especially to you, Mike. Believe me, I never wanted any of that to happen. I figured I'd lead Brack away from you once I had the stone; I'd jump in my jet and fly back to New Zealand and prepare a proper welcome for him, so I could defeat him an' get his stone."

"Then what? Rejoin the two halves somehow? And have the whole stone for yourself?" accused Billy.

"Of course not!"

"Then what?"

"Destroy both halves."

"NO!" shouted Michael. "Not my special stone!"

"It's much too powerful, kid. It'll eventually suck the life right outta ya. Mebbe not as fast as my step-brother, 'cause its power is split now, but it'll do it one day, sure enough."

"We ... *we trusted you*," said Billy harshly. "And you repaid us by *stealing* Mike's stone! An' that got us captured an' tortured by that psycho!"

"Look, I said I'm sorry - "

"That's simply *not* good enough! You had no right to steal it from Mike! Especially after all he's been through! That *sucks*! Who died and made you God?"

"Now look, guys, I did what I thought was best - "

"In *your* opinion. I thought we were a team! An' waitaminute, come to think of it, just how *did* you find where Brack was holdin' us, way at the edge of town in that abandoned building, eh?"

"Why, I ... I drove around looking for his white Porsche 918 Spyder - not too many $900,000 cars like that in a frontier mining town - an' luckily - "

"Wait!" said Billy. "How'd you know what car Brack drove?"

"I heard the cops talking about it at the motel. They'd received a Be On The Lookout for it from the Clearwater cops back east. The innkeeper said a car matching that description had been in his parking lot earlier that day."

"Okay," Billy said. Ethan went on:

"Well, as I was *saying,* after driving around, luckily I found the Porsche, parked at the back of the building."

Michael said: "He just told another fib."

"Hah!" said Billy. "Admit it, Delperdang!"

Ethan flushed crimson; a vein pulsed in his head and his hands balled into fists. He glared at Billy standing defiantly in front of him and the youth glared back, unblinking. Finally, Ethan lowered his eyes and said:

"Okay. Ya got me again. I used a tracking device. On the hem of Mike's shirt. I put it there at the bus station, just after we met him. So I'd never lose track of him. I mean, why not? It took us forever to find him in the first place."

"TRACKING DEVICE?" Billy shouted.

"Yep. Very sophisticated. Uses Global Positioning Satellites to track the wearer. Pin-point accuracy. Got several from my CIA friends, before I left their employ. They don't even know I have 'em. Or that I can hack into their secret spy satellites to use 'em."

Billy whistled softly: "You're a real piece of work, Delperdang."

"It was all for Mike's own good. I was trying to protect him from what happened to my step-brother."

"So *you* say! You should have at least *talked* with him first; with both of us! You had no right to slap a tracking device on hm, like he's some kinda animal that scientists are monitoring! An' you sure as hell had no right to steal his stone!"

Ethan lost his temper: "I have *every* right! I'm the only one alive who knows all about that stone! After years of research, I'm the one who originally rediscovered it, only to have my fool of a step-brother take it when I wasn't lookin'! I know what that rock really *is*, an' what it can really *do*! I've far more right to it than some small-town teenager who just uses it to turn into comic book superheroes!"

"Don't you mean small-town *retarded* teenager?" accused Billy.

"No! That's completely unfair! I'm sensitive to Mike's condition! Hell and damnation boy, the only reason I went back to that Chartrand bitch was to ream her out for her attitude towards Mike!"

"He just lied again, when he said that last sentence," said Mike, sightless eyes fixed on Ethan.

"Oh hush *up*, Mr. Human Lie Detector! OK, that wasn't the

whole truth, but trust me, ya don't wanna know the whole truth about that second visit! Now look, I treated you boys right. At my own considerable expense, I took Billy clear across this much-too-large country to find Mike. An' I tracked down Mike's birth mother, or the lady we thought was her."

"Yeah, but you had an ulterior motive," said Billy. "You just wanted to get your hands on Mike's stone. And, first chance you got, you swiped it!"

"Yes! We've just been through that! But I gave it back! Mike has it now!"

"Until the next time you swipe it, when our guard's down. We can't trust you any more."

"Chee-rist! Look, my patience is just about finished! I've told you that rock's too powerful. I'm the only one who can deal with it! That stone must be *mine*!"

"So you are a bad man too," Michael said softly. Yellow outlined his body, then he linked his fingers together and his hands enlarged and changed shape with a rubbery sound until they formed a perfect pink wingback chair, complete with comfy seat cushion. He scooped Billy into the chair. Then his legs grew and grew, stretching out of the ends of his sweat pants until they were 25 feet long. Ethan gawped in amazement.

Plastic Man towered over the campsite, head and shoulders almost invisible in the darkness. "You stay away from us, Mister Lying Scarecrow!" he yelled down.

"Look, I spoke too harshly just now! Sorry, sorry, sorry! I like you boys! Really I do! Cut me some slack, huh? You must realize I only did what I did with the best of intentions!"

Billy called out: "My Gramma says 'the road to hell is paved with good intentions', so SCREW YOU! Some so-called 'wise mentor' you turned out to be, you back-stabber! Let's go, Mike."

Plastic Man turned and stalked off through the forest, his impossibly-tall legs taking yards-long steps.

Ethan yelled after them: "Hey! Come back! You still need me! Hey!"

The nighttime symphony of crickets and frogs responded.

Left alone with only the crackling fire for company, Ethan said: "Well, hell."

His only reply was the plaintive cry of a loon out in the lake: a lonely warble that echoed in the wilderness.

సా సా సా ఆ ఆ ఆ

As soon as they were well away from Ethan, with even the glow of his campfire lost in the dark, Plastic Man stopped walking and shrank to normal size. Billy stood and faced his friend, asking:

"What is it?"

"Heh. I've no idea where I'm going. There's a bit of moonlight, but ... ah ... well, I'm losted. Hey, maybe I should become the Angel an' fly up an' spot the lights of that town Ethan found."

"Nah, Mike ... sorry, Plastic Man. That's the first place he'd look. He's probably on his way there now on that ATV. I noticed it had headlights."

The immense dark of the forest pressed into them. The night wasn't silent, but quiet: a profound stillness broken only by the wind combing through the trees, crickets, and occasional sounds of small nocturnal animals. Overhead, millions of stars sparkled against a coal-black canopy. They seemed close enough to touch, if a person could only just stretch high enough.

In the distance, a wolf howled. The mournful call was answered by another wolf, and this one sounded closer.

Billy, never a fan of the great outdoors, said nervously: "Ah, I think we need someone who's at home in the Canadian woods, an' I bet you know just the person."

"Sure do."

A yellow aura, then Billy faced a small, powerfully-built man sporting an incredible head of hair, long bushy sideburns, and steely eyes that glinted in the moonlight.

"Logan, I presume?" grinned Billy.

"Ya got it, bub. Now lemme sniff things out." He raised his head, breathed deep, and read the night air. He repeated the process twice more, turning each time. "Okay. There's a faint trace of wood smoke to the south; prolly a cabin. We can head there an' ask for shelter."

Billy touched Michael on the arm. "You're really him, aren't ya? Wolverine?"

"That's right, bub. The most famous X-Man, the greatest tracker 'n' hunter in the world, with a mutant healin' factor that's -" He stopped, looking at Billy's exasperated look. "Ah, but you know all that. Okay. Hey, did ya know we're bein' watched right now by a wolf pack 'bout ten yards away in the woods behind you?"

Billy gasped and spun around: "What?"

"Aw, don't worry, bub. They're more interested in the doe with the lame leg they've been trackin'. She's on the other side of us. The pack'll move on soon."

"If ... if they don't, do you have Wolverine's claws?"

Logan pulled back the right sleeve of his sweatshirt and tapped his muscular hairy forearm. "Yup. In here. A set of three in each arm. 'Course, they're only made of bone. I can't duplicate Wolverine's sharp unbustable metal claws 'cause they were bonded to his natural bone claws by - "

"Yeah, yeah, I know all that," said Billy impatiently. "So c'mon, lemme see 'em! Pop the claws!"

The small man sighed. "Ah, just like Melanie." He straightened his arms and, with a grunt of pain, extended the six long, bony claws.

"Ohmigod!" said Billy, mouth agape. He touched the white claws on one hand. "Totally awesome! My God, Mike, how I wish I could do that!"

After another admiring minute, Billy said his friend could retract the claws. With another painful grunt, Mike complied.

"Wow, thanks for doing that, Mike. Sorry it hurt ya," Billy said. "Y'know, I've been noticing that you now seem to take on the personality of the heroes you become. At the very beginning, I could tell it was still you inside, but lately, I'm not so sure. You even talk exactly like them. Like when you were the Hulk gettin' us away from Brack. Or like right now: you sound just like I imagine the comic book Logan would sound."

The small man snorted and fixed Billy with a look. "Whaddaya mean I sound just like Logan? I *am* Logan."

"Right, right," Billy said quickly.

"Now c'mon, follow me an' stay close. I'll lead us right to that cabin. But we can't go in a direct line; there's an old grumpy male black bear prowlin' between us an' the cabin, an' past him, two male skunks are havin' quite the fight over a female. Hope she's worth it."

൭ ൭ ൭ ൞ ൞ ൞

True to his word, Wolverine got them through the dense woods without incident and they came upon three rough cabins in a small clearing, obviously a rustic hunt camp. Smoke curled lazily from the chimney of one cabin and faint snores sounded from inside, but the other two cabins were cold and silent. The teens snuck inside the cabin furthest from the occupied one, where they found crude bunks each with sleeping bags and pillows.

Michael became himself again and the boys each chose a bunk and crawled inside a sleeping bag, fully clothed. They were asleep almost instantly.

The exhausted teens slept through the dawn, and the clatter and cursing of hung-over hunters setting off in hopes of blasting Bambi. When the boys finally awoke and cautiously emerged from the cabin, they were relieved to find themselves alone. They entered the hunters' cabin and gagged at the stench of male sweat and stale beer. The place looked like a bunch of college kids lived there: dirty clothes were strewn everywhere, furniture was upended and there was hardly a clear space of floor to walk on. The kitchen area was a horror show; the unwashed dishes piled high in the sink and the filth-encrusted stove made the mess Snow White faced in the dwarves' cottage seem like a minor clean-up. Empty beer cans were sprinkled liberally throughout the cabin, some roosting in unusual locations, like all along the top of the rafters: lines of colourful aluminium sentinels standing at attention.

Billy looked at Mike, and they both grimaced. They gingerly

THE HERO STONE

picked their way to the kitchen table, carved out a clear space from the clutter piled atop it, and helped themselves to a breakfast of juice and big sloppy peanut butter and jam sandwiches.

After they had finished eating, Mike peeled off his sweat shirt and pants and they examined the clothing closely. Just above the elastic on the pants' left cuff, they found a small rectangular piece of metal.

"Damn that Ethan!" said Billy, tearing the object off the pants. "Here's another tracking device!"

"Maybe you got one too," said Mike worriedly.

Billy shucked off his clothes, but a careful examination revealed no device. He said:

"Whew. That's a relief. Well, let's chuck your GPS locator into the fire here. I'll stir the embers an' get it blazing."

Michael nodded and moved to the fireplace. Suddenly, he stopped and turned to Billy, grinning. "No, I think I got a better idea."

After a flash of yellow, Wolverine reappeared. The diminutive mutant saluted Billy, took the tracking device, and grabbed a roll of duct tape from a side table. He left the cabin, loping silently into the woods. He returned about ten minutes later.

"What'd you do?" asked Billy, emerging from an odious outhouse that made the interior of the cabin look like the Ritz.

Logan chuckled: "I tracked down a stag - nice strong young buck - an' wrestled him to the ground. Don't worry, I didn't hurt him. Then I taped Delperdang's trackin' device to one of his antlers. When I released the stag, he took off like a bat outta hell! He'll lead Ethan on a very merry chase!"

Michael reappeared and both boys dissolved into gales of laughter.

"Very ... very clever of you to think ... of that, buddy," said Billy, wiping tears from his eyes.

"Thank you," replied Mike proudly.

"Now, we gotta get outta here before the hunters return. We don't wanna be like Goldilocks an' the Three Bears. We gotta find some civilization, where I can call my folks. We need their help to get home. My wallet was left back in Fort McMurray, with all my money and ID. The rest of your money was left there too. We just have the clothes on our backs."

Both boys had talked over breakfast and decided to return to Clearwater to make their stand against Robert Moses Brack. It was where Billy felt safest, because of his parents and their influence in town. As for Michael, it was where he had grown up, so he knew the town well, which gave him a comforting feeling. And the local police should be on their side now that they knew about Brack and had seen what he could do.

Michael shucked off his sweatshirt and became the Angel, grimacing in pain as the pair of magnificent six-foot wings grew next to his shoulder blades. Then he hoisted Billy into his arms and sprang into the air. It was the first time Billy had flown with the Angel, and he was thunderstruck:

"Wow! Oh wow! This is totally absolutely awesome! It's so *cool*!" he exclaimed as they soared over the forest, wind buffeting their faces and the mighty wings *thrumming*.

Mike beamed: "Thanks. Glad you like it. Glad I work out, too. You're a lot heavier than my previous two passengers!"

"Ah, get stuffed."

The Angel followed the narrow road that led away from the cabin. A small town hove into view about thirty minutes later, and they alighted on the outskirts. They had reached La Corey. The Angel morphed into Michael, who expressed relief at not to having to carry his large friend any longer. His arms ached. Billy gazed at him, all panting and sweat-streaked, considered saying "sorry", then suddenly decided that he was fed up apologizing about his body. The way he was, was the way he was.

That decision was an epiphany. It made Billy feel as if a huge burden had just been lifted from his shoulders. He felt liberated, released from a constant nagging pain. He felt *free*. He knew there would always be jerkwads who'd judge him by how he looked, who'd insult and demean him. But now he wouldn't *care* anymore; their narrow malicious minds were their problem, not his. He would refuse to let such idiots upset him any longer, denying them the satisfaction of causing him mental anguish. He would gravitate to people who appreciated him for who he was, not how he looked. And one such person was standing right next to him.

He put his hand on Michael's shoulder and squeezed, saying: "Thanks, buddy. Not just for carrying me, but for being my friend."

Mike blushed and said: "Aw, you're welcome."

They found a battered payphone outside a gas station and Billy called the operator, relieved that this was still a free service. He had her dial his home and reverse the charges. His parents, frantic with worry, were ecstatic to hear from their wayward son. Their happiness increased upon learning that Billy had found Michael. They were stunned and then angry at learning the teens were in Alberta. They and the police had been searching for them in the Maritimes, based on Billy's one phone call after he'd left that said he was heading east to look for Mike. Ethan had been right: Paul had promptly alerted the police, saying Billy had likely been kidnapped by Delperdang and that they were heading to Atlantic Canada to look for the runaway Michael Johnson.

Paul and Janet wanted to know what had happened to Delperdang: why couldn't he fly the boys home in his private jet? Billy said they'd parted ways with the liar and he'd explain everything when they met. His parents instructed the boys to go to the police station and tell the officers everything. They wanted the boys to stay with the police in La Corey while they grabbed the first flight out to Cold Lake, rented a car and came to collect them.

Billy, knowing that Mike would refuse to go to the police and worried that if they stayed in one place too long, Brack would catch up to them, insisted on flying home by themselves. Frustrated, his parents eventually agreed, and Paul McDonnell promised to arrange for tickets at the Cold Lake airport. He told Billy to wait by the phone until he called back to confirm the boys' travel arrangements.

When Paul did call back, the news was not good. In the

aftermath of the September 11, 2001, terror attacks in the United States, airport security procedures had become much more stringent. To pick up their airline tickets, both boys had to show photo ID. Since their wallets had been left in Fort McMurray, flying was out, no matter how much Paul yelled at the ticket agent for special consideration for underage children.

Then Janet McDonnell had a brainstorm: the boys would trek, likely by bus, to the nearest VIA Rail train station, where tickets would be waiting for them on the next cross-Canada passenger train back to Toronto: The Canadian. Paul and Janet would pick up the teens at downtown Toronto's Union Station and drive them home to Clearwater. They'd also wire some travelling money by Western Union to the General Store in La Corey.

And they made Billy promise to call them at intervals along their way home. Frequent intervals.

After hanging up with his parents, Billy dialled the operator again and had her call the Birski farm in northern Saskatchewan, at Mike's urging. Still no answer. In fact, the operator suspected the line was no longer in service, but she had no official confirmation yet.

When the travel money arrived, the teens bought bus tickets at the General Store, which also served as a bus depot. Their bus would take them southwest to Edmonton, Alberta's capital and the nearest city with a VIA Rail station. They also bought sandwiches and pop for the journey, plus windbreakers for each of them to wear over their sweatshirt. As they waited for the arrival of their motor coach, Billy noticed Mike's deep frown. He was sucking his knuckle furiously.

"What is it?" he asked, then horror chilled him. "Oh no! Your stone's not getting hot, is it? Is Brack near?"

"No," answered Mike around his knuckle. "But I don't wanna go back to Clearwater just yet. I'm really really worried about the Birskis, about what the Nastyman mighta did to 'em. We haven't been able to get 'em by phone at all. Mister Ethan couldn't get 'em either. So I wanna go there first, to check on 'em. Can we, please?"

Billy, seeing the worried concern in his friend's eyes, sighed. "Okay. We'll change our tickets for a bus to take us to Albatross Narrows in Saskatchewan, then after we see the Birskis, we'll grab another bus to haul us back to Edmonton where our train tickets will be waiting. But man, are my folks gonna be pissed at this little side trip. Y'know, when this whole thing is over, I'm gonna be grounded until I'm, like, really old. Like 30 or something."

Michael leaned over and hugged his friend. "I'm real lucky to have a buddy like you, Billy McDonnell. You came right across Canada just for me, an' now you're upsetting your mom 'n' dad just for me. I'll always remember this."

"Yeah, an' I'm sure my folks will too. That's what worries me."

Chapter 25

Gauntlet of Terror

Ever since he was little, Michael had been told not to play with fire. He'd been warned about matches and lighters, and severely beaten by his adoptive father when, at the age of five, he'd been caught simply picking up his adoptive mother's lighter from the floor where it had fallen as she passed out in another drunken stupor. That's why becoming the Human Torch - a being of fire - filled him with a delicious sense of naughtiness. But, despite being the Torch, he was still careful about fire and the things that caused it.

So if that was the case, then why did he have a fire in his right pants pocket?

Michael jerked awake. The bus had stopped. His stone was burning hot.

THE NASTYMAN!

He turned to Billy, still asleep in his seat by the aisle - his buddy had let him have the window seat and he had stared avidly at the northern Saskatchewan countryside as it rolled by until the gentle swaying of the bus had lulled him to sleep - and shook him awake, saying in a low urgent voice:

"My stone! It's hot! The Nastyman is here!"

"Wha-? Hey, why's the bus stopped?" asked Billy, siting up.

An elderly woman sitting in front of them turned and said: "There's some kind of accident up ahead, blocking the road. Our driver's gone out to investigate."

"Billy, we gotta *leave*," whispered Mike. "I can't fight the Nastyman here, not with all these people on the bus! They'll get hurted!"

THE HERO STONE

Billy looked past his friend out the bus window. It was about mid-day, judging by the sun. They were on a two-lane highway, with rolling fields of ranch land and grazing cattle and forest stretching into the distance. Here and there, a "rocking horse" oil rig broke the landscape, monotonously pumping its precious crude. A classic, beautifully-preserved Acura NX sports convertible - bright yellow with tan interior - was parked at the side of the road, just ahead of the bus. With a start, he remembered Brack liked flashy, expensive sports cars. That clinched it.

"Okay, c'mon! Let's get outta here," he said. Both boys rose, stepped into the aisle and started walking toward the open front door.

Their bus driver appeared at the top of the steps leading down to the door, smiling. Both boys blinked at his abrupt return.

The driver was a big man - big in the Billy sense, not tall. His ample stomach was locked in desperate battle with his blue short-sleeved uniform shirt, whose buttons strained to hold back the flesh yearning to burst free. Late thirties, with close-cropped brown hair and a lined face that had seen many miles of road, he had a ready smile and a booming voice.

"Not to worry, folks!" he announced. "Big ol' tree fell across the road up ahead. Police and a highway crew are already on their way and we should be moving again shortly. Here now, why don't you two boys kindly return to your seats and just relax, huh?"

Billy moved to comply, but Michael stood frozen where he was. His face was white and he said: "My stone is hotter than ever. It's almost burning my skin through my pants pocket. Billy, that's not our driver."

"What? Oh c'mon, Mike. Of course it is."

"Bil-ly ... that's ... *him!* Lookit the tattoo on his arm!"

Things happened fast after that. The smiling overweight bus driver glowed violet, shimmered, and became the lean wolfish form of Robert Moses Brack. He was no longer smiling. Passengers screamed and Billy was unashamed to be part of that chorus.

"Too bad you noticed it was *me* instead of your dead fat driver, but that ain't gonna save ya or your whale friend, *retard*!" yelled

Brack. He glowed violet, then a solid mass of obsidian shadow pulsated in the space where he once stood. A part of the shadow exploded outwards down the aisle straight towards the teens; an onrushing battering ram whose leading edge was an open mouth filled with rows of black teeth. Michael shone yellow, grabbed Billy's arm, then the teens were gone and the rear emergency door of the bus swayed open.

The shadow's thick appendage quickly retracted into the main body, which then erupted outside through the front door; a Niagara of stygian menace. Those passengers who had not fainted by now, screamed even louder.

Michael and Billy stood about four hundred yards from the bus, surrounded by the dust cloud caused by the Flash's super-speed sprint. "I can't run for long carrying you, Billy," the Flash said. "The friction will burn off our clothes and all our money."

Billy nodded, but he had other things on his mind. He was staring open-mouthed at the dark creature that had flowed out of the bus and was now advancing swiftly towards them. It was the first time he'd seen Brack's shadow form fully manifested. He was transfixed by the huge dragon-head with glowing orange eyes that swayed on a thin snakelike neck above the black cloud. As it neared, the inky cloud morphed into two giant bat wings and an awful *hiss* came from the monstrous red mouth filled with dozens of needle-sharp teeth. The youth realized with horror that those were the same teeth that had bitten Melanie, giving her the infection that had caused her leg to be amputated. He decided it was time to scream again.

Three white-hot fireballs slammed into the shadow creature. The thing roared in pain and stopped its advance. Billy turned and saw the Human Torch standing on the road behind him, his entire body blazing red-orange. The asphalt beneath his feet was already melting. Lying nearby was a pile of Mike's clothes.

"STAY AWAY FROM US," said the Torch through the flames enveloping his head.

The shadow *hissed,* a chilling sound like many steam pipes all leaking at the same time, and advanced again, faster than before.

A miniature nova sun of white fire hit the creature just below where its neck joined its body. The huge fireball exploded, sending shadow bits flying in all directions. Billy gaped, then cheered:

"ALRIGHT! Way to GO, Mike! Ya killed him!"

"NO. HE'S STILL ALIVE. LOOK." The Torch pointed with a fiery forefinger and Billy saw the shadow parts slowly oozing towards each other. "HE'S RE-FORMING. WE GOTTA GO. NOW."

Billy scampered to Mike's clothes and scooped them up. The Human Torch turned off the flames on his hands and arms, then became airborne, grabbing Billy under the armpits as he passed by. He soared up into the clear blue sky, angled southward and vanished from sight, leaving a long orange trail in his wake that dwindled by the second.

Behind them, the shadow thing finally reformed, becoming Brack, still dressed in the bus driver's now-loose-fitting clothes. Filling the air with vicious curses, he jumped into his Acura and awakened the powerful engine. He shot by the three cars stopped in front of the bus with the terrified faces of their occupants pressed against the windows, passed the bloody half-naked corpse of the bus driver, and swerved onto the left shoulder of the road, tires spitting gravel, to circumvent the tree that he'd felled to block the highway. He roared off down the highway in pursuit, looking for a road that led south.

The bus passengers unanimously decided upon intensive group therapy as soon as they returned to civilization.

༄ ༄ ༄ ༄ ༄ ༄

After flying about 20 miles over the countryside, passing small lakes and rivers but no towns or villages, the Human Torch saw another two-lane road running east-west. He alighted and flamed off. Michael reappeared, got dressed, then sat, exhausted, on the ground.

"Sorry, Billy, but this was as far as I could go," he said. "I'm too tired; I couldn't maintain my flame any longer. The Torch can only fly so far carrying somebody. Sorry."

Billy squatted and put his arm around his friend. "It's okay, it's fine. You got us away from Brack, didn't you? That's what counts. Y'know, you apologize too much."

"I do? Sorry."

"See?"

Mike looked at Billy, then both boys grinned.

"You got anything to eat?" Mike asked. "I'm real hungry all of a sudden."

Billy fished in the pockets of the jacket he'd bought back in La Corey. "I have half a sandwich left an' two chocolate bars. Here." Michael wolfed them down.

"So Brack's got a new trick," mused Billy as his friend ate. "Our bus driver: Brack made himself look just like him. If it hadn't been for your stone warning you, an' then seeing his horrible tat, we'd never have suspected until it was too late."

"Yah."

"Y'know, Mike, there's somethin' else, too. I'm thinkin' it's not a real good idea to go check on the Birskis after all, now that we have Brack hot on our trail again. We'd be leadin' him right to them."

Michael scowled. "NO! I'm real worried about them, about what the Nastyman might of done to them! We gotta see if they're alright!"

"That's all the more reason to stay *away* from 'em! We don't want Brack to attack 'em again, do we? That's if he attacked 'em in the first place, which we don't know he did."

Mike opened his mouth to protest further, then slapped his head. "Right! I should of thought of that! Thanks, Billy. I guess we'll just haveta keep trying to get them by phone."

"Yeah. So there's obviously no reason to keep travellin' east. If we go west along this road, we haveta come across a town where we can buy bus tickets to take us back into Alberta to Edmonton. That's where our train tickets are waiting for us. We make it to there, we'll be okay, 'cause then The Canadian train takes us home across Canada back to Ontario. An' there's a bonus: Brack'll be rocketing east along that road our bus was on, chasing us in that yellow sports car of his. He'll never suspect we've changed direction and are headed west."

"But how do we get to this town?"

"Well, until you get your strength back so you can turn into something useful, we walk."

And so they did. The sun was hot, but not unbearable, and the air was crisp and clean. But the sameness of the landscape made it seem as if they were not making progress at all.

After about an hour, and despite Michael's severe misgivings, a kindly rancher gave them a lift in the back of his pickup to a roadside diner. There, the teens treated themselves to a huge meal, which really re-energized Michael. They left the diner with a bag of sandwiches and pop and headed west along the highway again. The waitress at the diner had said the next town had a restaurant that was also a bus stop where they could buy tickets.

"I'm sure someone else will come along an' give us a ride soon," said Billy. "If not, then you can turn into somethin' not too obvious that'll get us there."

Mike's reply was drowned out by the searing crackle of electricity. A blue-white bolt just missed him and hit a tree, shattering it with a loud scream of tortured wood. Michael grabbed his friend and dove for cover in the ditch running alongside the road just as another electrical bolt shot over their heads.

"Damn!" came a familiar hated voice, "I just can't believe how lucky you are, retard boy! I thought I had ya there!"

"Brack again!" whispered Billy.

"Duh," said Mike, rolling his eyes. They started crawling down the ditch, but a shadow fell across them. They looked up to see Brack looming over them, energy crackling around his eyes.

"Freeze, boys. Or I fry ya," he grated.

Billy froze. Mike disappeared. Only his clothes remained, lumped together on the ground.

"What th' hell!" exclaimed Brack, then a miniature sand storm started at his feet and swiftly enveloped him. The sand swirled thicker and thicker until the electrical man was completely cocooned. Above Brack's head, two black pits of eyes opened at the top of the cocoon, followed by a black gash of a mouth, which yelled:

"Run, Billy! Run!"

The teen grabbed Mike's clothes and the food bag and ran, thinking: *Wow! Mike's become Sand, former member of the Justice Society of America until DC rebooted their entire comics universe in 2011. His body's made of silicon, he controls sand, and he can move through the ground at great speed. And sand doesn't conduct electricity! I bet Mike knew that from reading the JSA comics.*

Billy ran for what seemed forever, then stopped, panting. The ground came alive near him, sand swirled in the air, then a very naked Michael reappeared. He looked haggard.

"What happened to Brack?" asked Billy as his friend got dressed.

"I kept him wrapped in my sand body until I was sure he'd passed out. But when I let him go - an' I was going to grab his stone, I remembered what Mister Ethan said about not doing that before when I had the chance - he turned invisible and ran off. So I became the blind Daredevil, so I could hear him with my super-hearing, but two 18-wheelers roared by just then an' their noise blocked everything else out an' gave me a real bad headache thanks to my super-sensitive ears. So I came to find you."

The yellow Acura was upon them like a missile before they even heard the roar of its engine. The boys leaped out of the way as the car shot by, but Billy was just a little slower than Mike and the fender clipped him at the hip and spun him into the air. The boy crashed into the ditch and lay still.

"Billy!" screamed Mike. He picked himself up from where he'd rolled and started running towards his friend.

The Acura skidded to a halt, tires howling and smoking. Brack flung open the door and ran towards Michael, snarling. Frantic about Billy, Mike didn't notice the electrical fire until it seared him on his left shoulder. He yelled in pain and his left arm became useless. He flung himself sideways as another bolt burned past him.

Michael disappeared again, but this time there was no pile

of clothes left behind. Brack cursed, spun around, then noticed Billy's limp form. He called out:

"A-hey! Retard! Show yourself or I fry your tubby friend here! C'mon! Or we find out what cooked whale blubber smells like!"

No response.

"Okay, boy! I warned ya! I'm through playin' games!"

Brack's eyes unleashed a vicious blast of electricity straight at Billy. The lethal charge arced through the air. And stopped mere inches from the boy, exploding off in all directions, but leaving Billy untouched.

Brack cursed and let fly with another crackling blast. Same result. Then Billy disappeared.

"What the Goddamned hell?" the killer muttered. He walked to where the boy had been, and probed the area with his foot, but nothing was there. Both teens had vanished.

Suddenly, he was hit with what felt like a hard thick pole, end-on, except that he couldn't see it. The invisible force flung him almost a hundred yards down the road. As he struggled to his feet, he was knocked down again by a powerful wind that blew past him, then ended a moment later.

"Bein' invisible won't help ya, retard! I know the two of ya are around here somewheres!" Brack screamed, enraged.

He sent electric fire in all directions, trying to hit the invisible boys, but only succeed in destroying an empty roadside stand used for selling produce in season, five fence posts, two crows, and a $145,000 yellow Acura NX convertible. Which went up in a magnificent orange fireball.

"DamndamnDAMN!" he shouted, stamping his feet.

ൔ   ൔ   ൔ   ൕ   ൕ   ൕ

Billy regained consciousness looking at the concerned face of a beautiful blonde woman bending over him, asking if he was okay in the sweetest voice he'd ever heard. Well, besides his mom's.

"I'm ... I'm fine, I think. Nothing feels broken anyway, though my hip really hurts. Wow, was I ever lucky. Um, who're you?"

"Why I'm your bestest friend - oh! Waitwaitwait! I didn't want you to see me like this!"

The blonde vision disappeared. Literally. The light bulb went on in Billy's head:

"Mike? That's you, isn't it? My God! Now I recognize you! You're Sue Richards: the Invisible Woman of the Fantastic Four! Holy crap! Mike! You became a girl! You've never done *that* before."

The blonde reappeared, blushing crimson. Billy gawked at the definite female shape under Mike's track outfit. It was a voluptuous body which, combined with the beautiful face, blonde hair and that wonderful voice, stirred emotions in him. His brain screamed: *this is WRONGWRONGWRONG, because that's really Mike!* Billy closed his eyes and shook his head; this was too weird.

When he looked again, Michael stood there. He murmured, looking intently at his feet:

"Actually, I was a girl once before: Storm. At the Birski farm. I didn't like it. Totally gross."

Billy's head was spinning and not from the hit he'd taken from Brack's Acura. "Gross? Well, I wouldn't call it that. But weird? Yeah, it'd definitely be weird. Whew. So, um, what's it like having a girl's body, eh?"

"What you said: weird. Some parts are missing and there's too much of other parts. Looking down, you can't see your feet. You have to learn how to pee differently. I don't know how girls manage to be girls."

"Yeah, I can only imagine," sighed Billy. "So, then why'd you become her?"

"Well, I hadda think fast. See, I first became the Invisible Kid when he attacked me, but when the Nastyman said he'd blast you with his lightning instead, I needed a hero who could project a force field, 'cause I had to protect you. I sword I'd never turn into a girl again, but I had no choice. The Invisible Woman has a real strong force field, an' can turn herself and others around her invisible. She also can project an invisible battering ram, an' I gave the Nastyman a real good whack with that. But turning into girls is too strange."

Michael looked miserable. Billy stood, wincing at the pain in his hip, hobbled over to Mike, and gave him a quick hug, saying:

"Thanks, buddy. For protectin' me an' not leavin' me behind. Ya coulda got away real easy an' just left me, but you didn't. I'll never forget that."

Michael beamed. "You're welcome. There's no way I'd leave you at the Nastyman's mercy. We're friends. Friends stick together, no matter what, yes they do. Plus: he *has* no mercy."

"Hey, how did you get us away? We seem to be in a completely different area here. The Invisible Woman can't travel that far, that fast."

"No, but the Flash can."

"But we're still wearing our clothes. I understand how the Invisible Woman's power turned our clothes invisible along with our bodies, but how come they didn't burn off with the Flash's speed?"

"'Cause I only moved super-fast for a short distance. As soon as we were around the bend of the road, out of sight of the Nastyman, I slowed down to a speed that didn't burneded off our clothes. An' just before I became the Flash, I became Wolverine for a sec to fix my body where the Nastyman burneded it, so I could have two good arms to carry you. Then, when I got tired of carrying you an' running, I stopped here an' became the Invisible Woman again to keep both of us invisible an' protected by her force field 'cause I was worried the Nastyman would find us again. I only turned us visible when I heard you wake up, so's I could see you."

"Huh. Wow, good thinkin' buddy."

"Thanks Billy. An' now, I'm really hungry again and really tired, too."

"Yeah. I'll bet. An' I see you did some more good thinkin' - you thought to grab our food bag. So let's hunker down an' scarf our sandwiches, eh?"

The Flash had brought them to a derelict clapboard farmhouse, long abandoned, set back from the road. Behind the sad sagging structure, down a gentle hill, was a small lake with an equally-derelict boathouse, wearing the same cracked white paint with green trim as the house. The shoreline had obviously changed over time: the boathouse sat with turgid green water halfway up its sides. The doors facing the water hung skewed on rusted hinges, splintered and broken, giving the half-drowned structure a wide gaping mouth expressing perpetual dismay at its weed-choked watery grave.

The teens sat down on the slope of the hill to eat. While chewing, Billy stared for a long time at the ruined boathouse, then said: "That thing looks just like I feel."

Michael muttered "Yah" between giant bites of sandwich. As soon as he finished eating, he stretched out and promptly fell fast asleep. Billy followed suit.

Loud voices awakened Billy long hours later. It was dark; low clouds scudded across the moon and stars. He got up, careful not to step on his still-sleeping friend, and went to investigate.

Around the side of the decrepit farmhouse, four motorcycles were parked: two Hondas and two Harleys - large powerful touring machines of gleaming chrome and bright colours. Their riders, a mix of seven middle-aged men and women wearing expensive black leather outfits, were surrounded by a larger group of younger men. These men, 11 in all, had obviously arrived in the fleet of pickup trucks parked in a semi-circle around the bikers with headlights illuminating the area. A heated argument was in progress.

"I told you biker trash that this here's private property! You're trespassin'!" shouted one of the young men, a tall thin man with a huge cowboy hat and western boots with silver plates at the toes. Billy saw that he carried a baseball bat, as did most of his fellows. It was apparent that these men had also been drinking; they were red-faced, swaggering and swaying. Four of them still carried beer bottles, from which they took frequent pulls.

"And I already said that we didn't know; there's no signs posted and we only wanted a quiet place to camp for the night!"

one of the motorcyclists shouted back. "And we resent being called biker trash! We're all respectable citizens! For example, I'm a pharmacist and my wife here is a financial planner. We're all on vacation, touring through Alberta, and we don't want any trouble."

"Pharmacist? Hah! Great cover story! You're really a gang of Hell's Angels or somethin', prolly carrying drugs, an' lookin' to get high, an' have one a' your sex orgies!" the big-hatted cowboy shouted back. "We don't want your kind around here!"

"Okay, fine!" yelled another motorcyclist. "So we'll just leave! We'll get rooms at the nearest motel, and tomorrow morning we'll tell the local RCMP all about you nice hospitable people."

The cowboy who had been doing all the talking guffawed, a nasty laugh echoed by his 10 buddies. He sneered: "Leave? Well now, I don't recall saying anything about leaving, biker trash."

"What the hell are you saying?" demanded another motorcyclist.

Without warning, one of the young men lashed out with his bat, catching the biker who had just spoken in the stomach and doubling him over in agony. His lady friend screamed.

"I'm saying," said Big Hat slowly, "that we're gonna beat the livin' bejesus outta you men, have some fun with your women, then trash those fancy machines of yours into so much scrap metal before heavin' 'em into that lake."

The group of motorcyclists bunched closely together, facing outwards towards their antagonists with their injured moaning compatriot at their centre. They raised their fists and one woman said:

"We'll have the police on you assholes tomorrow. I know people in the Alberta judicial system and I'll personally make sure you're prosecuted to the full extent of the law."

"Haw! Why, you must be a lawyer," said Big Hat. "Well, lawyer lady, you first gotta survive 'til tomorrow to make good on that threat. C'mon, boys, let's do 'em! We got nuthin' ta fear from this gang of sissy bikers!"

The night air was split by a bolt of fire that arced from the darkness to explode at the feet of the tall cowboy. Dirt and stones flew up into the ring of attackers, causing many to swear in pain and surprise. A chilling, hollow voice boomed:

"WELL, PERHAPS YOU'LL FIND SOMETHING TO FEAR IN THIS BIKER."

A motorcycle glided around the farmhouse. Impossibly, it was composed entirely of flame, even its tires. It made no engine noise whatsoever; just the sound of crackling fire. It was a huge machine: from its long front forks to its big fiery seat with a tall backrest that sported a fanged demon's head at the top. But however spooky the bike looked, what sat astride it caused men to swear and women to scream.

Its rider was a tall, gaunt figure clad in ordinary fleecewear. With a flaming skull for a head. The hands that gripped the burning handlebars were skeletal bones.

"My God!" breathed Billy, still hiding in the dark. "Mike brought the original Ghost Rider to life! And then he created his hellfire cycle!"

"I HAVE COME TO WREAK HELL'S VENGEANCE UPON THOSE WHO DESERVE IT," announced the fiery apparition. He brought his ghastly bike to a stop between the attackers and their intended prey.

"What in *hell* are you?" quavered Big Hat, sensibly joining his buddies in backing away from the spectre, until they reached their pickups.

"HELL INDEED, SINNER. I AM THE DEMON ZARATHOS, THE GHOST RIDER. BUT I DON'T RIDE TO REWARD EVIL. I RIDE TO PUNISH IT. SUCH IS MY CURSE."

"Yeah? Well, punish *this*, freak!" Big Hat suddenly had his hands full of shotgun and he fired both barrels right at the Ghost Rider.

"NO!" screamed Billy as the thunder of the gun reverberated through the night. The blast hit the spectre - and had no effect whatsoever. The hellish creature didn't even jerk backwards at the impact. Another thug had likewise grabbed his gun from his truck, and now unloaded it into the demon. With the same result. Then all hell literally broke loose.

Deep in the sockets of the awful flaming skull, blood-red

circles blazed where eyes should be. Then the Ghost Rider fired bolts of supernatural hellfire from his hands at the attackers. Big Hat was the first one hit. The fire didn't burn the men. But soul-searing screams burst from each man as the demonic fire touched them and showed them terrible things.

It was over in seconds. Eleven thugs, made bold by equal parts alcohol and numbers, who had come for easy pickings, were reduced to drooling husks, quivering on the ground in foetal positions, overwhelmed by horrible visions of their past crimes and what awaited them in hell after their death.

The flaming spectre turned and regarded the bikers with blazing cavernous eye sockets. "WELL? WHY ARE YOU FOOLISH MORTALS STILL HERE? RIDE!"

They rode. Scrambling atop their motorcycles, thumbing them into life, they fled into the night.

The Ghost Rider watched them go, then swung his ghastly head around and looked right at where Billy was hiding. "WE MUST RIDE ALSO, YOUNG MAN. BEFORE ANOTHER DEMON – A MORTAL DEMON – SHOWS. HOP ON HERE WITH ME."

Billy looked at the supernatural cycle, its angry flames eerie in their silence, then at the Ghost Rider, who watched him impassively. *Hard to believe that's still Mike inside that flaming skull,* he thought. Pointing to the bike, he asked:

"Ah, will I get burned if I get on that thing?"

"ONLY THOSE WHO HAVE SINNED NEED FEAR THE HELLFIRE," answered the skeletal head. "HAVE YOU SINNED, WILLIAM BUTLER McDONNELL?"

"Ah, um, n-nothing m-m-major, I think," stammered the teen.

"WE SHALL SEE. MOUNT UP."

A skeletal finger beckoned. Swallowing hard, Billy walked up to the blazing cycle and gingerly swung a leg over the passenger seat. Closing his eyes, he plopped down behind the spectre, half-expecting to be burnt to a crisp, or to receive horrible visions.

Nothing happened. He let out a huge sigh of relief. Then he let out a huge yell of surprise as Ghost Rider gunned the hellcycle and they sped off. Billy barely had time to put his arms around his friend before the bike surged forward. The machine still made no noise as they rocketed through the night - a silent fearsome apparition trailing unearthly flames from bike and skull.

The demon lifted his blazing skull to the heavens and screeched, an awful predatory cry like that of a dozen eagles screaming at once. Billy quailed as he realized that the nerve-wracking sound was defiant laughter.

Michael. This is really Michael, the youth kept repeating. Then he started murmuring The Lord's Prayer. Just to be on the safe side.

Ghost Rider looked back at the trembling boy holding onto him and screeched again.

༺ ༺ ༺ ༻ ༻ ༻

On a supernatural hog of silent fire, travelling faster than a normal motorcycle, they arrived at the bedroom community of Sherwood Park, on the outskirts of Edmonton, just as dawn was breaking. Ghost Rider had travelled along Highway 14, a lesser-used route than the Yellowhead Highway, Trans-Canada 16. They stopped in a deserted field and dismounted. The demon re-absorbed his hellcycle back into himself with an eerie *sah-whoosh* of flame, then became Michael once more. It seemed to Billy that it was only with great reluctance that the demon allowed the transformation to happen. Mike looked drained, but put on a brave smile and said he felt fine.

The teens walked back to the highway and started walking towards Edmonton. A commuter kindly gave them a ride to the VIA Rail station downtown. There, they found their tickets waiting for them, just as Paul McDonnell had promised. They had a three hour wait before their train departed. They found a drugstore near the station, where Billy bought some Tylenol Extra-Strength painkillers for his aching hip. After grabbing breakfast at a nearby diner, they sat on a bench inside the train station. Despite their best efforts, they fell asleep, slumped against each other.

The PA announcing the imminent arrival of The Canadian from Vancouver awoke them. They stumbled down onto the

THE HERO STONE

platform and marvelled at the procession of gleaming chrome cars snaking into the station. They boarded without incident and settled into their comfy seats. Once again, Billy let Mike have the window seat. With a slight jerk, the train pulled out of the station and picked up speed, eager to resume its long eastward cross-Canada journey to Toronto.

"Ah, now *this* is the way to travel! An' these seats are so roomy, too!" exulted Billy, stretching. "Y'know, they serve full meals on board. We'll eat like kings all the way to Toronto."

"Yah, this is much better than riding in back of moving vans," said Michael with a wry grin.

"An' later, we can go to the Dome Car an' go upstairs to see the scenery from all sides through the big dome windows. That'll be cool!"

Outside, against the front of the grey slab snout of the VIA Rail diesel locomotive pulling The Canadian, was a man-sized patch of blackness, perched on the narrow coupling mechanism protruding just above the tracks. There was a male face at the top of the blackness and it was laughing, though the throbbing thunder of the engine drowned out the sound.

After a time, the human face disappeared, melting into the shadow mass, which then flowed down the grey-and-blue side of the locomotive until it reached the first of the silver cars hitched behind. The shadow flowed inside the car through a gap where the door met the floor.

Billy said: "That Ghost Rider was one awesome scary dude, Mike. Actually, I'm surprised you became him. He's not exactly a superhero, is he? Isn't he sorta in a grey area, part bad and part good? After all, he is a demon who uses hellfire."

His friend nodded. "Yah. Seeing the bikers gave me the idea, 'cause Ghost Rider is a biker too. He's a demon from hell, yah, but he does try to do good. But I dunno if I'll ever use him again - he really tired me out. Besides, he's way too spooky."

"I'll say. Ya even had *me* goin', the way you looked and talked. Man! But ya sure scared that gang of thugs spitless."

"Not scared enough that G.R. hadda use his hellfire on 'em."

"Oh, don't feel sorry for that bunch, Mike. They deserved it, considerin' what they planned to do to those motorcycling tourists."

"Guess so."

"Hey, I just hadda thought: why don't you become G.R. next time Brack shows his sneerin' face, then zap him with the hellfire? If there's anyone with sins on his soul, it's that murderin' bastard. It'd be great to see him reduced to a drooling vegetable."

Michael frowned and started sucking on his knuckle. "Oh, I dunno. Zapping him with hellfire would be nice, yah, but I just dunno if I wanna become Ghost Rider again. I dunno if I'd trust myself. I felt so ... so angry; a real deep, nasty kinda angry, like I really was a demon of ven - vengernance."

"Vengeance."

"Yah, that. I felt like I was losing control to the demon - but that's silly 'cause there's no such things as demons in real life, right Billy?"

"Right. As far as I know. But then, several weeks ago, I never believed in magical stones, either."

"Oh. Well, anyway, I shoulda thought about how risky it would be, becoming a demon. But I didn't. See how stupid I am sometimes?"

"You are *not* stupid. I've never called you that, and neither did Melanie. You're special. And quite clever at times, too. You've certainly been very clever using your stone, always picking the right character for the challenge facing you."

"Aw, thanks, Billy. Comics are one thing I know really well."

"Like I said the other day, when you change into someone now, you sound different. I mean the words you use: They're more adult-sounding, especially when you became Ghost Rider."

Michael frowned. "Really? I dunno why. An' with G. R., it didn't feel like I changed into him, but like something came into me."

"Huh. That's creepy. Well anyway, I do know one thing: I'm lucky to have you as a friend. You've never made fun of my weight, of how fat I am. You like me for me."

"Aw, c'mon. I'm the one who's lucky. You've never been mean to me either, even though I'm - you know - that R-word."

"Hey, anyone who can whup my ass at chess and checkers, an' who stands by his friends no matter what, is someone I respect, an' that's the only R-word that applies to you, in my opinion."

Michael gave Billy a sudden hug, which threatened to fracture a rib or two. "Thanks," he murmured.

Billy went to visit the bathroom, leaving Mike to stare at the wide prairie vistas rolling past his window. He felt happy about Billy, then he remembered about his other friend - Melanie - who hated him now, and that made him feel sad. The repetitive metallic *ta-dum ta-dum* of the train wheels, which had seemed such a happy sound at first, now seemed mournful.

Billy plopped back into his seat less than a minute later.

"Man, that was fast," said Michael, shrugging off thoughts of Melanie while still gazing out the window.

"Well, when ya gotta go, ya gotta go. Hey buddy, do ya think you could let me, y'know, hold your stone for a bit? This long train ride gives us a breather, so I wanna see if it, y'know, will work for me, too. Don't worry, I won't become anything obvious."

"Why? It didn't work for ya when ya tried it before, back in Clearwater."

"Oh yeah, I know. But I just wanna try it again. Mebbe it'll be different this time, huh?"

"Well, okay. But remember it didn't work for Melanie either." Michael's jacket hung swaying from a wall hook beside the window. In a rare break from habit, he had placed his stone in one of its pockets, because he felt safe in this shining metal cocoon that was leaving his nemesis far behind them with every turn of its steel wheels.

He pulled out the polished colourful rock and almost dropped it. It was blazing hot!

He jerked his head around to look at Billy, who was smiling.

"It's the Nastyman!" Michael blurted. "Very close!"

"Do tell," said Billy. Mike felt a sharp pain in his ribs. He looked down. Coming out of the sleeve of Billy's shirt was a long obsidian knife, its point digging into his side, drawing blood. Only then did Michael realize that Billy had changed his clothes; he was no longer wearing sweat shirt and track pants, but jeans and a patterned long-sleeved shirt.

"Billy? What - ?"

Billy's smile suddenly vanished and his eyes glazed over. He fell sideways into the aisle.

"Billy!"

Another Billy, identical to the first one but still wearing fleece, stepped into view. He held a fire extinguisher in one hand, which he'd used to hit the first Billy over the head.

Michael gasped: "Another Billy!"

"No, Mike. I'm the real Billy. *That's* Brack, the Nastyman." Billy pointed to the figure lying in the aisle, stirring and trying to rise. "Someone locked me in the john. I yelled an' yelled an' finally got a conductor to bust me out; he said it looked like some joker had spot-welded the aluminium door to the frame. Then I rushed in here an' saw you talkin' to me! I realized it was Brack, so I bashed him!"

"Oh. My. Gosh. I almost gave him my stone!"

Michael stood up and moved next to Billy in the aisle, clutching his stone tightly. Some of the other passengers in their car had cried out when Billy had whacked Brack, and two men were now angrily demanding to know what the hell was going on.

Then the teens saw the black knife that had stabbed Mike transform into a human hand. Brack groggily jerked to his feet, throwing off the hands of those trying to help him. A violet glow outlined his body, then his eyes crackled with deadly electricity.

"Everyone do exactly as I say, or they get fried," he said in a calm, cold voice that nonetheless carried throughout the train car. People gawped at the uncanny blue-white energy dancing around his eyes and fell silent, with some stifling screams. "Now you boys - you Goddamned infernally troublesome boys - you do just as I say or I'll fry all these innocents. You know I can do it and, more importantly, you know I WILL do it. *Capish?*"

Michael and Billy nodded, rooted to the spot.

"Good. Very good. Now what I want you to do is so simple even the retard can understand it," Brack said with an arctic smile. "Give. Me. The. Stone. An' no changin' into any stupid-hero; I see just the start of a yellow glow around you, boy, an' I start turnin' these nice folks into Cajun cookin'."

Wordless, Mike stepped forward, palm outstretched, his gleaming rock exposed. Brack stared at it with hungry eyes. A tiny spittle of drool escaped his slack lips. The predator stepped forward towards Mike, never taking his eyes off the multi-coloured rock. "Finally!" he breathed. He reached out to take it.

No telltale yellow aura surrounded Michael at the last minute. No awesome and appropriate superhero appeared, to whup the killer's ass. All Mike did was smile. And kick Brack as hard as he could right in the balls.

With a shriek of pain, Brack collapsed. His head became wreathed in electrical arcs. The foulest curses spewed from his lips. Then Michael grabbed him from behind with two strong hands. Muscles born of countless hours working out with weights, flexed. He lifted Brack high in the air and, with an inarticulate cry, flung him at one of the big picture windows lining the side of the car. Brack crashed through it and instantly vanished from sight with a howl of anger and frustration.

Panting, hair buffeted by the wind streaming in the open window, Mike looked at Billy. Awed, Billy said: "Michael, you don't need a stone to be a hero."

Mike grinned from ear to ear. Then both boys looked at their fellow passengers. They were staring at them open-mouthed.

Emerging from behind the seat where he'd been crouching with his younger sister, a teenaged boy stared wide-eyed at the gaping hole where the window used to be, saying: "Man, the conductor is gonna be pissed."

Chapter 26

Show and Tell

When the gleaming silver snake of The Canadian finally eased into downtown Toronto's Union Station, Janet and Paul McDonnell were beside themselves with worry. They had been told that the train had been delayed by 12 hours due to an "incident" out on the prairies, so naturally, being parents, they feared the worst.

In response to their anxious questions about the exact nature of the "incident", VIA Rail officials assured them that it was not a train wreck. They said that apparently some madman had snuck onto the train and assaulted several passengers, until one passenger did everyone a favour by heaving him out the window. His body had not been found. The RCMP were continuing to investigate.

The Canadian hissed to a stop and the boys appeared on the rear platform of the only train car with plywood boards covering one large picture window. That's when Janet and Paul knew for certain that the "incident" had somehow involved their wayward charges.

The teens barely managed to step off the stairs leading down from the train before they were engulfed by Billy's parents, hugging and kissing. Michael, surprised at being included in the family welcome hug 'n' smooch, and proud of himself for not flinching, grinned hugely. He wasn't used to this treatment; in his experience, when a parent touched you, it was to hurt you.

Later, on the long drive back to Clearwater in the McDonnell's blue Volvo station wagon, the teens received stern admonishments about their abrupt and foolhardy trek westward. Explanations were demanded.

THE HERO STONE

Billy and Michael had talked about this during the rest of the train ride home, following their latest Brack encounter, and had reached a decision.

They told Janet and Paul everything. About Robert Moses Brack. About the search for Mike's birth mother. About Ethan Delperdang. Even about the hero stone.

Paul pulled into a roadside service station and parked in the adjoining picnic area, which was deserted. He turned and faced the boys in the back seat with his most stern vice-principal look, the one that made hardened high school troublemakers glad that capital punishment was no longer allowed in Canada.

"What you've just told us is completely unbelievable, especially this stone thing. You boys aren't doing drugs, are you?"

Billy laughed. "No, Pops. It's all real, honest. Show 'em, Mike."

Michael brought out his stone and displayed it. Both parents stared at it and Janet touched it.

"It's warm," she said.

"Always," said Mike. "Except when it's near the Nastyman's half; then it gets real hot."

"And you believe this stone lets you transform into comic book characters?" said Paul with the same look he gave students vehemently denying doing something they shouldn't have been doing, despite being caught red-handed doing it.

"Yes, yes, yes, Mr. Billy's Dad," nodded Mike eagerly. "Watch."

A thin yellow glow enveloped his body and he disappeared.

"WHAT?!" yelled both senior McDonnells in unison.

"Oh, I'm still here. I'm just the Invisible Kid now. See?"

And he touched both parents on their shoulders. They both yelled again as they felt his invisible hands.

"Or rather, don't see," Michael giggled.

Another flash of yellow, and the Beast from the X-Men was sitting in the back seat of their Volvo, smiling with fanged teeth, heavyset body covered with thick blue fur. Seconds later, a slim blond teenager sat there, who stuck his arm out of the open rear window and calmly watched as his hand burst into flame, tracing the number 4 in the air with fiery fingers.

Then it was Michael again, grinning.

Janet and Paul stared at him, open-mouthed. The gum Janet had been chewing fell out, unnoticed.

They looked at their son. "So, Billy, it's really true?" croaked his father.

"Yes."

"And that means all the rest of your story is true as well?"

"Yes."

"Jesus."

It was the first time Billy had ever heard his father swear.

They drove the rest of the way home in silence. Michael wasn't sure how Billy's parents were taking this, and when he looked at his friend, all he got was a helpless shrug. So he said nothing and just stared out the window, sucking a knuckle. He grew anxious for the familiar sight of Clearwater and his old street. He'd been away too long. As much as possible, he wanted to return to the comfort of old haunts, old habits.

They arrived home in late evening. Mike marched into the McDonnell house without once looking at the house next door where he'd grown up with his cruel adoptive parents, now deceased.

§ § § § § §

The next day, Janet took the boys to the McDonnell family doctor for a thorough check-up, to satisfy herself that there were no ill effects from their trip. Meanwhile, at Michael's urging, Paul tried to contact the Birski farm by phone. A cold electronic voice told him the line was no longer in service. He then called the local RCMP detachment that served Albatross Narrows.

When Janet and the teens returned, with news of the boys' clean bills of health, including that the cut on Billy's stomach was healing nicely, they found Paul sitting at the kitchen table, face grim.

"The news is not good, I'm afraid," he said. "Your Brack fellow did indeed visit the Birski farm after Michael left, just as you feared."

"Oh no!" gasped Mike, going deathly pale.

"What happened?" breathed Billy.

"Quite a bit. But the RCMP officer I first talked to, was quite annoying. All he'd give me was standard police-speak: bare outlines and euphemisms. It's obvious I got routed to an officer used to speaking with the media. However, I did manage to pry a cell phone number out of him where I could reach the Birskis. Someone had loaned them a cell phone. You better all sit down and I'll tell you the whole story."

After they had done so, Paul continued: "I dialled the number and Jesse Birski answered. After identifying myself and reassuring him that Michael was all right, we had a long conversation." He paused.

"Well?" asked the lads in stereo.

"Okay, here goes," said Paul with a heavy sigh. "Brack drove into the farmyard. But when he tried to get out of the car, the Birski's dog went crazy, barking and snarling like this Brack was some sort of demon."

"Dog got that right," muttered Billy. His father went on:

"Brack slammed the car door shut and stayed inside until Jesse Birski appeared and dragged the dog away, still howling, and chained it to a tree in the yard. Then Brack stepped out, introduced himself, and asked to see you, Michael. He claimed to be your uncle and said he'd been chasing you across Canada, trying to catch you and return you to the group home in Clearwater from which you'd run away."

"Now that's a big lie, yes it is," said Mike.

"Yes. Brack became very upset when Jesse said you'd just left to continue your westward journey, even though he should have calmed down when Jesse told him you were on a bus to Fort McMurray and he could catch up to you either at the bus station there, or earlier in Edmonton where you changed buses, if he drove fast."

Paul paused and shook his head. "Then Jesse said something very strange happened, though now that I've seen what Michael can do, I don't doubt what he said. However, the police think he must have hallucinated, or been affected by the trauma of later events, because they certainly don't believe him."

"So what *happened*, Pops?" demanded Billy anxiously. Michael sat still, staring at Paul, face white.

Paul cleared his throat. "The dog had never stopped barking and growling, and had been flinging itself against the chain holding it, desperate to get at Brack. Mr. Birski couldn't get it to shut up. The racket must have been quite annoying and Brack lost his patience. He gave an awful curse and his body seemed to glow and then Birski said that a kind of blue-white lightning blast came from his eyes, aimed at the dog."

"Oh no! Not Lucky!" cried Mike.

"Don't worry, Michael. The dog lived up to its name: the blast missed Lucky, but just barely. It did knock the animal to the ground, however, where it lay stunned. Before Jesse could react, this Brack monster turned and unleashed that strange electrical fire at their barn. A large part of a side wall exploded and a fire started, which spread despite the previous day's torrential rain that had soaked everything. Jesse and his wife, Meredith, who had come out of the house, raced into the burning barn to free their livestock, leaving Brack standing there laughing the coldest laugh they had ever heard.

"Then a gun blast rang out and a bullet kicked up ground next to Brack's feet. An old man in a wheelchair had come out onto the front porch of the house carrying a shotgun. He called out to Brack that that was a warning shot, and if he didn't get back in his damned fancy car and drive the hell off their property, the next shot would bury itself in his chest."

"Captain Kenny, RCAF, retired," breathed Mike.

"Jesse, who had come out of the barn at the sound of the gunshot, said Brack stared at the old war vet, electric fire dancing around his eyes, and laughed. He started walking towards the house."

"Wow. So what did the old guy do?" asked Billy.

"Exactly what he promised. He shot him."

"Way to go, Captain Kenny!" Mike cheered.

"The man was very old and he hadn't fired a gun in years, so his aim was off," continued Paul. "He hit Brack, but not in the chest. Got him in the leg. Brack stopped, screaming in rage and pain. He yanked out a handkerchief and tied it over his wound, which Jesse said obviously was superficial since he didn't even fall down. Meanwhile, Grandpa Kenny, as Jesse called him, was reloading the double-barrelled shotgun as quickly as he could, but his hands were not as nimble as they used to be."

"Yah, he's got arthur-itis," said Mike.

Paul paused again. A pained look crossed his face. He said:

"Grandpa Kenny had just got the gun reloaded and was bringing it to bear on Brack when the devil unleashed an electric blast right at him. It hit the gun barrel, causing it to explode. The force of the explosion flung the old man sideways, out of his wheelchair onto the porch. He ... he caught most of the shotgun explosion."

The boys stared at Paul. A small "no" escaped Michael's open mouth.

"Then Brack turned those unholy eyes of his on the farmhouse and let fly. A chunk of the house exploded and another fire started, which spread just like the barn, since everything was made of wood. Meredith Birski had rescued the last of their animals from the barn when she and Jesse saw their house catch fire. They ran to it as Brack hobbled to his car and roared off in a cloud of dust, shouting curses as he went.

"They carried Grandpa Kenny off the porch and laid him on the lawn. While Meredith tended to him, Jesse raced into the burning house, called 9-1-1 for help, grabbed the first aid kit, and ran back out."

Paul stood and came over to where Mike was sitting, placing a hand on his shoulder. He said softly:

"I'm sorry, Michael. Grandpa Kenny died in his daughter's arms before the paramedics could get there. There was nothing the

Birskis could do, though they tried their best. He was too badly injured."

"Oh no, oh no, oh no," said Mike, despair filling him, face anguished. "Not Captain Kenny, RCAF, retired."

"His ... his final words to the Birskis were: 'I'm glad you two and that silly mutt are okay. Don't cry, kids. I've had a long and very good life. And I'm pleased as hell that I managed to hurt that bastard.'"

Silence filled the McDonnell kitchen. Then Mike jerked upright and fled to his room, slamming the door after him. They could hear his muffled wails.

"The house and barn both burned to the ground," said Paul.

"Did the Birskis give the police a description of Brack?" asked Billy.

"Oh yes, and of his car, and they said he was likely heading for Fort McMurray, because that's where Michael went."

"Well, at least Delperdang wasn't lying about the cops having a description of his car."

"The RCMP said they had issued an all-provinces arrest warrant with his and the car's description, and especially alerted their Fort McMurray detachment."

"How'd they describe Brack, because he slipped into Fort McMurray past their dragnet, as we very painfully found out," said Billy.

"Just under six feet tall, with a pot belly, blond hair, moustache."

"Why, that's not how he looks at all!" Billy smacked his forehead. "Damn, it's that new ability he's developed. He can change his appearance now. No wonder the cops couldn't find him. He can look like anybody."

The McDonnells ate dinner alone; Michael refused to come out of his room.

"I'm still digesting what Michael can do with that stone of his," Paul said, putting down his fork. "It's too unbelievable to wrap my head around it, and yet we saw it with our own eyes. I'm at a loss about what to do now, what authorities I should contact."

"None, Pops!" said Billy. "Seriously, ya gotta say nothing to nobody about it! Michael's greatest fear is somebody taking his stone away from him! That's exactly what the cops did when they arrested him, remember? An' that cost Melanie her leg!"

"Yes, son. Okay, we'll keep this to ourselves, at least for now."

"Pops! Promise you'll do nothing without talking to me about it first! Please!"

"Okay, I promise."

Janet chewed thoughtfully for a while, then said:

"This Robert Moses Brack monster, you both realize he'll track Mike here, don't you? Billy said yesterday that he's drawn to Mike's half of the stone. So, Paul, tomorrow morning, sure, we're going down to the police station and speak with Chief Arnott. We have to make plans on how to deal with Brack when he gets here."

"Yes," said Paul.

"Because he *will* get here," said Billy. "That's a given."

"And I'm not going to run from him any more," said a low voice from the kitchen doorway. The McDonnells turned and saw Michael standing there. His tear-streaked face was fierce. "Captain Kenny told me: 'You don't fight a bully by running away.' It's time to stand and fight, yes it is. That man needs killing."

Chapter 27

The Titanic Battle of Fetterley's Cliff

Michael and Billy were walking along the sidewalk from the McDonnell's house towards the corner store. It was a glorious spring day: sun shining, royal blue sky splashed with fluffy clouds of purest white, melodious birdsong, tree leaves of soft springtime green dancing in the mild wind, a neighbourhood cat being furiously chased by a neighbourhood dog.

The boys hardly noticed. Several days had passed and there was still no sign of Robert Moses Brack. Though Michael's stone stayed at its usual warm temperature, every deep shadow, every parked car, made the boys jumpy and suspicious. Billy's parents had insisted Chief of Police Frank Arnott provide the teens with 24-hour police protection, and the Chief had complied. Billy looked behind them at the grey unmarked car that slowly followed some distance back. He sniffed. He knew the police would be only a minor inconvenience when Brack attacked again. But he didn't tell his folks that; they were worried enough.

"So, um, how's ... how's your folks taking it? About my secret, I mean," asked Mike, sucking a knuckle and looking hard at his feet as he walked.

"They're still freaked out by it," answered Billy. "But that's to be expected, ol' buddy. It's quite a lot to take in and my folks are practical no-nonsense types. But they'll come around. Eventually. I hope."

Michael didn't find the tone in his friend's voice very reassuring, so he continued to suck his knuckle. They walked on.

"Ah, how are you doing now, Mike? About the death of your friend, that old war vet pilot?"

Michael said nothing for a long while. Then he cleared his throat and said in a voice both sad and angry: "I don't wanna talk about it. I really really liked him."

Billy patted his friend on the shoulder. "I understand." They continued down the street.

"Y'know, I was thinkin'," Billy said. "It's too bad a good guy didn't find the other half of your stone, instead of a twisted bastard like Brack. Can you imagine another superpowered person? You two could meet an' have a team-up!"

"Yah, but first we'd haveta fight, an' then become friends," said Michael. "That's what happens in the comics alla time."

Both boys laughed.

The purr of a powerful engine came up behind them and a silver-blue Audi TT convertible pulled up alongside. The top was down and the boys were surprised to see Melanie sitting in the passenger seat. The driver was someone they didn't know: an athletic-looking young man who appeared to be in his early twenties, wearing cargo pants and long-sleeved shirt. His face seemed familiar to Billy - did he resemble some famous movie actor?

"Melanie!" Mike exclaimed joyfully. "Wow, it's great to see you!"

"Mel?" said Billy, sounding cautious. "Well, um, hi there ... "

"Hi guys!" she sang out. "Awesome to see you both again!" She was wearing faded blue jeans and a multi-coloured shirt that seemed much too tight, though it really accentuated her bosom. She had left the shirt partly unbuttoned, revealing what Billy thought was a scandalous amount of cleavage. Even part of her bra was showing. *Damn, did her parents know she went out dressed like this?*

Michael suddenly remembered how they had parted, the harsh words she had said, and drew back. "Are ... are you still hating us?" he ventured.

Billy nodded agreement. "Yeah, before we left to wander across Canada, you made it pretty clear you wanted nothing more to do with us."

The sun caught Melanie's auburn hair at just the right angle, making it shine with rich highlights. She smiled a smile so beatific, so welcoming, that even the most miserable Scrooge would melt before it.

"Oh, guys, that's all in the past. I'm really sorry I said those nasty things. It was the shock of losing my leg, y'know? I've had time to adjust now and I've been talking with some people, including your mom, Billy. Well, actually, she talked to me. Boy, did she ever." Mel rolled her eyes, then went on. "Well, I deserved it. Anyway, I've realized it wasn't your fault and I hope, really hope, you both can forgive me." She gave another blinding smile. "Can you? Please?"

Billy's heart soared and he opened his mouth to blurt out "yes", but Michael beat him to it.

"Oh yes, oh yes, you're forgiven!" he gushed, barrelling past Billy and leaning over the car door to give Melanie a monster hug. "Great, great, great! We're friends again, yes we are!"

"That's wonderful, Michael!" she said. As Mike stood back, she looked up at Billy. "Friends again too?" She stuck out her hand.

"You bet," said Billy as he shook her hand, but he thought: *Huh? What's with the handshake? We should be hugging too.*

"Oh, please forgive my manners," she said and turned to the man sitting beside her. "Guys, this is Jonathan Stewart. He's been driving me to all my physio sessions since my amputation. Well, most sessions, anyway. He just returned from a trip to visit his folks. Anyway, Jonathan, this is Billy and Michael."

"Howdy. Heard a lot about you guys from Mel," said Jonathan as he reached past Mel to shake the boys' hands. Pleased to finally meetcha."

Jonathan had a firm handshake and a steady unblinking gaze that Billy found vaguely unsettling.

"So, um, you've been driving Mel around, eh?" asked Billy, then added with faint hope: "This your parents' car, or maybe an older brother's or sister's?"

"Nope. All mine," Jonathan said, causing a Grand Canyon

crack in Billy's world. "And Mel and I have become great friends. I don't just drive her to the clinic anymore. We've even been out on a date." He gunned the idling Audi's engine.

Mel blushed and Billy's world cracked even further. "A ... date?" he croaked.

"Yep. Just dinner at El Greco and a movie."

"El Greco. Right." Billy said numbly. It was one of Clearwater's best restaurants; a place, like the Audi, that was so far out of Billy's league that it might as well have been on Mars.

"Oh, I really enjoyed it," murmured Mel and gave Jonathan a sideways glance followed by another beatific smile. "Took a lot to convince my parents to let me go on the date, since Jonathan is 21 and I'm still only 15, but they finally said yes if we were back by 10:00, which we were." She looked up at the boys again. It was then that Billy realized her hair was different.

"Mel! You changed your hair colour!" he said.

"Yeah, I put it back to its original red-brown colour, much to my parents' relief. Waiting for me in our livingroom one day, Jonathan saw a photo of me from two years ago, before I coloured it blue, and said I looked much better this way." Another sideways glance at the man to her left, another smile. Billy started feeling nauseous.

"Anyway, guys, I'm much better adjusted now mentally - and physically too. I'm really getting the hang of walking around with this thing." Mel gave her left leg a thump; it made a solid artificial sound. Billy just noticed that her jeans leg was not pinned up, that there was something beneath the denim. Mel saw his surprised look.

"Yeah, I just got this prosthetic leg a few days ago. No more crutches! It was really cool how they got the upper part to fit my stump perfectly; you shoulda seen it! They took a cast of my stump an' then made a mould an' then shaped the fibreglass around the mould an' the result is I got something that fits me like a glove. It's like a giant suction cup where it attaches to my stump."

"That's ... um ... wonderful," stammered Billy, his mind still reeling. *A DATE!*

"Yeah, next time you come over to my house, I'll put on some shorts an' show you. Anyway, it's actually a temporary leg, for me to use on an interim basis, kinda like a training leg. So far, I can only walk with it for a short while each day. It will take a long time for my stump to fully heal, especially on the inside. So it'll only be in about a year before I can get fitted with a permanent prosthesis. An' then, the neat thing will be that I can get different prosthetic legs to do different things with, like one for running an' another for swimming. They'll just attach to the fibreglass cup that fits around my stump an' I'll be able to switch the legs myself using a little wrench. Now, I will admit that using this prosthetic leg gives me some awkward moments, but I've decided I will not let it get me down. The Unsinkable Melanie Van Heusen, that's me!"

She laughed and everyone laughed with her. Billy realized how much he had missed hearing her laugh, a joyous musical sound. He also realized that he was extremely jealous of this Jonathan Stewart guy spending time with Mel, especially driving her around town in his snazzy silver-blue sports car. He decided that getting his driver's license the day he turned 16 was his new life's goal.

"Hey Mike, do you still have that special stone of yours?" she asked.

The boys stared at her, mouths agape, then Michael said in a low voice: "Of course, but Melanie, it's supposed to be a *secret*."

She laughed gaily. "Oh, don't worry about Jonathan. He already knows; I've been telling him lots of stuff; he's so easy to talk to, y'know? Besides, we're all friends here, right? So what's the big deal?"

Michael frowned and started sucking a knuckle. "Well, you shoulda asked me first, before you told. Was supposed to be our secret."

Jonathan spoke up: "Hey, it's cool, guys. I haven't told anyone and I won't. Promise. But I would like to see this special rock of yours, Mike. It sounds really awesome. Could you show it to me, please?"

Michael hesitated and his hand drifted protectively to his right front pocket.

Billy said: "I dunno ..."

But Melanie said: "Oh, c'mon Mike! It's okay, really. Jonathan's a friend. C'mon, show him your wonderful rock." And she graced Michael with a dazzling smile just for him.

Mike remembered how she'd laughed and smiled that afternoon he'd carried her among the clouds as the Angel, remembered all the good times the three of them had had hanging out together, remembered how mad she'd been after she lost her leg because he couldn't get to her in time, and decided that he never wanted to have her mad at him again, that he loved seeing her happy because it made him happy.

He brought out the stone and showed it to the two people in the car.

"Wow, it's even prettier than I remember," marvelled Mel.

"Huh, yeah, seems to be a nice-looking rock all right," Jonathan said. "But I can't get a good look at it from where I"m sitting; the sun's reflecting off it so I mostly just see a glare."

"Here, lemme have it so I can show it to Jonathan better," Mel said and held out her hand.

Michael frowned, then Melanie smiled at him again and he found himself placing his precious stone in her hand.

She turned and showed it to Jonathan. "See? Look at those beautiful colours running through it. And it's so smooth and ... and warm. So warm, I'd even say it's getting ... hot!"

"Oh, really?" said Jonathan and jammed the Audi into gear and roared off down the road with an ear-splitting squeal of tires. The car disappeared around the corner before the boys could even react.

"MY STONE!" wailed Michael. It was the most heartbreaking cry Billy had ever heard. He blurted:

"That ... that sonofabitch *stole* it - and Melanie helped him!"

The grey unmarked police car that had been shadowing the boys suddenly screeched to a stop next to them. "Get in!" barked the plainclothes cop at the wheel. "I saw what just happened! We'll chase 'em!"

Hurriedly, the two lads piled in, Billy in front and Mike in the back. The cop put the pedal to the metal and the car sped off in pursuit, siren wailing.

"Can ... can this city budget special catch that Audi?" asked Billy, hanging on to the passenger grab bar for dear life and peering anxiously ahead.

"Certainly give it a try, young man. It has a powerful cop engine with cop suspension," answered the officer, swerving around the corner on what felt like only two wheels.

Then Michael said: "Hey! You're not Mr. Policeman!"

Billy looked at the man driving the car and realized that no one so thin and spindly would ever be accepted into the Police Academy, no matter how much they lowered their standards.

"Hello again, boys," said Ethan Delperdang and grinned his scarecrow grin.

༄ ༄ ༄ ༄ ༄ ༄

"Jonathan!? What the *hell* are you doing?" gasped Melanie, clutching Mike's stone in her left hand as she hung on to the passenger door handle with her right.

"Oh, don't fret, babe. Just playing a little practical joke, that's all," laughed Jonathan. The laugh had no humour in it. Breaking the speed limits and running at least two red lights, he had raced clear of the city and was now rocketing down a county highway. Luckily, traffic was light.

"Well, it's not funny and you're driving way too fast. Slow down and let's go back. Poor Michael will be frantic that we drove off with his stone."

Jonathan looked at her face and then at her chest. "Just hold on and shut up," he growled.

An icy feeling hit Melanie's stomach and she suddenly wished she'd done up a few more buttons on her shirt.

༄ ༄ ༄ ༄ ༄ ༄

"What are you doing here, Delperdang? And what happened to the cop who was in this car?" demanded Billy.

"The cop is having a nice little nap behind some bushes, where I put him. And I'm here to protect my property."

"*Your* property? Look, we've already been through this out West. That stone belongs to Michael, not you."

"That stone belongs to *me*! I told you before, it's *mine*! My step-brother stole it from me, then it disappeared after he broke it in two just before he died, and I've been trying to get it back ever since! That's *my* stone! Both halves!"

"Mister Ethan, it's my special stone, my hero stone," said Michael quietly. "It called out to me that day I was jogging in the woods and it always makes nice humming sounds in my head. It's happy to be with me, yes it is."

Ethan gave a long exasperated sigh. "Look, kid, you don't know what you're playing with. You don't know what that stone really is. It's a parasite. You have to realize that using it has a cost, a terrible cost. I already told you: It wears you out, uses you up. Billy, you saw the photo of my step-brother: died looking like a very old man, but he was only 28."

Ethan glanced at Mike in the rear-view mirror. "In time, it'll do the same to you too, kid. You've got grey hair at your temples already."

"What?" said Mike. Billy spun around to look at his friend. "Wow, he's right, Michael! I never noticed before. You've got grey hair there, just like a middle-aged person." Which, to a teenager, was someone who should start checking out cemetery plots.

"Now if you kids would kindly shut the hell up and let me concentrate on driving. I'd like to catch up to that psycho bastard Brack without killing ourselves," said Ethan grimly.

"But ... but that's not Brack in that Audi with Melanie. It's some guy who's been driving her to physio for several weeks now, some guy she obviously finds very attractive," said Billy.

"Uh huh," muttered the beanpole man and gave the car more gas.

Billy turned to Mike, asking: "Hey, if that *is* Brack in one of his disguises, why didn't you feel your stone get hot, either in your pants pocket or in your hand?"

"I dunno, Billy. If the Nastyman was near, it woulda been very hot, like all those times before. But it wasn't! So that *can't* be the Nastyman with Mel."

ഇ ഇ ഇ ഏ ഏ ഏ

The silver-blue Audi TT ground to a stop, spraying gravel and fishtailing, where Fetterley's Road ended in a wide clearing at the edge of Fetterley's Cliff. This was a popular teenage make-out and suicide spot, depending on how your love life was going. It wasn't where Jonathan had wanted to end up - he had taken a wrong turn - but it was deserted this time of day and that suited him just fine.

The car's wheels had barely stopped turning, when Mel flung open her door and heaved herself out of the car. Shoving Mike's stone deep in her jeans pocket, where its heat threatened to burn her flesh, she started running away in the awkward hopping gait made necessary by her newly-installed prosthesis on her still-healing stump.

Jonathan caught her easily. Spinning her around, he thrust his hand into her pocket and yanked out the stone.

"Hey, give that back!" she yelled and struck at him with her fists. He gave her a vicious backhand that knocked her to the ground, eyeglasses askew. Blood started seeping from a cut lip.

Jonathan stared at Michael's stone. "Finally," he whispered. "*Finally.*"

Melanie readjusted her glasses. Before her astonished eyes, Jonathan glowed violet and shimmered. The beautiful face of a young Leonardo DiCaprio melted, changing into the cold visage of Robert Moses Brack.

"*You?!*" she gasped.

"Me." Brack said, and smiled his arctic smile. "Hello again, babe. Surprise, surprise. Ain't you impressed with my new ability? I've been Jonathan all along. Since day one, when I drove you to your first physio visit. And you never suspected, you stupid bitch. In fact, I think you even had the hots for me. Now ain't that somethin': a woman with the hots for me."

"But how'd ... how'd you even know I had a crush on Leo when I was younger?"

"Ya still have a poster of him hangin' in your room. That was a big clue. Plus I flipped through your diary while waitin' for you to regain consciousness, that day I had you tied to your chair. Never could figger out why girls keep diaries. Full of personal secrets just askin' to be read by someone."

Melanie felt like she was going to either vomit or faint. Or both.

"Don' worry, sweetcheeks. I ain't gonna kill you. My way of saying thanks for your help in finally gettin' my hands on the retard's stone. And you don' have to worry about bein' raped either. Though the rest of you is still lookin' right fine, I don' do *cripples*."

Brack stared again at the rock in his hand, then with his other hand, he unbuttoned a pocket on the leg of his cargo pants and pulled out what looked like a flat black pouch. There was no visible opening on the black mass. As Melanie watched, the black melted into Brack's palm, revealing his own stone. Brack saw Mel staring and laughed:

"I been keeping my stone wrapped in my shadowstuff since returning to your jerkwater town. I figgered it would deaden the attraction between the two halves, so it wouldn't tip off the retard. It worked too. His stone only started gettin' hot when it was in your hand, when you were sittin' right next to me."

Brack held a stone in each hand. Both rocks were so hot, they glowed even in the sunlight. Brack didn't seem to feel the heat on his skin.

"Yes, yes, yes," he murmured to the objects in his hands. "You'll finally be whole again. Then you can stop *buggin'* me. Then I can do what I wanna do *all* the time. Then I'll be freakin' *invincible*."

Heralded by its siren, a nondescript grey sedan flew out of Fetterley's Road and skewed to a stop in the clearing amidst flying gravel. Three car doors sprang open and three highly-agitated males jumped out.

"STOP WHAT YOU"RE DOING!" commanded the tallest male, an impossibly-thin apparition.

"MELANIE, YOU OKAY?" yelled another, a teen almost as wide as he was tall.

"*GIVE ME BACK MY STONE!*" screamed the third, a teen who obviously worked out, judging by his chest and arms.

Brack laughed, an icy cascade of darkest malice: "You three Goddamned pests again! Well, you're too late!"

And with that, Robert Moses Brack joined the two D-shaped halves of the stones together.

"NOOOO!" shouted four voices in perfect unison.

"*Yes, oh yes,*" said Brack huskily.

A blinding yellow light enveloped the stones, then an equally-bright violet light, then a pure white brilliance so strong that it forced everyone to look away. A wild banshee wail filled the air. Brack screamed, but kept his grip on the stones.

After what seemed an eternity, the white light and keening wail died away. Brack stood shrouded in steam, which slowly dissipated with reluctant tendrils. Then, with an primal roar of triumph, he help up the stone for all to see. It was whole again, perfectly oval, with just a faint thin line down the middle marking where the break had been.

"Now the power is all mine!" he yelled. "Now no-one will ever again be able to deny me anything, or tell me what I can or can't do! Now I will - "

"Now you will please shut-the-hell-up, you twisted bastard," said Melanie and spun on her good leg in a perfect roundhouse kick, catching Brack full in the chest with the foot of her artificial leg.

The predator flew backwards and landed hard on his rump, a look of complete surprise on his face. Mel was disappointed to see he had not dropped the stone.

"You little *bitch*,"snarled Brack, getting to his feet. "I said I'd leave you alone, but now, now you'll wish you'd never been born when I get through with - "

This time, Melanie's artificial foot caught Brack square on the chin, snapping his head back so hard that the other three males heard his teeth clack together from where they stood across the clearing. Brack stumbled backwards one step, two, then three, then he was over the edge of the cliff and falling, leaving a trail of screamed curses in his wake.

Melanie planted both feet firmly on the ground and pulled her loose hair away from her face, tucking it back behind her ears. "How's that for a *cripple*, Mister *Bastard*?" she said. "I've been practising my kickboxing with this new leg, because *I-refuse-to-be-a-victim!*"

Then Billy and Michael were there, hugging her and babbling incomprehensibly. Meanwhile, the tall scarecrow ambled to the edge of Fetterley's Cliff and peered over. The bottom was a long way down and Brack's splayed body looked very small among the sharp jumbled rocks there.

"Girl, when you kick someone, you don't fool around," Ethan said. He looked around the cliff edge, hoping that Brack had dropped the stone before he fell, but the smooth iridescent oval was not there. *Hell and damnation,* he thought. *Now I'll have to get down there somehow, to retrieve it.*

"So it's over, it's finally over," gushed Billy, stepping back from Melanie. "And there was no typical climatic comic book battle between good and evil, between Mike and Brack. You took care of him all by yourself, Mel!"

The girl grinned. Even Mike managed a smile, though he was devastated at the loss of his special stone. He would no longer be able to become any of his beloved superheroes. But he was happy his two best friends were all right.

The ground trembled, ever so slightly.

"Well, now maybe things can get back to normal," said Billy. "Never thought I'd say it, but boring ol' Clearwater sounds pretty good after everything we've been through."

The ground shook again, harder.

"Hey, you kids feel that?" said Ethan. "Do you get earthquakes in this area?"

With a massive sibilant roar, like standing behind Niagara

Falls, a huge black shape shot up from the bottom of the cliff, soaring high over the cliff edge. Gigantic dragon wings of deepest jet unfolded and seemed to blot out the sky. A massive head with glowing red mouth filled with dozens of black needle teeth screamed defiance. It was four times larger than Brack's usual shadow creature. The thing's orange triangular eyes had bright blue-white electrical fire dancing around them.

"YOU DON'T GET RID OF ME THAT EASILY, YOU STUPID SONS A' BITCHES," said the creature in a booming voice that sounded like it was borrowed from Satan himself. "I'M SO POWERFUL NOW THAT I HAVE THE ENTIRE STONE. NOW I CAN DO TWO THINGS AT ONCE. JUST LOOK AT THIS MULTI-TASKING: SHADOW DRAGON AND ELECTRIC EYES."

Massive electric fire lanced from the black monster's eyes and exploded next to the dumbfounded foursome, knocking them down like tenpins. They lay still, unconscious, smoldering, their clothing shredded.

The black dragon-thing towered over the supine bodies, its awful mouth hissing in triumph.

"OH, I'M GONNA HAVE ME SOME FUN NOW."

Chapter 28

Armageddon

Clearwater was burning.

The downtown was a mass of flame and smoke, with many stores and offices engulfed. Dozens of dead and dying people lay strewn on the streets, sidewalks and parks. Firefighters racing to control the fires had been brutally murdered. Ditto paramedics arriving in their ambulances to tend the wounded, and police trying to restore order.

After seeing most of his brave men and women quickly and callously butchered by the black *thing*, Chief of Police Frank Arnott had ordered his surviving officers to pull back and leave the downtown to the creature. Arnott had his people establish a perimeter well away from the outer limits of the downtown, where they grimly hunkered down to await the arrival of the army. The commander of the closest Canadian Armed Forces base had needed a lot of convincing that what Arnott was telling him about the attacker was real and not some insane practical joke, and that, despite a meagre budget after years of government cutbacks, he should bring every piece of anti-tank ordnance and explosives he could lay his hands on.

"Now hold on, Chief. Normal procedure dictates that if local law enforcement can't handle a situation, then you call in the Ontario Provincial Police. If they can't handle it, then they contact the government which then, if the situation warrents, contacts me," said the base commander, irritated that proper procedure had not been followed. "So did you call the OPP before you called me?"

"The hell with all that! I called you directly," said Arnott, equally irritated that lives were being lost while proper procedure was being followed. "We need a rapid heavily-armed response to this terror!"

"Chief Arnott, are you saying it's a terror attack?" the commander asked.

"Hell yeah," said Arnott, "but not your usual -"

"That's all I need to hear," interrupted the commander. "We'll have a recce fly over in one hour. If they confirm your story, then we'll contact the OPP to deploy their Anti-Terrorism Squad. We'll also activate our own JTF2. So you'll have boots on the ground there in about four hours."

"Four hours! My city won't *be* here in four hours!" barked Arnott and slammed the phone down.

City Hall was ablaze, with the Mayor dead along with most of her staff. The carefully-manicured town square across from City Hall was in ruins with trees uprooted, park benches burned, the cenotaph commemorating the city's war dead shattered into a million pieces, the monument erected in 1967 marking Canada's Centennial blasted into twisted bronze shards.

Three telephone poles had been ripped up from a nearby street and rammed into the ground on a wide stretch of lawn near the centre of the ruined square, in a semi-circle facing the City Hall bonfire. Three people had been bound half-way up these upright poles with thick chain, taken from Sam's Hardware (before it had been set ablaze) wrapped around their torsos, supporting most of their body weight. They had been crucified to the poles, their arms stretched above their heads, with six-inch nails, also courtesy of Sam's, pounded through their hands and feet. The hands had been impaled one on top of the other, with one nail. Ditto the feet. Blood flowed freely from the nail wounds.

The crucified victims were Michael Johnson, Billy McDonnell and Ethan Delperdang.

Their clothes were in tatters, courtesy of the electrical explosion that had rendered them unconscious at Fetterley's Cliff. As each of them slowly regained consciousness, they screamed in agony as the pain from their impaled hands and feet hit them.

It was music to the ears of the black shadow monster that restlessly prowled back and forth along the section of street separating City Hall from the town square, shifting its gigantic shape from dragon to snake to *Tyrannosaurus Rex* to scorpion and back again. An ebon monster that howled its triumph to the smoke-blackened sky in a voice that was no longer even remotely human.

༄ ༄ ༄ ༄ ༄ ༄

As Melanie Van Heusen fought her way back into consciousness, at first she thought she was moving. As full awareness flooded in, she realized that she wasn't moving at all; things were moving on her, around her. Many things.

She was tied spread-eagled on the floor with ropes leading from her wrists and ankles to six-inch nails driven into the concrete. The floor *moved*: it was alive with insects and snakes. Hundreds of insects and snakes. Many of which were on her. Wisely, she fought the urge to scream, keeping her lips pressed firmly together, which was a good thing, as a scarab beetle was currently on her left cheek investigating a corner of her mouth.

She shook her head, sending multi-legged bugs and one small snake scattering. Her thick glasses had been replaced on her face following the electrical explosion. She looked down. All over her body, snakes and bugs were writhing and skittering in and out of what was left of her clothes. Again, she mastered the urge to scream.

Brack did this, she thought. *Tying me like this. Putting my glasses back on so I could clearly see what was all over and around me. Not gagging me so I could scream myself insane while bugs crawled into my mouth. Well, screw you, Brack.*

Looking around, she saw she was in a small room, with a low ceiling, three solid dark walls and a huge picture window instead of a fourth wall. Outside the window, she saw a long corridor ending in a pair of double doors with windows, through which daylight streamed. She recognized the place; she had visited it many times. She was in one of the display cages in the Insect and

Reptile House at the Clearwater Zoo, nestled in a ravine near the centre of town. Normally, there were just two species of snake in this cage. But Brack had added all the snakes and insects from the other exhibits.

Girl: Do. Not. Panic. You panic, you die.

She tested her bonds. Firm, unyielding. Brack knew his stuff; the knots were at the backs of her hands, where her fingers couldn't get at them, and the other ends of the ropes were knotted to nails at least two feet away from her hands. She had no hope of wriggling closer to one of the nails; she was painfully stretched to her limits. She wasn't going anywhere.

She froze, letting a large venomous spider wander across her forehead and down her right cheek, before stepping off to rejoin the writhing mass on the floor.

Yep. This is definitely Brack's work. God knows what he's done to the guys, but I bet he put me here because he figured I'd absolutely freak with all these spiders and snakes and bugs. Girls are usually terrified of these creatures.

But that asshole made one very big mistake: I'm not like most girls. I don't mind insects and reptiles. Not in the least. No way. In fact, I'm considering going to university to specialize in 'em. So all I gotta do is keep my big mouth shut, not make any sudden moves that'll encourage anything to bite or sting me, and work at getting one of my hands loose. At least it's daytime and most of these beasties are nocturnal and the zoo keeps 'em well fed, so they're either asleep or really drowsy right now.

A four-inch-long millipede travelled from her right shoulder down her bra strap and along the top of her bra. It disappeared into the darkness of her cleavage. It decided it liked it in there, because it didn't come out. Several spiders slowly explored her stomach. A Madagascar Hissing Cockroach, all five inches of it, skittered over her left ear and went into her hair. Something, she couldn't see what, was weaving in and out of her flesh-and-blood toes on her right foot (she had lost her shoes and most of her socks in the explosion). Two foot-long snakes toured her right leg and settled in neat coils on the floor between her thighs. She could feel their smooth skin against her skin, through the rips in her jeans.

Once again, she battled the urge to scream.

ക ക ക ക ക ക

After a while, the crucified trio were all screamed out, though low groans still came from Ethan. The pain in their hands and feet had receded into a constant dull throb, as long as they didn't move. Most of the bleeding had stopped, and the rivulets of blood down their arms and along their bodies had dried.

The shadow *thing* had gone into a five-storey office building a block away, one of the few not burning. Bodies of men lay strewn around the building and half out of broken windows on the upper floors. Soon after, screams - female screams - had started, from many different throats. The screams had lasted for quite a while, but had now mostly stopped.

Billy turned his head and looked at Michael. His friend was silently crying, tears carving paths through the blood and dirt caked on his cheeks.

"Hey ... hey, Mike," Billy croaked weakly. "C'mon, hang in there, buddy. If a fat guy like me can tough out this pain, you can too."

Michael sniffed and said in a cracked voice: "Yes it hurts real bad, but that's not why I'm crying. We lost, Billy. The Nastyman has my hero stone an' it's part of his stone now an' I'll never get it back, never, never, never. We lost."

Yeah, well, putting it that way, I feel like crying too, Billy thought. Aloud, he said: "Ya gotta buck up, Mike. We'll get out of this somehow. Someone'll come to rescue us."

Michael snuffled for a while, then asked: "Where's ... where's Melanie?"

Billy had been asking himself the same question since he regained consciousness and he didn't want to think about the answer. He prayed she wasn't in that building where all those women had been screaming. "I dunno," he said.

"How ... how long will the Nastyman leave us here like this?"

"Well, if he does what the Romans did, he'll leave us here until we die. Crucifixion was a slow, painful way of killing someone in the ancient Roman Empire."

Ethan coughed, groaned, and gasped out: "Geez ... kid ... thanks a bunch ... for the history lesson. Wonderful ... morale-booster."

Billy smiled in spite of his pain. "How you doing over there, Ethan?"

"Just ... peachy. Just ... like you boys ... I'm sure. Well, we're in a right ... proper pickle now ... aren't we?"

"Seems so. But someone'll come help us."

"Mebbe ... but don't count on it. Looks like Brack has killed many cops, firemen and paramedics ... and the bodies have all been left where they fell ... meaning no one's left to come get 'em."

"Huh. And you called me a morale-booster."

Another female scream came from the office building, a long wail of despair and pain. Billy couldn't tell if it sounded like Melanie. He tried to convince himself that it did not.

The scarecrow was overcome by a sudden coughing fit. His body convulsed and pulled at the nails, causing him to cry out in pain. A shriek of agony sounded from the office building, mixed with an animal shout of triumphant lust.

"Christ! What that Goddamned bastard must be doing to those poor women!" said Billy, wishing he could clap his hands over his ears and then ashamed of such a selfish thought.

Michael muttered something to himself. Billy looked over and saw his friend frowning so hard that his eyebrows looked welded together. His eyes were screwed shut and his lips were mouthing some inaudible mantra.

Then Mike's body went all blurry.

Ah Jesus, I must be passing out again, thought Billy. He blinked and shook his head, clearing the sweat from his eyes. He looked at Michael again. His friend was no longer crucified to the pole. The long nails were still there and the chain that had been around the teen's torso hung limply against the wood. But no

Michael.

Impossible! That's completely impossible! Billy thought and looked down. Mike lay in a crumpled heap at the base of the telephone pole. Billy saw a familiar yellow glow outline his friend's body; when it faded, his ugly wounds were gone.

"I don't believe this!" Billy gasped and thought: *Yeah, the Flash can vibrate through solid objects, and the Wolverine can heal his injuries, sure, but Mike doesn't have his stone any more!* Aloud, he said: "Mike! How the hell can you - "

Now hundreds of small thick orange rocks were growing all over Michael's body. In seconds, the strongest member of the Fantastic Four, the ever-lovin' blue-eyed Thing, stood there grinning his huge slash-mouth grin.

Billy gaped, speechless. He looked at Ethan. A funny smile ghosted across the scarecrow's face.

The Thing lumbered over and slowly, carefully, uprooted Billy's pole with orange rocky four-fingered hands and arms as thick as the pole itself. Billy gritted his teeth at the pain the movement caused in his impaled hands and feet. The Thing gently laid the pole down on the lawn, then bent and slowly pulled out the nail piercing Billy's hands. The boy screamed in pain. He gave a repeat performance when the nail pinning his feet was pulled free.

In a voice that sounded like it came from a gravel crusher, the Thing rasped: "Sorry."

He moved over to Ethan and repeated the process, causing more screams.

As the Thing turned back to Billy, he was greeted by a massive black battering-ram of a fist, which smacked into his broad rocky chest, sending him flying hundreds of feet backwards, clear out of the ruined town square.

༄ ༄ ༄ ༄ ༄ ༄

Some time had passed and Melanie had become sure of two things:

One: no one was going to come rescue her any time soon.

Where were the zookeepers, the cops, or even the general public? she'd asked herself countless times. She finally realized: *It's entirely up to you, girl, to free yourself. Somehow.*

Two: if she didn't get out of here before nightfall, when these drowsy and sleeping creepy crawlies all became active and started looking for food, then she was in big trouble. She'd been very lucky so far; despite all the creatures traversing her body, she'd only been bitten once, on her right calf, and she thought it had only been an exploratory nip from something not poisonous. She hoped. Though just after the bite, she'd had long moments of rising panic, where she fought to keep her self-control instead of going berserk, screaming and writhing in her bonds like a madwoman. Which definitely would have caused more bites and stings.

The cage was very warm, almost hot, simulating the tropics, the beasties' natural habitat. Mel was covered in a sheen of perspiration. But the sweat had a side benefit; it allowed her some movement of her wrists under the ropes holding them.

She had twisted her hands around so her fingers could reach the ropes leading to the nails. For a long time, she'd been picking at those ropes with her fingernails. So far, all she had to show for it were broken fingernails and a few cut strands. The rest of the thick ropes held firm.

Damn these ropes! I need something sharp.

She froze as a snake lethargically flowed across her chest and started down her right arm.

Hey, waitaminute! Snake fangs are razor-sharp.

The reptile slithered down her arm to her hand. As its head passed her fingers, Melanie suddenly twisted her hand and clamped her fingers around the snake's neck, just behind its head, like she'd seen scientists do when distending the jaw to take venom samples. The creature's mouth gaped open, revealing long deadly fangs, and it hissed its disapproval. Its long body thrashed around her arm and the floor, scattering insects.

Gritting her teeth, terrified that her sweaty fingers might lose their grip, Mel picked away at the rope with the snake's fangs. Its hissing grew louder and angrier, its body twisted wildly. The insects around her became more agitated as the writhing coils disturbed more of them.

Still she kept picking away. Something else bit her, on her left side just above the waistband of what was left of her jeans, but it felt like another nip, likely from a creature annoyed at being disturbed, nothing venomous. She hoped again.

After what seemed an eternity, she was overjoyed when the taut rope suddenly parted. Her right arm was free!

She heaved her furiously-reluctant rescuer away from her. It smacked into a wall and dropped in a mass of coils, stunned.

She reached over and, grunting, untied her left arm. Then, moving very slowly, she sat up, gently displacing the various bugs who'd taken up residence on her upper body. She untied her ankles then, equally slowly and gingerly, she stood up, moving bugs off her legs as she did so.

Carefully, with infinite slowness, she moved through the mass of snakes and insects towards the picture window. Finally reaching it, she pounded on it with her fists. It only vibrated slightly. It sounded very thick.

She turned and eyed the rear access hatch to the cage, but discounted it immediately; it was sure to be securely latched from the other side.

Melanie bent and grabbed her ripped jeans around her left thigh, tearing the denim more. She reached in and detached her prosthetic leg, releasing the suction cup from her stump and drawing the leg out from the bottom of her pants leg.

Brack made another big mistake when he trapped me inside here, she thought grimly, turning her prosthetic leg upside-down. *He caged a girl with an artificial leg.*

Balancing herself on her good leg, she swung the steel-and-fibreglass heel of her prosthetic limb against the display window with all her might. She was gratified to see a small crack appear. She hit it again, harder. Then again. And again.

The window finally shattered outwards. Gingerly, careful not to cut herself on the broken glass, Mel hopped out into the corridor, then hopped a good distance away from her prison. Looking back, she was relieved to see only a few creatures were following her out into the corridor, but nothing was giving chase. So far.

There was a bench against the wall and she sat on it. She bent forward and shook her hair, fanning it and running her fingers through it. Several squirming insects fell out, and she took great satisfaction squashing them with her prosthetic foot. She took off all her clothes - she was past caring if anyone walked in while she was naked - and thoroughly shook out each piece, ensuring that no bug or snake was hitch-hiking. More bugs fell out - and were summarily dispatched. She swept her rolled-up shreds of a shirt all over her body, especially the back where she couldn't see. Finally satisfied she was clean of insects, she examined the two areas where she'd been bitten. There was little swelling and only faint discolouration.

Thank God!

She reattached her leg, wincing as the suction cup snugged onto her still-tender stump. The foot was damaged, especially the heel, but she thought she could still manage to walk with it. She dressed again, though her tatters could not be called clothes by any stretch of the imagination.

She saw more of her former cellmates spill out into the corridor. *Time to go, girl.* With an awkward gait because of her damaged foot, she walked to the doors at the end of the corridor and discovered what had happened to the zookeepers. A woman in a staff polo shirt lay slumped in a pool of blood against the bottom of the door with deep ugly tears across her upper body, like she'd been mauled by something with huge claws. She was quite dead. The zoo had no large carnivores like lions and tigers and bears.

Oh my!

Fighting down a tide of nausea, Melanie stepped over the corpse and opened the door to the outside.

Stepping into the afternoon sunlight, she thought: *I've come to three major decisions. One: there's no way in hell I'm ever going into entomology or herpetology now. No Goddamn way. I've seen enough bugs and snakes, up close and very personal, to last two lifetimes. I'm going to become a marine biologist and study whales or something. Or I may become an exterminator.*

Two: I see Brack again, I'm going to kick him right in the balls, so hard they'll shoot up into his throat where I hope he chokes on 'em. First time he tied me up, it cost me my leg. This time, it was supposed to cost me my life. Bastard.

Three: I'm going to scream. Loud and long. I've earned it.

Melanie acted on her third decision then and there. Until her throat was raw.

༂ ༂ ༂ ༂ ༂ ༂

Michael Johnson was in the fight of his life and he knew it. The Nastyman, in all his monstrous black glory, had been hammering away at the Thing for some time, relentlessly. Chunks of the Thing's thick orange rocky hide had been broken off, the soft skin beneath oozing a dark oily fluid.

With the full power of the entire stone, Brack had formed a creature out of H. P. Lovecraft's darkest nightmares to fight Michael. Its top half was dragon-shaped with broad chest and sinuous neck, the bottom half was a thick snake ending in a huge scorpion's tail. Overall, the creature was almost three times the size of a *Tyrannosaurus Rex*. Two gigantic bat wings ending in razor-sharp points sprouted from its back, with deadly claws at the tip of the first wing joints, and its massive wedge of a dragon's head was almost all mouth. A red hell of a mouth crammed with long black needle teeth.

The hideous monster was the chimera tattoo on Brack's forearm brought to awful life.

Doggedly, ignoring the pain of his shattering skin, Mike kept fighting back, landing punch after punch on the black monster with huge piledriver fists. He made the creature stagger, but still the attacks kept coming. Neither combatant said anything; they fought in a terrible silence broken only by occasional roars from Brack and grunts from the Thing.

Their epic battle raged through the downtown, crashing into buildings, destroying parked cars, tearing up outdoor café patios and sidewalks. Michael realized that the Nastyman was much stronger than any time they had fought before. The teen kept his Thing shape; he was in too much pain to concentrate on changing into something else.

A terrible truth dawned on Michael: despite the Thing's prodigious strength, he was tiring and he was losing. With the Hulk, the madder he got, the stronger he got. Not so with the Thing.

With an inarticulate cry of rage, the towering black creature dislodged half of a three storey building with its powerful wings and sent it crashing on top of Michael. As the Thing disappeared beneath tons of falling rubble, his arms thrown up to protect himself, he felt a sharp pain as his left arm broke. He choked back a cry of agony.

No, I won't cry out. Heroes is tough. Heroes just keep fightin' no matter what, the boy thought.

Using his other arm and pushing with the Thing's massive legs, Mike dug himself out. Emerging from the wreckage, he found the grotesque chimera waiting.

"AWWW, HURT YOURSELF, RETARD?" Brack sneered in a deep hissing voice that chilled Michael to the bone. "LEMME BREAK THE OTHER ARM, GIVE YOU A MATCHED SET. I DUNNO HOW THE HELL YOU MANAGED TO CHANGE INTO THAT ROCK MAN WITHOUT YOUR HALF OF THE STONE, BUT I FIGGER ONCE YOU'RE LYIN' DEAD ONNA GROUND, I WON'T REALLY GIVE A DAMN."

The black horror flung itself at the Thing, bowling him over. Its giant jaws grabbed hold of the Thing's thick rocky neck, trying to sever it. The monster's orange eyes blazed malevolence. Meanwhile, the sharp claws at the end of its wing joints pummelled Mike's body and its deadly scorpion tail kept striking at him over and over, trying find the places in the Thing's rocky armour where the rocks had been ripped off, leaving vulnerable oozing flesh beneath. Mike's broken arm hung useless and Brack exulted each time he got in a solid hit on the injured limb.

Michael managed to get the Thing's broad shovels of feet up against Brack and heaved the creature off him. The Nastyman landed nimbly, coiled his lower snake's body, then launched itself back at Mike. The youth charged forward on legs like tree trunks and the two titans clashed.

They stood there frozen, like living statues carved by a nightmare: a small orange powerhouse against a massive ebony beast, limbs locked and straining, exerting powerful energies trying to throw the other off balance. Mike knew if he fell, he wouldn't be getting up again.

After what seemed an eternity of grunting and straining, the Nastyman cursed and shifted his grip on Michael slightly. That was enough for the Thing. With a shout of triumph, the teen stepped sideways and, as Brack stumbled forward, he hit him with a vicious piledriver with his right fist.

Brack went down and when he came up, scorpion tail darting at Mike, he seemed a little smaller.

This time Brack got lucky and the deadly hooked barb of his tail went deep into exposed flesh. Michael screamed in agony and jerked backwards, pulling free of the barb. The Nastyman roared in triumph and renewed his attack. Furious pummelling drove the Thing to his knees, head down, back hunched, rock chips flying off him.

Then Mike felt himself being grabbed by claws, lifted high off the ground, turned over, and brought crashing down with the small of his back impacting the massive upraised coil of the creature's snakelike lower body. The youth felt something in his back snap and suddenly he could not longer use his legs.

Laughing a devil's cold laugh, Brack flung the broken body of the Thing away from him. It skidded across the road and fetched up hard against the side of a building, where it lay unmoving.

The Nastyman turned and started slithering towards the town square, where Billy and Ethan lay, almost helpless in their pain, watching the epic battle in open-mouthed horror.

"Stop," croaked the Thing in a gravelly voice wracked with pain. "Come back here, Nastyman. We're not finished. You got a lot to answer for. Or are you a coward? Yes you are, aren't you? Just a great big momma's boy coward."

With a cry of rage, Brack spun around and charged the fallen hero. Grabbing a lamppost, Michael hauled himself upright with his good right arm and braced himself against the pole with the left side of his body and his broken arm, ignoring the white-hot pain that lanced through him, wobbling as his useless legs threatened to collapse under him.

As Brack slithered up to him, Michael evaded the snapping dragon's mouth and started pounding at the black creature with his massive right fist. The monster struck back with teeth, claws, and tail. Michael cried out in pain, but still he kept punching at the nightmare beast. Though he was hurting too much to notice, each punch he landed now caused Brack to grow smaller.

Suddenly the ebon creature gave a hideous scream and stopped its attack. It looked down at a length of aluminum pole jutting out from its chest. Its dragon's head twisted around on its reptilian neck and saw Billy holding the rest of the metal shaft - a broken flagpole - that he had rammed into the monster's back.

"*You leave my buddy alone!*" the bleeding teen yelled, eyes fierce, ignoring the pains in his body. "Leave us all alone! Go back to hell, you sonofabitch!"

The beast started laughing. Its laugh was more unnerving than its screech. "NICE TRY, FAT BOY, BUT YA CAN'T KILL ME THAT WAY. ALL YA DID WAS PISS ME OFF."

One of its huge bat-wings struck Billy, flinging the boy across the street into a parked truck as if he weighed nothing. Billy hit with a sickening thud and lay still.

"NO!" shouted the Thing. "Fight me, you Nastyman! I'm the one you gotta beat!"

The creature pulled the flagpole spear out through its chest and flung it away. Its black flesh closed over the holes in its chest and back; in seconds, it looked just like it had before. With another awful laugh, the monster resumed its vicious attack on the crippled Thing. Doggedly, Michael fought back with thunderous punches. Billy's brave attack had given Mike a much-needed breather, to get his second wind.

Finally, it could be ignored no longer: Brack was definitely shrinking. Where before the shadow beast had been four times the Thing's size, now it was only twice the size. Heartened, the boy kept up his barrage, landing blow after blow on the black hellspawn, ignoring the terrible punishment he himself was getting.

Suddenly, through his red fury, Brack realized what was happening to him. He was now the same size as his opponent! With a strangled cry, he broke off the fight and reared back, bat wings fanning.

"WHAT THE HELL YA DOIN' TO ME, RETARD?" he screamed. He screamed again as a big chunk of sidewalk smashed into him, courtesy of Benjamin J. Grimm, alias the Thing. The ebony monster shrunk some more.

Encouraged by this latest development, using his good arm, the Thing heaved his broken body at Brack, yelling his famous battle cry: "IT'S CLOBBERIN' TIME!"

The Nastyman yelped and tried to evade and Michael did indeed miss the monster thanks to his useless legs, but as he fell, the orange powerhouse caught Brack with a vicious uppercut - packed with all of the Thing's remaining strength - right on the jaw. The punch snapped his awful black dragon's head back, teeth clacking, and sent him soaring out of the downtown, still shrinking, in the general direction of the zoo.

Michael watched the black shape of his nemesis disappear. "That was for all the people you hurted and killeded, you evil mizzerble Nastyman, 'specially Captain Kenny, RCAF, retired," he muttered. Tears wound their way down the crags and valleys of the Thing's rocky face, unfelt.

The youth turned and started dragging himself with his one good limb toward Billy, then discovered he needed an immediate nap. He collapsed into unconsciousness.

Sometime later, as the Canadian army entered the battle zone, the soldiers found a half-naked overweight boy with puncture wounds to his hands and feet, cradling the bloody, shattered, completely-human body of his friend and crying piteously for help.

No one noticed an anorexic scarecrow, with similar wounds as

Billy, limping around the area where Brack had been before he'd been launched skyward, searching for something.

The medics were unable to revive Michael Johnson.

◈ ◈ ◈ ◈ ◈ ◈

Melanie Van Heusen had hobbled half-way down the zoo's wide central pathway towards the main entrance. The only people she had seen were lying in crumpled, bloody heaps. Brack's handiwork.

She was frantic with worry about Billy and Michael, about her family and her other friends. *Has Brack murdered everyone in town? And where are the police or the army?*

A high-pitched whistling reached her ears, increasing in volume. If she didn't know better, she could have sworn it sounded like a tiny scream.

A small black blob smacked into the pavement about five yards in front of her. She stopped, staring. The blob lay motionless for several seconds, then slowly started moving, snake-like, towards the grass and the shadows of the big elms beyond.

Mel hobbled closer and was shocked to see the crawling black blob was not a blob at all, but a familiar nightmare chimera about five inches long. She almost screamed in revulsion when she saw it had a tiny human head. The head of Robert Moses Brack.

White fury exploded inside her. She went up to the monster and kicked it with her good leg, sending it flying into the side of a metal garbage can. It hit with a resounding *whunk*, then dropped to the pavement. It started to move as Mel walked up to it, but it seemed to have become smaller.

The girl towered over the miniature creature. It screamed something defiant up at her, but she couldn't make out the words and she couldn't care less anyway.

"This ... this is for all those poor women you raped and murdered, you vicious scumbag!" she yelled and brought her prosthetic foot down hard upon the black devil. Its high-pitched curses were abruptly cut off as her foot hit. She bore down with her full weight, ignoring the pain that it caused in her tender stump, grinding it into the sidewalk.

When she lifted her foot, the creature's body lay twitching, scorpion tail writhing weakly. Brack looked up at her, tiny eyes blazing hatred, tiny mouth snarling something unintelligible.

"And this is for Billy and poor Michael and the horrible things you must have done to them, you Goddamn evil asshole," she said and stomped him again as hard as she could, with a strength fuelled by rage. This time, the beast hardly moved at all when she lifted her prosthetic foot.

"And this, this is for *me*." She mashed him a third time, so hard she cracked her steel-and-fibreglass foot. The impact sent a white-hot blaze of agony through her stump.

She stepped back, breathing hard. The black thing lay still.

"Seems I had one more bug to squash after all. A cockroach. An' I think I just insulted cockroaches." She looked down at her artificial leg and smiled. "Poetic justice, you sick twisted bastard. Killed by the leg you took from me."

She found a shovel used for shovelling manure - *more poetic justice*, she thought - scooped up the black blob and carried it over to the farm exhibit, where she flung it into the pigpen. She stood and watched as a big sow waddled over, sniffed at the blob, then downed it with three quick chews and a swallow. The sow belched satisfaction.

"That's poetic justice too, scumbag." She knew the pig's strong digestive juices would ensure Brack was gone forever. "Your horrible tat said 'life ain't fair' an' you just proved it."

Melanie turned and resumed limping toward the zoo's main entrance. Each step was torture; she had damaged her still-healing stump when she had squashed Brack with so much force. She didn't notice she was crying. When the army medics finally found her and sat her down, wrapping her in blankets, she started shaking uncontrollably.

Chapter 29

Explanations - of Sorts

It was one week later. Martial law had been declared, then lifted. Funerals had been held, many of them. The media had descended on the shattered city like locusts, sensationalising.

Clearwater had started to slowly rebuild its downtown. There was talk of a special memorial in the wrecked town square, once it was restored, to honour those who had died. Some folks had decided to move to another city, somewhere that psychopathic monster sexual predators were unknown. Other folks had decided to stay put, because psychopaths and predators could appear anywhere nowadays, dammit, so fleeing wouldn't solve anything.

No one knew exactly what had happened that terrible day, except six people and they weren't telling. (Billy and Melanie had told Janet and Paul McDonnell what occurred.) It was generally accepted that Brack had been the cause of it all, but how he had gained his supernatural abilities, no one knew. There were rumours he had escaped from secret experiments by the Americans, or the Russians, or even by alien abductors, but there was no proof. It was officially believed that Brack was dead, though there was no sign of his body.

The authorities had questioned Billy, Melanie, and Ethan about their parts in the disaster. The threesome's answers had been carefully vague and the authorities had come away satisfied that they had been victims just like everyone else. No one besides Billy and Ethan had seen the orange Thing battling the black monster. No one had seen Melanie finishing it off and feeding the corpse to a pig.

Michael couldn't be questioned; he was in a coma.

All four had been hospitalized. Michael's injuries had been the most grievous; the army medics who had first examined him had initially thought he was dead. He was covered in blood with terrible cuts and bruises. Doctors said the youth would never walk again - his spinal cord had been shattered - and his arm, broken in several places, would take months to heal.

Billy and Ethan's hands and feet had been cared for, though specialists said use of the appendages would likely be limited even after they healed. The hospital also treated Billy for two broken ribs and bruising, from when he had been slammed into the truck. Melanie had been treated for shock, pumped full of anti-venom, and kept under observation for 48 hours. She also received a new temporary prosthesis, with strict orders to limit her walking for the next month to allow her raw, damaged stump to resume healing.

Three days after being admitted, Michael suddenly sat up in bed, a huge smile on his face - a face totally free of bruises - and asked to have his cast removed please since his arm was all better now. He swung his legs out of bed and stood up, eager to walk to wherever he had to walk to, to get the cast off.

The attending nurse gawked at him, dropped her clipboard, and fled.

Doctors said it was nothing short of a miracle. The boy's arm and spinal cord were completely cured.

Later that day, a similar miracle happened to the hands and feet of Billy and Ethan: complete recovery, not even scars where the nails had penetrated. Ditto Billy's broken ribs and bruises. Clandestine injections of Michael's Wolverine blood into both Billy and Ethan, facilitated by a nurse friend of Janet McDonnell who had been sworn to strictest secrecy, had worked their magic.

Hospital personnel, still overwhelmed with treating the hundreds of survivors of the disaster, had many other things to occupy their minds besides three alleged miraculous recoveries. Besides, many felt that with all the trauma the citizens had suffered at the hands of the monster, folks deserved a few miracles.

With the continuing hubbub about Brack's rampage, these little miracles stayed under the media radar. The media were obsessed with assigning blame for the carnage and airing speculations about Brack.

With the McDonnells and a Community Living social worker present, Chief of Police Frank Arnott himself interviewed Michael. He asked many questions about the teen's part in the Brack affair and Michael answered them without a hint of power stones or superheroes. Arnott went away believing in Mike's assertions that he too had been a victim, but with a nagging gut feeling that the boy was hiding something.

A gym bag had been discovered by the police in the trunk of "Jonathan Stewart's" Audi TT convertible, with over $300,000 cash inside. A tag inside the bag identified it as belonging to Amy Harrison, and this established a link between Brack and the multimillionaire who had walked away with $700,000 in cash from her bank, and who had later been found brutally murdered along with her two teenage daughters and servants in the basement of her mansion.

ೡ ೡ ೡ ೞ ೞ ೞ

The foursome were now sitting in the shade on the back patio of Billy's house, sipping excellent lemonade made by Janet. They were finally alone and it was time for some answers.

"So, Mike, how come you can still change into superheroes without your stone?" Billy said.

"Well, just like before, I concentrate an' wish really really hard an' it happens," Mike answered.

"But how?" said Melanie. "We always thought you needed that rock."

Ethan coughed and said: "He did. But now he doesn't. Mike, you haven't needed your stone for some time."

The three teens stared at the man with the emaciated body. Billy said: "What are you talking about? This is no time for more of your lies."

"Roger that, kid. It's no lie. It's the stone's greatest secret. Mike's already proved it."

"But I don't understand," said Michael, frowning. "I mean,

it's neat I can still do it, but how can I?"

Ethan looked hard at Michael. "You just gotta believe. That's what you've been doing all along, right? You just have to *believe*. Yes, you needed the stone at the beginning. But after awhile, you didn't need it any more. See, it ... it kinda flips a switch deep in your brain each time you use it, and eventually you can flip that switch on your own, so you can do your own miracles after that."

"Pardon the language, but that sounds like total bullcrap," said Billy.

"No bullcrap, Billy me lad. I've told you before that the stone is only attracted to one person in a million, a person who's sympatico with it, who responds to it. The stone forms a relationship with that special person, it opens a doorway in their brain that lets 'em do wonderful things. But it's the person's brain that actually works the miracles, somewhere in that unknown nine-tenths region that scientists say we never use. The stone is just the enabler, the catalyst."

"Waitaminute," interjected Melanie. "We learned in Biology that the unknown nine-tenths of the brain belief is just a myth! It's Hollywood movies and TV shows that keep that myth alive."

"Yeah!" agreed Billy. "We're already using most of our brain, according to verified neuroscience research."

Ethan grinned at the two teens. "Well now, I don't believe that's proven 100% without a doubt. I think there's still some debate on the matter. Look, you can't deny what happened to your muscular friend here. Mike can now do all those wonderful things just by thinkin' of them, without usin' the stone."

"So I really am special, just like my teachers always tell me?" said Mike.

"You sure are," replied Ethan, refilling his glass with lemonade for the third time. "And it's a good thing you had your stone taken from you, before it sucked you dry."

The three youths stared at him. Ethan took a long swig of lemonade, smacked his lips in great satisfaction, and continued: "I've been telling you kids the stone is cursed. That kinda power always has a price. It's a parasite, draining its host over time.

The nasty secret about that rock is: You don't know that every time it lets you flip that switch in your brain, letting you do those wonderful things, well, eventually you're able to do it by yourself and you don't need it any longer. Nobody ever realizes that. So here's the nasty part: You continue to use the stone much longer than you need to and the stone drains you, uses you up until you die. Then it finds another victim."

"You're full of it," said Billy.

"No I'm not. Remember what happened to my step-brother, Dave? Hell, Billy, I showed you pictures of him! Even Mike here was starting to show definite signs of premature aging. He was going grey at the temples, remember?"

"I don't got grey hair no more," announced Mike.

"Yeah, it musta been because of that Wolverine blood, when you changed into him again at the hospital to heal all your injuries," said Billy. "It reversed the premature aging too."

"Yah, in the comics, Logan is way, way older than he looks 'cause of his special blood."

Ethan continued: "Because it was split in two, the stone's power was halved, so Mike and Brack hardly aged until near the end, when they started using their half-stones a lot. Especially Brack: his aging, the consumption of his body, really accelerated when he used the rejoined stone."

"So is that why he suddenly started shrinking; the stone was draining him?" asked Melanie.

"Yep," said Ethan. "He was using the restored stone full tilt, without pause, as that black shadow monster of his, rampaging through town, killing, destroying, raping and torturing those women he'd trapped in that office building, and, especially, fighting Mike. The stone started consuming him, slowly at first, then faster and faster at the end. When Mike's orange rock fella kept pounding away at him, that really accelerated the consumption. It was way more aggressive, faster, than what happened to my step-brother. Finally, even after he dropped his stone, Brack was too far gone; he still kept shrinking fast."

"That's right, he dropped his stone when Mike landed that last awesome uppercut on him, sending him flying," said Billy.

"Yep, he kept right on shrinking. So when he landed near Melanie, he was only about five inches tall."

"Why didn't he become completely human, after he dropped the stone?" asked Mel.

Ethan shrugged. "Dunno. Maybe, by then, he'd become like Mike an' didn't need the stone to stay a monster. But somethin' musta gone wrong, 'cause you said his head had become human, but the rest of him was still that awful chimera. I dunno why."

"But he's gone for good now, right? Dead? Really dead?" she said, pushing away mental images of Brack's tiny head atop the miniature shadow beast and what she'd done to it.

"I expect so, after what you did to him. An' a pig's gastric juices are very potent, as you know."

"So there's no way he's coming back?"

Billy interjected: "In comics, no one ever really stays dead."

Mike nodded. "Yah. Especially the vanillas."

"Villains, Mike." Seeing Melanie's concerned look, Billy said hastily: "But don't worry, Mel. I'm sure Brack's really dead. He won't be coming back. Besides, the bastard didn't read comics!"

They all laughed.

"Hey, Mike, I gotta ask: how come you chose the Thing to turn into, instead of a more powerful hero, like the Hulk?" Billy asked. "The Hulk would have been able to handle Brack better. He's the strongest one there is an' he never gets tired."

"Well, I needed someone very strong to get you two off the poles and remove those awful nails from you. The Hulk is stronger, yah, but he's much bigger an' clumsier an' I didn't want to make a mistake an' hurt you by accident. An' I didn't know the Nastyman would attack me so soon - I was only wanting to free you two - an' then the Nastyman attacked an' he started hurting me so much - so much that I couldn't concentrate to change into the Hulk or anyone else."

Billy reached over and patted Mike's arm. "Aw, forget it. You did just fine, buddy. You kept at it, you never gave up, an' you saved us."

Michael beamed. "I done good?"

"Ya done real good."

"So where is the stone now?" asked Melanie, looking right at the scarecrow man.

Ethan smiled, dug into a zippered pocket of his vest, and dropped the smooth four-inch-long oval rock on the table. It landed with a thud, sunlight reflecting off its multi-coloured polished surface. "Found it near where Mike last clobbered Brack."

The teens stared. Michael reached forward hesitantly and touched it. A huge smile wreathed his face.

"It still hums to me!" he said happily.

"Good for you, lad," said Ethan.

"But what *is* that stone, exactly?" asked Melanie.

Ethan looked skyward for a long moment before replying. "It's very old, kids. Older than recorded history. And it pops up from time to time, throughout history. It's the basis for all the legends we have of miraculous stones, or powerful medallions, or talismans. The famous legend of the Philosopher's Stone was based on it, though as you now know, it does a helluva lot more than just turning base metals into gold.

"In almost every culture on Earth, there's an ancient legend of a wondrous stone, or a talisman, or a medallion, that gives its wearer great powers and allows him or her to do great deeds. That's all based on this one stone.

"You saw how it let Mike and Brack do awesome things. Well, it's done that throughout history. Sometimes for good, sometimes for evil, depending on who possessed it. For example, the mighty hero of Sumerian and Babylonian legend, Gilgamesh, had the stone. King Arthur's powerful magician, Merlin, owned it. So did the terrible Russian monk, Rasputin - that's why he was so hard to kill.

"It's a known fact that Hitler was obsessed with the occult. Before and during World War Two, he had teams searching out rare mystical objects, because he believed that stuff would ensure his Reich lasted a thousand years. He had one team dedicated to nothing else but finding that there pretty stone. And if it weren't for the diligence and sacrifice of some brave people, Hitler's team would have found it. Instead, the stone's guardians ensured it stayed well hidden throughout the war, deep in the Australian Outback. Where, decades later, I finally tracked it down."

Billy said: "Who are you, really, and why are you so obsessed with it? And no more lies; we've all gone through too much to have any more of your lies."

Ethan grimaced. "Yeah, I regret the lies, kids. But you gotta understand: at the time, I thought it was for your own good that you didn't know too much. I was trying to minimize public exposure of the stone. I just wanted to get it back into hiding again. And for the longest while, I had no idea the stone had been broken in two and that murderous serial rapist Brack had one and was being drawn to Mike's half. The stone had never been broken before."

"You haven't answered my question," Billy said.

Sighing, Ethan said: "You should become a lawyer, kid. Or a reporter." He abruptly pointed a finger straight at Michael. "An' we've no need of that human lie detector fella you turned into out West, savvy?"

Mike smiled and nodded. Ethan went on: "Right, who am I really? Well, most of what you know about me is true. I'm an eccentric self-made multi-millionaire, retired. My hobby - obsession if you will - is stone lore. Mystic talismans. Medallions of power. After years of research, I concluded that all the legends of talismans or miraculous stones were based on one stone, that appeared at various times throughout history. That wonderful stone right there on your table. So, once I knew that, it became my obsession to find it. Which I finally did.

"Now you know that the stone doesn't work for everybody. It didn't work for you Melanie, or you Billy, or even me when I tried it after I found it in Australia. No matter how hard one wishes or concentrates, it only works for one in a million. It worked for Dave. When I refused to let him keep it, because I knew the terrible price it exacted from its user, my step-brother stole it from me and went off with it."

"Why didn't you tell your step-brother of the stone's secret, that you only had to hold it for a certain length of time until you didn't need it to flip that switch in your brain? It would have saved Dave from being used up so horribly," asked Billy.

"I only discovered that aspect of the stone recently, as I continued my research in the months after Dave's death and the disappearance of the stone."

"How'd it get over here?" asked Mel.

"The trauma of being split in two by my step-brother, just before he died, caused it to teleport away, all the way around the planet, from Australia to the opposite ends of this continent, where Mike and Brack eventually discovered its halves. It's the first time it's teleported itself, to my knowledge."

"Where did the stone come from, originally?" said Melanie.

Ethan took another long pause before replying: "I'm not really sure, young lady. There's conflicting stories. Some say it was made by the powerful magicians of fabled Atlantis, before it sank. In fact, one theory is that the energy unleashed by its creation was what sunk Atlantis.

"Other stories claim the stone is not of this Earth. That it came from outer space. There's many myths about strange rocks from space crashing here. There's stories that our mysterious rock was sent here millennia ago by advanced beings as part of their great cosmic Earth experiment, and that the stone caused humankind to make some great evolutionary leaps. Y'know in Stanley Kubrick's classic film, *2001, A Space Odyssey*, where the apes touch the black monolith and suddenly start using weapons? Well, suppose it wasn't a monolith the apes touched, but our colourful little friend here?"

The three teens looked at each other. "We've never seen that movie," said Billy. "Or even heard of it."

"What about the SF novel on which it was based, by Arthur C. Clarke?"

Three blank looks.

Ethan rolled his eyes and groaned. "Right. Modern kids; no appreciation for the classics. Anyway, another legend is that this stone is the true Holy Grail."

THE HERO STONE

"No way!" said Melanie and Billy in unison.

"We've seen the *Indiana Jones and the Last Crusade* movie. The Grail is a miraculous goblet that Christ drank from at the Last Supper," said Melanie. "We also learned that at church; everybody knows that the Holy Grail is the cup of Christ. King Arthur's Knights of the Round Table spent years searching for it."

Ethan shook his skull-head vigorously, threatening to snap it off his spindly neck. "Nope. With apologies to Indiana Jones and your religious teachers, there are many stories and myths about the Grail. Some stories, from pre-Christian Celtic lore and other myths of antiquity, refer to the Grail as a stone that fell from heaven that had mystical powers. Sound familiar? It's only when the Holy Grail became part of popular Christian imagination in the Middle Ages that it became cemented in widespread belief as a goblet or chalice used by Christ."

The three teens stared at Ethan, disbelief evident on their faces. Ethan shrugged and continued:

"Welp, whether by accident or design, through scientific or sorcerous means, who can say how it got here? We may never really know."

Michael spoke up: "What will happen to my special stone now?"

"Well kid, you don't need it anymore, as you know now," replied the scarecrow, finishing off the last of a huge pile of homemade chocolate chip cookies that had come with the lemonade. "And you've all seen how dangerous the rock can be in the wrong hands. Brack was an almost unstoppable rapist and murderer after he found his half of the stone, and more so once the halves were rejoined.

"So, I plan to take the stone back with me. En route to my home in New Zealand, I'll stop in Hawaii and throw the stone into the erupting crater of the Kilauea volcano on the Big Island. It's been erupting for decades. Madame Pele, the Hawaiian goddess of fire who currently lives inside Kilauea - according to native Hawaiian belief - will destroy it with her boiling magma."

"You're gonna *destroy* it?" asked Michael and started sucking a knuckle furiously. "Doesn't seem right. No sir, it sure doesn't."

"Maybe not, but it's the best, the safest thing to do with it. It's much too powerful to keep around. It's affected human history far too much, and not always for the better. I mean, just look at the havoc it let Brack cause, especially once Brack had the complete rock."

"Yeah, but look at all the good it let Mike do," said Billy.

"True, but it's still very dangerous."

"How do we know you'll really throw it into that volcano?" said Mel suspiciously. "Maybe you'll just keep it."

Ethan smiled. "You'll just have to trust me. Or you can come with me an' watch me do it. Just ask your parents if you can go an' I'll pay your seat-sale, standby, Economy class plane fares. Least I can do after all you've been through."

The three teens looked at each other, excitement in their faces at the prospect of a trip to Hawaii. Then Billy and Melanie's faces fell. Mel spoke:

"No, there's no way our folks would let the three of us go by ourselves on such a trip, not after all this. Especially with Mike and Billy taking off across Canada like they did. No, we're gonna be on a short leash for a long time."

Ethan shrugged. "Well then, it's as I said: you'll just have to trust me."

Several minutes later, Paul and Janet McDonnell came out and said they had something important to discuss with the children. Ethan took this as his cue to leave. Goodbyes were said, with handshakes and hugs all around. Billy was irritated that Ethan seemed to take overly-long with his farewell hug to Melanie, squeezing her body tight against his bony frame, a huge smile creasing his cadaverous face.

Then the scarecrow was in his newly-rented wreck of a car and they waved as it wheezed, clunked and shuddered down the street, obscured by a thick black exhaust cloud and likely searching for an opportune spot to expire.

Returning to the back patio, Janet and Paul sat down with the teens at the patio table. Paul cleared his throat:

"I've had our lawyer looking into Michael's affairs since his adoptive parents were murdered. My first instructions were for him to find any next-of-kin, but there doesn't appear to be any. However, he's discovered that the trust fund left by Michael's wealthy grandmother, to provide money to take care of him, is now considerably larger than anyone would've guessed."

He paused for dramatic effect. "It's well over three million dollars."

Billy and Melanie said "wow!" in unison.

Michael said: "Is that a lot?"

Janet chuckled. "Yes, Michael. That's a lot of money."

"All you'll need for the rest of your life," said Paul.

"Wow, no wonder those awful people let Mike have such a generous allowance for his weekly comics," said Billy. "It's peanuts compared to that fund."

"Yes, and the fund actually should have had a lot more in it," said Paul. "Michael's adoptive parents received a healthy amount each month, for his upkeep with some left for their trouble. But my lawyer discovered the Johnsons had been siphoning off extra money in secret for years. Now we know how they could afford those lavish vacations each year."

"Yeah, an' leaving poor Mike home with you folks each time," said Melanie.

"Mr. Billy's Dad, all that money, can I give some of it to those nice farmer people in Albatross Narrows, who were so nice to me, an' whose house an' barn got burneded down 'cause of the Nastyman?" asked Michael.

"Why, that's very thoughtful of you, Michael. Jesse Birski told me they were having trouble getting their insurance company to pay for the buildings. The adjusters can't figure out what caused the fires. An' their son can't help them much financially - or even physically - because of his job overseas," said Paul. "I'm sure we can arrange something. How much do you wish to give them?"

Michael frowned and sucked a knuckle, looking at Billy and Melanie for help. Then he brightened and said: "Enough to build them a brand-new house an' barn. Oh, an' enough for a new truck, too. The one they got is almost deaded."

"Well, that's certainly very generous of you," said Paul. "You're sure you wish to do this?"

Mike nodded vigorously. Billy and Mel both patted him on his shoulders.

"I wanna do something else too," announced Michael and looked at Janet. "Mrs. Billy's Mom, do you think you could ask your nice nurse friend to help us again an' interject some of my blood, after I turn into Wolverine, into those people in the hospital who got very badly hurt by the Nastyman, so they can get all better fast?"

Janet looked flustered. "Well, Michael, that's a very nice thing to want to do, but I'm worried people'll get suspicious. They're already perplexed with how you and Billy and Ethan recovered so miraculously. We're lucky they had all those other victims to tend to; it distracted them from investigating too deeply. But what'll they say if more miracles occur?"

Mike set his jaw. "Yah, it's risky, an' I know my secret identity must be protected, but it's something I really wanna do. I know it means more needles in my arm, an' I do hate needles, yes I do. But I wanna help fix some of what the Nastyman did."

Janet looked at Paul, then at Billy and Melanie. They were all nodding encouragement. She sighed. "Okay, Michael. We'll figure out a way to do it quietly. Somehow. Just those with very bad injuries, a few people at a time, starting with the worst ones."

"Oh, thank you, Mrs. Billy's Mom!"

"You're very welcome," Janet smiled. "Well, on a different topic, our lawyer was also looking into something else for us, Michael. Mr. McDonnell and I want to become your legal guardians, if you don't mind, that is."

"Huh?" said the three teenagers almost simultaneously.

"Yes," said Paul. "Michael, you're welcome to come live with us and consider us as your family now. Though you'd have to promise to curtail the use of your special powers." He saw Mike's blank look. "That means, don't use your powers a lot. Only rarely. So as not to attract attention."

"To protect your secret identity," added Billy.

Comprehension dawned in Michael's face and he nodded. Then he frowned and sucked a knuckle. A long minute passed.

"You ... you mean live here ... in this house ... with you and Billy ... all the time? Just like a ... brother?" stammered Mike, a smile hovering timidly on his lips.

"That's right, Michael. You'd be part of our family and we would look after you," said Janet.

Mike's shouted "YES!" sent birds flying in multiple directions for half a block.

༨ ༨ ༨ ༨ ༨ ༨

Billy was walking Melanie home, leaving Michael happily buried in several weeks' worth of comics that had piled up at the store during his absence. Knowing she was self-conscious about it, Billy completely ignored her awkward gait.

They had only walked three houses away from the McDonnell home, when Mel slipped her hand into Billy's. Billy almost swallowed his tongue.

He looked at her, startled. She smiled that beatific smile of hers. Billy smiled back and gripped her hand tighter.

"I ... I really meant it when I said I'm sorry for all the bad things I said to you, just after I ... lost my leg," she said. "It was a really difficult time for me, and -"

"No, don't worry about it," Billy interrupted. "I understand, really. Don't mention it ever again, okay?"

"Okay."

After a long minute, Mel continued: "I'm also sorry - more than you'll ever know - that I went out with that Jonathan creep. I never suspected he was really Brack."

"That's okay too. You couldn't have known. No one could. It was the perfect disguise. Plus he had that car."

"Yeah. That car. Sure was a nice machine."

Billy sighed. "Yeah."

"Well, thinking back on it all, I realize that you have something Jonathan could never have, even with that car and his hot DiCaprio looks."

"What?"

"Your heart. You're a loyal friend, to me and to Mike. And you're very sweet, too."

Billy blushed. He blushed even more when Mel kissed him on the cheek.

"Aw, c'mon, stop," he said. "We're good friends, but, y'know, I figure that's it. You could never ... ah ... have deeper feelings for a big whale like me."

"Don't be silly, silly. How you look is not important compared to who you are, inside. I've never thought of you as a whale."

"Really?"

"Really."

Billy suddenly felt like he weighed nothing at all. Melanie continued:

"Besides, you could never ... um ... have deeper feelings for an amputee, someone who's ... disabled."

"Now you're the one being silly. You're not disabled, as far as I'm concerned. You certainly had no problem taking care of Brack."

A dark shadow crossed Melanie's face.

"Oh, damn, I'm sorry," Billy said. "I shouldn't have brought that up. It must be awful hard to deal with. After all, you killed a man."

Mel stopped and gave Billy a fierce look. "No, I did *not* kill a man. I killed a cockroach, a small inconsequential *bug*. And I'm not going to talk about *that* again. Ever."

Billy squeezed her hand. "Good for you."

Suddenly, her lips were on his and he had never tasted anything so wonderful. She pulled back and said:

"Good for you, too, William Butler McDonnell."

༃ ༃ ༃ ༃ ༃ ༃

On the highway to Toronto and its Pearson International Airport, in a car that was amazingly still running, the scarecrow man allowed himself a loud, coarse laugh.

"Welp, once again, my carefully-manufactured 'Ethan Delperdang' character worked like a charm. Those kids bought most of the yarn I strung 'em. Well, admittedly, some of what I said was true. A few truths makes the load of bull easier to sell."

He pulled out the oval stone and looked at it.

"Throw you to Madame Pele? Yeah, right."

Another loud laugh.

"And what would I do without you then, huh? You've kept me alive for 700 years; I need you to continue doing just that. Those kids forgot the other fabled power of the Philosopher's Stone: long life. Well, you've certainly done that for me, my smooth friend. I was the only one clever enough not to use you for anything else, only the gift of longevity, a far more benign use of your power without any lethal side-effects. Well, besides making me look like a Goddamned corpse.

"I was so bloody lucky to acquire you early in the 14th century. Thank God I believed that old mystic, who said he found you in Venice among the exotic spices and silks brought back from China by Marco Polo in 1295. You let me survive the Black Death when it first swept through Europe in the 1340s and 50s, and again when it reappeared in the 1360s and 70s. That bubonic plague killed millions: almost half the population of England and nearly two-thirds of some parts of Europe. Entire villages were wiped out, including mine. So I became a nomad, wandering from country to country.

"I did allow myself to have a bit of fun with you during the first decades of my travels. The dancing mania I caused in July of 1374 in Aix-la-Chapelle in Western Germany still makes me chuckle. Hordes of men and women dancing in the streets in a pathological frenzy, until they fell from exhaustion or injury. Hah! Scientists still can't explain what caused it.

"Anyway, it's good to have ya back. I can't be far away from you for too long; weeks, even months, sure, but eventually I'll start to age. I was startin' to lose my hair before I got hold of ya again after that big fight with Brack.

"And that asshole who stole you from me: Dave, my so-called

step-brother - hah! I've never had a brother, step or otherwise - well, he certainly deserved what he got. As did all those others who have, over the centuries, managed to take you from me from time to time."

The scarecrow drove for awhile in silence.

"Now, putting aside all my crap about the unused nine-tenths of the brain, an' flipping some kinda mental switch, what you did to that Michael kid's brain, that's something new. Be interesting to see what comes of that."

Chapter 30

Memorial Flight

Michael was beside himself with excitement. "We're almost there!" he announced happily, face pressed to the window of the rented car.

Paul McDonnell turned into the long rutted lane with the weathered grey tin mailbox marked "Birski" at its head. He looked in the rearview mirror at his son sitting behind him and saw him smile.

"Thanks for taking Mike back here for a visit, you guys," Billy said. "It really means a lot to him."

"Yeah, thanks a whole lot, Mr. and Mrs. Billy's Dad and Mom!" called out Michael from the back seat.

"You're welcome, both of you," replied Janet, sitting in the passenger seat and smiling.

The Birski farm hove into view. The car's occupants grew silent when they saw the black ruins that used to be a sturdy farmhouse and barn. Paul stopped the car near a small house trailer parked on the lawn. As the McDonnells and Michael piled out, joyful barking sounded and a brown hairy meteor on four legs cannoned into Mike.

"Lucky!" he exclaimed, hugging the dog, which proceeded to thoroughly clean Mike's face with its tongue.

The Birskis came out of the trailer and introductions were made. They had been expecting visitors; Janet had called them a week ago.

"Oh, it's wonderful to see you again, Michael, and to know that you are safe," said Meredith Birski, giving the lad a big hug and reaching up on tip-toes to kiss him on the cheek. Mike grinned.

"It's great to see you and Mr. Jesse again too," said Michael. "But I'm really sorry about what happened to your house and barn. That's awful."

"Yes, but at least we're alive and we didn't lose any livestock," replied Jesse Birski. "The whole town's been so nice to us an' said they'll help us rebuild as soon as we get the insurance money, which doesn't look like it'll happen anytime soon. The suits in their glass tower in Toronto are arguing that our policy doesn't cover arson caused by an alleged monster with supernatural abilities."

"We're not going to get into all that right now," admonished Meredith sternly. "These nice folks only just arrived! Come sit at the picnic table here under the trailer awning and visit. I'll get you something to drink and eat. You all look like you need it; you've come such a long way just to see us."

Over cool drinks and delicious homemade bumbleberry pie, Jesse admitted that the hardest thing to accept was the loss of a lifetime of memories: keepsakes, antiques from Meredith's parents, their stamp collection, and their old family photo albums. Mike got very sad and the McDonnells commiserated with their loss; things that could never be replaced.

Then Michael brightened and announced that he had brought a special gift that would help them to get something back. Janet produced an envelope from her purse and gave it to Michael, who presented it to the Birskis with a flourish.

The middle-aged couple were stunned when they opened the envelope and read the cheque inside.

"That's ... that's quite the amount!" said Jesse. "And it's for us?"

"Yes, yes, yes, for you," said Michael with a huge grin. "It's for a new house an' barn an' even a truck, yes it is!"

"I made enquiries and the amount should cover all that," said Paul.

"But ... but how? Why?"

"It's Mike's money," said Billy. "From a large trust fund his rich grandmother established years ago an' which we only just found out about. Mike wanted to do this for you, to thank you for your kindness to him, and to replace some of what that Brack assho- um, criminal took from you."

The Birskis looked at Michael, who nodded feverishly.

"Oh, but we can't accept this," said Meredith.

"No, we certainly can't," echoed Jesse. "We've never taken charity from anyone."

Mike leaned forward across the table and clasped one of Meredith and Jesse's hands. He looked them both straight in the eyes and said quietly:

"I want you to have this money. It means a lot to me to give it to you. I won't be happy unless you take it."

The Birskis looked at each other, then back at Michael. Jesse opened his mouth to speak, but Mike said:

"I"m also doing it for Captain Kenny, RCAF, retired. In his memory. He was a very special person an' I really really liked him an' I'm very very sorry he's ... he's deaded."

Big tears started rolling down Mike's cheeks. It was the first time that the death of the old pilot had been mentioned. Meredith gave Jesse her "No Arguments" look and said:

"Thank you, Michael. You're very kind. My father, Captain Kenny, was very special to us too and we also miss him a lot. We accept your wonderful gift in his memory."

Jesse said nothing, but nodded, looking away across a field and swiping at a speck of dust in his eye.

Meredith insisted on cooking dinner for everyone. Despite the trailer's cramped kitchen and scaled-down appliances, she managed to produce enough food to feed a football team, and of a quality that would make a gourmet wax poetic. They ate at the outdoor picnic table, gorging themselves.

Afterwards, Michael helped Meredith with the dishes while the McDonnells were toured around the farm by Jesse, including visiting the "Miracle River" that was reviving their arid land and that of their neighbours. When the last dish had been stowed away, Meredith left the kitchen and returned with a small brown envelope, which she handed to Michael.

"Here, son," she said. "It's from my dad, from Captain Kenny. In the short time you were with us, you really made an impression on him. He wanted you to have it, if you ever returned here. Luckily, it was in our safe deposit box at our bank in town; we fetched it here after learning that you folks were coming."

Mike opened the envelope. A yellowed folded paper lay inside. Opening it, Mike saw a poem was printed on it, but his attention was drawn to what had been placed inside the folded paper: A worn cloth badge insignia of white wings with RCAF under a crown in the centre.

"It's his pilot's wings from World War Two, when he flew Spitfires against the Nazis. And that poem was his favourite. It was read aloud at his funeral. In fact, it's a favourite of aviators everywhere and it's the official poem of the RCAF. He told me that you should have these keepsakes, because you let him soar among the clouds again and it was the best flight of his life. He said you'd understand. Do you know what he was talking about?"

Michael nodded, swallowing hard. "Yes, Mrs. Meredith. I do."

༂ ༂ ༂ ༃ ༃ ༃

Late that night, Michael and the McDonnells retired to Albatross Narrows' one and only motel. Tomorrow, they would go with the Birskis to the local cemetery and pay their respects to Captain Kenny.

The family had adjoining rooms, with the boys in one and Paul and Janet in the other. When Billy was sleeping soundly, producing a *Symphonie Nocturne* of snores reminiscent of powerful turbo-prop aircraft engines coughing into reluctant life, Michael got out of bed and padded softly into the bathroom. He closed the door, flicked on the light, and brought out the envelope given him by Meredith. Using the complimentary sewing kit provided by the motel, he carefully sewed Captain Kenny's pilot's wings to his pyjama bottoms, just below the waistband, checking carefully to ensure it was secure.

He slipped outside and went around to the back of the motel.

A three-quarter moon in a cloudless sky illuminated a vast field of canola stretching out before him. He gazed at the carpet of yellow flowers waving in the stiff night breeze, then looked up at the sky. It was full of bright stars, shining against an ebony backdrop.

A perfect night.

He shucked off his pyjama top, leaving his bottoms on. He concentrated and grunted in pain as twin, white, six-foot wings erupted from his back.

Michael raised his face to the sky and opened his magnificent wings wide, letting the wind fill them and slowly, gracefully lift him into the night sky. As the motel fell away beneath him, the wings started beating with powerful strokes, *thrumming*, and the youth was soon soaring high and free. He started doing loops, turns, and power-dives, imitating how a fighter plane acted in aerial combat from war movies he'd seen.

Cool wind buffeted his face and body, blowing away the tears from his eyes as soon as he formed them. He said:

"You fought the Nazi bullies in World War Two, to protect our freedom. You fought bad guys right to the very end, never giving up. You were a true hero.

"This flight's for you, Captain Kenny, RCAF, retired."

Here is Captain Kenny's favourite poem:

High Flight
by
John Gillespie Magee
RCAF World War Two Fighter Pilot

Oh! I have slipped the surly bonds of Earth
And danced the skies on laughter-silvered wings;
Sunward I've climbed, and joined the tumbling mirth
Of sun-split clouds--and done a hundred things
You have not dreamed of--wheeled and soared and swung
High in the sunlit silence. Hov'ring there,
I've chased the shouting wind along, and flung
My eager craft through footless halls of air.
Up, up the delirious burning blue
I've topped the wind-swept heights with easy grace
Where never lark, or even eagle flew-
And, while with silent lifting mind I've trod
The high untrespassed sanctity of space,
Put out my hand, and touched the face of God.

EPILOGUE

It was six months after the horrible events in Clearwater. The media had moved on months ago in their relentless search for other crises on which to breathlessly report. In downtown Toronto, five figures stood before an imposing building on the sprawling University of Toronto campus.

"This is it," said Paul McDonnell. "One of the foremost centres for medical research in Canada."

"The research team headed by that Nobel-winning doctor are waiting for us," said Janet McDonnell. "Let's not keep them waiting."

The group entered the building: Paul and Janet, their son Billy, Billy's girlfriend Melanie, whose gait now looked almost entirely normal, and a short, muscular, hairy man who moved with the lithe grace of a predatory animal.

Bank Manager Brianna Van Heusen, Melanie's mother, had used a contact made at her weekly Rotary Club of Clearwater meeting - the CEO of their regional hospital - to arrange this meeting with the U of T medical research team, a team that specialized in disease research. The hospital CEO was a old friend of the team's celebrated leader, Doctor Kee Teo, and had paved the way for Brianna's phone call to him.

Brianna had promised Dr. Teo that what the McDonnells would bring him would likely cause a breakthrough in curing incurable diseases and would almost certainly result in another Nobel prize. That got his attention.

Paul and Melanie had been carefully vague when they'd asked Brianna to arrange this meeting; Brianna didn't know any further details. She had told Dr. Teo that all would be made clear when his team met with the McDonnell group.

The group was led into a conference room and senior members of the multi-disciplinary research team filed in. Everyone took their seats and introductions were made; the short, hairy man was introduced as Logan Xavier. Then Paul explained that Logan had unique blood that rapidly healed injuries and cured diseases. He said the man was willing to donate sufficient blood for the research team to analyse and conduct experiments, in an effort to understand what was in the blood that allowed it to perform its miracles. He said they hoped this healing factor would enable the team to synthesize cures for heart ailments and incurable diseases like the many types of cancer, diabetes, Parkinson's, AIDS, the Ebola virus, MS, MD, and others.

After Paul had finished, there was a long silence. Then Dr. Teo and his researchers expressed their polite, but firm, skepticism about Paul's claims. After listening to their comments for several minutes with growing impatience, Logan, who was wearing a T-shirt, pulled a pocket knife from his pocket and opened the blade. He cleared his throat loudly until everyone was looking at him, then sliced his forearm from elbow to hand. The shocked cries and gasps from the research team was nothing compared to their reaction when the bloody gash healed itself in seconds right before their eyes.

The hairy man grinned and pulled up his T-shirt, exposing washboard abs. He sliced straight across his stomach. Again, the shocked researchers witnessed the flesh heal in seconds.

"Works the same way if I break a bone, or get inspected with a disease or poison," Logan said, smiling.

"That's 'infected', Logan," said Paul. "I apologize for this graphic display, ladies and gentlemen, but we thought we'd have to do this so you would take us seriously. You see now that we're telling you the truth. We have seen with our own eyes the curative power of that blood. It healed our own son from terrible injuries - twice. Imagine what that blood could do to a cancer patient. Or a child with polio. Or a senior with Alzheimer's."

The room erupted in a cacophony of questions, all of which Paul sidestepped by saying: "My answer to all your questions is with a question of my own: Do you wish to have samples of Mr. Xavier's miraculous blood for analysis and experimentation?"

Dr. Teo and his team most certainly did.

The only proviso was Paul and Janet's insistence that all their identities must be kept secret. They wanted no publicity, no acknowledgement whatsoever. In fact, today's meeting never even happened. Though it violated their usual protocol, the researchers agreed.

Arrangements were quickly made to draw samples of Logan's blood. Before the procedure started, the hairy man looked at Melanie and said:

"See? I didn't forget what you talked to me about when we rested on that hill after our first Angel flight, Melanie. So this is me being brave again."

Mel smiled and patted his arm. "You are the bravest person I know. It's a very good thing you're doing here. It could change the world of medicine an' save countless lives."

As the blood was being drawn, Billy and Melanie each gripped one of Logan's hands, talking to him and calming him, because as the man said repeatedly with eyes squeezed tightly shut, he *really really* hated needles.

༄ ༄ ༄ ༄ ༄ ༄

Dr. Nashrin Singh was a senior researcher on Dr. Teo's celebrated team. After the meeting with the Clearwater quintet had ended, she went outside to the designated smoking area. She fished out a lighter and a pack of cigarettes from her purse, extracted one, lit it, and inhaled deeply. She sighed in satisfaction. Stowing the pack and lighter back into her purse, she brought out an ordinary-looking smartphone. It was not her usual phone. This one was encrypted. She speed-dialled a number.

"Yes?" a curt male voice answered.

"Codename: Alpha Flight," she replied.

"Hold."

Seconds later, a woman's voice snapped: "Speak."

"Agent MD 27, Commodore."

"Been awhile."

"Yes Ma'am. Haven't had anything to report in awhile. Listen Commodore, you won't believe what I just witnessed this afternoon ..."

The End?

About the Author

Since 2003, **BRUCE GRAVEL**'s light-hearted stories have delighted readers of newspapers like the *Peterborough Examiner* and the *Globe & Mail*, and magazines like *Maclean's* and *Association*, among others. His first book, *Humour on Wry, with Mustard*, a collection of 88 funny tales, was published in 2008. His second book and first novel, *Inn-Sanity: Diary of an Innkeeper Virgin*, was published in 2009. His third book, *Humour on Wry, with Mayo featuring Travels with Fred, the World's Worst Tourist*, collecting 51 chuckle-worthy yarns, appeared in 2010. In 2012, *Humour on Wry with Ketchup* was published, featuring 32 funny stories.

In 2015, Bruce shifted gears, releasing *The Hero Stone*, a fantasy adventure novel for readers aged 13 and up, starring three teenagers, including one living with an intellectual disability. 2015 also saw the publication of *Every Season has a Story... Summer*, an anthology of eight interweaving short stories by eight Peterborough authors, of which Bruce was one. His contribution was a tale of adventure and secrets.

Email him at: bruce@brucegravel.ca

Made in the USA
Charleston, SC
28 March 2016